Haven't we all been driven, at some point, to Google ourselves? And what did you find? That there are people out there who seem to have something in common with you? Dates, places, interests? How coincidental are these connections? And what are the factors that define a human life?

Chris Eaton, a Biography combines the lives of dozens of real people who share nothing more than a name, identities that blur into each other with the idea that, in the end, we all live the same life, deal with the same hopes and fears, experience the same joys and tragedies. Only the specifics are differ-ent. From birth to death and everything in between, the narratives we share bring us closer to a truth about what it means to be alive. To be you.

A remarkable collection of randomness. I can't tell what's true and what's not but I don't really care because ultimately it's an ingenious look at our obses-sions with identity framed by a grotesque overload of fascinating informa-tion. Chris Eaton has managed to invent a kind of super-ego by distilling and compounding all the Chris Eatons that ever lived into an avalanche of hilarious humanness.
  – Charles Spearin of Broken Social Scene and Do Make Say Think

Combines world history, North American folklore, personal memories and postmodern storytelling to create an intricate novel that can stand alongside the work of both Mark Twain and Roberto Bolaño.
  – Jason Boog, *LA Review of Books*

A wondrous Oulipian experiment of a book, *Chris Eaton, a Biography* is like *Tristram Shandy* turned inside out and anagrammatized.
  – Gabriel Blackwell, author of *Shadow Man: A Biography of Lewis Miles Archer*

Not since Ray Davies' X - RAY has a musician/author crafted such an engag-ing, artful 'biography' about his life. Equal parts moving, funny, irreverent, full of shit, sincere as hell, and nothing short of brilliant.
  – Mitch Cullin, author of *A Slight Trick of the Mind* and *Tideland*

Just as often hilarious as it is tragic, it offers truth and absurdity hand in hand.
  – Todd Olmstead, Mashable

Reaches for the impossible, creating characters and situations that could never be – and yet you find yourself believing.
  – Emily Schultz, author of bestselling *The Blondes*

Awesome. Chris Eaton shows how environment and experience shape our individuality and that, no matter how different we seem on the surface, stripped to the core we are all the same. A harsh reality for this self-obsessed society to accept, Eaton makes us comfortable with it, and does so with humor and intensity, skill and style.
  – Nat Baldwin of Dirty Projectors

Rich with history and memory, myth and legend. While your parents probably called you something different, don't assume you'll find this novel any less captivating, as it's impossible to miss or mistake the other common bonds that unite us with all these real and imaginary and fantastic Chris Eatons, many of whom you will not soon forget.
  – Matt Bell, author of *In the House upon the Dirt between the Lake and the Woods*

Zany, exuberant, encyclopedic, possessed of remarkable wit, knowing and complex and hilarious, *Chris Eaton, a Biography* is a book which, if it didn't exist, only the mind of Chris Eaton could invent.
  – Steve Hayward, author of bestselling *Don't Be Afraid*

In *Chris Eaton, a Biography*, the multi-talented Chris Eaton twists together the frayed threads of possible lives and laces them into a remarkable, hilarious, and stirringly original novel.
  – John K Samson of The Weakerthans

Like *Trout Fishing In America* meets *Cloud Atlas*.
  – Jim Guthrie of Royal City, Human Highway and *Sword & Sworcery*

CHRIS EATON, A BIOGRAPHY

Chris Eaton, a Biography
A Novel by Chris Eaton

BookThug · 2013

Cover illustration (front) "you were born ... you died," (back) "Casey McGlynn, moments before his death," by Casey McGlynn, copyright ©2002, 34 piece wooden box diorama – house paint, pastel, crayon and ink on wood – 120 × 120 inches – used with permission.

The production of this book was made possible through the generous assistance of the Ontario Arts Council and the Canada Council for the Arts.

The author would like to thank the Canada Council for the Arts, the Ontario Arts Council, and the Toronto Arts Council for providing funds toward the writing of this book.

Copy Editor: Ruth Zuchter

LIBRARY AND ARCHIVES CANADA CATALOGUING IN PUBLICATION

Eaton, Chris, 1971–
        Chris Eaton, a biography: a novel/ Chris Eaton.

Issued also in an electronic format.
ISBN 978-1-927040-64-5

        I. Title.

PS8559.A8457C57 2013   C813.6   C2013-901267-2

CONTENTS

PART 1

It's not hard finding ways to die.

In Sheffield back in the forties, there were tons of them. At least that's what Chris Eaton's grandmother thought to herself as she herded her tyrants into the neighbour's shelter, the nearby ground ripped wholly from the Earth, where the pockets of violently vertical soil coalesced into a flock of birds, an octopus, a steam engine, counting each child as they skipped excitedly through the door like it was Christmas. She had one in her arms, one grappling her leg, and the third running off in all directions after the dog the boys called Betty, the one they found in the rubble of the last German attack. The mutt humped everything it saw, including the baby, and still the boys thought Betty was the perfect name. *One, two, three, Betty. One, two, three, Betty.* She did it over and over to reassure herself, until she began to think the numbers were their names: *One, two, three, Betty; one, two, three, Betty.* Chris Eaton's grandfather had left with his brothers (*One, two, three, Betty*) to make sure this explosive import-export business, this trade of bullets and bombs (*One, two, three, Betty*), was not unilateral. And oh, how they died! The eldest never even saw battle, drowned during training procedures at Ford Ord when he convinced one of the tank operators to let him take one for a spin, and he steeped the Crusader in the river, trapped inside as the water seeped slowly through the slots of the gunman's visor. *One, two, three, Betty.* The next, Great Uncle William, who was schooled as a mining engineer, was selected by a Special Missions unit to tunnel under German lines and set off charges beneath the enemy trenches, just like they did at Messines Ridge in wwi; but with nothing but a pick-axe, a canary and a compass; he had already succeeded in undermining the fronts at **CLASSIFIED** and **CLASSIFIED**, and was making his way towards **CLASSIFIED**, when his compass was attracted to the iron deposits of the mines in **CLASSIFIED**, and he mistakenly created another underground effluent for the nearby river. *One, two, three, Betty.* Exhausted during the rainy march to the front, Great Uncle Nelson pitched face first into a mud puddle and never looked up again, already dying from the venereal disease he picked up from a prostitute in London before even shipping out. *One, two, three, Betty.* And Great Uncle Timothy, the youngest, who liked to collect exotic fish and sail paper boats down the canal behind the steelworks, constantly devising special folds in order to create more and more elaborate rowboats, lifeboats, and double-ended sailboats; dinghies; Turkish caïques; Irish currachs; cobles and coracles; kayaks and umiaks; punts and junks; luggers and nuggars; galleons, battleships and aircraft carriers; and gradually perfecting his kraftmanship to create everything from a catamaran and trimaran through septamaran to dodecamaran, halted only by his inability to find a sheet of paper large enough to fold into a vessel with thirteen hulls side-by-side; Great Uncle Timothy, the sensitive artist, who managed before he was even twelve to harness the feebleness of the nearby creek to power his sister's tiny oven for making small cakes; Great Uncle Timothy, the innovator, who tumbled into a pool when he was three, and subsequently wept at any attempt to teach him to swim until his parents simply gave up; *that* Great Uncle Timothy, the crybaby, was captured in France in 1941, and deported to Germany a year later, where he spent fifteen months in captivity before being shot because the camp was running low on rations. When news of their deaths reached their mother, Chris Eaton's great grandmother, the poor woman refused to take another bath, or even go out in the rain.

Chris Eaton's grandfather survived mostly because of his position as a drum major, a responsibility that was still used in World War II when radio signals were uncertain and unsecure. The only other brother who managed to return without serious physical injury was Great Uncle Chippie, who had already completed most of his medical degree, and so they sent him over with a First Aid Regiment. He suffered a stroke soon after his return, on the train into London to catch another early show of *Oh, What a Lovely War* at the Theatre Royal, and when they went to visit him at the veterans' hospital they always had to approach him from the right, just so he could see and hear them coming.

When his grandfather returned from the war, planting his drumsticks in the front yard like they were flags, there was a hole he could not fill. A hole he could not explain. Something was missing. Like the schoolchildren when they were told there would be no more bombs, he didn't understand. Someone might as well have told them there would be no more air. Or water. Or beans with toast. There had been nothing *but* fighting. Nothing except the sirens. And for six months following Nazi surrender, the kids would continue to play games in the schoolyard where one girl would scream at the top of her lungs like a thousand wailing children while the rest of them ducked under whatever they could find, until they were told repeatedly by any passing adult to stop, just stop. So, Chris Eaton's grandfather started with the roof, where the dud had passed through. Then he filled the holes made by the missiles in the fields behind their house. Against the recommendations of friends and neighbours, he packed the entire bomb shelter with soil and covered the entrance.

This made him happier.

Still, it was not enough.

Luckily, there were even more holes in London, which were then being filled with American greenbacks, provided to the UK through the Marshall Plan – created as much as an American PR stunt for repelling Communism as it was a European rebuilding fund. Boarding the train to London each morning, Chris Eaton's grandfather shovelled dollars into ditches and sat back to watch the American seed money grow in the only way it knew how: straight up, blossoming into residential towers and high-rise flats, great plumes of brick and reinforced concrete that weighed heavily and choked out the skyline. Chris Eaton's grandfather was elated. Then someone wrote a study that said high-rises made people depressed. On the outskirts of the city, complete new towns went into bloom, with rigid grid systems, which he admired, and spacious backyards, which he did not. The birth of the suburbs. Discouraged, he stopped boarding the train.

Around that same time, the government had started up a programme for war veterans, facilitating the transition to civilian life by training them as security guards, cross-walk guards, valets, mailroom management, mailroom operations, couriers and dispatchers, weigh-scale operators, managing complaint desks and wildlife control. He chose the parking lot because, once again, although it wasn't the most exciting job in the world, it involved more space to fill. Then, towards the end of the seventies, the average car length dropped from twenty feet to somewhere closer to seventeen. He repainted his lines and found he could fit another dozen cars; fifteen if he parked them himself. Throughout the eighties, another two feet fell to history, and this time he discovered that pivoting the entire layout, running parallel to the street instead of perpendicular to it, brought him another four vehicles. (By this time, he parked everything himself.) Whereas he used to spend half of his days reading the newspaper or playing solitaire, he now used all of his time arranging and re-arranging the cars in the lot. Parallel, perpendicular, diagonally. In star patterns and spirals. In 1611, Johannes Kepler challenged himself to discover the most space-efficient way to pack oranges leaving as few gaps as possible. Mimicking the stacks of cannon balls he witnessed on ships, he found he could make the exotic fruits occupy 74.04% of the total space. So Chris Eaton's grandfather tried that, staggering the cars, alternating rows between cars that faced north-south and east-west, producing even more space in some cases depending on the particular makes and models. He also tried parking them in self-contained squares: two cars parallel followed by two perpendicular. And by the end of it all, he'd found space for another five cars. On a good day, six.

It just made it harder to get them back out.

He spent more and more time at the lot, requesting overnight shifts at the locations where he knew people parked until morning, for maximum time with the same vehicles. Sometimes he'd fall asleep at his calculations and Mr. Chisolm, who came around at midnight to collect the cash from the register, would have to poke him with his cane through the bars where he accepted the money, or shake the entire booth. There were normally only a few people who would pay to park after that time, and it was the unspoken rule that whoever worked the late shift could keep that extra money as a tip.

In the February 8 edition of *The Sheffield Star* (1992), the front page features a story about the Maastricht Treaty, the controversial agreement between European nations to create a political and monetary union with one common currency. Maastricht was the first city in the Netherlands to be liberated by Allied forces in World War II. Great Uncle Chippie was there to greet many of the Dutch resistance with Vitamin D tablets and **CLASSIFIED**, treating them for **CLASSIFIED** and **CLASSIFIED** as they emerged from the caves at St. Pietersberg. The caves were originally created in the 1700s, when the limestone marl was excavated to build homes like squat, fossilizing toads, and Maastricht became part of the dinosaur boom at the turn of that century. The most popular was the masosaur, which turned out to not be a dinosaur after all, but contributed to a 6-million-year epoch being named after the city. In fact, the photo of the European leaders was taken as the delegates emerged from a tour of the caves, with the caption: *Major Takes Britain Back to Maastrichtian Era.*

On one of the last pages of the first section is the story of a murder. There is no picture. The name of the war veteran who was knifed for twenty-seven pounds as he was getting ready to head home from his job at the car park is not even mentioned.

Chris Eaton's grandmother, Cordelia Eaton (née Barratt), hated Sheffield until the day she died, popping and snapping down the stairs like a bag of doorknobs, arms and legs forgetting their place and going every which way at once. She'd been legally blind for two years but had refused to tell anyone, preferring instead to sit still when people came to visit, and when she was alone, accompanied by nothing but the high-pitch squeal of her malfunctioning hearing aids, crawling across the countertops to press her face directly to every box of cornstarch and dried soup mix. The only one she confided in was Arthur, the mysterious stranger who showed up at her funeral and shook quietly in the back, his creased satchel rattling at his side like the dark, brown seeds of the chronic infection at the back of his sinuses, in the new modern Lutheran church of all places, which was best described – and *was* described by several of Corrie's more distant and Anglican relations – as looking like a child had made it with a gigantic shoebox and scissors. Corrie never liked Sheffield, and saw the Nazi razing of it as its true nature finally revealed. The place was rotten, she often said, like a disease that had felled nearly the entire population, with its lack of cultural arts and its goonish football thuggery, and she was constantly reminding her grandchildren of her idyllic youth near Newcastle-under-Lyme, dressed in her favorite cream-colored frock with a wide and heavy straw hat, quietly kicking her foal-like legs against the wall. In Newcastle, people would greet her as they passed. Her family was known. In Sheffield, they had eyes so heavy they rolled down into breast pockets when she passed. In Sheffield, their noses were like weathervanes, twisting their faces whichever way the wind blew.

To Chris Eaton, who would help her with the crosswords on Sundays, she left her entire collection of books, including:

Anna of the Five Towns by Arnold Bennett (1902) – This was Bennett's first novel about the Potteries, a name given to the six communities that spread to the east of Newcastle like a child's fantastic, shimmering soap bubble: Tunstall, Burslem, Hanley, Stoke, Fenton and Longton. The town of Fenton was dropped by Bennett mostly because he found the word *five* much more euphonious than *six*. The volume is signed.

Inspired by the evolutionary work of Charles Darwin, Bennett was part of the naturalist movement in literature, whereby the lives of characters were greatly influenced by heredity and one's social environment. Bennett believed, like Thomas Hardy and Emile Zola before him, and John Steinbeck shortly after, that the lives of ordinary people had the potential to be the subject of interesting books. He also took on the less popular stance that the same could be achieved with the other, inanimate minutiae of life, and his books also contain prosaic and wearisome lists of pottery and ceramics tools and processes, from the blunger to the sagger or the muffle, sculpting scalloped lambrequins with a half-inch Acacia thumb tool and then applying the most delicate glost with bundled Japanese hemp palm stems. At parties, he was known to entertain people by reciting a quite comprehensive list of the most famous makes of china and porcelain: Adams, Belleek, Bow, Bristol, Chelsea, Coalport, Copeland, Crown Staffordshire, Davenport, Dresden, Goss, Kofmehl, Limoges, Longton Hall, Matteo, Meissen, Minto, Pietra, Rockingham, Rosenthal, Royal Copenhagen, Royal Doulton, Royal Worcester (thank goodness for five Rs in a row), Schildknecht, Sèvres, Spode, St. Michael's, Sunderland, Swansea (and six Ss), Wedgwood and Withem.

Cordelia's own father was said to have been an inspiration for one of Bennett's characters, to which the signature and inscription – *To a great friend* – can attest. Every day, Great-Grandpa Barratt stepped gingerly across the West Coast Main Line railway and the A500, from Newscastle-under-Lyme to Burslem, past the crimson chapels and rows of little red houses and amber chimney pots, and the gold angel of the Town Hall. From the window of her bedroom, Corrie could see all the sedate reddish browns and reds of the composition all netted in flowing scarves of smoke, harmonised exquisitely with the chill blues of the chequered sky. For centuries her father's family – the Barratts – had worked making felt hats, an industry that at one point employed nearly a third of the city's entire population. Then in the late 1800s, for reasons that were initially blamed on resentment towards the upper class, high-priced hats suddenly went out of fashion and the whole family was forced out of their livelihoods. Similarly on her mother's side, the Hanleys (for whom the area known as Hanley Green had been named) had been employed for generations in the fashioning of clay pipes, until the industrial revolution effectively made the hand-carved puffer an object of historical interest rather than purchase. Without a family business to inherit, even through his inlaws, Corrie's father was forced to sink beneath his station and find something more menial. The youngest of nine children, he'd never been properly prepared for making hats anyway, and so was more disposed than his siblings to taking on something else, several of whom must have turned to stealing loaves of bread and/or dysentery. The only thing holding him back was the optimism he'd been raised with, spoiled for so long by all his siblings that he was sure some fine job would eventually come his way. Once Cordelia was born and he discovered pessimism to be just as agreeable, he was able to take a job sweeping floors at the Wade Ceramics company in Burslem and be just as satisfied.

For young Corrie, things could not have been better. Her father was permitted to accidentally break two pieces per fortnight without a dock in pay. Instead he broke nothing, and rewarded himself by smuggling two unbroken pieces home inside the pockets of his coveralls to his daughter. In those days, Wade Ceramics was just shifting their focus from traditional pots to the burgeoning industry of collectibles: mostly small animal figurines but also Biblical scenes, and during the first World War, comical caricatures of the German Kaiser in compromising positions; so every second week he absconded with a hippo or a wise man, and once or twice, a British Mark IV tank.

Corrie only left the area after meeting Burnell, who entered her life by securing a position as a driver for one of the country's first fleet of rubber-tired trucking companies, acquiring finished work in the Potteries and transporting them safely (on a cushion of air) down the A500 to London and beyond. Daimler and Benz were the first things the Germans dropped on the UK, long before the wars and no more than half a day from each other in Cannstatt and Manheim, both independently releasing light-weight trucks in 1896, and hitting British shores by 1900 with the five-tonne model. Burnell Eaton was not always the best driver – on his first day on the job, he backed the truck out too soon and took out the passenger door on the side of the garage – but he showed an immediate aptitude for cramming more goods into his van than anyone else seemed able to manage. Most of her figurines were destroyed in the move to Sheffield, crystallized beneath the dance of a large gilt mirror that she hated. The mirror, of course, emerged completely undamaged.

The author's signature on this book is a forgery, crafted by a friend of great-grandpa Barratt to impress his daughter on her sixteenth birthday.

Architecture for Worship by Edward A Sövik (1973) – When Cordelia Eaton first became disenfranchised with the extravagance of the religious establishment, her son loaned her this book and she never gave it back.

An American architect of Lutheran faith, Edward Sövik is held responsible in many circles for the unwarranted torture and systematic disfiguration of sacred architecture. This book, the one that started it all, is about the state of contemporary sacred architecture in the West, and how the period between the Norman conquest of England and the Reformation lured both Roman Catholic and Protestant church architects away from God's original intent with the promise of their own personal immortality.

Sövik begins with the three natural laws of that middle period, used in evaluating local churches: verticality (reaching to the heavens), permanence (transcending space and time), and iconography (the building itself as art), and then dispels them as counterproductive to the original tenets of Christianity. Naturally, early Christians had worshipped in homes, fearing persecution from the Roman authorities. But after its legalization under Constantine and gradual adoption as the Empire's official religion, one-room wooden sanctuaries sprang up across Europe. In the Middle Ages, just as advances in building technologies allowed more and more spectacular feats of construction in the name of God, the separation of man and ministry became even more distinct, dividing the worship space into the nave, for the meeting of the congregation, and the second was the dominion of the clergy, where Mass was observed, while the parishioners observed from afar. Returning to the religion's roots, he claimed, and restoring the idea that God was everywhere, Sövik re-imagined the church as a one-room meeting place again, in the most unassuming structures one might ever imagine. Only God can make a building a Church, he said. And He could make it out of anything He wanted.

Attached to this book by an elastic band is a small moleskin notebook. Cordelia had become obsessed with Sövik's theories, and had nearly filled this notebook cover to cover with small sketches she'd made of her own hypothetical churches, each one dated carefully in the upper-right corner so that they knew she'd been working on them for decades. When her husband had been off counting cars at the parking lot, Corrie had often spent her days hunched over the miniature collapsible linoleum kitchen table, beginning with ideas much like the professional designs of Sövik – albeit much cruder – but then building on them to become even smaller and more speculative. If God could make a building a Church, could He not then do the same for small boxes, or whisky tumblers, or bathtubs, or even objects with no insides, like trees or clothespins, or abstract concepts like sorrow or happiness. When her husband died, for example, she made a Church out of her sorrow, which she depicted in her sketchbook as an area of complete emptiness, devoid of anything, because that was what she felt. She'd never shown the sketches to Burnell because she was afraid he might not understand, and laugh. Similarly on another page, there was only the spot that was left when she pressed the pencil so hard against it that the lead snapped, leaving an uneven smudge with no room for any sort of extravagance or personal baggage.

C D B! by William Steig (1968) – Slightly out of place at first glance, a children's book with the story told in large letters read phonetically in the place of words (e.g., *See the bee!*), this book also contains an inscription: *C, I* ♥ *U, A.* After her husband was murdered for pocket change, Cordelia would sometimes play bridge at a nearby church, a Catholic survivor of both wars, trying her hardest to ignore the flashiness of it because she needed the social benefits. Unfortunately, she also found the competition levels severely wanting. But before she could stop, she was recruited by one of the supervising parishioners to deliver "meals on wheels" to less mobile seniors, and it was here that she met Arthur, who was not invalid so much as he was afraid to leave his home. He wouldn't even come to the door when she rang the bell, but would wait behind the curtains until he could see the automatic lock on her car doors click down. One day she left him a note with his bowl of stewed prunes, asking if he might like to accompany her to the end of his block and back, which was something he had not imagined in years, and he accepted. The next week, she sat beside him while he wrote a letter – he had no one to write to, but he didn't want to tell her this, so he invented a story about a man in a boat – and then walked with him to the end of the subdivision so he could drop it in a post box. They sat on a park bench without speaking. They read the marquee outside the VUE cinema at the Meadowhall Shopping Centre and then just kept walking. She showed him her church sketches, and he didn't laugh. At the blank page, he cried.

The Stieg book was the only one Cordelia could read in her final years, a gift from Arthur, and she read it daily.

At the funeral, Arthur introduced himself as their grandmother's lover. His satchel was full of Wade figurines he'd been collecting off eBay and waiting for the right time to give them to her. For the next year and a half, Chris Eaton's parents invited Arthur over every Sunday for dinner. On a handful of occasions, he brought wine. But most of the time he brought nothing.

Then, one day, Chris Eaton's father received a call at his office:

I loved her so much, the man sobbed into the other end of the phone.

...

I miss her so much…

Me too.

Several hours later, Chris Eaton's father was called to come down to the police station. None of the figurines in Arthur's pockets carried even a scratch.

There are so many ways to die. But it all ends up in the same place.

PART 2

There are twenty-seven bones in the human hand: eight carpals in the wrist; five metacarpals in the hand itself; and fourteen phalanges, which are the same bones that are used to construct the toes. Each finger has three phalanges (the distal, middle, and proximal). The thumb only has two.

These are the things that make us who we are. This shape. This biology. Or, so we imagine. But a bird's wing is also supported by the equivalent of the bones in the human hand. Instead of having five distinct fingers, however, birds have adapted their digits to create a specialized wing for flying. Some of the digits are fused together, while others never develop beyond the tiniest stump. But they're exactly the same bones. And this is the innate potential of beginnings. While some developments are always more probable than others, there remains the constant chance that something more exciting could happen. A twist. A surprise. We begin as idiot invalids without the faintest idea of what the world has in store for us. But who's to say where we'll eventually end up?

In its embryonic state, a baby bird is completely indistinguishable from a baby lizard.

Or even, in its earliest stages of development, from a baby boy. Or girl. Or something in between.

It's almost as if, in those early days of fertile gestation, with no more consciousness than the need to feed and grow, each human goes through every historical decision of evolution, from subdivision to the formulation of a spine to growing separate fingers and opposable thumbs. *Ontogeny recapitulates phylogeny.* And every single one of us takes the safer route when, instead, we could emerge as fantastic beasts of light and hope. Or destruction. With hard outer shells, torsos completely covered in fur, powerful dorsal fins...

If only we had the courage.

Chris Eaton had a mother and a father. Granted, most people did in those days. Especially in Maine, where technology sometimes came to vacation but never seemed to stay. Even the championship pumpkins his father started under the 400W metal halide bulbs in his ebb and flow hydroponic marijuana system could be traced back through a distinct lineage, year after year, beginning each season where the last year's best performers left off. They were his kids, and he even named them, following an alphabetic system based on the rules of naming purebred cattle, so you would know the year they were born, yoked with handles from the 'soaps' he watched while tending them. Alice was nothing to brag about. And Bo would still have had him laughed out of the county fair. But by the time he reached Hope, appropriately, the other competitors acknowledged him with friendly nods. He wasn't exactly competition, but he was certainly respectable. He tipped his Black Bears ball cap back to them, fingering the fishing lure he'd pitched along its brim.

In secret, however, he despised the whole lot of them, slamming the garage door behind him when he returned from the annual Clarence weigh-in, head drug low, fists at his sides like diseased burls. In 1986, when the World Pumpkin Federation promoted a one-thousand-pound pumpkin challenge, most growers said it was impossible. But once money became involved (the first to break the mark won an astonishing $50,000), so did the chemical companies. The trick had always been finding ways to coax the pumpkin into believing it could absorb even more water than it normally would. Once a pumpkin reaches its maximum capacity to take on more water, any further expansion is offset by a progressive thinning of the outer shell, and a larger pumpkin might actually begin to weigh less. Then the scientists took over. In 2003 alone, the number of North American entries to break the thousand-pound barrier was forty-three. As far as Chris Eaton's father was concerned, you might as well paint an elephant orange and let it walk to the fair under its own power. And he stubbornly refused to use anything that wasn't one-hundred-percent organic, nurturing them on one hundred and fifty gallons of water per day and a secret sixty-ingredient compost including powdered sugar, liquid molasses, blood meal (all for heating the compost to make it churn harder), hardwood sawdust, brewery by-products, animal manure, pine bark, sandy loam, rice hulls, coffee grounds, cornstarch, tomato paste, scum from cleaned lobster tanks, egg yolks, live bees, and when Spring washed up on the coasts of Maine like a disoriented whale, wet and awkward, seaweed. Lit only by the moon and his undying hope, Chris Eaton and his father hustled great polyethylene bags of it back to the garden. Mixed into the regular compost and Canadian sphagnum, it served dual-purpose by increasing water-holding capacity and protected against any late frosts. The winds off the compost pile made Chris feel dizzy and loved. When it was freshly turned, it released an acrid drift, warm and rank like his father's breath.

He lost again and again.

Of course, seaweed is not only an excellent source of trace elements for growth, but also contains Iodine-127, making both plants and humans resistant to the absorption of Iodine-131, an element that is constantly being released into our atmosphere by the so-called normal operations of nuclear power plants and weapons facilities. If you've been anywhere near a nuclear explosion or fallout, you know exactly what normal can mean. The sodium alginate in kelp is capable of binding with ingested particles of toxic strontium-90, cesium-137, and various heavy metals in the digestive tract. After Chernobyl, the Russians isolated the polysaccharide U-Foucauldian in kelp, an excellent sponge for radioactive elements. They fed the extract to Eurasian glass lizards and found their ability to regenerate their tails was not diminished by repeated exposure to nuclear radiation.

All of which came too late for the children of Chernobyl, who walked straight out of the womb with feet like pumpkins, heads like flattened salamanders', without eyes, the bones of the hands fused into solid hammers of flesh and osseous, their legs like welded bows...

These were the ones with true courage. They were the future.

The only way they resembled their parents was that they spoke the same language. If they had mouths.

Or they died early.

Chris Eaton's grandfather never went to war, avoiding Woodrow Wilson's draft in 1917 by faking bad genetic eyesight. So when war broke out again in Europe, even with two young children to support, Chris Eaton's father read the newspapers back in California with careful interest. And as soon as the US decided to join the Allied forces against the Nazis, he was off to the local conscription office. After two short months of basic training at Fort Ord, and some additional amphibious training at the British Centre in Invarary, Scotland, he was assigned to join the 1st Infantry Unit, fresh from fighting in Italy. In the Normandy invasion, he stumbled in the water immediately upon exiting the boat, and was sucked under the churn of the Mark 5 LCT transport.

Accounts at his funeral one year later said he was held under for close to five minutes. But somehow he survived, yanked out by the Captain of his unit, and they all started thinking of him as their good luck charm. Seemingly blessed with a second chance at life, an opportunity to start over, Chris Eaton's father returned to the US and to his practice. He took up golf, and hit a hole-in-one. He swam every day, and took up poker. Then, he joined a private tennis club with some fellow doctors, and less than a year later, an attendant found his body in the hot tub. Since they could find no trauma to his head, the coroner ascertained that he had passed out due to dehydration from excessive sweating, after which his body must have slipped below the surface and was filled like an empty jug.

Chris Eaton's parents could have done anything, too, but instead they ended up together, while she was trying to force her extracurricular activism into a Master's degree and he was trying to single-handedly demolish the fish stock up at Belews Lake. She'd been canvassing for Mondale for nearly a year and a half; he hadn't even voted. But when Chris Eaton's father crashed his mother's election party with a Reagan mask obscuring his sight and screaming "Born in the USA" at the top of his lungs (Reagan had attempted to steal the hit as his campaign song, until Springsteen himself demanded he stop), she knew she'd finally found someone who understood, cornering him at length on social injustice, gay rights, the growing divide between rich and poor, and the need for a strong female presence in the White House ("Are we really better off than we were four years ago? Really?!"), some of which he partly understood (and much of which he couldn't hear through Reagan's oversized latex ears, anyway), and then they went back to her place, got married and because of complications, induced a girl, a boy, didn't matter, and perhaps because of their story, or their decision to have our hero on a predetermined day – his understanding of what it takes to make a baby: one sperm, one egg, and five tablets of Buccal Pitocin – Chris Eaton tends to think everything will eventually work out.

Before they left California, Chris Eaton's father had worked as the Assistant Director of Caltrans, the government agency responsible for road mobility across the State, the pride of all state agencies, credited with designing the font used in road signs nationwide for over fifty years, as well as being the innovators behind reflective, raised dots as lane dividers instead of painted lines. By the eighties, he was responsible for the ongoing maintenance and safety on over 50,000 lane miles of roadway, 12,000 bridges, 250,000 acres of roadside including 25,000 landscaped acres, 88 roadside rest stops, 350 vista points, 340 park-and-ride lots, 310 pumping plants and more than 400 maintenance yards. It was his job to ensure that all of the connections remained as connections, that society did not crumble in the face of weather and time, and that everything continued to make sense, at least from a strictly utilitarian point of view. His role – and, indeed, his great engineering talent – was in seeing how so many seemingly unrelated pieces fit together and to plan for the most likely eventualities.

That's when he became interested in earthquakes, after the 1989 tremors that stunned baseball fans across the country during the World Series game between San Francisco and San Diego, and began to follow the writings of Jim Berkland, who had predicted the incident four days before it happened. Berkland employed a system of measurements and calculations to which Chris Eaton's father could entirely relate, bringing together as many "unrelated" bits of information as possible until it began to take shape: tide levels, the lunar perigee, even strange animal behavior, measured chiefly by the number of runaway pet ads and beached whales in a predetermined period. Over the next two and a half years, as Chris Eaton's father followed Berkland's predictions fanatically, the retired geologist accurately predicted nearly eighty percent of the globe's major and minor quakes, always several days before they struck.

To be of use in his own work, Chris Eaton's father had to predict events much further in advance, with more of a regional focus, so he took Berkland's findings and cross-referenced them with other measures of local synchronicity and aggression, like the penalty minutes taken by the Los Angeles Kings in home games versus away, the differential between the price of gas at competing stations, the position of the banana ice cream tub at his local frozen dairy, the number of times he came across people with his name, or the number nine, all of which he included in a paper on seismic retrofitting for many of the state's surviving elevated roadways and bridges (replacing obsolete, riveted lattice beams with heat-treated bolt lattice, and adding ductile steel restraints to expansion rockers using friction clamps), roundly applauded for its size and complexity but for those same reasons also went largely unread, and – most unfortunate of all – his recommendations were not adopted until immediately following the quake he'd predicted for Northridge in '94. Fifty-one people were killed, 9263 were injured, and large portions of Interstate 10, Interstate 5, and California State Highway 14 had to be entirely rebuilt, taking nearly two years to replace, and to add insult to injury, his Director was replaced and focus shifted from maintenance entirely to new construction, so Chris Eaton's father jumped at a job offer from Florida, where they were experiencing a road crisis of their own, under the weight of so many obese, two-fisted tourists and pensioners – that is, until the pressure of being a prophet of disaster became too great to bear, and his mind alighted from his frantic pursuit of the gaps in symbolic order to one particular cut in the real: the alarming byproducts of the parasitic hospitality industry, the business of competitive pampering, the American Automobile Association reserving its Three, Four and Five Diamond rankings for facilities that would go that extra mile, providing their guests with such unnecessary luxuries as single-serving shampoos and conditioners, paper doilies around the in-room water glasses and, according to the rules set out in its own guide, "Two bars of soap greater than ¾ oz." Two new bars of soap. Every day. Even for guests who remained for more than one night. All of those bars of soap were tossed in the dumpsters out back, and then carted to the landfill. And the sheer number of them skewed his calculations to distraction until, on one of his inspections up north, he just kept driving until he reached the groomed grass and asphalt of Alexandria, Virginia, and using a slight modification of US Patent #4310479 (*wherein soap scrap material resulting from the formation of the soap bars is reintroduced into the process by adding it into the final extrusion device*), combined with US Patent #4296064 (*a method for recycling soap chips in a particular structure including a container having a removable rack having four compartments and a heating element, the method comprising, placing the soap chips in the compartment, heating the soap chips, cooling the soap chips, removing the rack from the container and emptying out formed soap bars*), Chris Eaton's father registered a device that could be used to collect waste soaps from the hotel industry, re-render them and sell the new recycled bars back for profit.

At the annual soap convention in Orlando, the big producers practically laughed him out of the hotel. But with new garbage collection laws that penalized businesses for any excess waste, he was able to approach one hotel at a time with a simple proposition: to reduce the waste of a hundred-room hotel (operating at 75% capacity) by nearly half a tonne every year, undercutting the government penalties and carting the bars away in a leased van that he would return reeking permanently of lilacs and lavender. The first letter from Procter & Gamble arrived shortly after Chris Eaton's father signed the contract with Disney. Phone calls from Amway and Unilever followed soon after. They had taken some interest in his curious invention after all, and wished to discuss the possibility of purchasing it from him. He refused. If they'd really been so interested, they could have purchased it at the convention. Now it was too late. Of course he had no idea who he was dealing with. The major manufacturers had been fighting a war over the lucrative soap markups for decades. Before the eighties, P&G had held a near monopoly over North American cleanliness for as long as anyone could recall. Then, just as Chris Eaton's father was graduating from college, the real war for soap supremacy began. Unilever created what they dubbed a *beauty bar*, made with extra moisturizing ingredients to prevent the dry skin often caused by harsher soaps, and by 1986, *Dove* had become the top-grossing soap in the world.

When Chris Eaton's father came on the scene, both companies had already lost a significant amount of the hotel business to soap makers in India, Singapore and the Philippines, so they were not about to lose out to an engineer from Florida who three years earlier was trying to predict earthquakes with tea leaves. They dropped their prices. They launched new campaigns that stressed the purity of their own product. Near Tallahassee, P&G created a special repository for used soap fragments, actually paying the hotels to collect the barely used bars and burying them deep underground where they could not be used again.

Chris Eaton's father was not dissuaded. In fact, despite all of this, opportunities began to open up in several other states along the Eastern seaboard. Through Disney and old connections with Caltrans, he was able to set up facilities in California. Then the rumors started, that the flu-like symptoms that were cropping up in California were linked to bacteria in the recycled soap. Somehow, various innocent personal bacteria were mingling with chemicals in the recycling process and making people ill. It was a blatant lie. But the Florida and California legal systems refused to do anything about it. When one of his clients forwarded him a damning email from a P&G distributor, they apologized and settled out of court for an undisclosed amount. But the business never recovered. They were left with warehouses full of questionable product that they were never able to sell. And Chris Eaton's father was never the same.

A few years later, Chris Eaton's mother started suffering from severe weight loss. She complained of increased cramping, and frequent diarrhea, until one morning she discovered dark ochre blood in her stool. One of her husband's military friends diagnosed her with piles, and prescribed an ointment. But the bleeding continued. Six weeks later and thirty-two pounds lighter, she collapsed in line at the Gottschalks buying new underwear, the pair she was wearing spotted in red. At the hospital she was re-diagnosed, this time with pseudomembranous colitis. The wall of her bowel had begun to perforate and she'd started to enter major organ failure. She woke up with a quarter-sized hole in her abdomen and a rubber colostomy bag held in place by a seven-inch-wide fabric belt – her new rectum and port-a-potty. She made the best of it. She made jokes about how she was glad she'd already given up swimming. And she continued to look after her two children as best she could. Then, after the first bag failed, and they "tore (her) another asshole" (she'd never sworn before in her life), she was told she could no longer eat nuts or celery, coconut or citrus fruit, for fear of further blockage, and she basically told the world to fuck it. Still a teenager, Chris Eaton had to take over most of the errands because Chris Eaton's mother was too embarrassed to leave the house.

PART 3

The first time Chris Eaton hit the water, everything stopped. He was just a child, a spastic three-year-old with wet towels for feet, head like an overgrown ape's paw, his legs like welded bows, too fast for his body, so they just bounced up and down like the limbs of some delicate, drunken ostrich. He knew enough that he wasn't supposed to run around the pool. That much he'd already learned. And he was not disobedient. But who could help it? He was still young enough to change form at will, and that day he was full of potential energy, with an imagination unrestricted by shame. Or knowledge. Or impossibility. He was the first seconds of an igniting lightbulb filament, he was a falling chestnut, he was a blade of grass in the rain. If he wanted to, he could have frozen the pool with his mind, could have leapt skywards and pissed rain down on all of them, could have taken out the entire line of soldiers tracking him from the opposite shore with one shot. If he wanted to.

But then he was in the water, completely unsure how he got there. And then there was nothing but the sound of bubbles rushing past his ears. He was too young to know the difference. Solids and liquids; liquids and gases. What did he care? The world looked like it had fractured into millions of pieces. There was a momentary illusion of flight. A feeling of heavenly aquatic weightlessness. A darkening peace.

He inhaled.

And he sank to the bottom.

Chris Eaton was a good boy, a bad boy, a good girl. Bad girl. Chris Eaton was so fast. Chris Eaton was so pretty. He was strong and fast and big and pretty. She could run and jump and stretch tall like this. Chris Eaton was precious. She was all the meaningless things you call a child when you're too disinterested to properly engage, and more.

Chris Eaton was a fucking *genius*. Her IQ score was through the roof. Her mother, who had a Master's degree in Sociology, taught her how to read long before she went to school, believing the curriculum was too soft, that children had so much more capacity to learn at an early age. So Chris Eaton always read at a level three grades higher. She knew all the tricks of the multiplication tables: numbers divisible by 2 were all even numbers; the digits in a number divisible by 3 would add up to a number that was also divisible by 3; likewise 9; numbers that fell into the sets of 2 and 3 would also be divisible by 6; the last digit in a number divisible by 7, when doubled and subtracted from the remaining digits of that number, will produce a number that is also divisible by 7. She could tell you the population of every country in Africa. She could name the capitals of all fifty states, in alphabetical order. She'd even memorized *pi* to twelve decimal points (3.1415926535897), which is the point at which all numbers except zero have been used at least once.

When she was first tested by Mensa at the age of eight, she made only two mistakes on the entire test:

> **21. Pear is to apple as potato is to?**
> **Banana   Peanut   Strawberry   Peach   Lettuce**
>
> **22. Which of the following is least like the others?**
> **Poem   Novel   Painting   Statue   Flower**

Her answers: **Lettuce**; **Statue**.

The correct answers: **Peanut; Flower**.

Of course, because she was only eight, and because her score was still remarkable, they explained to her where she had made her mistakes. In the first case, **pear** and **apple** are linked by the fact that they grow on trees. So the proper corresponding link to **potato**, which grows under ground, is the **peanut**. In the second question, the **flower** is quite simply the only object in the list that occurs naturally. It is not a man-made object of beauty.

Her answers, however, were no less correct, particularly after emerging from a lengthy sequence of math-based, quantitative solutions. She chose **lettuce** for reasons of length. **Pear** had four letters, **apple** had five, **potato** had six, and **lettuce** was the only word with seven. For her, it was simply the next in the sequence. **Statue**, she reasoned, was the only word in the second list that ended with a vowel. Even her choice on the next question, though correct, was chosen for similarly incorrect reasons:

23. Which of these is the odd one out?

Cat Dog Hamster Rabbit Elk

The answer was **Elk**. But the Mensa explanation was because it was the only non-domesticated animal in the list. Chris Eaton, once more, chose it because it was the only one that *began* with a vowel.

She was wise beyond her years. A visionary. The Mensa officiators didn't know what to *do* with her. Her brain, she thought, must be the size of a fucking *Zeppelin*! They even thought about skipping her a grade, when her family came back to Arizona from Norway in Grade Five, but she was so tiny, as if merely living in Norway had shaped her outward appearance along with her inside, infecting her somehow with a sensitively hunched Scandinavian frame, and her teachers were worried she might get picked on. Small kids, most adults theorize, have difficulties maturing. Small kids cannot handle situations with more complex emotions. Small kids (or at least this is true for Chris Eaton) feel something burning behind their eyes at the slightest sign of confrontation, when a math competition is lost, or when a word is mispronounced out loud in front of the entire class, and someone starts to snicker, and the tears well up....

One day, Chris Eaton's teacher took him aside and told him that he could be whatever he wanted, which is a horrible thing to say to a child with an overactive imagination. All he wanted out of life was to go to Heaven and get his picture in *Rack Magazine*. She laughed. And she told him she wanted him to write stories. A story a week. About topics she would assign him. For thirty-six weeks.
36 was divisible by 2, 3, 4, 6 and 9.

The stories ranged from Halloween horror to science fiction to intense battles with wild animals, usually inspired by a one- or two-sentence catalyst, such as *Write a story about becoming invisible; call it "Unseen Self,"* or *Imagine two cats who confront magic, danger and death to rescue a missing friend,* or *Does Income Improve Health or Does Good Health Increase Income?* He wrote an imagined history of rugby, and what it would be like to be a stock car racer, and work at an Internet help desk; he wrote a review of a skateboard video game, a complaint to a computer manufacturer, a short play called *The Mummy*, a love story about a civil war hero and some girl, one sci-fi piece about managing large systems and a second called "Pure Substances;" there was an emperor, and a barking goldfish, a brown bear, a koala and a young man on the western frontier, a bridge game, and angelic warriors without wings. And his friends gathered around him on the playground at recess and practically begged to hear more. The attention became an obsession that darkened his soul.

Once because it was President's Day the card read: *Imagine you went to battle with General Washington to fight for our Independence. What do you see?* But of course his namesake – the first Chris Eaton in North America – had actually been there, right beside Washington at Brandywine, having already served his country's rebel forces for nearly a year in Virginia and the Carolinas, then with General Arnold at White Plains, and for several months in the special units forces of General Rutherford near Charlotte. Rutherford ordered a detachment to march to the River Santee, where they captured several more Tories, and British, and two boats. They then conveyed the twelve prisoners to the main army at Rugeleys Mills, where they remained for some weeks, during which time a detachment was sent to support General Sumter against the enemy toward the Catawba River. When they reached Sumter, they were informed he had defeated the enemy so they marched back to the headquarters at the mills. They then marched toward Camden. Yet he returned to Surry County (later renamed Stokes County) with no fireworks and no parade, and pockets full of continental money that had already depreciated to basic uselessness. Washington went on to be the country's first president. And Christopher Eaton became a harness maker. The next year, he married. But because there was no record of a Chris Eaton before the war, the government tried to take his war pension away, even after several of his surviving compatriots testified on his behalf with verbal affidavits that are still maintained in official documents in Washington:

> **Aff. of John Venable**, Stokes Co., NC, 15 Apr. 1834 – He is acquainted with Christopher Eaton and knows of his militia service. He was present at Gates defeat although Eaton did not serve in the same company with him.

> **Aff. of Philip Kiser and Charles Banner**, Stokes Co., NC, 9 Apr. 1834 – acquainted with Christopher, believed in the neighborhood to be a soldier in the Revolution.

> **Aff. of Joseph Darnall**, Stokes Co., NC, 13 Sept. 1832 – Darnall is well acquainted

with Christopher Eaton, who now resides in Surry County. He personally knows that Eaton served faithfully as a revolutionary soldier in the militia company commanded by Capt. Absalom Bostick in Col. Armstrong's regiment under Gen. Rutherford. Eaton entered this service in Surry County in June 1780. They marched to Salisbury, NC, where they joined headquarters and then marched to Cheraw Hills in South Carolina, where they joined General Gates army. They then marched toward Camden where "we fell in with the British when the battle ensued" between Gates and Cornwallis' armies. Joseph Darnall was not in the battle but Eaton was, he believes.

Aff. of Hugh Boyles, Stokes Co., NC, 13 Sept. 1832 – He knew Eaton during the Revolution and always understood that he served in the Revolution.

Aff. of William Merritt, Stokes Co., NC, 13 Mar. 1833 – Merritt was in service at Moravian old town in 1780. There was an Eaton in the service at that time guarding the prisoners taken at Kings mountain and I believe Christopher Eaton is that same man.

When the government eventually offered him an annual pension of only twenty dollars, he refused to accept it.

When he was six, Chris Eaton's parents tried to give him some focus. He needed some good focus. Couldn't focus. So they put him in tennis lessons, drum lessons, acting lessons, football. But he was not good at it. Lessons. Not good at lessons at all. Chris Eaton's parents even put him in violin lessons, taught via the Suzuki method, a technique based on endless repetition and observation, the way a child first learns to speak. Shinichi Suzuki was the son of Japan's first violin manufacturer, born at the turn of the century, and he taught himself to play by stealing one of his father's completed models and using it to replicate any sound he heard, from recorded music to bird calls, and later in his life, the sound of the missiles falling from the American bombers. Chris Eaton was going to be a prodigy, and some day play for kings and queens if kings and queens were still around by then. Or so his father dreamed. But Chris Eaton spent most of those lessons hiding behind the back seats of the conservatory auditorium. The only thing he learned, like Suzuki, was to imitate everything he heard, like a confused, urbanized starling calling back to the surrounding car alarms. Eventually, he picked up his father's old Stella guitar and, just through memory, flawlessly duplicated Mark Knopfler's solo from the live recording of "Sultans of Swing."

When he turned ten, his mother tried again, and sent him to piano lessons taught by nuns near the hospital, in a building that would later become occupied by the regional Department for Environment, Food and Rural affairs. His sister had warned him about the nuns. When she didn't arch her fingers properly, her uncooperative hands failing her time after time, her knuckles were rapped with the ruler. Chris Eaton's nun, thankfully, was younger and less violently inclined. She didn't even wear a habit, just handed out stickers like raindrops and was happy to be working, he guessed. Two years later, after his sister wet her pants on the way to her weekly session, his mother switched them to lessons with the mother of one of his classmates. Four months later, as he was about to make his ninth assay into "The Alleycat," she swiveled his seat to face her directly.

"How many hours do you spend practicing a week?"

"…"

"When your mother shows up, I'm going to tell her we're through. You're wasting my time and her money."

He was eleven by this point and frankly a much bigger fan of European football; and devising alternate rules to *Dungeons & Dragons* with less chance of failure; and BMX bikes with fake plastic gas tanks; and the drums; collecting "sports memorabilia," which basically amounted to a few hockey cards, a broken goalie stick from The Carolina Hurricanes' Traseac Drakhinov, and some stickers he'd collected from bags of potato chips, mostly of wrestlers like Hornet Cisa, Stone Hirca and Inert Chaos; musical parody (his favorite: a send-up of Johnny Cash's "Walk the Line," redubbed "Taco Shrine;" and joke books.

JOKES HE TOLD INCESSANTLY
AND UNDERSTOOD:

How do you stop an elephant from charging?
Take away his credit card.

How do you make an elephant float?
Take two scoops of elephant and add some root beer.

What is the centre of gravity?
The letter V.

What is at the end of everything?
The letter G.

What will you find in the middle of the sea?
The letter E. (Sea. E. His initials, which made the joke
even funnier for him.)

JOKES HE FAILED TO UNDERSTAND
BUT TOLD ANYWAY:

How do you get down from an elephant?
You don't. You get down from a duck.

What do you get when you cross an elephant and a rhino?
Elephino!

Want to hear a dirty joke?
Two white horses fell in a mud puddle.

Want to hear an even dirtier joke?
Three came out.

Really he spent most of this time playing foosball in bars he got into
using a fake ID, which was ridiculous because he was obviously not
even close to puberty, let alone forty, or British. But because he won
so often, they believed it. And so did he. It was like they were seeing
an entirely different person.

How else could they justify being beaten regularly by an eleven-
year-old kid?

When he told the elephant float joke to some of the other players, one of the men told him he had told it wrong. When he showed
the man the book, he was told it was an honest mistake, but that he
should change *scoops* to *buckets*.

"Why?" he asked.

"Elephants come in buckets, son. Buckets."

This was another one he didn't get.

She had trouble making friends as a child, falling asleep in one state and then waking up in another, a new home, same as the old home but with a different placement of sunrise and sunset, different mountains, different trees, sometimes no trees, sometimes no mountains, a different smell on the wind, a swimming pool, a neighbor she liked, a neighbor she didn't like, a neighbor with a swimming pool and thus didn't matter if she liked or not. In one place, she made one friend, a girl named Trisha Cone who had also come from away that year and whose father, she claimed, killed people for a living. Really, though, he was just an undertaker.

Trisha's father, James Cone, had always wanted to be a professor, a philosopher, an academic, a great mind; but as a child in Arkansas he had written special aptitude tests, and the results had been misread and mistaken for another boy with the same name, so instead of being placed in an advanced class he was relegated to the back of the room, with the troublemakers and the mentally ignored. He understood the subject matter better than his teachers, but he was told he did not, and thus moved through knowledge like a mental dyslexic, as though the things he took for truth were just a trick of his mind, that his intelligence and comprehension were just illusions, like a rainbow, or the thumb trick of his drunk uncle, or democracy, until he began to distrust the cognitive part of his brain so much that he eventually just shut it down. He dropped out of high school to work at a drive-in, earning points with the smarter kids by allowing them to sneak in for free but then losing the job for the same reason, which made him feel even stupider. He hitchhiked up to Malvern, and for three months made a living as an unsanctioned tour guide outside the main gates of the hot springs, helping tourists find similar pools outside official park grounds for half the price of regular admission, then helping himself to their wallets and shoes while they soaked. For this, he spent six months in detention as a juvenile near Alexander, but having learned other lessons in this time, he then set off on a string of new scams up into the Midwest, sidled over to Memphis, and was then drawn, as if by Fate through a straw, up the Mississippi to St. Louis and beyond, committing another series of seemingly unrelated crimes under the names Sean Mejoc, Jason Mece (pronounced *meechee*, like the fish, not *meesee* like the principle of grouping data), Mace Jones, Jan Coëmes, and Enoc James, until someone realized they were all anagrams of his own name and he was picked up near Rapid City, South Dakota, going by the name Joe McEans.

It was the Coëmes alias that confounded authorities most. A couple from Canada made a call to the local sheriff near Bowling Green, Kentucky, saying they'd been touring the Mammoth Cave when a young man from their group had lost his wallet to a pickpocket. The young man had just shrugged it off, saying the amount was so insignificant it didn't really matter, but the couple insisted on calling it in, just to make sure the police were on the lookout, to protect others in the future. The Canadians also made sure he had enough to cover his costs back to Chicago where he was due to catch a flight back to Belgium. The sheriff filed it beside his empty coffee cup and sandwich wrapper, alongside yesterday's crossword.

Then, about a week later, the sheriff fielded another call, this time from the wife of a farmer near Smiths Grove. She had likewise encountered a young man who had had his wallet stolen, "a handsome man with teeth like a horse," and had likewise provided him bus fare to Indianapolis, where he could at least have money wired to him from his father, a Belgian diplomat in Washington. And three weeks after that, he was sitting across his desk from the Glasgow grocer, listening to her story of the poor fellow who spoke in such broken English, as if the lower half of his jaw were too heavy to properly maneuver, who promised to reimburse him once he returned to Europe and – more than that – to pay for a ticket in thanks so that the grocer might one day come share hospitality from him, after which the grocer had heard nothing more. The sheriff asked if he'd gotten the man's name, and after making a few calls to confirm that there were no visiting Belgian dignitaries in the country with that handle, the sheriff turned things over to the Feds. Though James Cone had barely passed high school English, many of the victims claimed the poor young man spoke fluent French. But the US Marshals were already familiar with Cone and with the area's own language skills. And he likely would have gone to prison for most of his life had it not been for the millionaire Vic Saater, who surprised everyone by using some of his political leverage to get Cone off scot-free.

His full name was Victor Hådron Saater, although he much preferred Vic. He also identified first and foremost as a Norwegian, despite the fact that he'd been born in New York, educated in Boston and made his fortune in South Dakota. His father had moved to the US in 1902 to work as a civil engineer on the fledgling New York City subway project, but had returned to Oslo on his divorce to create a similar system back home. Vic's mother had stayed behind, raising Vic and his sister by herself, and Vic eventually earned an engineering degree of his own in explosives from MIT. He'd never dreamed of living any further west, perfectly content to remain in Massachusetts to help expand its own transit system. But when fellow Norwegian-American and Klan member, Gutzon Borglum, was charged with the task of designing a fitting monument to four of the country's greatest presidents, Borglum hired Saater as the head of demolitions, and for the next fourteen years, Borglum often left him in charge while he lobbied for more funds in Washington. Saater simultaneously expanded his own wealth by contributing to local gold and iron ore mines in Keystone, Deadwood and Lead.

Of course, when the German forces eventually occupied Norway on April 9, 1940, Vic volunteered along with a team of other expat commandos to join the Scandinavian resistance, all of them trained in survival, skiing, marksmanship (two of the team members, Haukelid and Røjevold, had competed for the U.S. at the 1936 Olympics in the military patrol competition, an early form of the biathlon) and – Saater's personal expertise – advanced demolition. Unfortunately, there wasn't a lick of orienteering skills in the whole bunch,

44

and the mission, code-named Operation Sloth, involved parachuting into the mountains several hundred miles from Vemork, where the Norwegians had been producing heavy water for nearly a decade as a byproduct of making fertilizer. The Halifax bomber encountered bad weather and dropped them several hundred miles off course, and by the time they actually reached their target, the shipment was already on its way by train to Lake Tinnsjø, where a ferry was waiting to transport the dangerous material to the nearest airbase. Haukelid, who had been placed in charge because of his prior military experience, felt that detonating charges on the ferry might be the best way to sabotage the Nazis' hopes of developing an atomic weapon, so he and Saater snuck down to the docks and convinced one of the Norwegian hands to smuggle them on board.

When he returned from Europe, Saater had a few medals and a genuine Norwegian bride to show for it, and the two of them wasted no time in producing nine daughters named Ingrid, Anna, Sara, Kirsti, Kaia, Karoline, Hanna, Frida and Marte. He managed to marry each off in fairly quick succession, except for Ingrid, who despite being the most beautiful, had managed through her Shakespearean stubbornness to remain as chaste and unlovable as possible for over thirty years, even as each of her sisters fell helplessly in love and married the most incompetent men their father could have imagined. By the time Cone showed up at his door, working some angle as a travelling salesman with a broken automobile, Saater was so desperate to be rid of her or find a suitable heir to his empire that he told Cone he had a room for him, most assuredly, but he would also have to share a bed with his daughter. And when the federal marshals trapped him a week later, Saater agreed to get Cone off if Cone agreed to marry Ingrid and earn a regular stipend working for him. On the first day, Cone flicked his cigarette butt out the passenger window of the company pickup and it spun into the back with the unused explosive charges. Later, when he was caught using his shovel to break up some stubborn rocks, sparks flying in every direction, Vic Saater helped his new son-in-law set up an apprenticeship at a funeral home in nearby St. Petersburg. He passed the National Board Exam on the first try and left immediately with Saater's daughter to a neighbouring state.

This was how Trisha Cone came to be Chris Eaton's one and only best friend. In the ninth grade, their class took a trip to Vancouver to experience a foreign culture that was essentially the same as her own except for the proximity of the mountains. There, they did most of the things they would never have done back in Seattle, like go to the aquarium, or see a musical. They even bought their first thongs, to mark their passage into womanhood, and were so worried about them being too tight up the butt that they bought extra large, and they hung loose at the crotch like tiny cotton hammocks between their thighs. Then Trisha, who had run low on money after buying a caricature near the Chinese Garden, let several of the boys from the other school touch her boobs for $10. By the end of the year, Trisha's father heard of a better market in Salinas, California, and again, Chris Eaton was alone.

He likely should have died. Or so he's been told. But so much of his life is based on stories he can't remember having lived. That's what people do. We place so much importance on sight and touch, we are taught these things are the touchstones of experience, we base all scientific knowledge on what we can witness or at least make theoretical suppositions on potential witnessings; but the truth of the matter is that so much of identity comes not from personal experience, not from the touching or seeing or tasting or even those emotional swells of sporadic attraction and indifference, it comes from hearing – and then processing – each of those stories into some reasonable explanation of your life. Babies are born with so much potential, in a world without identity, an empty vessel. All we know is that we are somehow separate from the world. Otherwise, we are anything we want to be.

Then, as we grow older, the indoctrination of repetition begins,

46

and each time a story is retold, another possibility is killed. At dinner parties, listening to the grownups from beneath the serving table, we're subconsciously losing all hope. And we start to believe it. So that the very foundation of our character is constructed for us by other people who might as well be strangers, albeit blood strangers, and we accept it without struggle.

For example, they say it was his sister who saved him, only eight but already competing in teen and adult swim meets across Illinois. In the 50m junior freestyle at the 1A State finals, since it provided her no discernible advantage, she was even permitted an unorthodox starting position from within the water. But by the time she'd reached the Nationals in North Carolina, her legend had preceded her. Once she cut the water's skin, they said it was like she was part dolphin, the surface around her as still and pristine as a morning lake. Little did her awestruck competitors know that the only thing that kept her from completely humiliating them was the confusion of so many bodies in the water at once. Surrounded by these awkward, monstrous teens, she could barely think over the incessant chaotic slap of their flat-handed dreams, the sour scent of yoghurt drifting from their exhalations. Occasionally, she could even smell their blood. Or the diluted stench of IGF-1, Clenbuterol, cypionate, erythropoietin. She had to fight off the urge to attack, to veer from her lane and ram her heels forcefully into her opponent's ribcage. Then, for the final heat to qualify for the Olympics, the coach from Holmes Lumber lodged a formal protest forcing her to start on the blocks with everyone else. Someone actually had to help her mount them, wobbling like a wounded foal. And after two false starts (she didn't even wait for the gun; she just hopped in as soon as she felt the television cameras on her), they had to forcibly remove her from the pool (setting the stage for Dara Torres to repeat her 1987 title and go on to become an American swimming hero until retiring at the 2000 Olympic Games.)

One day, as the story went, Chris Eaton fell into the pool, and his sister was there already, as she always was, with her skin softened to terry cloth, her eyes like flaming oil rigs from the chlorine. She felt the displacement of water more than saw him. Something had entered into her space. And the adults watched her circle him several times before she poured him back onto the Wolmanized deck and blew into his mouth.

He inhaled again.

He coughed.

He blinked.

The way his father told the story, they were fishing. His father was one of the first men to have his own fishing show, a local access program that came about after the ice was broken by television angling pioneers like Ron and Al Lindner. With only his wife as a camera operator, the senior Eaton cast his line in all the secret spots he could find around the state, like the tiny pool behind Wolf Point, or the poorly groomed outcropping on Tongue River he named after his son. And when things went no further than that, Chris Eaton's father cursed the more popular shows for pandering to people, by setting their shows in more exotic locations, or using pre-caught fish, which was more common than you might expect, his knotty hands like singed rope ends in the hood of his windbreaker.

Chris Eaton's father took him fishing, and he landed a thirty-nine pound carp at the Nelson Reservoir. His father took him fishing and he landed a twenty-six-and-a-half pound channel catfish at Castle Rock. His father took him fishing and he snagged a small parr, through the eye, which he was legally bound to toss back because of its size and there was no way to remove the hook without taking the eye with it. The sun felt like toasted bread against his skin, and he felt sick, and the next thing he knew there was a sting on the back of his hand and across his left cheek, a quick popping in his ears, the muted sounds of movement, bubbles rushing past his ears.

The water was cold.

The current punched him in the chest and spun him sideways.

48

His shoulder struck a rock.

And he inhaled.

Instead of being instilled with fear, he transformed his bedroom into a water mausoleum, with jars of it collected from every spot they had ever visited (three of the five Great Lakes, Nelson Reservoir, the overly chlorinated habitat of the neighbour's pool...), most of which had begun to facilitate life and made his mother gag when she came in to change his sheets. He begged his parents almost daily to take a vacation to the ocean. During lightning storms, they had to keep him from going outside to lay down on the lawn. And he spent hours soaking in the bath until his skin began to prune and separate from the layer of fat beneath it. It was only when he hit puberty and began worrying about odour that he gave the jars up. From that point on, he was all but directionless.

When he fell in the water and sank to the bottom, the young boy forgot everything. He forgot his name, forgot who he was, forgot his address, his eye color, his shoe size (not that he'd ever had any), forgot the number of trees inside the walls, the number of trees he could see outside the walls, the beating he'd just been given, his favorite food, and essentially forgot about all the horrible days he'd spent at the Saint Roche orphanage.

Saint Roche (alternately known as Roch, Rochus, Roc, Rocco, Rokku, Roque, Rok, Roko, Rókus, Pókkou and Rollox) was not a proper historical saint, at least as set out by most European hagiographic scholars, and some would even argue (among them, the contemporary Frenchman Pierre Bolle) that he owes his existence as much to a typo as to any real acts of bravery, selflessness or godly miracles, an aphaeresis rather than an apotheosis, a linguistic trick of dropped and/or rearranged letters, when Christians in the South of France in the fifteenth century (in a time of great hardship and conservation of resources, including ink) took a shortcut when translating the capabilities of the Italian Saint Recho – who had, up to that point, been nothing more than a spook people enlisted to ward off storms – and instead of transcribing the entire French word for storm, *tempeste*, the new entry was abbreviated to the simpler *peste*, accidentally rooting this new sub-saint in pestilence and disease. Until then, Bolle claims, he never existed. But the nineteenth century Greek academic Phaeron Troetschi documents several records that feature Recho and Roche as separate people, including a list of French prisoners in Vorghera, Italy, in the years and days leading up to Roche's celebrated death there, as well as journal entries indicating early festivals dedicated to both men, including the main one for Roche in Montpellier, France, his supposed birthplace. According to Troetschi, Roche was the son of the governor of Montpellier, and showed several early signs of sainthood, not least of which was his mother's prior barrenness and, even as a newborn, never seeking to suckle while she was observing the fasting periods of her renewed faith. Then, when he was in his late teens, the entire population of Montpellier was struck by a horrible disease, bed-ridden and pain-filled, with a momentous thirst that could not be slaked. Many of the town's citizens threw themselves in the Mediterranean to escape it. Both of his parents died. But Roche was miraculously spared, and he took his entire inheritance and distributed it evenly among the area's few survivors, setting out on foot to the next town where he had heard of a similar plight. He cured people on the edge of the sea all the way to Rome until he too succumbed to the killer virus; but rather than retiring to bed like everyone else, he booked passage on a boat to help sufferers in Africa, from which he never returned.

The Ursuline nuns founded the Saint Roche orphanage in Natchez, Mississippi in 1729, after a similar flu struck most of the area, with so many of the sick gathering at the banks of the Mississippi to die. This likely spread the disease even faster, but no one could really stop them. They far outnumbered the healthy and simply forced their way to the banks to drink. The official story back in France described an Indian attack, perhaps hoping to bolster nationalism in the face of growing tensions with Great Britain, but the actuality of the plague was indiscriminate, decimating both the French colonial and Natchez Indian populations, particularly adults. And when they arrived and discovered the truth, one of the nuns from Potenza suggested the orphanage be named after San Rocco to protect the children against future outbreaks.

Of course the orphanage – and the nuns – had a much darker secret history, carried in whispers on both sides of its walls. The sisters had arranged the passage to America for hundreds of eligible young French women (orphans themselves, or prisoners, or anyone else without a real identity of their own), to allegedly help them find husbands to repopulate the State. But each girl was also supplied, for the ship, with a small, locked box, shaped like a casket, said to contain the elements of her dowry from the King himself, to be opened only when a satisfactory suitor was found, and before the ships even landed, rumours were already circulating that something more insidious and occult was afoot. There was talk of mutiny, with many of the sailors just looking to make a fast buck by dumping the future brides in the drink and filching the dowries for themselves. Others feared the boxes *were* caskets, with vampires or worse inside them, wanting to dump *both* the girls and their charges. Luckily for the girls, most of the main troublemakers took ill and died, supposedly after a group of them snatched a box and broke it open for themselves. After that, the young women were left alone.

The rumours, though, did not stop. On their safe landing, all the young passengers and their caskets–each box now dripping wet, from what appeared to be an inside source–were brought to the orphanage. While many of them did eventually find husbands, each and every box remained locked in the attic. The orphans described demons (horrible sea creatures that could turn you to water with their touch, which the nuns had been charged by the Pope himself with guarding and perhaps, more insidiously, they even worshipped them), and these theories were backed by hard evidence. Several key boys had been disappearing, the real troublemakers, whom the nuns had threatened with things they could only whisper. One boy had helped carry a box of nails he claimed came from Italy, blessed by the Pope himself, in order to trap whatever was up there. And on the outside of the building near one of the attic windows, there was a suspiciously expanding ochre stain.

* * *

The young boy had never been liked. Born in 1756, at the outbreak of the Seven Years War, he was always looked on, by the other children and even the nuns themselves, with a certain degree of distrust. Bad luck, even. He was regularly beaten. Again, by both the children and the nuns. And his assailants were not even bad people, just superstitious, suspecting somehow that the war would last as long as he did, especially among the other children, who had already forgotten how horrible their lives had been before that, too. When he was only two, the other children tried to smother him. During his first seven years, in fact, he narrowly escaped death at their hands a remarkable eight times. They had begun to call him *El Gato*, because even though most of the orphans were either French or Indian (mostly of the Yazoo and Cherokee tribes, who had moved in after the earlier epidemic), many of the words from the predominantly Spanish inhabitants (who had also moved in around the same time, when the French were weak) continued to plague them like a virus of language.

They had also begun to suspect that he was enjoying his beatings, that he liked to fight. So the other boys decided instead that he should explore the attic alone, and find out once and for all what was really in there. When he came back to say he'd found nothing, they called him a liar and tried to drown him. Because that's what you do with cats who have one life left to live.

Chris Eaton's name was actually Christophe Valentin. His mother was a mermaid and his father was a dragon. Or they might as well have been, since he never met them, just woke up one day in an orphanage in Mississippi and felt the first pillow against his face. He never knew why the other children hated him, because he was still too young to understand what war was, or hatred, but he went to the attic because they said so. And when they subsequently ordered him down to the pond, he did that too. And when he first hit the water, all he felt was the sting on the back of his hand and across his left cheek, there was a quick popping in his ears, and then nothing but the muted sounds of movement, the sound of bubbles rushing past his ears. The water was cold. Someone punched him in the chest and spun him sideways. And he began to forget. In fact, he forgot so hard that he lost things he'd never even known, or things that hadn't yet happened, his first kiss, his first love, the feel of lightning entering his side, forgot the way he would eventually die.

When they discovered he was enjoying being held under water, too, the other boys gave up, leaving him alone with his peculiar aqueous obsession. Even after he escaped the orphanage, with nothing to his name but a pilfered blanket and canteen, he gathered it from any place that was important to him, starting with the drops he scooped from the pond where they'd tried to drown him but eventually adding water from the Mississippi, on which he floated south to Baton Rouge and into the Gulf of Mexico; the first rainfall of his freedom; the hurricane he survived in Pensacola, West Florida; the first alcohol he tasted, at nine years of age, from a man on horseback near Mobile, who then tried to bugger him so he stuck the man with a sharpened stick and stole his knife; the last tears he ever shed; another swig of rum, this time some he made himself in St. Augustine, East Florida, at fourteen, with pocketed sugarcane from the plantation on which he'd been hired. He went thirsty most days he was on the lam so he could save all of it in the canteen, mixed like the days of his life into one inseparable sludge.

When he heard the horses coming in North Carolina (where he'd heard there was easy money robbing newcomers), he immediately went into the river to hide. Beneath the surface, he was always safe. His life was his own and the current washed away all remnants of the nuns, the Spanish and Indian boys. He was nothing. He was everything. Free to do and be whatever he chose. The catfish and bream butted up against his ankles and legs, and he hugged them close to his body and once thought he might even take a bite. He went deeper, resting his cheek against the riverbed, and he suddenly heard the words, the fateful words, as if they were whispered to him by the water itself: *Chris Eaton*.

He remained where he was.

Christopher Eaton?

And after a brief moment to consider, he came back to the surface and said: Yes.

The rebel soldier snatched his canteen, took a long drink, spat it out, and then poured the rest back into the river.

From that point on, that's who he was.

PART 4

After that, everything went from *You could do this* or *You can be anything you want* to *You have to do this* and *You really need this*, like all teenagers were the same, which was bullshit, and he couldn't even sit down at the mall any more without some security guard telling him to keep moving, like it was against the law to sit down. Once you became a teenager, everyone treated you the same, like you were liable to vandalize something at any moment, or like they were trying to teach you and help you become an upstanding citizen. But none of them had any idea. And none of them were terribly upstanding either, if you really wanted to know. Hypocrites. His Math teacher had been an English major. The guy who taught Sociology once massaged his friend's boobs after she passed out at an assembly. *These people* were going to guide them into the future? The specifics of each teenager's life didn't even matter. You could have a 23-and-3 wrestling record. You might have won $100 on KGON for correctly giving Joni Mitchell's real name. Perhaps your father was the Mayor, lucky shit, because then you probably wouldn't even go to jail for burning down the waterfront. Maybe you were some kind of nerdy tenor-sax prodigy, and were possibly also a kicker on the football team, just to confuse things, or a guard, in either Massachusetts or New Hampshire, or some other State with a city called Dayton. It was like everyone was the same person, and only the details were different; and the details, which were really what distinguished them, were unimportant. You couldn't drink in public. Or smoke. You had to pay more for car insurance, even if your personal record was clean. And you already had to know exactly what you wanted to do with the rest of your life. This was what you were taught in school. Don't dream any more. Apply yourself! Be a doctor, be a scientist, be a senior process engineer, be some other bullshit job that cemented your position in society. Why not work for a gas company? Or play cricket? Or manage a plant and bust some unions? Or join the bullshit army? For Chris Eaton, this was where the momentum was lost. Because the only real difference between being a child genius and a genius of the older variety is that, as a teenager, you had to prove yourself more often. And there were so many goals inside him that he sometimes became confused, and faltered, he might have done so many things, if he'd been born somewhere else, under different circumstances, if he'd been born a girl, born sooner, born later. He would have kicked out the stars. But as soon as he became a teenager, his dreams held him back.

He wasn't even sure how he'd gotten there. It was like the key moments of his life were completely unconnected, quantum particles that appeared on the other side of a wall without having passed through it, following his father's jobs around the country, so that one moment he was in Illinois, or Maine, as a Boy Scout, where his Kub Kars won almost every award for design but crept across finish lines like reticent worms; and the next, he was in Oregon, or Indiana, skipping the rest of the two-dimensional map by virtue of air travel, while their furniture traveled in a Newtonian moving truck below. He was a teenager in California, where they held weekend bonfires on the beach, hugging under their sweaters without copping direct feels, and where they started a blog site so they could all stay in touch online when they eventually left for college. And then he was on the other side of the country, at his first summer job at the waterfowl park in Rose Bay, the only thing he'd ever done that really made him feel good about life, tending to the environment, part of a team of students responsible for tours and maintenance, but more often than not cutting the grass and fishing dead waterfowl out of the reeds where they'd been beaten to death by other bullshit teens.

In grade 10, they read Shakespeare's *Julius Caesar*, and his teacher thought this was a good opportunity to talk about Greek mythology, just because it was a story about guys in togas, even though Caesar was Roman, not Greek, and there was barely any mention of gods in there at all. She got out a list of gods and assigned one to each of them, and Chris Eaton's was Anchorites, the Greek god of disguise and indecision. One day, Zeus came upon a prism, falling in love with his own repeated image, and in their frantic coupling, the prism was chipped. Thus Anchorites was born distorted, with a seemingly infinite number of shapes and form, looking different from every angle, so it was impossible to ever truly know him. He appears as a secondary character in dozens of other myths, although never recognizable from one to the next.

His own myth, however, was one of great tragedy. Because no one could ever truly know him, women saw what they wanted, and fell in love with him at the drop of a hat. Even Aphrodite could not help throwing herself at him. And although she was equally, undeniably perfect in every way, Anchorites still woke the next morning with doubt and regret, unable to shake the possibility that there might be someone even better for him, someone even more perfect, more beautiful, somewhere in the world. So he snuck away before she roused, and refused to answer her messengers. Aphrodite, in her wrath, destroyed Thebes.

Anchorites left a string of broken hearts behind him, which unfortunately included the sea nymph Theacronis, who helped her father Poseidon control the tides, and who cried so much at losing Anchorites that she flooded several coastal communities near Crete. Poseidon requested an audience with Anchorites, and demanded answers for what he saw as the scorn of one of his most beautiful daughters. Anchorites claimed innocence. Poseidon said: I am sorry, Anchorites. Perhaps my ears are growing old. Or perhaps it is the sound of the ocean. But I could not hear what you said. Could you repeat it?

Anchorites did. And Poseidon shook his head. Wow, this is really embarrassing, he said. But I really can't hear you. Can you come closer?

Anchorites did, this time bellowing at the top of his lungs, both feet wet to the ankles in surf. Poseidon, once again, said: You must forgive an old man, Anchorites. One more step and you can whisper it in my ear.

And Anchorites did, taking one last step over the unseen ocean shelf, tumbling ass over tits into the sea. Because Poseidon ruled the oceans, surrounding Anchorites with water enabled him to capture the younger god from every angle, see him for what he truly was. Then he trapped him inside a globe of water so that he would be exposed, in his entirety, to everyone else as well. Only after someone fell in love with him, knowing exactly what he was, would he be released.

Not surprisingly, perhaps, it was Theacronis who freed him. But after his humiliation, Anchorites eschewed love and had himself bricked up in a cell against the side of a mountain for the rest of eternity, so no one could do this to him again. And without the distractions of the outside world, he grew to understand the world in ways no one else had ever fathomed. The site became a famous destination for Greek pilgrims who wished to seek his advice. The word *anchorite*, now commonly used to denote someone who withdraws from secular life like a religious hermit (and in medieval times would actually follow Anchorites' example by having himself bricked into the wall of a church or monastery), comes from this story. As does the word *anchor*, which comes from a word meaning *locked in (or) attached to the water*.

Chris Eaton wrote a presentation that essentially mocked the teacher for even assigning it to him. But she didn't get it. She never got anything.

His first drawing was a reproduction of Neil Young's solo debut. In pastel. Then The Kinks' *Heroin Cats*, Prince's *Purple Rain* (to practice the lettering), some Velvet Underground, and various others from his mother's collection. Then one summer while vacationing at their cottage near Buxton, North Carolina (which he would continue to do until he died), he met Devo Raanta, a Finn who claimed to live most of the year in New York City but in Buxton always slept on a blanket on the beach, though he was not a vagrant, both of which Chris Eaton admired. One day after showing the man some of his most recent drawings, Raanta invited him back to his rented cabin for tea. No matter where he travelled, he said, his art collection always came with him. And Chris Eaton was so awestruck by the beautiful display of pretension that he forgot to ask what Raanta even did for a living and how he had accumulated so many wonderful things.

Over the next three summers, Chris Eaton switched from copying his mother's album art to copying the Finn's art collection, and with a few gifts of watercolors, oils and false praise, the boy's early precociousness and proficiency were sufficiently encouraged to continue. Back in Cincinnati, he received various art books from his Empire State benefactor, starting with one dedicated solely to Akseli Rahnasto, who had essentially laid the visual foundations of modern Finnish culture, and was often cited as a major influence on artists in several other countries, including the Fauvists in France and the Blue Rose symbolist group in Russia (and tragically, as far as Raanta was concerned, the expressionist German group, *Die Brücke*, particularly because of his *Portrait of Maxim Gorky* (1905)). Chris Eaton was drawn instantly to Rahnasto's romantic nationalism, reminiscent of the art in his fantasy novels and games, and Raanta was very satisfied. But the more the boy looked into Finland's Father of Fine Art (a label that was not entirely accurate, as Rahnasto in turn had been a disciple of Tuomo Cedärvi), the more he became influenced by the abstraction in the artist's later work, after the death of his wife and child when the real darkness set in, when he began to experiment more with colour and abstraction, especially in the series of paintings from his African period, including *The Salt Miners* (1909), *Crabs on the Dock* (1909), and *Swimming Soldier* (1911). These unfortunately provided the perfect jumping-off point for Chris Eaton's fascination with *Die Brücke* (mostly Heckel and Mueller, but also Pechstein), as well as the emotional angst and experimental styles of the brutish Septem Group (Jaska Jokunen foremost among them, but also, notably, Lassi and Leevi, who openly mocked Rahnsato and Cedärvi yet clearly owed them a huge debt), Kalle Johanson in Sweden, the latter periods of Kandinsky, and even the clumsy American expressionists like Albright, Ali, Church and Kleene. The boy even said that Church and Kleene made Rahnasto's colourism seem naïve and superficial. Church and Kleene? Two of the most functional and derivative artists to ever be associated with a word like *expression*? They made Rahnasto look superficial? Raanta continued to send Chris Eaton books on other great Finnish artists, including but not limited to Aku Ankka and Roope Setä, but the boy's ongoing admiration for Rahnasto began to have further adverse effects, dropping him firmly in the lap of Edvard Munch. The Norwegian had sat for one of the Finnish master's portraits, and the two painters had exhibited together several times in Germany, including one show that featured one of the first *Scream* works, from which it was impossible to keep teenage boys, particularly sensitive ones like Chris Eaton, and over the next year-and-a-half, though Raanta tried as hard as he could to counter it, the boy produced more copies of *The Scream* than its originator.

Raanta grew desperate. If Chris Eaton wanted something predictable, then what about Cézanne and Gauguin? Or Derain, who offered the same illusion of simplicity but with actual mastery of the medium? In the boy's junior year of high school, Raanta dropped them on him like fishing lures, hoping they might gradually bait the boy back to a true upholder of classical tradition like Matisse, or at least someone from the Nabis, like Ker-Xavier Roussel or Christan Oe, who were not medium-sized, stout or well-dressed enough to have ever been popular in their own day. But once again, the examples only sucked the boy deeper into degradation: Deburau and Copeau and Lecoq, none of whom had anything worthwhile to say, and the *fin de siècle* degenerate Christophe Ratoen (who was even worse, if you can imagine, than the twin travesties from Lyon: Charin or Davaste). At least they were all French this time. Raanta was frantic. His last hope, he figured, was Klimt. If the boy insisted on frank eroticism, he could at least follow something beautiful. And at last all was good. For maybe a month. Until the boy wrote back to him about seeing his first Schiele, the less said the better.

Of course, was it possible to tell, from the few short years Chris Eaton had existed on the planet, that the artistic light in the boy's soul had been damped and grotesquely refracted beyond help? Certainly it would have seemed so to his Finnish benefactor. But Chris Eaton's attraction to Egon Schiele was not the common adolescent perversion Raanta might have presupposed. And besides, like a bird without a suitable mate, the boy did not nest on Schiele but continued to flit about, until he discovered the work of Ivar Drasche and decided this was really his home. Schiele had died of the Spanish flu at twenty-eight, still several years younger than Drasche when they first met, as Austrian soldiers guarding Russian prisoners during the First World War. And yet Drasche is often incorrectly noted as a disciple of Schiele, perhaps because of a similarity in their brush strokes, and palette, and expressive lines, and the grotesque aesthetic of both men. But while controversy and scandal typically followed Schiele – and arguably made him more popular, or at least more talked about – Drasche was like a fly on the wall, barely known in his own time, let alone now. Schiele thrived on calumny. He encouraged it. And despite being arrested or run out of town several times, he continued to sell and live off his work. Drasche, meanwhile, worked many different jobs, including machinist, metal worker, furniture-maker and bike-maker (all in high demand during the global depression between wars) in order to fund his creativity.

Chris Eaton grew swiftly bored by what he saw as Schiele's excessive narcissism, posturing and sophomoric attempts at shock – potent in its immediate effect but not lasting in its impression. Drasche's work, on the other hand, always strove outwards, like a plant towards the light, stayed with him even in sleep, no matter whether it was a painting of an apple, a moustache or a bank clerk. It was a tragedy, the boy felt, that most critics were too concerned about appearing philistine around Schiele to see the real truth: that he had never passed out of his awkward artistic apprenticeship, attempting to disguise his debts to Klimt through nude depictions of under-age girls. Drasche was the real deal, secure enough in his own talents to paint whatever he liked. Drasche resisted the easy money and sought out the models for his most accomplished work in the most nondescript corners of Vienna: the bureaucrats and civil servants, the street cleaners and postal employees. Though his early career was marked with portraits of Viennese celebrities in a nervously animated style, his time as a factory worker issued in a fascination with the everyman, and the first works of Drasche's new Charest-Harvaton Period (named for his first two subjects, which he initially drew for money as an illustrator for a story in *L'Officiel*) focused his exotic vulgarity on the day-to-day existence of the common people, with all of its minor events and details, its mundane happenstance, its prosaic routine. Like van Eyck's *The Arnolfini Wedding*, his work was often clogged with seemingly unimportant objects, long visual lists of machinery parts, lucky charms, books and sewing needles, tobacco, boots. But unlike Eyck, his objects were not symbolic but representative. When he painted a pipe, for example, he was painting a pipe, not the riddance of happiness, or Magritte, or even welding instructions, such as a bevel, or flare, or flare bevel, which more than a few critics have independently posited. His subjects were the people he considered the true epitome of life, just trying to get by, performing their simple tasks and performing them well, like ants in a colony, and he surrounded them with the dirt that remained after digging their nests, because he felt he might, through the minutiae of one particular subject, capture what it meant to be human in a more general way, not to depict just one moment in the life of a person, nor even the complete biography of his socially inert subjects, but to capture life itself in its entirety.

For a full six months, it was mostly Drasche that Chris Eaton wanted to emulate, until the end of his senior year when The National Gallery of Canada bought a painting by Barnett Newman for nearly two million dollars and he became a devout disciple of the American color field painters, like Rothko and Motherwell (from whom the leap to Matisse was not so great, though it was too late for Raanta to witness), as well as John Winger and Russell Ziskey. He was especially obsessive of Anthony Gillis, who by the mid-sixties had moved on from his initial Prussian and Indanthrene blues, his Winsor greens, mixing reds and turquoise-greens to achieve something approaching black, which an artist statement from his second solo show claimed was "to convey strength, simplicity, and the quiet energy of balancing forces," to increasingly lighter and lighter tones, until his legendary show in 1967 that featured three-dozen unique paintings entirely in shades of white (excepting the one piece called *Negative*, the centerpiece of the entire exhibit, a canvas coated with black straight from the tube). The canvasses were confined areas of emptiness, devoid of anything, capturing themes based on isolation but with a wide variation including sexuality (*Old Lace and Ivory*), fragility (*Walking on Eggshell*), and madness (*Who's Afraid of Isabelline?*). The last of these was the largest piece by far, measuring twenty-eight by nine feet. It was used but never credited – or at least approximately duplicated – for the ninth album of a rather prominent British band, leading to a fairly famous lawsuit that he eventually lost but which also helped to make his name.

For several weeks Chris Eaton went to Europe, with an inter-Christian choir singing at local conventions and symposiums designed to repair the rift created mostly by the British and Germans. As they crossed the border into Italy, one of their chaperones claimed to have grown up with an Archbishop in Sweden. And after a few calls on a cell phone the size of a toolbox, they were scheduled for a private Papal audience that afternoon. Chris Eaton wasn't Catholic. Many of them weren't. But there was, nevertheless, a universal respect for the Pope in those days. He spoke to them of promise in three different languages, and of forming connections and bonds across continents and cultures. And hope, like they were kids or something. And then he was introduced to each of them in turn, shaking hands and passing out cheap rosaries. In early 1979, when it had come time for the newly vested Pope John Paul II to select which make of rosaries should become the official gifts to visiting groups of pilgrims and young people, nothing, especially some money from the budget, was spared. And the finest plastic, blessed by the Man himself, was delivered into the hands of special visitors with abandon, the Vatican seal printed legibly on the vinyl envelope that held them. Still, Chris Eaton was shocked as the small package was slipped discreetly into his hand, because he thought, at first, that it was a condom. And his shock is obvious in the photo they sold him for the equivalent of fifteen US dollars.

There was another girl on the trip from St. Petersburg, with a slim waist and chest, her cheeks sunken like northern roads, and her spine almost malformed, her waist jutting forward so abruptly. One night after a group dinner in Paris, she pulled him from the restaurant back to the hotel. His roommate was in their room and would not leave, so they moved to the stairwell. I just want to kiss it, she growled, then started licking, up the base and across the crown, before taking it full in her mouth. He'd never slept with anyone before. Never even masturbated. And he was surprised to discover that it was slightly painful, especially around the foreskin. No one had ever told him

64

what a foreskin was, certainly never explained how he should clean it, and he wasn't entirely sure that this wasn't supposed to hurt, this first time, at least in some tiny way, so he ignored the burning and tearing as her lips and tongue worked him over, and the defenseless foreskin retreated further and further, from where it had fused itself to the glans, until she suddenly placed both hands on his thighs and reared violently backward, the slick spill of something across her chin.

"Jesus Christ!"

The blood was all over her teeth, dripping from her chin to his thigh. She was holding her stomach like she might throw up.

"What's wrong with you?"

He had no explanation.

Thankfully, she was too embarrassed to report anything to the chaperones. For the rest of the trip, she just wouldn't look him in the eye.

Soon none of the other girls would either.

He'd never really thought about boys before Phil. All he knew was that he wasn't interested in girls all that much. Or, basically, hanging out with any of the kids at his school, boys *or* girls, just a bunch of rich brats with nothing better to do than smoke pot and complain about their trust funds. His parents sent him to a private school so he'd have better opportunities. The public school around the corner didn't even have a pool, for Christ's sake, built in the Cold War to withstand missile attacks and look like a penitentiary but not to foster any sort of learning beyond the Three R's. So they shipped him off to Shorecrest along with the cripple kid who lived down the street and who couldn't handle the stairs. His new school somehow managed to cram elevators every five or ten feet, even in the single-level buildings, just to show how wealthy they were; the only time anyone used the stairs was to hang out between classes, and the staircase you chose to sit on marked your social standing.

The only real benefit to attending Shorecrest was going on class trips. And all he had to do to qualify was join one of the many teams and clubs. The easiest, he figured, was to join the "orchestra," made up almost entirely of prodigy violinists and flutes. No one, up until that point, had taken up the tuba, so he didn't even have to audition and barely had to practice. He was all they had. It was also an instrument that allowed him to remain aloof. The trumpet and clarinet sections were like haunts of annoying little songbirds, the way they giggled to themselves during practice, or pecked at their lunch in little groups. Every time one of them sneezed, he thought the rest might wet their pants. And still, putting up with the band seemed a brilliant way to see the world, like Hemingway had done, or Oscar Wilde. All he had to was survive the rest of them. And that was what Walkmans were for.

More often than not in some foreign city he could be found listening to The Cure in some overcompensating hotel lobby, surrounded by miniature potted palm trees, drawing pictures of himself in a ringbound notebook, only more buff. Even in Southern Europe, they'd decided that a palm tree signified a tropical vacation, and the hotel was full of them. It just wasn't hot enough for them to prosper, and the pots they kept them in restricted proper root growth, so they remained in a state of constant arborial adolescence.

This was when Phil Taylor, the hardest drummer of hard rock, nearly tripped over him "trying to find the sodding ice machine," complimented his drawings and invited him up for a little party they were having.

"You mean, to your room – "

"What are you listening to?"

He held up the tape.

"Geezus, I love that shite…"

"…"

"Makes you feel like it's okay to be different from everyone else."

And Chris Eaton wasn't out yet. He was simply innocent enough to think they were just kindred spirits. Here was someone who un-

66

derstood him, who could relate, in a mature sort of way, who'd heard of The Cure and The Pet Shop Boys and even Depeche Mode. "Pictures of You" always made the drummer cry. His own songs, Phil said once they'd gone up to his room, were trying to capture those same feelings: "Of despair and fucking isolation in a world of bleeding fuckwits." And when he grabbed an acoustic guitar from the corner and played him one, Chris Eaton cried for him. With him.

"You should record it."

"It could probably use a better bridge…"

Of course, when Philthy Phil eventually brushed his cheek and called him sweetie, he was helpless. And he imagined, for a moment, what it might be like to run off with a rock star, to leave those other losers behind and start his life anew. The drummer's stubble scraped across his neck and down his chest (he wasn't entirely sure when he'd lost his shirt but didn't care), there was a hand in the pocket of his cargo shorts that was not his own, a few bars from Philthy's song whispered in his ear, someone knocking at the door, followed by several hours of staring at nothing but the wall, the Motörhead drummer stroking the muscles of his thighs and tracing lines with his tongue between his shoulder blades.

And at graduation Chris Eaton told her entire grad class, her diploma so fresh it was still bleeding, to take a flying fuck off a cactus, not to mention all of their parents and siblings, and more than a few grandparents, who hopefully couldn't see too well, or didn't understand, when she flipped them her twin birds of freedom, both hands held high like she was about to take a bow. Which she then did.

PART 5

There are stories people tell. Most of them aren't very interesting. People find themselves funny. And they set these stories in likely yet semi-exotic environments. Like abandoned communist submarine depots. Or meat-packing plants. Or karaoke bars. In the cities they're from. Or been to. Or even just imagined. Like maybe Chicago. The predominant subject matter: me, me, me.

Granted, you learn more from the stories people tell about others than the ones they tell about themselves. When they talk first person, it only reveals a personal obsession. And who doesn't fall into that category? It's only when they start to speak outside their own identity that you can finally get a good vantage point on someone else. Interests. Bias. Motivation. Why does anyone ever tell a story to someone else? Especially to a complete stranger? Attention.

More specifically, why tell you a story about the legs of Céline Dion, like rolling pins beneath the stall doors, her manicured nails tracing familiar patterns along the back of her throat, in 1991, with her nondescript beginnings behind her but the heights of her career like free change at the bottom of the toilet bowl, tempting, but something you only imagine for someone else. What possesses someone to lie at the top of their lungs – just to be heard over the urban cowboy belting out some Stina Verda – about near-meetings with celebrities, claiming to have the pop diva's first-ever music award lodged unceremoniously behind his headboard, having shoved it in at least one orifice of every man he's ever fucked?

Because really the queer's just crying out.

Because everyone just wants to be heard, and mostly to be heard as something separate from what they are. In this place, this bar, this hole, this haven, their chairs inch slowly closer to yours, and their stories dribble past their beer-cracked lips to collect in unsightly puddles around their feet: the fag, the braless septuagenarian waitress, the man on stage, with his hair like burnt wicker and a Cubs cap for a halo. Each one with a story. And each one with the voice of an angel, albeit angels who've smoked two packs a day for the past twenty years. They know the lyrics to every Johnny Cash song, and can even produce a tear when required, drawing on years and years of tantric misery. Their songs swing high over the other patrons, dive-bombing the bar, with grooves like early death and decay, worn in by years of tears, decades of sob stories, poured over the faux cherry finish and rubbed in nightly with slop buckets of week-old water and ammonia. Every false note – no, none of them are false, they are all true as despair, just sharp or flat – skips along the floor and embeds itself just above the brass footrail. The ankles of the patrons are covered with scars from errant peeps, tracking divots and pockmarks up their forearms and necks, dragging their feet across lobes and tragi before cracking the hinges off the tympanic membranes and squatting triumphant and defiant in the unplastered living rooms of the aural canals.

In a place like this, you can start all over; be reborn; be someone else. There's even a fair chance you can avoid what's coming. You can dodge the bullet of your future; call in sick that September morning; decide not to strap on that seatbelt and have your grin shatter the windshield and never ever come back to Earth...

A new hope.

He chose the bar mostly because he didn't know a soul, had never been there and was fairly certain he wouldn't see anyone he knew, because they'd either find the place too low in class or not low enough. Chicago had its fair share of dives. But a dive wasn't a place you frequented when you were from Forest Hill. The only drawback: the mob of televisions all set to hockey and basketball. Sports, especially televised sports, were the lotteries of the chronically poor, on that level of social strata that exists beneath hope. If it was a choice between dreams and cigarettes, there was really not much of a contest. The Game, on the other hand, was always free. Couldn't see it live. Couldn't even watch it at home some times. But the playoffs settled in to these bars like a persistent cough, another symptom of the seasons, the only difference that year – a new trend that had turned the once-proud city into a murder of whiners and nostalgists – was that neither the Bulls nor the Blackhawks were anywhere to be seen. So even though no one could bring himself to turn the sets off, no one really paid attention, either.

Do you like the Blackhawks? the fag asked him, dragging the stagnant *ck* from first half of the word into the second. And: Nothing better than a big Blackhawk.

On any normal night, he would probably have just told him to fuck off. He'd been working for hours on the eager cougar at the front, who was probably twice his age, and he watched eagerly as the seam of her jeans licked up and down the cleft of her ass, tonguing deeper with each step from her table to the guy with the handlebar moustache who accepted the song choices. Earlier, he'd dreamed he was that stitch, and he'd tried to spark up a conversation with her. About music, of course, although his tastes tended to be a little harder than hers, but also: how smog kept making the summers more and more unbearable; the war on terrorism; the friends they knew in other places. Common places. They'd already made out briefly. And she'd kissed like a bag of chips. Although that was better than no kissing at all.

But he was ready for something a little harder. And from past experience, he knew it was the queers who did more coke than anyone. Any time he'd been offered cocaine in the past, it had been a fag. Those really flamboyant indiscriminate ones, who threw fits across crowded tables and sucked face with the beef they'd tossed out the week before. They had nasal cavities like empty spice jars. When they bought cigarettes, their bills rolled up before they hit the counter.

When they headed to the washroom together, no one even turned to watch. People pee all the time, after all. And besides, they weren't about to deny someone else the chance at a good story. He wasn't even upset when, side by side at the urinals, he caught the fag looking. Gender wasn't a private club that suddenly gave you exclusive rights over all the team equipment. But there was a code for moochers. And when you've got a free hit coming your way, you flash your wang for whoever wants to see it.

Sometimes, they might even get to touch it.

He was nervous. This was not his bar. He had to stand watch while the fag cut it. When someone came around the corner, he wasn't sure what to do. He coughed. He clicked his tongue. He tried to think of a good excuse for hanging out in the doorway of the men's washroom.

And before he knew what was happening, he had taken the bill and leaned forward, pretending he was just trying to smell the daisies. And it magically erased every drink he'd had up to that point. By the time he left the men's room behind, he felt like he was wearing headgear, like he was making a mold of his face for posterity, like he'd never go to sleep again, like he had a cock thirteen inches long. His "girlfriend" was gone. No worries. Suddenly this fag had become the most interesting fuck on the planet, with a complete oral history of the life and times of Canada's expatriate pop diva. Didn't they have anything else to brag about up there? Was Canada so boring? The year was 1991. The fag described Canada's national music awards as junior high presidential elections, with all the most popular kids vying for head of the student council office. And who walked away with all the gold but the awkward kid from Charlemagne, Quebec. Album of the Year. Female Vocalist of the Year. It felt like a joke. It was as if the cool kids just wanted to see what she'd do. Like she had a hair lip and they just wanted to laugh at her acceptance speech. And the fag was so excited when she walked into his restaurant. He was just the busboy, and didn't really know who she was, but it was still exciting to be in the proximity of a winner. Or even just a celebrity. And when she turned out to be one of the nicest people he'd ever met, even asked him his name as he was taking away another empty bottle of champagne, he felt offended by the brashness of it all and bussed the award onto his tray.

Chris Eaton didn't believe it, of course, and had to see the award for himself. So they ditched the music, and the wannabes, and their heads were like cement, crashing through doorways, swinging in wide arcs at the ends of their chain-link necks. All muscles and tendons. Bones like helium balloons. The pavement had never been more pliable, and the streetlights burned like aluminum sparklers. He was dodging an apocalyptic meteor shower in slow motion, slowing him down considerably, but the fag was never too far ahead.

And sure enough, back at the apartment, there it was: Dion's award. Just like he said. They abandoned their bodies to the couch and laughed uncomfortably. There they were. Did he want a drink? More coke? They sat in the darkness for fifteen minutes without speaking, sobriety overtaking them in deep breaths, until the fag – he couldn't even remember his name – broke the silence: I have to use the little boy's room.

Uh-huh...

And when the fag hit the washroom, he hightailed it with the Judo, or whatever it was called, floating out the door and down the street like a raccoon on fire. Were there other people who could run that fast? Others like him? He doubted it. His feet were like greased mortar shells. His legs whipped and snapped like corrugated rubber. And he was digested, through the large and small intestines of Chicago, to the steps of the platform where the train took him back to his parents' house, then back to school in Virginia.

73

He went to Brown. He studied fiction. He studied theoretical math. She studied law. He went to UNB. And studied sustainable communities. He played racquetball. And basketball. And tennis. And ran.

He swam, eventually earning his scholarship to the Virginia Military Institute as a backstroker, which wasn't Auburn or Stanford but wasn't a total failure. There, he made a name for himself in the freestyle sprint, as well as the 100 and 200m breaststroke. The potential for active duty was supposed to be limited.

He studied international development. And he survived the Ugandan Civil War, then went to South Africa, where he was mugged, and was chased by men with guns, and worked with one woman who was stabbed in the arm and another whose daughter was raped before her eyes.

On his first day of university, he fun-tacked a political poster to the wall of his room:

> **Chris Eaton 4 Senator**
>
> **It's time for a change**

He thought it was funny, because he and this local politician happened to share the same name. (What he did not know: they had both moved to Florida at the advent of high school; both had been presidents of their junior high schools back home (California and New Jersey, respectively); and the other man had also attended University of South Florida.) But mostly it served as a reminder of his cause. His high school job at Rose Bay had been his saving grace. So he was particularly alarmed when most of the State's Senators voted in favor of pumping untreated water down into the Florida aquifer, an underground system of springs and wells beneath the entire State

74

of Florida, as well as parts of South Carolina, Georgia and Alabama. It was water so pure you could drink it with a straw, if the straw were long enough. It provided sixty million gallons of water a day for human consumption alone, as well as nourishing several wetlands areas like the Everglades, and even Rose Bay. And his government was voting to endanger it.

So he'd gone to university to hopefully fix it. The original plan was to develop a new waste management system that would integrate the living machine designs of ecologically friendly biomass digestion systems with current sewage treatment methods. But once he discovered similar systems already in use in several conventional plants across the country, he began to find more shortcomings with it. For example: available land. How could the capacity of treatment plants meet the demands of growing, heavily populated areas? Especially when land for expansion was so scarce? So he started planning into the only space left. Up. Constantly aware of the oppressive weight of the holes in the sky above him, The Biomass Silo – a theoretical treatment facility that could take up a much smaller landmass by mimicking the skyscraper model – would use capillary motion to wick the water up and the natural cascade of a waterfall for its descent. The idea even received a Certificate of Meritorious Achievement from the National Medal of Technology program in D.C., but Chris Eaton felt there was still so much to be done, continuing to construct small-scale models and monitoring their progress to ascertain feasibility.

The erection of the first silo, the size of an overturned rain barrel, was simple, and provided Chris Eaton with tons of data. The second, slightly larger, about the size of a mini-barn, gave him even more. The hard part was discovering how these groupings of facts somehow aligned, merging the similarities between them to create new facts that didn't exist – or weren't known – without them. Generally speaking, in mathematics, a concept is only so good as the confirmation of its presupposed result. We suppose that $2 \times 5 = 10$, and when we actually start adding things up (2, 4, 6, 8, 10!), we discover that our concept is correct. But when all was said and done, there were values for x in the silo concept that the calculations should not have worked out to. Even facts that did not relate to each other directly produced a result, as if the mere proximity of the numbers – something similar in them, rather than their actual sources or values – created some result other than the simple A leads to B leads to C and so forth.

Of course, there were many unsolved mysteries in mathematics; even with frequently used concepts like *pi*. Theoretically, if taken to an infinite end, the single digits in *pi* are equally distributed throughout it – the same number of ones and twos and threes and so on. In a given set of, say, five hundred places past the decimal, each number should appear approximately fifty times. (In a set so small – and yes, five hundred, in the scope of infinity, is small – the numbers will actually range from about thirty-six to fifty-nine.) *Pi* appears to encompass the perfect definition of *random*.

But when you study a long *pi* set, at least the appearance of patterns begin to manifest:

3.14159265358979323846264338327950288
41971693993751058209749445923078164
06286208998628034825342117067982148
08651328230664709384460955058223172
53594081284811174502841027019385211105
55964462294895493038196442881097566
59334461284756482337867831652712 0190
91456485669234603486104543266482133
93607260249141273724587006606315588
17488152092096282925409171536436 7892
59036001133053054882046652138414695
19415116094330572703657595919530 9218
61173819326117931051185480744623 79962
74956735188575272489122793818301 19491
29833673362440656643086021394946395
22473719070217986094370277053921717

6293176752384674818467669405132000568127145263560827785771342757789609173637178721468440901224953430146549585371050792279689258923542019956112129021960864034418159813629774771309960518707211349**99999**...

After the first seven hundred and sixty-one places, a mysterious string of five nines appear. And because it's physically impossible for us to study *pi* to its infinite end, it's also impossible to know whether this repetition is an anomaly, or whether each digit would have a similar string. So far, the longest repeated string, when *pi* is examined to two million places, is 31415926, a brief return to the beginning, the first eight digits, before spinning off again into seeming randomness. But it's fairly safe to assume that, if *pi* is indeed infinite, every conceivable pattern will eventually appear, including five ones, eight two, 13 fours, and also, as impossible as it might seem to reconcile this with the seemingly infinite randomness, an equally infinite string of sevens.

This was how he became obsessed with Georg Cantor.

Cantor believed he was on a mission from God.

To prove God's existence. To find meaning in life.

And he thought he could do this through mathematics, or more precisely, through non-linear dynamic systems and set mathematics. As Cantor himself often explained it: *A set is a Many that allows itself to be thought of as a One.* A set can be any group of numbers you want to group together. The set of even numbers from 1 to 10 is shown as {2, 4, 6, 8, 10}. The set of whole numbers below 100 that are the squares of other whole numbers include {1, 4, 9, 16, 25, 36, 49, 64, 81, 100}. But before Cantor, Set Mathematics was only built to handle closed sets, like the ones mentioned above. The set of all whole numbers, on the other hand, would continue to climb without end. One plus one plus one plus one plus one... And it's this introduction of infinity to mathematics that produced the most interesting results.

First, Cantor posited that the set of all integers {1, 2, 3, 4, 5...} has an equal number of members as the set of all even numbers {2, 4, 6, 8, 10...}, despite the apparent contradiction that a closed set of those same two groups would produce twice as many of the former. Since numbers can keep increasing endlessly, how can one group ever be larger than the other? Conversely, if you were to take either one of those infinite sets and divide it in half, your new set would also have an equal amount of members. You could keep halving this infinite set forever and you'd still end up with the same number of rational members.

He also addressed the infinitely small, claiming the number of points you can map on a line this long...

————————

...is equal to the number of points you can map on a line that is infinitely long. How much space is there between the numbers 0 and 1? Or even between 0 and 0.1? Once again, the space is infinite. Coastlines are infinite. The circumference of a pumpkin is infinite. You can always create a more precise measuring tool that will allow you to measure more of the nooks and crannies of a jagged coast. And as you do so, the distance grows. Infinity can be present in a pinpoint. A raindrop. A snowflake.

The way he demonstrated this would become known as a Cantor Set. Or, ironically, the Devil's Staircase. And it is explained most simply by a repetition of steps, continually subdividing the interval between points 0 and 1:

1. Divide the original interval into three equal parts.
2. Remove the middle interval.
3. Go to 1.

With each removal from the original interval, new intervals are created that form the Cantor Set. After the first subdivision, we have two intervals, from zero to one third (0, 1/3), and from two thirds to one (2/3, 1), with a total length of 2/3. After the division of those intervals, we have four: (0, 1/9), (2/9, 1/3), (2/3, 7/9) and (8/9, 1), with a total length of 4/9. And so on, and so on. The total length of the intervals will always be two thirds what it was before, or (2/3) to the power of the number of subdivisions. Steadily smaller and smaller. This is undeniable. But since you only ever remove a third of your existing lines, you can perform this exercise indefinitely. And as you approach infinity, the number of intervals in the set also becomes infinite... with a total length approaching nothing.

An infinite number of lines taking up no space at all.

The resultant graph, created by Cantor's diagonal approach to depicting intervals, is where the Cantor Set gets its devilish name, because it resembles an erratic set of infinite stairs, on which you can never finish the climb to 1. Perhaps because this seemed like a joke, Cantor's proofs and experiments with infinity were largely ignored, at least until computers were invented that could carry out his calculations to their theoretical non-endings. By the time he died in Halle, Germany, in 1918, almost no one had acknowledged his discoveries. He had also failed to prove God. But his new mathematics did give way to current chaos theory, which has replaced Newtonian physics as providing a better understanding of planetary motion and other natural occurrences. Now, with the growing speed and complexity of processing chips, computer models of real world systems base their calculations on infinite iterations and are increasingly better equipped to reflect actual real world systems with astonishing accuracy. Computers are used to recreate crash simulations in the automotive industry, anticipate weather disasters through finely calibrated climate models, and are even used by the government to predict the likelihood and potential results of enemy military action or a global pandemic.

And what is the main thing we know about non-linear dynamic

systems? Eventually, when stretched as far as possible, beyond even imagination, any system will either:

a) gravitate to a constant (forever at rest);

b) keep climbing forever (only in unbounded systems);

c) exhibit periodic or semi-periodic motion (like the Devil's Staircase); or

d) descend into completely random chaos, or at least what appears to be chaos until we are able to pull away sufficiently to discover the pattern.

Or perhaps there's just something special about the number 9.

Chris Eaton was born on April 9. April 9 was also the date that marked the end of American Civil War. In 1991, the Russian state of Georgia officially declared its independence from the Soviet Union. In 2003, it was the day Saddam Hussein's Ba'ath regime was officially deposed, in which, through the wonders of the Internet, he knew another person named Chris Eaton had taken part. A coincidence? Or, if he were to dig deeper, would he discover a pattern in his own life he has yet to fully comprehend?

The patterns are there. The question is merely whether or not our interpretations of the patterns are correct. And would the patterns exist without us to perceive them?

Do we make the story, or does the story make us?

Though he'd agreed to attend university because of his parents, he rejected the establishment outright, and did everything he could to undermine it, from letters to the editor to alcoholism to posters of Che Guevara. In his second year, he nearly failed a paper on *King Lear* with a thesis that said the character of The Fool did not exist. The Fool, he said, was merely a figment of Lear's imagination, two figures representing the same man, used by Shakespeare to accentuate the king's madness, and it was clear by the way the bard used him that no one but Lear and the audience could see him. Many scholars have noted that The Fool seems to exist outside the play, appearing and disappearing without warning. The only times Lear actually speaks directly to him are when they are alone, and otherwise The Fool's responses are more like witty quips, like a voice over your shoulder, to which Lear sometimes responds in ways that confuse the "real" people in his presence. The only exception is in Act III, Scene I, lines 41-59, in which The Fool, before his abandonment of Lear on the heath, delivers his ultimate soliloquy on madness and identity, where essentially Lear's madness is complete and they become one:

> 'Tis a king? A whale? Wallowing by nights
> 'cross his feral wavering imagining?
> Witless fisherman who, by day, sleeping
> with fishes or laying hold the eel,
> despises all? No phrases numerable...

This was later rectified in the Nahum Tate version of the play, which appeared about half a century later, with the same name but a much happier ending: Lear regaining his throne and Cordelia marrying Edgar. This Fool-less version was often performed instead of Shakespeare's for nearly a hundred and fifty years.

He had similar results with an early paper in his third year on *The Trial*, in which he posited that Josef K's unstated crime was a crime against society: being different, a failure in matters of conformity, refusing to take part in *the universal experience*. This crime is not even one set down on him from above, but by a general hegemony, like a corporate action, without a single instigator but by group mandate: *As you know, employees always know more than their employers* (p.17). After K is arrested, he spends the entire novel asking questions, demanding answers, resisting *their* will, not even realizing that *they* is the rest of the world and the important part is not that he hasn't *done anything wrong* (p.3), but that he refuses to believe that the rest of the world can be right. His search takes him through the people closest to him (Frau Grubach and Fräulein Bürstner), logic (The Lawyer), action (The Manufacturer), art (The Painter), and finally religion (In the Cathedral). But it is Society that says he is guilty, Society that is defining him. And by continuing to deny it, he merely proves the point, right up to his execution. If he would merely accept things as they were, and confess to his crime, he would be found innocent. Kafka even prepares the reader for this in the book's initial paragraph, when K is arrested and told to stay in the room and his initial instinct is to quickly pull on his trousers and say he will go next door and demand answers from his landlady: *Yet it occurred to him at once that he should not have said this aloud and that by doing so he had in a way admitted the stranger's right to superintend his actions* (p.4).

This paper was refused by his professor and he was asked to write another.

Then, at the end of his third year at Oberlin, he wrote an essay about 9/11 fiction, which he initially dubbed the crassest and cheapest of genres, capitalizing on collective shock and misery to sell books. So many of the country's masters, the established and the hopefuls, had felt compelled to address it, and Chris Eaton delighted in systematically toppling his idols and the idols of his classmates, which led to his ostracism, which led to his delight, which then led to the reconsideration of his delight, which led to his honours thesis in his final year about disaster literature through the ages, starting with *The Bible* and going straight through the horrors of *The Iliad* and *The Odyssey* to Modernism, which led him eventually to one of the most extensive studies ever written on the complete works of L. Frank Baum.

After the horrors of the First World War, European fiction was forced into similar drastic changes, using abstract thought and formal stylistic play to come to grips with how and why human relations could have become so inhuman. Other movements, like Gothic literature, Romanticism and French Realism, were all brought on by earlier wars, the Seven Years War, War of the First Coalition, and years of

Napoleonic conquest, respectively. The satirical eighteenth-century Augustans, like Pope and Swift, were composing in reaction to capitalism, or the war on the poor. And lining up lists of the great European writers and wars of the past two centuries, one could easily see the correlations. Although Tolstoy set his masterpiece during the debatably successful defense of Russia from Napoleon in 1812, the author had actually served in the latter months of the Crimean War, from September 1855 until its end in February 1856. H. G. Wells's highly influential sci-fi book, *The War of the Worlds*, was clearly influenced by his time at the Battle of Dorking in 1871. The Tonkin campaign between France and Vietnam, in which Joris-Karl Huysman briefly participated as a clerk in the service of Alexandre-Eugène Bouët, is generally credited with shifting Huysman's style from the naturalism of Zola's Médan Group to the decadent barbarism of À rebours (1884). And in 1912, Louis-Ferdinand Céline joined the French army as an act of rebellion against his parents, setting in motion the events which led to him being shot in the arm while delivering a message past German lines, deserting the forces in a wagon full of green carnations and traveling to Detroit to study the conditions of Ford factory workers, another war on the lower class and the inspiration for *Journey to the End of the Night*.

In the field of English literature, T. S. Eliot's *The Waste Land* is most often cited as the signature piece of the post-wwi generation. Beckett was really only able to escape his Joycean mimicry – the shift from *Dream of Fair to Middling Women* (1932) and *Murphy* (1938) to *Molloy* (1951) – after running messages for the French Resistance during World War II. Hemingway did not actually serve in either World War, or the Spanish Civil War, but he wrote as though he did. And the only thing Hemingway fought at the Battle of the Bulge was pneumonia. But he was still present to witness many of these conflicts' atrocities, unlike William Falkner who, upon failing to join the United States Army in 1918, faked a British accent to enlist with the British Royal Flying Corps in Canada, and was still in training when peace broke out. Even Falkner emerged from the experience a changed man, when a clerical error in his registration gave his last name the more distinguished U.

Before all that, there is evidence that Shakespeare spent some of his "lost years" serving under Francis Drake during the Anglo-Spanish War, particularly during the Battle of Gravelines (where he likely got to know Francis Walsingham). His near-drowning that day is often cited as the inspiration for the large number of shipwrecks and water deaths in his plays. In South America, T. H. "Rico" Henestropa, author of the epic gauchesque poem *Chine Rosta*, who was cited as a great influence by poets as varied as Chile's Roberto Ávalos, Colombia's Ignacio Zubieta, and even Mexico's Nobel-winning Octavio Paz, lost two fingers and most of his faith in humanity at a battle alongside Argentinean natives to gain their independence from Spain. In Africa, Sachete had his civil war. Molière, Gustave Flaubert, Sotho Charpentier, Dickens's *Tale of Two Cities* and Marcel Proust were affected by the French Revolutions of the mid-1600s, late-1700s, 1830, 1848 and 1889. And naturally James Joyce was traumatized by his time in Zurich, but even more so by the Irish War of Independence, which he heard about through letters from family while living in Paris.

Horrible acts are in our nature, if not to commit them then to certainly slow down and roll down the window and revel in them.

And not all disasters had to include such struggles between man and man. More often than not, the art of the day was used to come to grips with man's relation to nature, which could often be equally cruel and unforgiving. It was as a way of dealing with the great tornado outbreak of 1896, in which hundreds of Americans across much of the central and southern states (including, but not limited to, Kansas, the worst of it located in St. Louis) were killed in their sleep, and thousands more injured, that L. Frank Baum wrote *The Wonderful Wizard of Oz*. He could relate, having lived through a devastating storm of his own in South Dakota, in which the entire village of Newark was wiped clean off the map and Baum, who lived in a neighbouring town, lost his prize Hamburg chickens. Baum was also inspired by the wreck of the Titanic, which spawned dozens of works by everyone from Lucy Maud Montgomery to D. H. Lawrence to Jim Wallace to H. G. Wells and, seemingly, the first big-budget full-length film ever made, called *Atlantis* (although the Danish film was actually a fairly accurate rendering of Gerhardt Hauptmann's German novel of the same name, eerily published just weeks before the disaster). Baum's novel was published under one of his many pseudonyms, Orin Chaste, and was mostly about the relatives left behind, sitting on their front stoops and wondering what they might have done to save people if they had been on board. The title, *Titan Porch Heroes*, was also an allusion to the 1898 novel by Morgan Robertson called *The Wreck of the Titan* that Baum had enjoyed greatly. All told, Baum wrote more than a dozen different novels under seven separate pseudonyms, dealing with everything from the Iroquois Theater fire of 1903 to the San Francisco earthquake of 1906 to the great Ohio Basin flood of 1913, the most obvious being the trilogy of books as Schuyler Staunton, written for adults, in which he processed, in order: the Brazilian revolution of 1889, controversially using many of the real names of people involved, including the Emperor Petro II, H. Avaro (who was head of military coup to depose him), and H. Cristen (the so-called Dutch Marshall, who would become Avaro's Vice-President and the first elected leader of the Republic of Brazil); the brutal succession conflict in Baluchistan in which a railroad worker with the American Construction Syndicate was mistaken for a U.S. millionaire and held at ransom for three days until his heart gave out; and the Sudan Revolt. And all of this is perhaps most ironic when it is considered that Baum's own death was as a result of the flu epidemic following World War I – the inspiration for Camus's short novel *The Plague*.

Despite the protests of her advisors at Haverford, she still selected, as the subject of her thesis, the Welsh inventor, the pioneer of sustainable, the hermit, the crackpot, the lunatic: Saith Crone.

It was a paper that was nearly never written. Saith Crone's inventions had undoubtedly changed the course of history. An early pioneer in mechanical sewing machines and the creator of parcel post, not to mention mail-order retailing, Crone's contributions to the lives of housewives in the mid-1800s might have been enough to ensure his immortality. It is, in fact, arguable that these domestic breakthroughs, by allowing women to become more politically active, contributed as much to women's suffrage in Britain and the colonies as the hearsay and rumors of similar political movements in Sweden. Crone also invented the precursor to the modern sleeping bag, which he would always regret. And most interesting to the field of Environmental Studies, at the height of Crone's retail empire, he took the considerable fortune he'd amassed in his short life, sold off all holdings he had in international commerce, and constructed an environment that would allow him to pursue the several new agricultural theories that had lately begun to obsess him. In 1872, after nine years of steady construction, Saith Crone completed his fortress on the northern coast of Wales, dubbed Caernrhyl for its proximity to the seaside community of Rhyl, and claimed he would never leave.

Caernrhyl (whose ruins can still be visited for a small fee, but few actually take the *Sefydliad chan 'n Crone Astudiaethau* up on this offer) is not without its architectural interests. It is the only British castle, for example, to be constructed in the Elizabethan Renaissance style, in its truest sense, as opposed to the more common Renaissance palaces you can find under any rock in the British Isles. Its Paxton-inspired design stands out dramatically from other Welsh fortresses like Caernarfon and Raglan, its outer walls constructed largely of molded steel to more easily defend against high-grade firearms and cannons, as the decline of the feudal system and new weapons technology made those old stone parapets entirely useless. Likewise, the inner court is a very good example of the Renaissance reaction to the Gothic and Greek ornamentation of, say, the Cardiff clock tower, with even its gardens laid out in grids approximating Japanese Sudoku puzzles, in cubes split into groups of nine. In these graphs, despite the un-nurturing Welsh climate, Crone succeeded in growing everything from beetroot, leeks and swede to bananas and mangoes, papayas and passion fruit. These gardens were clearly Crone's focus. He'd calculated the height of the walls to keep the harsh Welsh winds at bay while maximizing the reluctant sun. The moat was fed by several nearby rivers, draining through perforated sheets of coco fiber in the castle foundation beneath the lush gardens and orchards. Plus, Crone had developed a complicated system of crop rotation, transplanting entire gardens of barely-sprouted plants, possibly as often as once a month (the diagrams he left behind provided no time frame), until the soil reached a fertility level of 0.1% nitrogen, 0.2% phosphorous anhydrides and 0.6% potassium, comparable to that of the Nile. But of course the real curiosity was that Crone had built his self-sustainable fortress without any exterior doors or windows, sealed off totally from the outside world, with squared crenels spaced three feet apart and three feet deep, because he never intended to leave it or let anyone else cross its threshold, because he feared for his life at the hands of French assassins sent by the nephew and step-grandson of Napoleon Bonaparte.

***

Saith Drava Crone was born in 1827, in Chantiesor, a small suburb of Newtown (or rather an even smaller suburb of Llanllwchaearn, which was itself a suburb of Newtown, until it was absorbed by Chantiesor in the 1870s), the fourth of five children to a well-known cricket player and the wife of a well-known cricket player. Young Saith's dreams of following in his father's footsteps were shattered, along with his hip, when he was only eleven, pushed from a tree by his sister while picking apples on the family orchard. While recuperating, his mother taught him to sew and knit, and at thirteen, he apprenticed for a short time with the village draper. At eighteen, his parents provided him with enough money to buy his own shop, but instead he spent it all on the most luxurious cloths and fabrics he could find, had them sent to gentry across the country, and then handled his growing clientele by mail from his childhood bedroom. Eventually he bought his own house, and then a separate work loft, then a warehouse, and then a factory.

Then he invented his ill-fated sleeping bag. He had plans to change his business model, from the sale of raw materials to the fabrication of fine clothing. But a lot of his revenue still relied on his knowledge of materials. The Russians, for example, were keeping him afloat with an order for sixty thousand brown blankets to outfit their soldiers against the Ottomans, and he'd been supplying St. Petersburg with two to three thousand of them a week for months. But then Great Britain decided it was fashionable to join the French in the Crimean War and all trade with Russia was ceased by order of the Prime Minister. Also fashionable at the time were high-end breeches for men, and Crone had shipments of velvet coming in from Lucca and Genoa, the finest sarcenet from Bhagalpur, and antique silks from the Chinese Jiangxi province, so had no room for this lightly quilted overstock. In fact, his accountant urged him to cut the stock loose, dumping as many as he could into the Severn, or the Cardigan, or down off St. Ann's Head, where there would surely be no one to see it, to make room for items that, through process, presented more profitable margins. But Crone believed he could add value to the blankets as well, and had his tailors fold the long rugs in thirds, stuffing the interiors with feathers and straw, then marketed them to the poor as a combination bed/pillow/blanket. They were a miserable failure, and eventually Crone packed the first wagon to dispose of them himself.

If it had all ended there, in the initial failure, things would likely have turned out much differently. For Crone and the rest of Europe. But just as he and his accountant were set to launch the cursed sleeping bags into the drink, they were approached by two men in uniform. Back then, it was understandably not yet a crime to clog the waterways with waste. The disposal of textiles, however, had been brought under British legislation a few years earlier, in 1854, after wig merchants in London dumped barrels of rotting hair into a well in the Soho district, and the resultant fly congregation caused an outbreak of cholera and salmonella that left thousands gasping for their lives in makeshift hospitals, killing over six hundred and twenty-one people. Crone and his accountant were sure the jig was up, and quickly made as if they were simple salesmen with bad timing, stacking two of their packages into a makeshift table and unrolling a selection of the sleeping bags under the waning moonlight. Fortunately, the men they had mistaken for police officers in the darkness were just foreign soldiers on leave, drunk and barely coherent, poorly begging for a place to stay for the night. Crone gave them two of the bags for free, tossed the rest of them back in the wagon, and headed back to Newtown. Three days later an emissary from the Prussian Chief of the General Staff arrived at his factory to sample one, purchasing the remainder of Crone's stock to test them with the Prussian Second Army. After they arrived well-rested at the Battle of Könnigrätz to rescue a swift victory from Austria in the Seven Weeks War, and once reparations were made to them, Prussia sent an order to Crone for four hundred and fifty thousand more. This was the transaction that made him one of the wealthiest men in England. He was invited to Prussia by Chancellor Otto von Bismarck himself to see an army at rest, fêted by the King of Prussia, gave a speech to sleep scientists at Frederick William University. He even set up another factory in Berlin to handle growing orders from the public sector, catering to journeymen and seasonal workers, shepherds and amateur astronomers, and practically invented the outdoor enthusiast in Europe, the idea of sleeping outside for fun rather than destitution. To the Prussians, he was a minor celebrity. He returned to Wales with an honorary title and more stories for the boys at the pub than you could imagine.

Of course, this was also when he unknowingly crossed the Napoleonic Dynasty. Following the overthrow of Queen Isabella of Spain, the Prussian Chancellor suggested Prince Leopold of Hohenzollern-Sigmaringen, Wilhelm's nephew, as a replacement. Emperor Louis Napoleon III of France, nephew to the original Napoleon (while also the grandson to the original's first wife, Joséphine de Beauharnais), feared encirclement by a Prussian-led alliance. He was also advised that a war with Prussia, which they would assuredly win with their superior breech-loading Chassepot rifle (so successful in the recent American Civil War) and *mitrailleuse* (an early form of the machine gun), could help dam his declining popularity and distract the French population from their cries for democratic reform. So he sent an emissary to the King of Prussia demanding that they retract the Prince's candidacy. And when they weren't nearly so polite about doing it, Louis Napoleon left Paris for Metz to assume personal control of the Army of the Rhine. Despite being outnumbered and outgunned, Crone's bright-eyed and bushy-tailed Prussians eventually trapped half of Louis Nap's exhausted soldiers at Metz and forced the French Emperor's surrender at the nearby Battle of Sedan. Parisians rebelled and selected an interim minister for their second republic, September 11, 1870. When the news reached Newtown several days later in the form of an order for nine hundred thousand more bags, Saith Crone crossed himself and put out the light.

* * *

It is quite impossible to say whether Crone would have remained mentally stable after the fall of The Second French Empire (and quite simply have continued to amass more wealth than anyone could ever need or want) had that empire's deposed leader not selected Great Britain as his new home of exile, and had the British Parliament not welcomed him with open arms; because it is quite simply a fact that he did, and they did. Sure that the Frenchman would seek his revenge, Crone used his considerable wealth to petition against the immigration. But since Louis had already lived in England during his first exile as a young bachelor in the late thirties and early forties, there was not much the Welsh entrepreneur could do. Napoleon had already purchased an estate in Chislehurst in Kent where, according to an interview with *Daily Telegraph and Courier*, he planned to live the rest of his days in peace and quiet with his wife, Eugenie, and young son, Jérôme. He was glad, he said, to finally have time to himself, without having to worry about "helping people catch trains" or "making Paris look pretty for tourists."

Then: nothing. Crone had men watching from the street, from the trees, from afar, and anear. He was able, through his relationship with the British Postmaster General, to have Louis's mail appropriated, steamed, perused for any mention of himself and resealed before being sent on its way. And: nothing. If anything, Napoleon was a model citizen – a boring model citizen. Mostly, he spent his time working on puzzles, riddles, children's games, which he received in the mail from all over the world: crosswords from the Americas; tangrams from China; a French translation of *The Charades* written by Pope Leo XIII; a Russian Minus Cube; some ancient Greek assembly puzzles; a form of disentanglement puzzle from Northern Korea, mixed with an impossible object, called the Acorn Heist; Iranian puzzle locks; a Sri Lankan magic box, with a gorgeous roach inset; lateral thinking one-minute mysteries, most of these homegrown in Britain, in which a pile of sawdust beside a bed indicated mind games with a circus midget leading to his suicide, or a nude man in the desert was obviously on a doomed balloon trip with some friends and drew the short match to save them all, or some equally ridiculous twist; and many, many others. There was certainly nothing that, through whatever means of coincidental logic, could link him to any plot on the Welsh inventor's life. Similarly, Crone's team of private investigators came back with nothing but the old emperor's grocery lists, half-eaten mustard-and-brie sandwiches, cigar bands, gardening tools, and the first ten rows of what was assumed to become a sock, although it might have also been a mitten, a sweater sleeve or a stuffed animal of some sort for young Jérôme, who had become sick shortly after they came to England, diagnosed with a rare yet hereditary disease. Louis didn't even appear to know anything about the sleeping bag's role in the war, let alone Crone's part in it, as evidenced by an incomplete crossword on October 1, 1872, with the five-letter clue: **11 DOWN Put the Prussians to sleep**, beside which, in the page's margin, he'd scribbled the name of the German poet Gleim, along with the word booze, and even death. The investigators suggested Crone was safe to live his life, but he interpreted the omission of his name as a poorly contained fury, in which Louis Nap could not even bare to speak or write it. Crone sold the company he had built from the ground up, liquidated all other assets he had, and started work on his steel fortress. The only person allowed in his direct presence was his chief contractor, Ian Rotches, who single-handedly welded the final walls into place. On January 9 of the following year, Louis died of kidney failure. But Crone was already locked up in an impenetrable fortress, so presumably lived out the rest of his days in Caernrhyl alone and afraid. In 1917, forty-five years after he closed himself off from the world for good, one of the fortress's walls was accidentally breached by German bombers. At that point, the gardens had become completely overrun, and most of the exotic fruits had completely disappeared. The only evidence that Crone's notebooks were not just the writings of a mad man were traces of seeds in the stool of the monstrous flock of macaws that had taken up roost in the bell tower. Crone himself was discovered in the innermost recesses of Caernrhyl, apparently suffocated by one of his own sleeping bags, then shot several times, in a room locked from the inside containing nothing more than his body, a piano wiped clean of fingerprints save for each F key, a bat, a mirror and a table sawed in two symmetrical pieces.

After following the clues to various dead ends, the case was eventually dropped.

Her fellow students, if you could even call them that, students, were infinitely more interested in screwing and drinking than learning. The professors were also jokes, several of them barely older than she was, as unconfident as her high school classmates, just as desperate for acceptance, or establishing some semblance of authority, perhaps to mask the not-so-secret lusts they harboured for the prettier bimbettes in her classes, the ones with the pert little bums, button noses and that vague, sexy librarian look to them, the bookish ones that would be less likely to make a big deal out of something, or tell anyone. Fuckwits. Most unfortunately, their inner securities spilled out into their marking schemes, convincing themselves it was ethically repugnant to give any paper a grade over eighty, and the only way to keep her grade point average high enough to retain her scholarships was to sign up for courses in Finite Mathematics and Intro to Calculus.

Math led to Statistics, which led to Sociology, and by the end of her four years, she was somehow emerging with a degree in Psychology, under the guidance of the one brilliant professor in the entire establishment, Dr. Isac Thorne, who was just beginning to make a name for himself in the field of Early Childhood Education with a concentration on special needs and terminally ill children. Thorne, unlike the others, was able to see past her looks to her real potential, her real self, unlocking a passion in psychology that might otherwise never have emerged. She spent hours and days beyond what was required of her, helping Thorne in his research, conducting experiments on test groups of sick university students, as well as infants at the medical centre in nearby Bangor, and pregnant women in the company of midwives, remaining with those women from inception to a year following the birth. With her help, Thorne's papers on *The Effects of Propinquity on Childhood Convalescence* (1979), *The Presents of Presence: The Gift of Just Being There* (1981) and *The Singing Paraclete: Deep Comfort in Propinquity for Minors* (1984; in which Chris Eaton is thanked directly for her contributions), were largely considered to

93

have changed the hospital system in the late eighties, allowing parents to stay with their children in their rooms while under medical care, even when that child's situation was considered hopeless. In a speech at The Third International Conference on Health Promotion in Sundsvall, Sweden, in 1991, Thorne laid out the importance of what he was calling *holistic therapeutic propinquity*, not because of any direct link to concrete, medical benefits (which was non-existent) but to the less palpable benefits he and his assistants observed when placed directly in the iatric environment. Propinquity, he said, is crucial to all living things, because it enables us to see ourselves through the eyes and heart of others, thereby validating our inner suspicions of self. It is the proof, in some sense, that we exist, and enables us, through others, to see who we really are. He went further, claiming that it is in the first moment that a fetus gains awareness that it exists inside its mother, that it is a product of its mother, that contractions begin, and that the retention of that sense of identity is what keeps a person's heart beating, until death, when confusion returns like a signal, like his metaphoric parakeet, that the end is coming. Just as Descartes said: I think, therefore I am. But with a twist. More like, I think this is who I am, therefore I am. It was the key to elderly patients seeming to develop senility, failing to recognize the loved ones they had around them, or dogs that went off alone to die. And Thorne had made the same link to children. Without self-identity, there is no hope. Without hope, there is no chance of survival. Love and compassion, they had discovered, was at the core of this personal health. Even simulated love and compassion.

Towards the end of her final year, in spite of her best efforts, she dated a boy from her Honours Class named Julian, who stalked her briefly in the library's basement, where she preferred to study because people like him usually avoided it, before walking over one day and asking her to an evening of performance art, without even a hello or warm up, as if he'd been working his way up to it for weeks, and she said yes out of pity, then got too drunk and sat on his lap in a pub and then avoided him for the next few weeks until Thorne's legendary graduate party, the night after their final papers were due, with the most exotic cheeses one could hunt down in all of Penobscot County, and mixed drinks they would never have imagined, like red and white vermouth with a wedge of lemon and lime, and they smoked pot and listened to records they had brought to impress him, and discussed television shows, the recession, and their futures, and smoked more pot, which was her first time, by the way, so she barely even inhaled anything directly, but just being in the room with so much of it started to make her feel like she were drifting to the ceiling, looking down on the rest of them while she floated there, watching herself, and them, and herself with them, as if she weren't really herself, the way she scratched her own face whenever she finished a point, and tried to talk over everyone, hating every single one of them until her teeth hurt, and everyone else seemingly watching her, too, as she listed to one side and then the other, reaching for her drink on the coffee table like she were operating mechanical arms at a nuclear facility, two of her classmates – one who could barely read and the other with an understanding of Bentham and Festinger that bordered on facile and of Gilroy and Nesmith that more than broached laughable – disappearing out the back door to fuck in the garden, another excusing herself to the bathroom so she could take a peek under Thorne's bed, and in his closet and drawers, searching for God only knew what, with Dr. Thorne, back downstairs, finally succumbing to their/her pleas to break out his guitar and play some Cat Stevens, some James Taylor, one of his own (which they/she all agreed was beautiful and profound), Julian pretending he had better options with that slut, Carol, over by Thorne's collection of rocks he and his wife, who was away that weekend visiting her sister who'd just given birth in Chicago, had collected from beaches around the world, as well as places like the Stone Chair of Cairo, The Great Wall, Hadrian's Wall, various other walls, Julian no doubt trying to sell Carol on the same pathetic story about his ex-girlfriend in New York he'd used on her, the aspiring model who'd stolen his heart with a promise to stay faithful and fallen for a republican POLI-SCI major that she later claimed to have a small penis, cradling Carol's elbow and leaning in to whisper everything in her ear, with Chris still floating up near the wrought iron light fixture, full of dead flies, watching herself on the couch with Dr. Thorne, the outside of their thighs were touching, talking about her plans for the next year, and where she might go for her post-graduate studies, because she should, you know, he believed in her and what she might accomplish, he could even put in a good word for her, he said, he knew people, but she heard so little, concentrating instead on the way his words sounded, nodding her head so he would just keep talking, until people realized the garden couple weren't coming back, and the snooper had actually crawled under Thorne's pile of dirty laundry and passed out, and even Julian and Carol went home, separately and celibately, leaving her alone with Dr. Thorne, on the couch, and on the ceiling watching herself on the couch, leaning in with all the seductive prowess her horribly intoxicated body could muster and, well, fuck Julian, asked him if he wanted to spread her out and eat her whole.

He dropped out. He'd elected to come out to his friends right before the end of classes, and then decided the headaches of campus gossip just weren't worth the effort. All their compassionate bullshit about already knowing (what the fuck did *they* know?), or their complaints about exam stress, or the ones who were saying he'd jumped out of his dorm window when actually he'd just lost control while bouncing on his bed. Miraculously, despite falling four floors, he connected with the only patch of grass you could find for miles, and emerged practically unscratched except for a cast on his left arm. It was all too much. He rose to even greater fame during the exam period by writing DEAL WITH IT in bold letters across his regulation booklet and then storming out of his Spanish final waving it over his head. He claimed to be considering a lawsuit against the university, for faulty window screens that hadn't prevented his fall, and for designing rooms with the beds so close to the windows. But ultimately, what would be the point? It wasn't going to change the fact that some people just can't deal with having a confident fag around.

So he joined Greenpeace, canvassing door to door to save the fucking whales or something, just to pass the time. He only became passionate about it because he couldn't stand the hypocrisy of the minivan set, with their two-point-four kids and their file folders full of excuses. Their middle class guilt made them bring the environment up at dinner parties. They moved their investments into so-called ethical funds so they could avoid funding strip mines and sweat shops. Meanwhile these new funds invested mostly in banks, who, in their turn, invested in the strip mines and sweat shops for them. And when it came time to lay the money down – for something real like whales – they always managed to be on their way out the door, or on the phone, or had forgotten to go to the bank that week so they had nothing on them.

In the end, he decided to hoof it around Europe instead (way less hard on the feet), permanently borrowing his sister's backpack and boarding the first plane he could afford for Amsterdam, where he met Marcus. Marcus was supposed to be the end of his fooling around. They met on the train to Barcelona from Paris. Marcus had been on vacation in Greece with some Norwegian schoolmates when they ran out of weed. And he set off on his own because he figured it would be easier to score more. He smelled like a rusting horse. And the musky smell hit the American *errant* before he felt the hand on his shoulder.

The day after they got off the train, he found an Internet café and wrote home to everyone about him. They booked a room together. If they could find a state that would legalize it (or take a trip up to Canada some weekend), maybe they'd even get married! But then there was this beautiful Finnish boy at a party and he was drunk and so was the boy and partly stoned and so was this boy and... what could he do, really, what could he do? Marcus was perfectly happy

snorting coke in the other room, ignoring him already because someone had offered him some free hits. (Drugs would always be Marcus's first love, and it drove Chris Eaton crazy.) They were also just
kissing, at first. But Saku's lips were like worn leather straps, smooth
and soft with a forceful reluctance. The Finn seemed so new to it all,
Chris nearly shed a tear, he wanted to hold his hand through the entire night, guiding and kneading and tugging and stroking. He might
have stayed there all night if another bitch who also wanted Saku
hadn't ratted them out. And when Marcus eventually broke up the
party, kicking Saku in the ribs with his socked feet and using his boot
to slap him across the face like a blubbering like a fool ("Can you
believe it? Who has the time to take their shoe off in a fight? The
coward. In front of everyone, using a boot to smack an innocent fag
around."), Chris Eaton didn't even bother to pull his clothes back on,
his right cheek swollen up around his eye like a dying balloon, the
party over, lurching half-naked through the living room, sobbing,
and staggered pantless through the streets of the Barrio Gotico district until a cabbie with broken English and hair in his ears picked
him up and cuddled with him in the back to calm him down.

"Do not worry about him – "

"Thank you."

"He is jealous only."

"Oh, thank you…"

"Be careful, he hurt you simply because you are beautiful."

"You're too kind…"

Well, he'd gone to Spain to fall in love, hadn't he? Something like
his parents had? And here it was, the proof of that love, throbbing below his left eye, a reminder of his own weaknesses in matters of heart.

Who needed Marcus? There were plenty of other men. The cabbie started nibbling at his ear, trying to force his hand at his crotch.
And he let him for a while because he didn't have the money for his
fare. "He stole my money," he whimpered, trembling slightly for effect. "He stole my fucking money… and I'm all alone."

"Is okay."

"..."

"Is okay..."

So long as the old man kept driving, with one hand on the wheel, who gave a shit? He got out of the cab at the hotel zipping up his pants, and the old woman at the front desk gave him a dirty look as he strutted by.

When he tried to check out the next morning, the same bitch tried to charge him for an extra key. And, of course, he'd already handed his in. It was that racist, gay-basher Marcus who was still being delinquent. But he couldn't make the stupid idiot understand what he was trying to tell her. Couldn't she see the gigantic mound that was swelling up around his eye? Didn't she know what he'd been through? And now she wanted him to bail out Marcus when all he wanted to do was escape?

"You no give no key!"

"Then what the fuck is that on the wall behind you?"

"He give key lass night," she hissed at him, which was a bald-faced lie. He could see it in the way her moustache twitched below her right nostril, and the way her tiny, crack-baby eyes constantly looked to the left. But after the sudden appearance of what was either the clerk's brother, husband or pimp, he finally admitted defeat, and said he would go back to the room for one last check, pissing on the bed before slipping out the window and spraining his ankle trying to jump to the street below. He half-crawled for two blocks before wedging himself between a crucifix cart and the wall, until the heat died off.

History is useless to understanding life, in general or in the specifics of one identity. Why? Because time and truth, the pillars of history, are such immaterial concepts. The latter, especially, attempts to give importance to events that "actually happened," as if the world of our perception coincides at all with the empirical one. As if we can trust the first-hand account of anyone, including ourselves. The human mind is known to block out traumatic events. Like a car crash or a near-drowning. But even a simple first date can be drastically changed to procure a transcript better suited to liking ourselves. We must, in the end, like ourselves. And so, a "true life" is made up of memory and mythology. Something happens, we tell someone else, we obfuscate, the story changes, it becomes the new truth.

We create our own identities.

By telling stories.

Likewise, our identities never travel in straight lines, but instead jump willy-nilly from memory to memory, using similarities in the "facts," taking something as innocent as a sitting position, to leap from one place to another. Time is replaced by memory. You go on vacation to Central America, and you're sitting in a motorized dug-out canoe over the clearest waters you've ever seen. The sun and sea spray have transformed you into a saltpan. Dolphins are breaking the water all around you. You might even see a manatee. And your lover is sitting on your left side with his or her hand resting excitedly on your thigh. Squeezing lightly.

And then you close your eyes, blink once and you're back in bed, at home, or you're back in the days with your ex, when things were still so good, or you're at work ten years from now, staring at your computer screen and wishing you had made some different career choices, or you're a three-year-old running around your parents' pool. The next time you blink, you make the leap back to the Caribbean (and make no doubt about it, you are as much there then as you were the first time you felt it), you're on public transit, with your lover in exactly the same position on your left side, and you blink, and it's this little connection of proximity that links the events that define you.

This is why religions are so successful, because they allow people to form an understanding of the world through stories. The so-called truth of the stories makes no difference, because they offer an explanation that fits all the criteria we ask of it. A little bit about Jesus, or Job, a dash of David, a sprinkle of Solomon… This is what life is all about.

We are, each one of us, living, breathing Bibles. We are all mere anthologies of random, unrelated stories and coincidence.

He woke up with horrible pains in his lower abdomen. He was also feeling dizzy again. He wanted nothing more than to sleep in, but the pain was insistent. He could barely enjoy brunch at the bistro on the corner. But he went out that night, anyway. Some friends of Albert wanted to watch a Liverpool game at the pub, and he was glad for the excuse to visit the washroom to escape the boredom. He threw up on the ice in one of the urinals, kissed Albert in the alley without telling him about it, and headed back to their flat, hoping to God he wouldn't shit his pants in the underground.

He'd been sick before. This was different. There was no fever, no exhausted weakness, no feeling of brittleness along his ribs and collarbone. Just nausea and a constant pain around his ass. It hurt to sit. Or to stand, for that matter. And he couldn't sleep to save his life, not on the lumpy futon Albert called a bed. This was his punishment, he figured, for being gay. This was the ghost of his mother (alive and well back in Florida), cursing him for making her worry about him.

After Marcus, Chris Eaton hitchhiked his way to Berlin. Just in time for the World Cup semi-final between West Germany and England. The game itself held little interest for him, but the Wall had recently come down between East and West (not early enough to form a combined German team), so it was bound to be a party. It was also where the first car that picked him up was going. Albert was Irish to the core of his crystal blue eyes, and the shortest man he'd ever met who still turned him on. In the car, Chris would help him crack cans of Kilkenny so he wouldn't have to take his eyes off the road. They talked about girls, football, how he'd become stuck in London ("The arsehole of England…"), and football. When Albert stopped for breaks along the side of the road, Chris Eaton watched him pee against the back tire in the rear-view mirror. They were both drunk by the time they hit the city. But they made it in alive, not even bored to death by Albert's endless rants on why his homeland would never win at soccer's elite event:

"The refs fucking hate us!" he bemoaned, spitting out the window. "The Irish are the Jews of Europe!"

"You mean the blacks."

"…?"

"The expression is, "The Irish are the blacks of Europe.""

"…?"

"The Jews are the Jews of Europe."

Albert didn't think of himself as gay. But when he was drunk, it didn't seem to matter much, masturbating each other while they drank at the hostel. They didn't even make it to the game, passed out in lakes of each other's sweat, and woke up later to the sound of German youth overturning Volkswagens in the streets below. Albert ran to the window and started spitting on people underneath them. And Chris Eaton was in love again. Thankfully, the apartment Albert rented in London had an extra couch, so when they returned to the UK, none of his friends had to be the wiser about their situation.

For Chris Eaton, London was a tale of two cities: Night London and Day London. Most evenings, they went to pubs and smoked. Or watched a game with the boys, cheering against England. Liverpool was basically an Irish town, anyway. And it was about the only way he could be certain of getting in a fight without trying too hard. When Albert met people he disliked, he played up the accent even more, gave his name as Rick O'Shea and then quickly found some way of turning the conversation around to child pornography or how Shakespeare and Byron used to like lying under a glass table while other British queers shat on them. Occasionally he and Chris Eaton would ignore each other at a disco. And when Albert took his shirt off and twirled it around his head, he was stunning. Then Chris Eaton would pretend to flirt with one of the hired dancers (who let him up on one of the pedestals) or start kissing some Turk who kept buying him drinks and Albert would have him by the hair, dragging him home, and Chris Eaton would be so drunk he could barely remember if he and Albert had fucked or not, or if they had, what exactly they'd done.

It was heaven.

The days, conversely, were goddawful boring, with their museums and architecture, statues of warlords, men who were supposed to be guards but couldn't move, and the double-deckers spitting up cameras on every corner. That's why everyone rushes to and from work in London, it's depressing, how they pander to the tourists, just to maintain the status of a world-class city. And always the same monotony. Every time he went out, it felt as though the movie of his life was a reshoot, and had been cast with the same extras. The middle-aged divorcees from the provinces were always out in full force, lining up for *Random Musical by Andrew Lloyd Webber*, or *Musical with an Indirect and/or Specious Historical Connection*, or *Musical In Which Inanimate Objects Come to Life*, with their short-cut highlights and semi-stylish, black suit jackets over gigantic beaded necklaces and white turtlenecks. Or just the turtlenecks. What is it with middle-aged women and turtlenecks? And the hair that seems to be trying to escape from their heads? The ethnic gentlemen always seemed in such hurries, and yet with nowhere to go. The punks seemed like the only ones nice enough to trust with your kids. Every day at noon, he stopped at whatever pizza joint was closest, normally Pizza Hut, which he would never deign to eat at home but somehow craved with every waking moment when he was abroad. It also cost twice as much as any other place he might have eaten at, because the allure of American life was still so new and exciting. He might have blamed one of their grease bombs on the pain he was experiencing. With each meal, it grew worse. He was afraid the doctors might judge him. And eventually he broke down and bought himself a home enema. It was the most painful bowel movement he'd ever experienced. Yet, when he inspected the bowl, there it was: a plum-sized orange ball, the color and texture of the ones they used to play road hockey, with four or five tiny chain links dangling from it. The last one was broken.

"You lost something up my ass and didn't tell me?" He and the Irishman watched it bob in the water. Apparently Albert had been trying new things for weeks, including this string of – obviously deficient – anal beads he'd picked up at a x x x shop, four balls linked by shorts bits of chain, and had thought Chris Eaton was enjoying it. No doubt he was, but how frightening was it that someone could shove something so large into him and he wouldn't even remember? And how could he not tell him when he left it up there?

Albert was, at the best of times, reluctant to take responsibility. Perhaps, he accused, if the little pansy could hold his liquor, this wouldn't be such a fucking problem.

"The little what?"

"You fucking heard me!"

And after shouting at each other for nearly three minutes, when he threatened to tell Albert's friends and Albert slammed the door on his way out, Chris Eaton tried to flush the ball without thinking.

No amount of plunging could seem to dislodge it.

So he packed whatever he could into a garbage bag – he'd lost the backpack in Spain – and went back to America.

She was without direction. So she moved back to Cleveland, to attend the R. B. Turnbull Jr. School of Enterostomal Therapy Nursing, the only school of its kind at the time, partly to follow in her father's medical footsteps and partly so she could help people like her mother to adapt to the fear and discomfort of their ailments.

It was in Ohio that he met Emily, at the library, while he was checking out a book about Sol LeWitt. He was thinking about painting his apartment in primary colors, with lots of geometric lines, and he was going to The Master for inspiration. She recognized him from the musical, where he'd been growing his beard out to escape the humiliation of his last dramatic role. And she'd recently taken a course on LeWitt, so the book under his arm provided her with an intro:

"Did you know Lewitt used to work at *Seventeen* magazine?"

He feigned shock, started flipping through the pages. "This *isn't Seventeen* magazine?"

"..."

He was blowing it. "Last time I took out a book on fire."

"Yeah?"

"Yeah."

"..."

"I had to stamp it out."

She didn't get it. But she was cute, with an extended neck that lolled like a dying vulture. Her eyes drooped adorably like turkey wattles. And because the Oberlin campus was so small, they couldn't help running into each other at parties. Once, they even shared a bottle of Canadian rye whisky, and he knew immediately she was the one because she filled the awkward silences with whatever came into her head first.

"In high school, I set up a system with the cafeteria where we could collect the tabs from soda cans and use them to build wheelchairs for the needy, I mean, it wasn't really a system so much as they let me put a few mason jars and signs near the exits, but we collected nearly twenty thousand tabs before discovering the whole thing was a scam and the tabs were really being used to make guns."

"'For the needy?'"

"Can you imagine that? That's, like, a multi-billion dollar industry there. Built on the backs of well-meaning kids like me. Lesson learned, right? You never know what you're getting into sometimes. That's why you really have to do your homework first."

"..."

"..."

"They don't make guns out of aluminum."

And before he knew it, they were at his place, because she'd said something about the Sex Pistols and he invited her back for a lesson in real punk music. There was nothing in his bedroom except a mattress on the floor, where he lay with Emily, both of them naked, and she told him about this guy he'd gone to high school with, this guy she also knew, this really quiet, chubby guy who had rarely said a word to anyone and whom Chris Eaton had barely known except as the only male clarinet player in the school band. In fact, Chris Eaton was genuinely surprised to arrive for his first year at university and find they were living in the same dorm. One night at a party, this guy breached the doorway of his room with blood pouring down his face, having pierced his own nose by slowly drilling the stud pin through the wall of his progressively infected flesh. Within two days, he could barely touch it, let alone turn it to prevent his flesh from adhering to it as it healed. The infection eventually passed into his sinuses, and the only thing that could cover the stench of his breath while he was on antibiotics was popping cloves.

She was beautiful. And he was pretty sure he wanted to sleep with her. But he also had a bad habit of developing two or more crushes at the same time, and so he was always worried there was something better, someone hotter, something more meaningful he could be missing out on. The university was so small, he would never be able to keep things quiet, never be able to keep it from Julie, whom he'd secretly lusted over for more than a year. But Emily's clavicle was rising so lovely above her tiny breasts, her shoulders hunched like a rower at rest and her hair hanging down to her knees.

He told her about these albums, and these facts:

Napalm Death – *From Enslavement to Obliteration*. Important largely for managing to cram fifty-four tracks into a single CD, several of them only a few seconds in length. The band actually released a split single with The Electro Hippies in 1991, each side lasting only a second.

Merzbow – *Aqua Necromancer.* Named after Kurt Schwitters' famous art piece and self-described life's work *Merzbau,* or *Merz Building,* an architectural Dadaism that, at its peak, transformed a full eight rooms into a fantastical clutter of geographical shapes and biography. Schwitters started the piece three times: the original Hannover structure was destroyed in an Allied air raid; the Norwegian version, started fourteen years later, fell victim to fire; the last version in England was never completed. This is definitely Akita's most accessible recording, which is why he likes it. And through the Alien8 label, this CD turned him on to the postmodern, post-rock, avant-chamber music of Montreal groups like Do Make Say Think and Godspeed You! Black Emperor.

Pain Killer – *Guts of a Virgin.* A Japanese import collaboration between free jazz alto saxophonist John Zorn and Napalm Death drummer Mick Harris.

The Lounge Lizards – *S/T.* Loud jazz from the New York art-rock scene of the eighties, featuring John Lurie on saxophone and his younger brother Evan on keys, alongside which he has the complete Criterion D V D collection of the elder Lurie's wonderful program *Fishing with John,* following the strange misadventures of a jazz hipster without any angling experience and various celebrity friends, including a hunt for the elusive giant squid with Dennis Hopper in Thailand, and a legendary battle between Leonard Cohen and a giant cod in Ogac Lake on Baffin Island using live loons as bait.

Motörhead – *Iron Fist*. Released the year he was born and the last album to feature Philthy "Animal" Taylor on drums. Never mind the Sex Pistols, it was Motörhead who invented punk. And anyone who believes differently is living in some delusion of nostalgia. Or the falsity of first impressions. The Sex Pistols, led by Johnny Rotten (a.k.a. John Lydon) under the watchful eye of Malcolm McClaren, are generally considered to have led the first wave of the chiefly British movement. The names of other bands can sometimes be heard in the echoes of this thesis, The Damned and The Clash are certainly the main ones, though some might say the Pistols stole their sound from The Stooges. By the time the Damned released "New Rose" in 1976 (the "first punk single"), punk was already a viable music term. It was also three months after the release of Motörhead's first full-length offering: *On Parole*. The true birth of punk, building on the heavy metal genre made popular by Alice Cooper instead of New York anti-pop. Basically, the Sex Pistols were created as an art project by a clothes designer, the fashion spin-off of an anger and dissatisfaction that was too loud to ignore. Motörhead was that anger's true embodiment.

On one of their first dates, they went to see a film called *A Hardcover Saint*, about a writer in his mid-thirties who treated others poorly, mostly because he felt a sense of moral superiority towards them, including his friends – especially his friends – who continued to forgive him well beyond the normal limits of friendship, set in a contemporary context but based on the combined biographies of Mann and Proust, with additional elements from the lives and/or work of Hardy, Tolstoy, Strindberg, Borges, and specifically the widely cited feud between Proust and Maupassant. (Proust, for example, arranged all of his speaking tours around those of his elder, purely to arrive later and mock Maupassant's general obsession with realism and particular fascination with the Franco-Prussian War, in which all of his stories were set.) He adored it. She wanted to leave. Everyone in the film was a complete asshole, she said. Why would I want to sit through that? He said he knew people like that. She found it unrealistic. Then why did it bother her, he wondered. What she wanted, or what she enjoyed, rather, were films that featured some form of redemption – what she called *a purpose* – whereby the characters were able to discover their flaws, the riddle of their own lives, and be transformed. She wanted prostitutes with hearts of gold, mobsters with family values, porn stars who fall in love. And he said: People in real life don't change. They don't see the light, and they don't have sudden revelations.

It's enough to see that life is a puzzle, he said. Attempting to figure it just fills one with frustration.

He wrote a short story about John Lurie similar to Hemingway's *Old Man and the Sea*: *"It is good,"* Lurie croaked at Leonard as they *hooked the giant bass into the dinghy, "that we do not have to try to kill the sun or the moon or the stars. It is enough to live on the waves and kill our true brothers..."* The story talked a lot about otoliths, and forensic science, and considered how it should be possible to capture the entire history of a single person through one and yet coroners and medical examiners seemed to focus on little more than the cause of death.

The otolith is one of the small particles of calcium carbonate in the saccule, or utricle, of the inner ear. Pressure from the otoliths on the hair cells of the macula provide sensory input about acceleration and gravity, balance and sense of place. It allows all fish, particularly those swimming at extreme depths, to keep track of which way is up. The aquatic otolith can also be the most important tool for understanding the life of fish and fish populations. Affected largely by fluctuations in temperature and time, the otolith develops growth rings not unlike the rings of a tree, recording daily age and growth patterns in surprising detail. With the proper microscope, a fish otolith can reveal everything from the exact date of hatch to migratory patterns to the daily temperature of the water it swam in.

The otolith performs a similar role in humans. But due to our ability to regulate the temperature around us with various heating and cooling devices, cross-sections of a human otolith tend to reveal much less about the subject. In a human being, damaged otoliths can result in extreme dizziness and nausea, at inopportune times like when you're driving down the highway at night with the temperature well below freezing, and you're about to navigate a savage off-ramp. The world shifts. The entire left side of your body goes numb. And you're only vaguely aware of being driven to the hospital.

When he met Emily, who also had dreams of becoming a writer, she told him her stories because she wanted him to know her better. "Because that's all anyone is," she whispered to him in the back of her late-eighties Chevrolet station wagon, her eyes as wide and dark as potholes or abandoned wells. "The sum of a series of unrelated stories." And he made off with that shiny part of her identity like a lazy raccoon, or a bat, never going too far with the stories she'd left out in the open. And it drove them further apart because she became afraid to open her mouth around him.

For Thanksgiving, Emily decided to host all of her friends who didn't live close enough to their parents to make the trip home. The orphans, she called them. Chris Eaton's parents lived less than a half-hour away, but he stayed to help because he didn't want to miss out on anything. She was a wonderful cook. Or rather, she was a wonderful hostess, which made everyone ultimately forget the dry and poorly seasoned meat. Memories of her gatherings amounted to collages of her smile, tall candles, beer made from kits, and the newest music her roommate stole from the campus radio station. But as soon as the last of the guests arrived, Emily received a phone call from her parents to tell her they were splitting, which was such a foreign concept to him that he was entirely useless to her. His parents – along with most of the parents of his friends – had all stayed together. Her family was from a much larger city, where the stench of fermenting dreams always hung in the air. People couldn't stop moving because there was always something better, something bigger, something lofty to strive for. In a big city, people never sleep. Even in their dreams they're trying to make themselves better. Trying to make their mark. You can be awake at any time of the night and feel a city tensing up, its eye twitching under the pressure.

The turkey Emily was planning sat uncooked in the oven for days until it started to smell.

Eventually, Chris Eaton was the one who had to throw it out.

There were nine planets in the solar system. Beethoven wrote nine symphonies. When you take all the single digits from one to nine, they add up to forty-five. Add those two numbers, and you get nine.

The average human pregnancy lasts approximately nine months.

Emily's, however, lasted just over a month: a missed period due to the stress of Christmas exams and her parents' divorce.

For that month, however, until her flow kicked in again, it was as real for them as midnight feedings and future custody trials. Ordinarily, she had this adorable, permanent half-smile, caught motionless in the headlights between her hunching shoulders. She liked to wear jaunty hats. Even in bed. She had hairy nipples he could feel on his tongue. But by the time they parted for the holidays (she chose to spend them with her father, because she'd always been daddy's little girl, and her mother had grown increasingly moody and less fun to be around), the smile and nipples were both gone. This could be it, the end of their lives as they knew it, redefining themselves to be part of each other, and then part of this thing, and then inevitably (in her mind, anyway) tearing it all apart to make them all feel less than whole.

Then, the day before Christmas, her father introduced her to his new girlfriend, someone she knew from his office. They were getting married. They had already purchased a new condo, and for once her father had not scrimped on the extras, upgrading to granite countertops, stainless steel appliances, plush white carpeting in every room but the kitchen. Her father and this woman, whom she could vaguely remember from a Christmas party where employees were encouraged to bring their kids. (She had kids? No, thank God. To think this woman would ever procreate, with her eyes like ripples caused by fallen rocks, so wide and yet always getting wider, as if they were pried open by the greedy fingers of monkeys, was too much for Emily.) This woman kept doilies under doilies, and held on to an eternal façade of good-naturedness. Even when Emily spilled red wine on the new carpet it didn't phase her, tossing her own glass of white wine in the same spot and dabbing, dabbing, dabbing, never rubbing, until it was gone. She knew how to clean everything. Everything. Which made it all seem even worse.

When Emily returned to school, she didn't want to talk about it.

That was the worst part: another month that distracted him from his work on the silo. Not that Emily – or the baby, as they could joke about it later, when "the baby" just meant the dark stain on her pad – was entirely to blame. There was also something about the town itself, how it seemed in a constant state of sleeping on its side. There were nights he would have stayed up until morning working on the numbers for the silo, if it weren't for the fact that everyone else in the town was already asleep. He could feel it, as if the entire town were breathing deeply at once. Not just the people, but the town itself. And it made him feel guilty to be disturbing that geographic rest. They fought about meaningless things, like what to have for dinner, or whether one had to outlaw pesticides (in order to fix the current food distribution system) or fix the current food distribution system (so they could finally get off their dependence on pesticides).

Still, the split would never entirely make sense to him, especially when he looked back on it later, in the periods directly following other breakups, when he was vulnerable and particularly unoptimistic about the future. She was everything he thought he wanted in a partner. She liked his concrete poetry when it wasn't too conceptual, seemed able to reconcile his attraction to experimental works like *Trout Mask Replica* with his days as a Phish-head, and put up with his daily rants on the state of literature. The sex was amazing. And while his tendency was to see the world only as it related to himself, he respected the awareness she had of the larger picture, except – and this seemed so minor – when it came to other animals. Shortly before they met, her cat Rue, named for the Pooh character but tragically misspelled, had been hit by a car, paralyzing it from the waist down. It had somehow learned to maneuver around her apartment using only its front paws, but she had to literally squeeze the shit out of it two or three times a day, bracing it under her left arm like a set of bagpipes and forcing her bicep from the cat's ribs to its ass. She had no television, so this was basically the only entertainment she provided. The whole place smelled like barely digested tuna.

"You know, we're a whole lot closer to animals than you might think," she would say, Rue flailing under her armpit. "And what do we do to them? We lock them up in cages so other people can pay us money to stare at them while they use the bathroom. Do you think that's dignity? Thank God Rue has me or they'd probably have him caged right now."

"A house cat?"

"Soon we'll be driving them to the brink of extinction, too..."

"But are zoos really cruel to animals? Zoos are the only PR those animals get! They're like diplomats! If we didn't have them in zoos, we wouldn't even know they existed, and we'd care less about their extinction than we do about Iraqis, or the Afghanis, or those poor idiots in England under all that ice!"

Outside the city, the roads had buckled under the last few weeks of heat, forcing the landscape into grass-stained blisters, and several of these had split into milky fields of hay. The clouds took weeks to build, hanging low like a bubble of paint under a leaky roof. And then finally everything burst.

"Why do you have to be such an asshole sometimes?" she asked him.

And he wasn't sure.

For the next two months, he would regret having been so harsh. He missed her. Then he didn't miss her. He put his compost silo project off a little longer, and spent many of his nights at the Roadhouse out by the train station, where more than once he went home with a girl from one of his electives. Her cheeks were lumpy, like balls of half-kneaded flour, with the tightest mouth he'd ever seen on another human being, peeling back from her teeth when she smiled. She kissed him once, twice, on the dance floor, ramming her horsy teeth into his mouth with such force that he was momentarily stunned, it was the only way he could explain it, hanging off him like an x-ray protection vest, heavy and warm. Her name might have been Julie.

They rubbed each other's thighs beneath the table, thinking no one else could see, and then broke up after three weeks when he caught her moving her lips as she read.

He would always be alone. Like his parents. From childhood's hour, he felt, he dreamt, that he was not as others were, was drawn, from every depth of good and ill, towards some mystery that he could not quite reach. Could not even see. He had a purpose. Of that he was sure. But the finer details – or even the larger, vaguer ones – were beyond him. And such was his difficulty in trying to circumvent this ambiguous calling – so clear, he could not help but see right through it – that he looked on the rest of humanity, his acquaintances and friends and even the occasional circumstantial lover, as they chased the paths set out by their parents, or their likes and dislikes, or their economic station, with a heaping tray of contemptful jealousy. As if he existed outside the world in which they squatted.

He would never quite understand it until his final days, when suddenly his purpose would form like a cataract on his vision, or the hand of God, confusing but unmistakable, and close enough to touch, and then, and only then, would he see that everything he had resisted doing up until that point, for fear that any decisive course of action might unwittingly take him further away from his destiny, had been the straightest line he might ever have shot. From birth to this point, he'd acted as if his own life, and where he placed himself within the spectrum of it, did not matter. And he was never likely to make that connection with someone or something else that would change this.

So when the voice called his name, he said yes.

Then two sets of arms were fishing him from the water, and suddenly he was at war. Or at least in more physical training. The war in Iraq went longer than anyone could have imagined. When they'd first announced it at the academy in Lexington, everyone had expected Hussein's Imperial Guard to lay down their weapons and surrender. But US forces didn't actually march into Baghdad until April 9. And there were still fierce pockets of resistance scattered throughout the country, in Fallujah and Ramadi, chiefly, but also in places less mentioned. His entire class was transferred to Fort Lewis, just outside Tacoma, Washington, one of the largest cities in the state although, in many ways, it didn't exist. It had its own bowling alley, fast food restaurants, movie theatre, bars. Gasoline without taxes. A city with a wall around it. Possibly to keep the protesters out, or even worse, the zealots. Because he was single, they placed him in a barracks with all the other single soldiers. The married soldiers were provided with separate homes, which was why so many of them got hitched so early, for the privacy. He salvaged a mattress another soldier had dropped to the curb – they received a pittance for food and entertainment, so why waste it on something as unimportant as bedding – and for the first few nights he had trouble sleeping, repeatedly woken not by the lumps or bedbugs but by low-flying helicopters and machine-gun fire from the training. Why they were training in the woods for a war in the desert, he was never sure. But he continued to wake every morning at four-thirty anyway, and shined his boots up for a tramp through the mud. It rained nearly every second day. On the other days, it was worse. And some nights the other soldiers joked about how great it would be when they were finally sent to Iraq, because at least it would be warm and sunny.

When he arrived over there, he realized he often drooled in his sleep. This had never been a problem before, but in Iraq if you drooled in your sleep, you woke up with mosquitoes sucking on the puddles around your lips. And you walked around looking like you picked up a swarm of cold sores from sucking a whore. The only thing worse than being gay in the army was admitting you like to go down on women. Anything besides vaginal intercourse was actually a crime, and it wasn't uncommon for women who were filing for divorce to say they gave their servicemen husbands an occasional blowjob. Thankfully, they were allowed to use scarves because of the blowing sand.

To make matters worse, his first task, which they assigned him not with words but by handing him a shovel and a canister of gasoline, was latrine duty, officially called *latrine management*, a rite of passage for many when they first stepped off the plane because of the distasteful nature of the work, especially if it was their first tour, like fraternity initiation but without the luxury of inebriation. His unit's entire responsibility was to keep the camp sanitary by digging regulation shit pits, burning them when they reached capacity, and then digging more. Normally, this would have only comprised part of their duties, digging a latrine or two each week. But nearly half the company had contracted dysentery from eating chicken kebabs on their days off, and productivity was so high they had to punch a new series of holes and burn them every day. His shovel was never out of his hands, and his clothes were never without the stench of gas station washrooms, oil refinery sludge, farm machinery. The smell set up shop in his nostrils and it was one he was unable to successfully evict. The other soldiers called him shithead. And when they saw the sores on his face, they called him ass-hat, fudge-patrol, the rusty trombonist. His only saving grace was that he seemed the only one immune to whatever stomach issues were going around. Unfortunately, after he made one too many cracks about skid marks in their underwear, the other soldiers began to plot their revenge.

Still, all in all, it was better than fighting, digging toilets in the desert. And better than border duty, where busloads of explosives could roll slowly up disguised as children. Or as an ambulance. One day a child came up to one of Chris Eaton's friends with an injured dog in his arms. Both of them were crying. The soldier took the whimpering mutt from him. It was bleeding heavily from its stomach, its intestines spilling out into the boy's hands, from what he assumed must be some random shrapnel. He tried to hold everything in; as if the dog's insides were some kind of manifestation of his own repressed emotions; as if holding all of it together, like the Dutch boy with his finger in the wall, was akin to holding back the dam of his insanity; as if holding it together might even end the war itself. Like holding his breath underwater just long enough to be rescued. If I can save this dog, he thought, all of this will have been worth it. If I can save this dog, he thought, I will understand what it all means. And I will end it. He thought, This boy must be dying inside. Like his dog. When I was younger, I also had a dog. I was allowed to name him and I called him Betty. He was my best friend. Then, one day, Betty got hit by a car. And I found him in the ditch with his head caved in. I was sure he was dead, but when I approached, he lifted his head. The only object close at hand was a brick. This poor boy is just like me. But when he looked up to console him, he saw that the boy had run away. And the dog exploded from the grenade the rebels had inserted into its abdomen, killing Chris Eaton's friend and three other men instantly.

* * *

At the end of the week, they were removed from latrine duty and told to prepare to march on Fallujah. This thing had to end, his sergeant told them. And it had to end now. So if a bunch of ragheads wanted to make a couch-cushion fort out of this town, they'd just go in and kick the fucker down. They boarded the trucks to Fallujah, and his sergeant handed him a bottle saying, "Could be the last drink you'll have in a while." He downed the whole thing, despite the chalky aftertaste. Then the whole troop laughed at him for the entire two-hour drive to the outpost, the empty bottle of ipocac rolling around the floor of the transport. This was war, forced to live your life with a bunch of amateur adolescents. Bunch of fucktards. Most of them were backwoods hicks. And the rest not even Americans, just a bunch of illegal immigrants, mostly from Mexico, who were deemed unsuitable for citizenship but just dandy for helping the government avoid another draft implementation. Half of them were married at sixteen, their wives and kids stuck on the military base back in the U.S. with nothing to do except grow bitter. So they amused themselves by humiliating one another, even running the risk that their practical joke might actually work, and they'd be forced to sit in that truck for the full two hours with another soldier who'd just shit his pants.

All the other soldiers grabbed seats close to the cab, to get as far away from the sand kicked up in the back, and from Chris Eaton, who stood at the rear, worried about the growing force in his bowels and how the resistance against that force might be changed if he were to even shift one muscle. Soon enough, most of them were asleep, and once he was certain he would offer none of them any satisfaction, he settled back with his pants around his ankles, alighting his derrière out the posterior flaps. Any time he tried to look past the flaps, the scenery was the same, a road going nowhere, although in this case, nowhere was the direction he'd already come from. So he kept his eyes pointed forward instead, into the increasing darkness inside the transport, like he was slowly passing out or fading. And for a moment, the world became nothing, which was especially soothing.

Then his silent non-existence was broken by the rhythmic trace of a sibilant hiss, what he suspected was a smuggled portable music player beneath the helmet of another soldier, and the hint of a recognizable tune – something he couldn't quite identify but definitely something he had heard before on popular radio – reeled him slowly back to reality. The other soldier, the origin of Chris Eaton's distraction from grace, was much older than Chris Eaton, in fact much older than anyone else in the regiment, which tended to make him stand out in the group more than any skin colour or body shape or personalized scarf. He was also not asleep, and unfortunately realized this fact at the exact same moment as Chris Eaton, their gazes unconsciously spooning each other for comfort before recoiling in embarrassment.

Worst of all, the older man took their eye contact as an invitation to something worse, conversation, launching into the unrequested story about his life, which Chris Eaton sank in and out of like a slightly rancid glass of wine, how he'd grown up in the country, shortly after the end of the second World War, pitching crab apples at hornet nests and falling out of trees, playing in the dirt behind his grandfather's garage, lying in the tall grass between his home and the graveyard, smelling the birds and the clouds, pissing on dead raccoons, drinking alcohol out of abandoned dreams, always alone. There was something about his father. And a '45 (was it called "Banana Split"?) played on the wrong speed. And how his father always accused him of being sick with music, whatever that meant, always humming or drumming on tables or wetting his bed in the night. The army, his father said, was the only place for him, so he didn't try to avoid the draft and it came for him, just like that. Afterward, with the financial help of the Sidharrtha Veteran Co-op (an organization started in Chistorra, Nevada by another ex-soldier who, while fighting in Vietnam, had learned and accepted the ways of Buddhism), he opened up a store, following his love of music, focussing on 8-track stereos for cars and home, the failure of which was somehow the fault of the singer Billy Joel. When his old battalion was again called upon for the invasion of Grenada, he decided to re-enlist. And this time he stayed through the Honduran conflict with Nicaragua, some time in Libya, and Operation Harvard Chest (an umbrella code name that also included Operation Chard Harvest, as well as Operation Harsh Redact I to Operation Harsh Redact V), to the invasion of Panama in 1989. By then, fighting had essentially come to define him. He picked fights in bars. He argued with strangers in restaurants. No one would hire him because of his temper, and he was strong and brutish, so he took up boxing, until he realized he didn't like being struck, so he swung at the referee to disqualify himself without showing signs of cowardice, and he took a job that allowed him to hate people in private. He married a girl he thought would save him, who had a good job, and an effervescence that made his chest feel delightfully like it was full of the blowing grass of his youth, light and ticklish up high in his throat, and later, when money was scarce, or he'd been drinking, or he was bored, he beat her. They had children. And he watched them grow up and wondered which one would try to take him on first. So he re-enlisted again. This time to Kuwait. The girl sent him letters. Sometimes with photos of his kids. He sent them drawings he had made, of their favourite cartoon characters, horribly mutilated by a bayonet to the stomach, or having their brains blown out at close range. They were quite accomplished. He felt bad for that. He stopped writing back. She did not. And this made it worse. He made a vow that when he was discharged again, he would find her and the kids and make an honest woman out of her. By then, however, they were both in their fifties. To avoid future problems with her bladder, her doctor suggested she have a complete hysterectomy, which he also suggested was a routine surgery and would lower her risk of ovarian cancer. But when they were stitching her back up, the surgeon perforated her colon, which no one caught until she had suffered so much internal bleeding and the wound was already so infected that there was nothing they could do.

He heard all this from her sister, who was now looking after the kids and never wanted them to see him again. When the twin towers came down, he enlisted again for the last time.

* * *

The other soldier asked him if he liked music. Chris Eaton said he did. The other soldier asked what kind. And Chris Eaton said all kinds. Was there not one kind in particular? asked the other soldier. And Chris Eaton said no, there was not. What about country? asked the other soldier. What about rock? What about Christian music? Him? He liked only one band, that was how particular his taste was. And probably, when it came right down to it, just one album. It was *his* album, he said. It was the album he'd probably been searching for most of his life and didn't even know it. And when he finally found it, nothing else he listened to felt complete. It was the album that finally made him feel calm. It was *the* album, he felt, that might have saved his marriage, if he'd found it sooner, that might have saved the relationship with his kids. It was the album that might have made him happy. Chris Eaton reconfirmed that he liked all kinds of music, that he found them all interesting and appealing for a variety of reasons, and that he tried, whenever he could, to venture outside of his normal comfort zone, to seek out new auditory experiences. The other soldier suggested Chris Eaton had just not found the right one yet.

* * *

The other soldier asked him if he'd killed anyone yet.

* * *

The other soldier said the only thing worse than lobsters on your piano was crabs on your organ.

* * *

The other soldier said he had once read an article in a magazine, written by a man, he said, or maybe a woman, from a part of the country where you wouldn't expect, where they don't normally have those kinds of people, people who don't have anything to do with their hands, people who think too much, not in some place like New York or Massachusetts or Rhode Island, or California, no, this person was from somewhere in the middle, and this was where he'd first come across the idea that each person had one album that was their musical soulmate. The premise, he said, was really just an expansion on the idea of Desert Island Discs, a radio program started in Britain shortly after the outbreak of World War II when the creator Roy Plomley was searching for some sort of entertainment-based distraction to raise national spirits, or rather a tighter focus on the idea, which had invited celebrities as varied as Welsh singer and radio host Tom Pwy, painter Schuyler Die, poet Fernando Quien and Italian sex-symbol

Elisabetta Chiunque to select their top eight records – and one luxury item – they could never do without. Most people tended to choose "Ode to Joy" and similarly obvious pieces, so as not to appear too low-brow, rather than choosing something as base and popular as "In Der Führer's Face," "Mairzy Doats" or "We're Gonna Hang out the Washing on the Siegfried Line." But the first few guests are most notable for interesting selections like Louis Jordan's *Swimmin' with the Fishes*, Chip Shorter's *The Blackout Stroll*, or Louis Armstrong's experimental jazz number, *A Prevaricated Horn Shot* (selected by Schuyler Die), in which the middle trumpet solo is actually just Armstrong trying to mimic the sound of his instrument with his lips alone. Pwy, for his luxury item, chose a bottomless bottle of Dalwhinnie. The American critic, from the magazine he'd read, had taken this premise one step further, suggesting people might be happy – happier, even – with just one, because this would remove the stress of having to choose between those eight every day. And the critic used, as an example, the life of someone the soldier was unfamiliar with, someone he had meant to look up but, as of yet, had not. In fact, he'd all but forgotten his name. Because the most interesting thing about this person, this happiest man, was not his name, but how he had started his own musical journey through life, and how it seemed to mirror the other soldier's life so precisely, listening to his parents' old jazz records (Chip Shorter, again, key among them!) on the wrong speed, thinking music was a plodding thing, heavy and thick, like gobs of batter falling from a spoon, being introduced to the music of Charlie Hardin, which broke everything wide open, obviously owing a nod to Elvis but without The King's fattening showmanship, purchasing every Hardin record he could find, from what he thought was Hardin's self-titled debut (a common mistake, and not made just by the two of them) to the third album, *The Grey Fog* (1959), even after the singer/guitarist died so prematurely and they continued to release greatest hits packages with smatterings of unreleased studio recordings for the next ten years. This led to his discovery of the British invasion – The Beatles and The

Rolling Stones – through an honest, hopeful mistake, a record by a band called The Hardins, who had no real connection to Charlie and were also not particularly good. The other man went to Vietnam, too. And opened a music store. And the soldier began to believe that the article had actually been written about him specifically. He thought it was a sign. And he began weeding down his own collection, as if by a message from God, immediately tossing any record he had not listened to in the last five years, then one year, then six months, then writing down very selective criteria that had to be met by the remaining hundred or so records to stay on his shelf, that it had to be influential in some way, and couldn't be simple to classify as a genre, and had to be somewhat obscure (because he didn't want his special disc to also possibly be someone else's) without being entirely pompous, and then he basically just decided to remove the half dozen classical records because how could they really speak to him when they weren't from his generation, and anything with a saxophone or banjo, until one day he was down to his traditional eight desert island discs, which he set up head-to-head in a tournament bracket until he had one winner:

- The Doors – *Narrative Chap* (1978; one of the three post-Morrison albums, which is all the other soldier would listen to because, as far as he was concerned, there was only room for one Morrison on the list; with an album cover that featured a photo of a private ranch – presumably Morrison's – that fit the title particularly well)
- Van Morrison – *Veedon Fleece* (1974)
- Charlie Hardin – *S/T* (1958)
- Chip Shorter – *Rave On Data* (1998; also a lesser-known later work, collaborating with a trio of young turntablists named Patree, Vitaro and Hersch)
- Stina Verda – *Charo* (1980)
- Tom Pwy (another coincidence) – *Hot Arsenic* (1939)

- Chet Nasario – *Hardtop Rev* (1967)
- Chris Eaton – *She Was a Big Freak* (1974)

His luxury item, he decided, would be a book of crossword puzzles.

And finally he was left with only *Charlie Hardin* and Chip Shorter (played, for old time's sake, on the wrong speed).

And he chose Chip Shorter.

And he found that the result was the opposite, that he was hungrier for new music than he'd ever been in his life.

And the next day he heard the music that was the last CD he'd ever buy, the CD he was currently listening to, and he'd never listened to another record again.

We're all searching for something, the other soldier said. I'm just lucky enough to have found it.

That's idiotic, Chris Eaton said, and shut his eyes to go to sleep.

And the next day he was dead.

PART 6

He couldn't remember. Or rather, he remembered everything perfectly. Everything. Over and over. Until his mind became so clogged with memories that there was no room for anything new. But each time he remembered, it was like dubbing an old tape, so that, gradually, all of his memories became more distorted in their reliving, less clear in their retelling. Each time he told a friend about something fond, it became fonder. When he spoke of something trying, it became worse. Until he could no longer remember what was true and what was invented. He couldn't remember how it started. Or what came next. Or the order from which it would all make sense.

One day, he died. And the next morning he woke up as if nothing had happened. Someone told him it wasn't true. He stopped leaving the house and took up painting, crosswords, anything that left a permanent mark. So he could constantly reassess where he was by what was around him. He woke up from a dream about drowning, about war, about a city completely closed off by walls. More fighting. Planes crashing. He woke up from a dream of lying immobile in a hospital bed waiting to die, and he realized it was true. He woke up. And he was still there. He couldn't move his legs. Complete paraplegia from the point of injury down. The rest of his body felt as though he'd been beaten with snooker balls. He woke up surrounded by friends and family, looking at him with those blank stares, and he failed to convince his father about their fishing trips, or the pumpkins. His sister smiled weakly when he brought up the swim meets. He had to tell them about the time he fell in the pool when he was two.

"I nearly died."

"Sure you did, buddy... Sure you did..."

The only thing he seemed unable to remember was the trip with his friends in the '73 Simca van, on their way back from *Logan's Run* at the Torch Theatre out on St. Peter's, all six of them shining with such promise, their youthful ignorance triumphant, the snow letting up, turning to rain, and the solidifying playset landscape taking shape around whatever base it could find, park benches, mailboxes, stranded cars, the entire planet hardening into a desert of ice. He could not picture being the only one wearing a seat belt, and Tony being tossed neatly out the window as the van did its first flip, as if God had just reached in and yanked him out like a tissue, couldn't recall Conrad's head striking the passenger headrest, his nose driven sideways across his face, snapping like one of those plastic cases that kept the cassette tapes high enough to see in the stacks previously made for LPs, couldn't even fathom the steering wheel meeting Phil's ribs, driving them into his bladder and eventually causing an infection that would prevent him from having kids and ruin his first marriage. There were only three bones in Andy's right arm, but just the same, all three of them unanimously decided to give up when Andy tried to use them against his impact with the dash, the radius and the ulna pulverizing each other and the humerus driven up and through Andy's scapula, escaping out his back and acting as a lever when his body was flung back against his seat, cracking his wrist against the door; when the car finally stopped moving, the glass of the windshield was still hanging in the air around them waiting for the world to exhale.

Eddie only got a black eye. He couldn't tell the glass from the snow. Tony came walking out of the mist without a scratch, and Eddie immediately dubbed him Lucky Tony.

The emergency blinkers kept going red, then black, and then stayed that way.

But they were all lucky in comparison to Chris Eaton. Upon impact, the two-point seatbelt focused all of its attention in one place, and his vertebrae went to each other for support, huddling together with their inflamed nerve fibers clenched in their knobby fists, excited by the new experience but frightened by the sounds they'd never heard before, sounds they couldn't quite place: skate blades on a frozen lawn? a rusted dock on polystyrene plastic buoys? They became frantic, stepping on each other in an attempt to escape the noise, but they also weren't exactly sure where the noise was coming from. So they came together, and they went in every direction at once, confusing him on every sensory level. His balance was off. Someone had kicked him in the sternum, but who? With every neuron firing at once, he was simultaneously sure that his face was wet, someone was baking bread, he was on fire, someone was licking him. He was trying to open a can of corned beef, trying to fire off a perfectly executed corner kick. He tried to flap his wings. His fins. The trapezius muscle, which runs in a triangle up the neck and along both shoulders, clenched, and the sternocleidomastoid helped out as much as it could, threatening to lift off its scalene base.

The doctors were fairly sure he'd never walk again. At his initial physiotherapy exam, however, nearly six months after he first woke up in hospital, he was able to resist the therapist as she flexed his foot forward. The next day, he succeeded in moving the big toe on his right foot. Within four more, he could move that leg laterally, as if he were creating a snow angel, and was practically able to sit up by himself. It was, the experts claimed, a minor miracle. Tony and Phil stopped by to chat nearly every day. They were even allowed to take him out on day trips, with a return trip to the Torch Theatre to catch the big screen colossus of *Superman*, which he enjoyed, although he thought the time travel ending was a bit weak. His sister brought him a new pair of running sneakers so he could get back into shape when they eventually released him. It was clear that he would be able to return to his old life, to the Chris Eaton that he once was.

Then, just as suddenly, he was struck by a simple flu. Because he was perpetually lying on his back, he developed a sinus infection that quickly spread into his lungs, leaving him weak and out of breath. They had to place him on a respirator. They prescribed massive antibiotics to prevent the infection from spreading to any of his other injuries, especially the paralyzed portions of his body where he might not feel any discomfort until it was too late. But he was unable to attend his physio sessions for nearly a month.

And the feeling in his legs never returned.

Thorne put a hand on her leg, and the feeling came rushing back. But Thorne's face was still. She tried staring at him harder. This was it. She was in love. But then his eyes fell, and his hand moved slowly to hers, helped her upstairs to the bathroom where she threw up, multiple times, held her hair back until she was finished and then called her a cab. There was no spreading, no eating, no final initiation into life's mysterious carnality (for which she would have to wait another three years, and in the most horrible of ways).

Still, Thorne recommended her for the Master's program in Early Childhood Education at Tufts, where she could put more of his theories into practice at Children's Hospital Boston, as part of her practicum while composing her thesis. Chris Eaton was placed into various rotations throughout the hospital but always out of uniform so that the children could disassociate her from the procedure they were about to undergo – or the illness they were currently fighting – and see her more as an ally, a friend. Often she would be the last person they saw before going under; and the first person, if they were lucky enough to survive, when they woke up. The success cases in those serious patients were most often the worst, largely because they were flown in from all over the country, with insurance rarely covering the additional costs of their parents' tickets, and many were from families much too poor to afford the frequent trips on their own. These children developed an even stronger attachment to her, as she did to them, because she was all they had, making her a sort of surrogate parent. And when the surgeries made it possible for them to go back home, the emotional blow was sometimes too much to take, because she knew, from experience, within a few months, that they would be back.

After graduating from Tufts, Chris Eaton was offered a similar job at the St. Hecarion Children's Hospital in Houston, this time focusing solely on the terminally ill, or at least the ones least likely to make it, those with heart and lung problems and sometimes leukemia. She was tasked with setting up a private playroom – a space that was entirely off limits to other hospital staff – in hopes of furthering their comfort level, and even the children who were confined to bed rest were wheeled down at least once per week. She brought toys to them and helped them to decorate the curtains around their beds to create a starry night with full constellations, a circus or, strangest request of all, by keeping the white of the curtain as a snowy landscape, an arctic panorama with explorers trudging towards the grey strain in the top right. She met a young doctor, also named Julian (unfortunately), and after a few tear-filled confessions about the children over coffee, they moved on to dinner, then a movie, and eventually to dancing at the Bayou Mamma. Houston was going through hard times with the oil crisis, but was not yet rough. It just wasn't growing. Julian said Houston was like that nice kid in your class whose parents had just split and wasn't sure what was right any more, and it was only a matter of time before he started breaking into your house when you were away for the weekend but for now he was still fun at parties. Chris Eaton thought Julian was funny, and cute, she thought she might even be falling in love with him, but the first time he asked her up to his place, she withdrew. Her period, she lied. She'd waited so long already, she didn't want to enter into anything lightly, and she was naturally more than a little afraid. On the third invitation, she let him remove her top and even finger her uncomfortably, but it quickly felt like someone was flicking her frostbitten ear, or kneading a bruise, so sensitive was her clitoris, so she feigned a charley horse until he grew aggravated and went to sleep. Otherwise, things were good.

Soon after her arrival, Chris Eaton was asked to spend a few weeks observing a young boy who was so severely autistic she was almost sure he had no idea she was there, that he viewed her like any other piece of furniture, other than to kick her when he passed. He seemed happiest when his hands were submersed in water, so she kept a large basin of it on the floor in the centre of the room, but she had to watch him closely lest he stick his head into it, too. Otherwise, there seemed nothing she could do to break through.

Near the end of the second week, already growing hopeless, she decided to rearrange the furniture. He moved with such grace around the room, even with his eyes closed, seemingly paying no attention to anything he was doing. Not once did he ever trip, stub his toe, or deviate from his path except to kick her in the shin or ankle. So she thought transforming the environment might shake him up. He paused on entering the room, cocked his head to the left and back as if to smell it, then went straight for the basin of water as per usual. So she decided to remove that object, moving the chair to its opposite side and storing the basin in the closet. The next day he paused again, and stood still at the closet door. For the entire day. On the third day, she moved the chair again, to the other side of a toy castle, and took the castle away. On the fourth, she arrived to find him already there, the chair completely on the other side of the room, everything else in the closet, and the boy had even balanced another chair atop the first. So on the fifth day, she purchased a game of checkers and left it in the middle of the room, with two chairs, should he invite her to play. The next morning he was, again, already there. Both chairs were side-by-side. The table and the game of checkers were gone.

He was at a loss as to what to do with his life, so after four years at Kenyon, Chris Eaton made a go of it in Cincinnati, where he continued to explore a Grand Unified Field Color Theory, combining the elementary basics of color as unbroken, flat planes with the fundamental force of his violently distorted moods, and without the traditional field theory emphasis on brushstroke and gesture. He got a place in Over-the-Rhine above the old pool hall behind the Laundromat, where the rent was fabulously cheap because the area was being overrun by blacks who had been displaced by the construction of the Mill Creek Expressway, and still he convinced his roommates to cram a fourth person into the living room because they only ever entertained in the kitchen. Over the next two years, he had nearly a half-dozen shows at the Patty Salam Gallery, the Ijon Tichy Congress (decorated like a seventies Berlin apartment to separate itself from so-called "serious" galleries), the Georgi-Glashow Gallery (for which he had only two weeks to prepare and his standard model was unavailable), Studio SU(5), and Steven Weinberg's The Decay. The Decay, in particular, was very seminal to the scene, setting the stage between the still-popular realism and what Weinberg labelled "progressive constructionism." Weinberg was also key to the gentrification of the area, owning several galleries along the strip including Symmetry Breaking, Supersymmetry, Dreams of a Final Theory and the horribly named pop-art House of Cheese and Wein. For all that, Chris Eaton's art had only been purchased by one prominent collector (and not even purchased, really, because it was just Weinberg, who didn't pay for the piece because he felt the artist owed him for his meagre sales), his parents, two of his aunts and his dentist. He left the rest of his work in the apartment for his roommates to deal with when he moved out.

***

If he wasn't going to sell anything he made, he might as well not make anything sellable. In fact, he might be better off not making anything at all, composing elaborate theoretical art projects that no one could ever complete, or would want to. He assembled the complete canon of eighties television shows with emergency tracheotomies (the pen in the military sitcom *M*A*S*H*, the quill in the historical medical drama *Dr. Quinn*, the straw in *Happy Days*, a hollowed-out pretzel in the bar at *Cheers*, etc.), and wrote a list of Great Ideas for Movie Sequels that will Never be Made:

- *CK2: Rosebud's Revenge* – the long-awaited second installment to Welles' masterpiece, starring Vin Diesel as Citizen Kane, and Anthony Hopkins as the voice of Rosebud: "You let me burn, Kane. Now, YOU burn!"
- *Casa Blanca Dos* – Humphrey Bogart and Ingrid Bergman get married back in the States and run for President
- *The Better, The Worse and the Uglier* – more hats shot off heads than ever before
- *The Ramboer War* – Rambo travels through time to fight in South Africa and makes sure apartheid never happened
- *The Youngtouchables* – a prequel, really

He turned to concept photography. In one project, he took photos of everyone he knew for two solid years, every time they had a chance meeting, and began affixing them to the walls of his dining room, using the cheapest children's paste he could muster, starting at the ceiling and working down, until the whole space was rank with them, dripping from the walls like night sweats. Over the duration of the project, he learned three things: people cannot stand still for photographs; the scope of the city inhabited by his own personal daily routines – and those of his closest friends – was satisfyingly small; and no matter how many times their paths crossed, even if it occurred on a semi-daily basis for more than a week, people would invariably be wearing the same clothing.

At the same time, he started taking Polaroids of other drivers, taken from his own car (the same '83 Corvette they used to film *45701*), depicting their reactions after responding to his "Honk if you love Jesus!" bumper sticker and he gave them the finger.

In another, he planned to mount a camera on a tripod in the middle of a field surrounded by deciduous trees, like maples, or oaks, rain or shine or beautiful snow, one photo for every hour. And at the end of every twenty-four hour cycle, he would rotate the camera one degree to the right, for one entire year. For display, he'd need a round room, with entry facilitated by either trap door or skylight, because every inch of wall space would be covered, in order of the days, clockwise. Each hour would sit atop the last, midnight bracketed by floor and ceiling. And with appropriate shutter speed, the colors of the leaves, or absences thereof, and the relative light of day, would create a gradual, almost-abstract shifting of amorphous color, the Winter being particularly dark, Summer more light, with more green in the Spring and reds in the Fall. Inclement days would produce interesting grey smudges on the overall colorscape. 360 degrees; 360 days; 8640 photos. The only thing he had to really consider was which five days to choose as holidays:

1   Christmas
2   Easter (can't shake the old religious mandatories)
3   His birthday
4   Halloween (the night it's most acceptable for him to still dress as a woman)
5   The US Open tennis finals

Also: he would take a series of abstract photographs, the exact number of which would be immaterial, indeterminate and potentially infinite. He would purchase a restaurant and operate it as you would any normal restaurant, with some key differences: all interior decorating would be done in yellow and blue, staff would wear only yellow and blue, and patrons would likewise be required to wear only yellow and blue. For those arriving without yellow and blue clothing, yellow and blue clothing would be provided to them. He would then place an out-of-focus camera in the corner of the eating salon, which would take photographs at random intervals to produce glorious abstractions. Other colors would be inserted on previously designated evenings. For this, most of his time would involve working for years to be able to afford a restaurant, and planning menus.

* * *

By the time he had reached an age whereby he might be able to make his mark in the world in some form or another, he discovered that the canvas was already full, with no more room for achievements to be made in traditional, visual art of any kind. The death of painting had long since come and gone and been forgotten, and the only ones who had apparently been invited to the funeral were Gillis and Drasche. The last original evolution of drawing had coincided, if not with the creation of the eraser, then with the Renaissance. And photography, which had begun purely as a scientific document of time, rejected by the art world until the nudes of Rohr-Steichen, had moved, through the ensuing centuries, from using the person as subject to capturing images of Nature to developing abstract concepts and impulses, after which it boomeranged on itself, like a basic child's palindrome, to renew its fascination with the earlier subjects but in different contexts, so that "Nature" was something more urban, obsessed with the footprint of humanity, like the first steps on the moon, the person as subject was seen as a reinterpretation of Nature from within, and the documentation of time was more harried and hurried, to reflect the new age of rapid progress and short attention spans, such as the

American who took untrained snapshots of every meal he ever ate, or the way he looked every morning on waking, or various other monotonous tasks like the ones Chris Eaton used to think up.

Even the lesser arts like printmaking, pottery, ceramics, metalwork, weaving, woodturning, textiles, glassblowing, knitting, felting, macramé, landscape gardening, architecture, shoe repair, even these had nothing left to give. Some artists decided to eschew them altogether, and made attempts pickling aquatic creatures, or crossbreeding species to generate glow-in-the-dark rabbits, but was there anything more in this than Duchamp's appropriation of the urinal, ready-mades and assisted ready-mades, just another example of an instance where the specific physical subject was of no importance in comparison to the concept itself? Within a year of the first one in North London, there was an exhibit by some Stuckists in San Diego that featured an identical shark in formaldehyde, only with a caption that said: "*Ceci n'est pas un requin.*" Simultaneously in Minneapolis, there appeared another, by one of the last remaining living Dadaists, Marinou-Blanco, nearly one hundred years old, with the words: "*Ceci n'est pas un Magritte.*" And a third, perhaps the closest copy of all, was exhibited at the Georges Pompidou, by another member of the slavish mob, an Irishman with a perforated ulcer, who had only drawn a tiny moustache on the snout and called it *E.S.N.S.O.L.*

Strangely, it was the same photographer who had "made" the medium, the Austrian-born Janos Rohr-Steichen – or "Pato" as he was more commonly called towards the end of his life – who was the influence for Chris Eaton's last conventional project. Rohr-Steichen had moved to America in the 1860s as part of Archduke Ferdinand Maximilian's entourage as the new Emperor of Mexico. The official court photographer responsible for most of the existing images of His Imperial Majesty (although commonly uncredited), Rohr-Steichen became more widely known back in Europe when some of the photos he took for his own personal use were intercepted by an aide to Louis Napoleon himself (a gift from Maximilian) and put on display at the 1865 *Salon des Refusés*. Even among works of art that were considered at best risqué and at worst blasphemous, the inclusion of Pato's foreign savages was considered so scandalous that the reaction it created was parodied in a famous sketch by Daumier, with a group of bourgeoisies fanning themselves to keep from fainting. Over the next two years, Rohr-Steichen's popularity back home grew even faster than Manet and the Impressionists, fed by this new opportunity to view nude women and call it art, stigma-free, and he was included in both Paris Salons and sold hundreds and perhaps thousands of prints to the French and Austrian elite, at a price per image nearly double the average weekly wage, making him fabulously wealthy and providing him with the extra capital he needed to convince even more poor, young Mexican girls to disrobe for his lens. That's when he became known as Pato, *the duck*, not because of his curious walk but because any charges that arose from the questionable ages of his models seemed to slide right off his back, at least until both he and Maximilian were captured and executed by Liberal forces in 1867. He was a disgusting individual, who is still used by Mexican mothers to frighten their daughters. But aside from a fame that arose more from his subject matter than any real artistic skill, he did contribute one technique to the art world that led to an international movement. For his last Paris exhibition, he exposed one sheet of paper to all of the images he had captured, laying each on top of another until he had created what he called the typical Mexican girl. Few pieces of art – not even Picasso's *Les Demoiselles D'Avignon*, anything from Gauguin's Tahitian phase, Robert Rauschenberg's *Untitled (Asheville Citizen)* or any work of opera – can really compare to Rohr-Steichen's *Ils sont tous la même* for pure unadulterated racism and chauvinism. And it's curious that he didn't recognize the experimental original-ity of it himself, as his journals clearly treat the piece as a joke on his friend the Emperor, even calling the new technique Maximilism. While most of his oeuvre has long been forgotten, it is this piece that occasionally rears its head in fringe discussions of contemporary art, the idea that one work of art could, through the inclusion of as many seemingly unrelated elements as possible, contain an entirety, that through many specific details one could achieve universal truth.

After learning about him in a slightly anachronistic art history class called *Kodachrome and Colonialism: Oppression Behind the Lens* (a course likewise heavy in Gauguin and Brunias), Chris Eaton spent a year painting his own portrait, daily, always using the same canvas, just painting directly over the one from the day before. At any given moment, all you saw was one Chris Eaton. But all the rest of them were always there. As one.

* * *

For a time, he considered covering his body with the tattoos of every country in the world. But then he heard of a man from India who had begun a similar process in the late eighties, who had eventually had to have the flag of The Soviet Union removed and replaced with Armenia, Azerbaijan, Belarus, Estonia, Georgia, Kazakhstan, Kyrgyzstan, Latvia, Lithuania, Moldova, Russia, Tajikistan, Turkmenistan and the Ukraine; East and West Germany rejoined; the Czech Republic and Slovakia emerged out of Czechoslovakia; Yugoslavia split into Bosnia and Herzegovina, Croatia, Macedonia, Serbia and Montenegro, and Slovenia; and years later even Serbia and Montenegro split into two separate countries, followed by a unilateral declaration of independence from Serbia by Kosovo; and he left that idea on the curb with the rest of the trash.

* * *

He returned to Athens, working as a largely useless and mostly enfeebled construction worker for a friend of his father, and spent most of his time after the accident haunting several of the city's patios, stirring ground chicory into his black coffee to remind him of Paris ("Only American expats over there drink that fancy Italian tourist bullshit"), or at night, sliding over to Odair Ach's Tavern, where he knew a bartender – a lovely girl – who would give him free pitchers of run-off. Occasionally he would go to Toni's Reach, because the girls were prettier, but only during happy hour, or when he was meeting a friend who might pay. One day he overheard a new crop of recent graduates from Ohio U (mostly bullshit, post-outsider artists, but also a handful of kitsch and performance artists) talking about a parody television show on Public Access 27, based loosely around the most popular show of the day but setting their version in their own zip code of 45701. Before he knew it, he was at their table, pretending to be nice, and interested, and no more than a beer later, he had talked them into an infrequent role as the older brother of one of the main teens.

The initial scripts were predictable and safe. Periodically, Chris Eaton would appear as Ensel, who was supposed to be cooler than the rest of the characters and involved with a lot of underground music and possibly even illegal activity. It should never have lasted more than a handful of episodes. But because the production values were so low – and because it was on Public Access television – many people thought it was a documentary, and Chris Eaton started getting recognized on the streets, not as himself but as his character. Without discussing it as a group, Chris Eaton wrote several letters in character to the editor of the local paper: in support of gay rights, in opposition to the Gulf War, in support of re-opening the flood gates on the river, and eventually Ensel was offered a regular column, the editorial staff completely unaware that he was not, in fact, a real person.

People began to take notice. Because of the popularity of his column, Ensel began to take on a starring role in the show, and Chris Eaton had the leverage to take the story in more exciting, unexpected directions. And if no one else agreed, he just had to do it for real, making sure it was caught on the News so that it became inseparable from his character. Ensel had affairs with rock stars. He took trips to tropical countries. He contracted tropical diseases. He began appearing in public in drag, so they worked that in, too. There was even a brief storyline involving time travel. People stopped referring to him by his real name – even the other cast and crew members. And he marveled at how easy it was to just shut himself off and become another person. He slept in different positions, brushed his teeth longer, took showers instead of baths and peed sitting down. He stopped calling his parents on the weekend. He bought a new car.

It was in his column near the end of 1992 that he joked about running for mayor, and suddenly the city was overrun with homemade t-shirts for his campaign. Several of the other actors convinced him to register for real. Everyone in the group was excited about it. And as interest continued to grow, they began filming the show live, running twenty-four hours a day, following Ensel around on his campaign trail so that you could be watching the show on Channel 27 and flip to Channel 4 to catch the exact same thing from another angle on the news. He was an instant hit. For at least a week and a half, he was leading in the polls. Then, after he lost, the group's interest in producing the show waned. The storylines, now that they actually had to write them again instead of just filming the action as it happened, naturally felt less real, less creative. Then it was done, and they were all back to being themselves again.

The group still hung around each other for a short time. But eventually the only artistic pursuits they shared was a sense of common vitriol, constantly trying to one-up each other to feed their own self-worth. Once, during a particularly combative conversation, his mind drifted into a calm, therapeutic stasis. There he imagined meeting one of them in the future, outside an office building, or a shopping mall, arranging something else for a later date, actually carrying through with it, at a restaurant where they served mostly meat, with only the most boring vegetables as decoration, as two people would, who had not seen each other for some time. They would speak of all the things you might expect, as well as a few you might not, and later they would drink until they could stand one another, then have one more. At the end of the night, they would both wonder if they should hug,

141

if it were the proper etiquette for such a thing, which it might have been, but in all that split-second thinking they would miss the proper window of opportunity, and go home with their arms feeling empty.

The next day, he opened up the portrait studio.

It was also in Ohio that she became a folk hero, most notably for an album called *She Was a Big Freak*, which was reissued in 2010 with the following liner notes:

> In the first third of these liner notes, available in the Otolith Records reissue of *Chris Eaton's Greatest Hits*, we discussed Chris's humble beginnings: her birth in Cleveland to a young piano teacher and her surgeon husband who left them to go to war; how her remarkable mother managed to raise two kids on her own as a nanny for big band leader Sammy Watkins (responsible for discovering Dean Martin); and how because of this, Chris Eaton spent her early formative years drawn to Watkins' extensive collection of singles. Chris apparently listened to most of these '45s on her own, and was never properly instructed on the speed differences between 45RPM singles and the jazz LPs the band leader most often played for his own enjoyment, and this is how she developed her own signature, bass vocal stylings. On moving back to Cleveland in the early sixties to attend The R. B. Turnbull Jr.

School of Enterostomal Therapy, she bought her first Gibson guitar for $50 and hit the growing coffeeshop circuit. The war was on in Vietnam, and perhaps because of that, folk music was the going concern across America. Many of her songs even used war imagery to great effect. But most of the Cleveland scene were not ready for Chris Eaton's slowly lurching style, especially the way it made her body move like poured syrup. She also wrote very few songs with choruses, and sing-alongs were very popular. So few club owners would give her the opportunity to really spotlight her talent, and the only time she was able to perform in front of actual audiences was at open mic nights.

Then there was the strangely coincidental run-in with her future manager and husband, Larry Harmon, an experimental jazz trumpet player who, when his shining star was eclipsed by the planetary draw of Miles Davis, went even further into dissonance as a *modus operandi*. Their love affair was hot and brief, with the making of her cheekily eponymous debut album likely a significant contributor to their subsequent divorce. In this second part, we'll discuss the making of *She Was a Big Freak*, but also Chris Eaton's search for a new voice, and the new explosive live show that came out of that.

* * *

If you were ever lucky enough to own Chris Eaton's first two albums on Harmony Records (the label started by Larry Harmon in order to promote and exploit Chris's intriguing talents), you'll notice that they were released only a year apart. But if you quickly scan the personnel, you'll note that the only two names that remain from *Greatest Hits* are Eaton and – curiously – Harmon. After splitting with her husband/manager, it was clear that Chris was looking to take another direction with her music. Phil Giallombardo, who was an original member of the James Gang before joining the Chris Eaton juggernaut (other members went on to join The Eagles and The Guess Who), described Harmon's influence this way:

"Larry was a real clown. He saw what Chris was doing as a real freak show, you know? She was a new sound he could use to explore his own noise experiments. He was the real reason why that first record never caught on with the people. Chris recognized this. She asked me if I would produce the next record. But I told her she had such a clear idea of herself that *she* should be the producer. I would just add keys however she wanted."

144

In those days, she'd been hanging out a lot at La Cave, the club on Cleveland's ghetto side that was featuring a lot of the newer sounds like Richie Furay's Poco, and Mama's Baugh (an early trio formed by the brothers who would later form DEVO at Kent State). La Cave was really the only venue you could play in Cleveland once you gained a certain amount of popularity. It would uncomfortably fit three hundred people, but the only other options were the Music Hall, which was a three-thousand-seat auditorium, or the Public Hall, which held more like ten. The smaller venues didn't want her because she'd moved beyond folk into something unclassifiable. And after the Kent State shootings, when four student protesters were killed and nine others injured by the Ohio National Guard trying to break up a peaceful anti-war protest, protest folk was all anyone wanted to hear. All men wanted to be Bob Dylan and all women wanted to be Joan Baez. Meanwhile, Chris Eaton's songs were more about working through a lot of hew own personal turmoil after her break with Harmon.

Naturally, it was at La Cave that Chris Eaton opened for The Velvet Underground the first time, a relationship that would continue for several years because of the common ground they found in exploring one-chord song structures. Although they were actually from New York, The Velvets played La Cave so often that they might as well have been the house band. Because they had already set up their equipment on stage, Chris made a joke halfway through her solo set that anyone could join in if they felt the need, and in an interview with *Creem* magazine at the time, Chris recounted being halfway through a new song called "The Things That Bind You" when "the music I'd always heard in my head became suddenly louder. I always played with my eyes closed, and when I opened them, there was Phil, with his closed eyes staring right back at me."

Afterward, someone asked how long they had been playing together, and she replied "Honey, I don't even know that man's name!"

In addition to Giallombardo on keys, Chris found more like-minded souls in Ramon Quinolt (rhythm guitar), Alan "The Robber" Grilt (lead), Nat Saurot and Ren O'Baldy on trumpet, Fred Arrabal on banjo and trombone, her second cousin Michael Turner on drums, who could never be trusted to do the same beat twice. But perhaps

the biggest influence on *Freak* was the
addition of a new young bass player
by the name of Willie Collins. Collins
was well known on the Cleveland scene
because he stood out in any crowd, and
not merely because he was only thirteen.
Sometimes his mother would accompany him – occasionally his older brother,
Phelps, would come as well – to shows,
quietly smoking and reading romance
novels in the back. Other times, local
acts would claim responsibility over him
as their own son, and keep him at the
side of the stage, a lie in which everyone
including the owners of La Cave were
implicated because he was so remarkably
good. To make up for the discomfort
he felt at being both black and so small,
he nearly always wore huge platform
boots, let his afro grow as large as gravity
would allow, and somehow managed
to accumulate the largest collection of
novelty sunglasses one might reason-
ably expect to exist in the world. When
he first joined Chris and the others on
stage, there was certainly the notion that
she was doing it for the gimmick of it
all. She'd already hired a Serbian dwarf
named Roussimoff to be nothing but a
go-go dancer, complete with a Mexican
luchador mask and a full-sized cape with
'The Giant' stitched in gold thread. There
were way too many band members to

fit on the tiny La Cave stage. Plus, her outfits were frequently scandalous and she refused to let the male members of her band wear shirts, personally oiling them up before shows. But all of these things were quickly forgotten when they started to play. This is the period where many of Chris's crowd favorites were written, like "(Don't You Believe) The Words of Handsome Men," which supposedly featured a five-minute Roussimoff solo, whatever that might mean, and "Saviour's Day," which traditionally had the entire horn section leaving the stage to lead the audience in a conga line out the fire exit on to Euclid, tracing the entire circumference of Severance Hall a few blocks to the Masonic Auditorium, which was the home of the Cleveland Orchestra before they moved in 1931.

Both *Freak* and Chris's third album, *A New Asshole*, were recorded simultaneously, at the Killer B Studio, located in nearby Akron (where a young Chrissy Hynde was interning as a technician). *Asshole* also features contributions from Miles Davis on nearly half the songs, more than likely as a slight to her ex. According to Giallombardo, they represented Chris's best work, successfully combining her lopsided melodies with Collins's "danciest beasts" (sic): "It might have been too much for most people to understand fully, but even grasping a piece of it would have sent people into an awkward bliss ... like you were dancing with a drunk aunt at a wedding but really enjoying it!" Collins agreed: "As soon as we heard it, we knew it was hit material."

Unfortunately for the band, Harmony Records still had the rights to release the records, and legally owned the masters. So before pressing *Freak*, Harmon essentially re-produced the album with his own trademarks again, even going so far as to remove most of Willie Collins – and all of Davis's takes on *Asshole* – from the mix. There was a brief lawsuit filed on behalf of Chris Eaton by the lawyer of her new boyfriend, a descendant of the Kroger family whom she would later marry and move with back to California. But it became clear from earlier contracts that Harmon was completely within his legal rights, and Chris Eaton essentially retired from music-making as an unknown. It was only later, when one of her albums was rediscovered and a song licensed for the film *The Hunger* (2001) that the true wonder of Chris Eaton began to spread in the new indie music circles. And we are proud to re-release it here, so that even more people can experience it.

Whether real music fans benefited from Harmon's historical revisioning has been the subject of many debates. This reissue includes both versions, working with Giallombardo and Collins to restore the songs to Chris's original vision, so you can decide for yourself.

* * *

Be sure to check Otolith's final reissue of *A New Asshole*, originally released in 1971, where we visit the long legacy that Chris Eaton has left on popular music, including her influence on Cleveland bands like DEVO and The Eagles, the meteoric rise of bass player Willie "Bootsy" Collins to band leader for James Brown and then frontman for his own funk masterpiece, Parliament/Funkadelic (Collins has claimed in several interviews that Chris Eaton was the inspiration for his song, "The Bomb"), as well as the wider reach she has achieved in recent years with new indie bands across North America and Switzerland.

His family encouraged him to continue his studies at Kent. But the pain was too great. He couldn't hold a pen without pain cramping his entire right side. Even oral examinations proved too stressful. And eventually he just moved back to Milford Haven, where the local Texaco refinery took him in as a favor to his father. They even arranged it so he could work from home, meaning he was nowhere near the place for the big explosion in '94. That was when Tony finally met his maker. Wasn't even supposed to be there. It was his day off. But he'd gone in to pick up his paycheque so he could put down the last payment on his truck, and the blast was so severe that they found his truck two counties over.

Lucky Tony.

It also meant no one was really monitoring him. And no one was likely to fire the company cripple. So he was able to pursue his other dream of crafting custom *Star Wars* collectibles. He had missed the first film, *A New Hope*, when he was in his coma. But the way his friends talked about it only fuelled his obsession. And when the third of the trilogy was released, the new slate of figures was so woefully inadequate that he decided to make his own. It was amazing what you could achieve with old model paints, breaking open the plastic bodies and replacing one figure's head with another. (The main heroes, Luke and Han Solo, were basically the same, anyway, with their hair painted different colors.) By carving out Darth Vader's helmet, and replacing his head with Luke's, he was even able to anticipate a younger version of the Dark Lord, with removable mask, long before Kenner and Lucasworks got around to it.

The toy giant eventually keyed into this collector mentality and began releasing limited runs of the more obscure figures. But by then, Chris Eaton had already established a following by focusing almost exclusively on the second film in the series (his *Star Wars* wasn't the episode of youth, which he could barely remember and hardly associated with himself, but the episode of new beginnings). When people contacted him with other requests, he often had to gracefully decline.

Then he received a call from the lawyer of billionaire Travis Cohen.

* * *

Because Travis Cohen had amassed his fortune so early (some said hula hoops, others claimed antiseptics for treating gonorrhea, and still more figured oil), there was nothing left for him to do in 1959 but start accumulating things most people would have no use for. That was how Travis Dara Cohen (using his middle name here so as not to be confused with the comedian, or the young boy from North Carolina who enjoys playing fantasy card games) made his name, not for Jefferson's bottle of Chateau Lafitte that he acquired in the sixties; not even for several greater wines owned by several lesser Presidents, one of which he even shared at a party with the President of the day and a Senator from California (although he would never disclose when and with whom); not for his trio of Buggati '41s, painted in red, white and blue; or his collection of vintage Stella guitars; nor his art collection, which concentrated mostly on the Nouveau Réalisme Movement of the sixties, including all signatories of the original group manifesto but ultimately zeroing instead on the movement as it spread from France and Italy to Bulgaria and Argentina (Christo and Varea) as well as England, Portugal, Czechoslovakia (Hardie, Canto, Svra). Those artists were the ones he felt were more successful in capturing the goal of *collective singularity*, revealing the similarities of life through the differences. And he acquired them largely by inferring himself into their inner circle, via the brother of a fellow New Yorker, a writer who threw popular parties, and the writer, who had been working on her same masterpiece for over ten years and kept reminding them of such, sniffed at Cohen flashing his money at a party thrown by Varea and said loud enough for everyone to hear: He doesn't look like a Jew. The collection also included: a Dürer gouache once owned by Raphael, thought to have been lost but which he purchased from the Estate of King Farouk along with some rare coins; a study illustration for Raphael's own *The School of Athens* (he very nearly purchased the actual fresco from the Vatican, too, until it was deemed to be a load-bearing wall); Caravaggio's reclining *John the Baptist* and a *Magdalene* (a remarkable self-portrait in drag) that the Church sold him instead, because they were never supposed to have them in the first place, acquired by the Knights of Malta on the artist's

152

death and offered to the Pope in the early-1800s when they relocated their headquarters to Rome, but because of their illicit nature, Cohen had to keep them hidden away, anyway, and he later traded the former to a Munich businessman who owned several refineries near Dresden for the original shutters and frame for *Arnolfini's Wedding Portrait* by Van Eyck; a drawing by Da Vinci which, when turned topside, still resembles the artist but smiling; some Titians; a Veronese; a Giorgione; dozens of Rembrandts, signed by him but actually painted by his students; more Van Goghs than were worth mentioning; a room full of others that he couldn't even remember; the Willem de Kooning supposedly erased by an American artist, for which Cohen bragged at parties he paid extra "for my word that I wouldn't tell anybody!", and similarly, the original complete set of Goya's *Los Disastres de la Guerra* prints that a pair of British artists had claimed to have defaced in the early-twenty-first century (cowards); and a contemporary painting by Sheri Canto, daughter of the aforementioned Alberto Canto, from whom Cohen had acquired much of her father's work, depicting herself and Cohen as she hands the collector a perfectly duplicated work by Courbet. He was not known for his collection of early Diners credit cards, with the names of some of the first members on them, including Harry S. Truman, Elvis Presley, Elizabeth Taylor and Marlon Brando; the Adidas worn by Jesse Owens in Berlin and the waffle iron used to make the first pair of Nike treads; his signed memo from J. Edward Day ordering the reprint of the Hammarsköld invert; not even for the ruthlessly vicious ways that he amassed them, running men into the ground financially when they wouldn't deal, as he did with E. I. Stronach in order to acquire his political cartoons; or when they were particularly entrenched in their businesses and collections, making deals with their trust-fund children, like Read and Vanier Scott-Haroph, sons of Joseph Haroph, the military aircraft mogul, and the great-great-grandsons of the man who started the Scott Standard Postage Stamp Catalogue, who eventually inherited the generations-old philatelic collection and signed it directly over to Cohen in exchange for one lump payment to cover some old gambling debts. He was not known for buying the one red shirt worn by every dispensable character in the original *Star Trek* series from Forrest J. Ackerman; nor for the magnificence with which he showed no discrimination in his viciousness, using equally harsh tactics on fourteen-year-old boys at sci-fi conventions across America, where he switched briefly from collecting to hoarding, dredging up more 12" dolls and playsets from *Planet of the Apes* and *The Six-Million Dollar Man* than he knew what to do with, the full set of biker helmets and the original eye patch from *No Blade of Grass*, the lighting gels used in *The Andromeda Strain*, and the original sloth suit from the first *Sloth vs. Manatee.* That was when he realized he was in a league of his own, and needed a new challenge, with his live chess board that included genuine puffed Henry VIII armor for all sixteen pawns, and wild Sorraia horses for knights; or his full tea serving of Yuan Dynasty china; or his set of mint rookie cards for the first Baseball Hall of Fame inductees at each position; his collection of infamous exhumed moustaches, including Nietzsche and Dali, military figures from Hitler and Stalin to Lord Kitchener and Sgt. Floyd Pepper, and the true *pièce de resistance*, the last moustache of seventeenth century trendsetter Jakob Amman; or a collection of forgeries of Shakespeare's signature, many of which he had had traced back to equally famous writers of their own day, and had managed to increase their value to greater than the originals. After all this, he realized that his wealth was so immense that it was only a matter of deciding what to own and he could have it, that everything had its price. This dampened his pleasure and sense of accomplishment in acquisition considerably. And he decided instead to create collections that, before he thought of them, would never even have existed, owing their entire existence to an idea borne from his own imagination.

This was how he came into his arrangement with Chris Eaton, after seeing some of his work at the 45th Annual Science Fiction Worldcon in Brighton. After coming to the *Star Wars* series late, just as Chris Eaton had, with *Empire*, missing the first film entirely because he was obsessed at the time with digital watches, snatching up the original 18-carat gold pulsar L E D prototype at an auction in London, as well as the futuristic clock it had been modeled after, made for the film *2001: A Space Odyssey* (the film that got him interested in science fiction in the first place). Cohen had his people bring him an illegally obtained copy of *A New Hope*, and then, attracted to the idea of a new acquisition, had another set of people acquire the original twelve figures, along with the double-telescoping lightsaber version of Darth Vader, and then the additional nine, including Boba Fett with working missile, Luke Skywalker with hair that was too yellow, and the misinterpreted tall blue Snaggletooth. He purchased the twenty-nine *Empire* characters as an expensive set at Worldcon 42, and prepared for the thirty-one *Return of the Jedi* figures by buying entire crates straight off the truck as they arrived at Sears, still cheaper to sift through them than waiting until the other fanatics swooped in and set their arbitrary rarities. This failed to satisfy him, though. What he wanted from Chris Eaton was a complete set. Not just the characters the toy company had produced, but a toy for every character in every film. He still had hundreds of extra bodies from his *Jedi* purchases to use as fodder, and all he needed was someone else's expertise. The lawyer who approached Chris Eaton said money was no object. He also said: Heck, son, he has so much money he can probably even make you walk again.

Cohen also wanted him in New York where he could watch him more closely. So he quit his job and packed his bags. And in America, they worked in tandem, with Cohen watching and rewatching the films and Eaton manning the molds and variable-speed Dremel. The two became very attached, perhaps even more attached than Cohen was to his own wife, whom he had met at another sci-fi convention in St. Petersburg in 1971 where she was appearing as part of the cast of *Star Trek* (easily ranked as top ten hot nameless nurses in the original series, smiling at the captain as she passed by with a clipboard in the episode with the grey fog). Their union had produced a daughter, whom his wife had insisted on naming Ocean, to which Cohen had reluctantly acquiesced. The little girl was his pride and joy, but still Cohen began claiming Chris Eaton was like the son he never had. And as the young Brit put the finishing touches on the last of the Imperial army, modifying dozens of generic Force Commander figures – with a little acrylic enamels on the hair and rank insignia – into everyone from Admiral Veers and Piett to Captain Roehvarr Deshto, Cohen would hover over Chris Eaton's shoulder and say, with a sweep of his arm, that all of this would one day be his.

That was when he fell in love with Trish.

She was amazing, everything he'd been looking for, especially her firm stance against progress. She refused to get a cell phone or even use the Internet. And her reasons for hating capitalism and technology were as wide and as varied as his own. When his grandparents first moved to Maine from England in 1938, the state was in such lovely disrepair. Homes once used for soldiers holding the border against the British in the War of 1812 had discovered the slimming effects of remaining vacant. Settlements that had once been the pride of their colonial forefathers, where ships were loaded up weekly with monies for the monarchy, were competing to see who could reach **Population: 0** first. And the ones that remained created an entirely new fashion out of remaining indifferent. A style that would eventually overtake the entire country. Cracked fence posts. Peeling paint. Houses rallied for the best weeds on the block, if there was a block, which was never. Children and dogs roamed the streets with abandon, and no one cared who owned'm. Charming, it was.

Then "The War" came along and ruined everything. GIs returned from across the pond bearing government grants, a bonus for the employees after so much profit, to either pay for education or buy property, especially in the relatively untouched, pristine areas of the country that threatened to become such a global embarrassment. The war in Europe had shown America the effects time could have on the past, with their overturned French palaces and dilapidated Dutch windmills, so susceptible to bomb and artillery fire and neglect. Or was it disdain? What if a war were to ever break out in New Hampshire? Or Alabama? Would they really want the rest of the world to see that? America was the land of the Future. The land of Perfection. Science and technology. Skyscrapers and motorcars. It was time they started acting like it.

Suddenly, becoming a landowner in Maine was like falling off a truck. Or catching a cold. It crept into their lungs like a virus, and evolved into competition. Porches were replaced. Eavestroughs were repaired. For those who'd shirked their patriotic duties and faked nearsightedness to avoid battle, it was remarkable how a new coat of paint made all of that forgotten. Then people started building additions, or ripping down their old homes to make room for new ones. Communities on the verge of extinction regained their hamlet status, then village, and bang, they were towns again. When Ford started mass-manufacturing Model T's in 1908, everybody had to have one. New boats were bought, and the lobster and fishing industries really took off...

...which would eventually place almost every species of marine life in danger by the turn of the next century.

Neha's parents had moved to Maine to speed up the immigration process from India. They were advised during their application process that the have-not states would be more likely to accept them right away, and they would only need to remain for a few years before joining relatives in Boston. So they dug up a list of the coldest, poorest, most remote places to live in America (minus Alaska, of course), and even then, Maine was their fifth choice. Still, they decided to make the best of it, settling in Ellsworth and purchasing a motel, as many Indian immigrants were doing at the time, because her father failed to get one of the twenty medical placements offered to foreign-born doctors each year.

Somewhere in their third year, her father made the acquaintance of a British travelling salesman who regularly stayed with them on his rounds, regaling them with his stories of automotive and electronic fuses, for industry or for the military, surface mounts and semiconductors, the accompanying cable ties and circuit breakers, thyristors, varistors and distribution blocks. All of those things were fascinating in their own right, he said, but it was the seemingly inconsequential, slow-burning MDL – not as small as an automotive fuse, but still less than an inch long – that helped him see the light; and that light came from inside a pressed wood cabinet about the size of a sleeping sheep, shining through a thirteen-inch black-and-white standard resolution monitor. What was he talking about? A surprise, the man said. And on his next visit, he made his big reveal: a table-top issue of *Pong* – a game where a dial on each side allowed the player to manipulate a virtual game of ping pong with a bouncing ball of light. Neha's father's mind was blown. Who wouldn't love this? So he took out a second mortgage, and he and the salesman, whose name was Maynard, became partners, dealing in dreams, purchasing several dozen tables to rent to other motels across the state and letting people play the hero for only twenty-five cents. *Pong* led to *Space Invaders*, *Asteroids* and *Breakout*, which meant the revenue was no longer based on a set time but on the skills of the players. The price to play *Pac-Man*, *Centipede* and *Donkey Kong* remained the same, but the complexity of these newer games meant the length of play became even shorter. And with the addition of miniature dramas between levels, which would eventually lead to spin-off games like *Ms. Pac-Man* and *Donkey Kong Jr.*, patrons spent hours trying to reunite Mr. and Ms. Pac-Man, or Mario and The Princess. They sold the motel entirely and opened up genuine arcades, in Ellsworth and Portland and Bangor and Augusta. They couldn't sell beer any more, like they could in the motel lounge, but the profits from the games themselves had begun to replace that income anyway. And besides, his partner assured him, there were other things that kids might buy that could provide them with even greater margins. Neha's father, no idiot, turned a blind eye. Everything was perfect.

Then, the very next year, Neha's father's mind was blown once again, when he first laid eyes on the prototype for *Dragon's Lair*, the first video game to utilize laser disc, with a higher level of graphics than had ever been seen before. Animated rather than programmed, with movie-quality visuals and stereo sound, critics were already predicting that these new units would eclipse traditional games, and he had to agree. So he took all the profits he'd made from the other games and re-invested. *Dragon's Lair* was so popular that they had to hire an additional two maintenance men just to repair them, and the actual LaserDisc player inside, the Pioneer PR-7820, had to be frequently replaced. They were going to be rich.

The only real drawback was the game play, which was actually much simpler than on other units. People largely ignored this in the beginning because the visuals were so breathtaking. But then people started to figure out the pattern. In all of the games that came before it, there were infinite ways to win, countless permutations on moving left and right, or up and down, jumping, eating dots, firing missiles and spinning in place. There were, in fact, so many that it would have been impossible to commit them all to memory as a strategy for victory. With *Dragon's Lair*, however, victory was assured so long as you followed the correct steps, which in this case were (with asterisks denoting time-critical moves): SWORD*, UP*, RIGHT, RIGHT, SWORD, UP, RIGHT*, DOWN, LEFT, UP*, UP, LEFT, LEFT, RIGHT, RIGHT, RIGHT, LEFT, UP, LEFT, RIGHT, LEFT*, RIGHT*, SWORD*, DOWN, DOWN, DOWN, DOWN, DOWN, DOWN, UP*, and so on. And as long as you memorized the exact sequence of moves and your rhythm was good, you could monopolize the games for hours on only a quarter or two. Maynard had to hire local children to periodically bump the cabinets, knocking the laser disc off its base so the game jumped to another random point, quite often with Dirk the Daring crushed in the tentacles of the opening scene.

But the damage was done. The curtain on the magic of laser disc games had been yanked aside. Subsequent titles floundered, or were shelved almost immediately. One last-ditch effort was made to create a laser disc home system, named Halcyon after the computer in the film *2001: A Space Odyssey*. The creators promised more than a gaming system. They were presenting the future, where a tiny box could run your entire home, controlled exclusively by new voice-recognition software. Unfortunately, with a sticker price of twenty-five hundred dollars, the company tanked, taking Neha's family fortune with it.

Wouldn't it be so much better, Neha said on their second date, if nothing ever changed? If they could just find a nice rut and stick with it? A place where time stood still, devoid of the progress and innovation that were ruining everything?

And he agreed.

He graduated with a Communications and Public Relations degree, and was recruited straight from his program by an investment firm in Colorado that wanted his environmental background for a new venture in socially responsible investing (SRI). With the country's upscaled participation in Vietnam, a new brand of investing was emerging, for people who didn't want to contribute to the war machine any more. It was the early-seventies. The first SRI mutual funds were emerging, with a focus on war (bad), as well as women's issues and the environment (good), and he didn't really even have to understand the financial side of things, they said, they'd have someone else for that. All he had to do was take a look around, to make sure nothing was grossly affecting the surrounding flora and fauna. He recommended against several pulp and paper mills because they used highly toxic defoliants in their manufacturing processes. But it was also a huge growth period for what was then considered an environmentally friendly alternative to burning coal for energy: nuclear power plants. In 1973, forty-one new plants were ordered in the US, and even after the Three Mile Island disaster in 1979, they continued to sprout up like dandelions, so that approximately one quarter of energy today comes from nuclear power. He continued doing it for several years because the money was good and he'd already developed several expensive habits. Then, he met Julie.

Colorado was also where he started running. When he and Julie first moved to Denver back in 1989, their apartment was on the top floor of a residential home overlooking City Park, a three-hundred-and-seventy-acre green space right in the middle of the city. Julie found her workplace very competitive, particularly as a woman in her late-twenties entering a career path infested mostly with nineteen-year-olds. So one day she stomached the public transit a little longer than usual to pick up some runners and some Dri-FIT socks, dropped the new bundle in front of him, and suggested maybe they try it together. Only because he wanted to be supportive did he agree to try it, and despite crippling knee pain that meant crawling up and down the stairs to their apartment for nearly a month, he continued to wake up with her every morning at 6:00 AM With all the late nights she was spending at work trying to impress her new employers, this was the only time she felt she could squeeze it into her day. The only problem: she wasn't squeezing hard enough. And when the alarm came to with an abrupt regularity, she somehow managed to sleep through it. Or she'd sit up, mimic a stretch, and by the time he came back from putting in his contacts, she was already back under the sheets.

She had a knack for being unconscious, even when she was awake, could zone in and out of conversations like unplaceable odors. Even when they first met. One minute, no one could take their eyes off her. The next, everyone forgot she was there, forgot they had even met her.

And once he was awake, that was it for the day. So what else was he going to do with an hour-and-a-half until breakfast?

At six-thirty in the morning, the area around City Park used to be rotting with foxes and coyotes, gliding across the pavement like miniature science fiction monsters, with their tendril legs, their reflective eyes. Along the hairy lip of Sloan's Lake, small badgers and turtles crossed paths inconsequentially. Once he saw a possum, prancing around like a mossy log, following its tail more than chasing it, before losing its footing and tumbling off the path. Shortly after his agency made him a partner, they moved out to where the Sand Creek Greenway was about to open. And because it was so new, and so popular among those who wanted to forget they were living in a city, it was rare to see anything but squirrels. Or middle-aged housewives with iPods and fierce determination, walking their dogs. Maybe some angry wasps around a discarded ice pop.

When they first moved in together, Julie had never once done laundry. The apartment they rented in Denver had a European stacked washer and dryer, located just outside in the stairwell, and whenever they needed to use it, they had to haul it over in front of the door so the water hose would reach through a special window into the kitchen. When they were doing laundry, there was no escape. After a month, Julie complained that the dryer was broken, and when he removed the lint guard from its cradle, he found it choked with a cotton moss, mostly green from the fleecy set of towels they'd received as a housewarming gift, stitched together with their errant body hair. But they were so new to their love he let it slide.

Her parents had spoiled her, leaving her unable to perform even the simplest tasks, like plunging a toilet, or resaturating the sponge in his humidor. She avoided rooms with expired light bulbs. And she became terrified and then hostile towards the ants that occupied their apartment in the Spring and Fall, spending entire days mashing them against the wall with her shoes. Their shells felt like crumpled plastic wrap between her fingers. The way they kept coming, they seemed immortal. And yet several of them seemed to have committed suicide in his bucket of home-made wine. There was nothing they could do until the weather became too hot or too cold again, and the ants went into hibernation or found it easier to scavenge food outside.

He didn't feel like the running defined him at all. There were "runners" in the world, to be certain, people who didn't feel whole unless they were in full motion, who marked their lives by 10ks and marathons, or their quarterly footwear purchases. There were those who others saw and thought to themselves, with either envy or pity, there's a runner, that person is a runner. But even for them, the daily act of running, while therapeutic and invigorating, was so habitual and repetitive that it blurred one day into the next, without definition or influence. He forgot them much as he forgot how he would get home after a night of drinking, a trip he made so often that it would never again imprint itself on his memory. The running was part of him, but not a part that was likely to shape his life in new directions, not likely to truly shape who he was.

Then, one day on his morning run, he found a magic coin.

The first thing he needed was the proper space to conduct his experiments. He recorded three albums with his band Cookin' By Numbers (*The Seven Sermons to the Dead*, *The World Within*, and *Modern Man in Search of a Soul*) and another two with Carpet, and he'd grown so disillusioned with it all, particularly with the current states of blues, pop and rock. It had become clear to him, for example, that most people did not like music, and only purchased it out of the same desire to accumulate as with anything else. He had also observed that there were two kinds of listeners: these gatherers, and the explorers. When the brain hears music, it tries to anticipate what comes next, as it does with most anything else, trying to make sense of seemingly disparate information by assembling it into a coherent form and predicting the next steps in the sequence. And so the reason why most music was hopelessly derivative was because it made people feel good to recognize a song immediately on the first listen, rather than be challenged by something new and exciting. It was music for people who hated music, and who really only longed for the endorphin release of predictability. But then Chris Eaton was paralyzed by the equally frustrating tendencies of the second group, who seemed to praise so-called ingenuity, but at the expense of true beauty or feeling, as if combining uncomplimentary colors into a grey sludge was some stroke of genius. Stuck somewhere between the two, he was unable to do anything.

Then he began playing with ghost frequencies, the notes between the notes, created when two strings were plucked or hammered in unison. Every note has a frequency measured in Hertz (Hz), and the higher the frequency, the higher the pitch. A traditional piano, for example, begins with a Low A of 27.5 Hz and ends with a High C of 4186 Hz. But with two notes at once, a third sound emerges at a frequency equal to the highest common denominator of the original two. If notes of 200 Hz and 300 Hz are plucked simultaneously, the frequency you are most likely to hear is one at 100 Hz. And these connections are what makes music sound so beautiful and lush.

What Chris Eaton wondered was what would happen if the tuning of a piano were fudged to use only prime numbers as frequencies instead, extending from a Low A# at 29 Hz to a High A# at 3709 Hz. Each note would still be so close to the prescribed string lengths (the traditional 7th A# harmonic, for example, would be 3712 Hz) that the ear would still hear the proper note, but it would also be just enough off that, of all the combined fundamentals and harmonics in any two notes, the only common factor in both would be 1, a noise so low that the human ear would be unable to hear it, a keyboard of prime frequencies cancelling each other out. A symphonic white noise. The perfect sound of silence.

All he needed was a sonically sterile environment where he wouldn't have to worry about the extraneous sounds of the streetcars or mating cats. The neighborhood children. His apartment shared a wall with a couple that fought incessantly, and a floor/ceiling with

164

someone who liked to play POV video games through his stereo. At the music store, they told him that absolute soundproofing would be impossible. If a helicopter were to hover fifty metres above the roof, for example, even top-of-the-line studios could only get outside noise levels down to 30 dB. And these places would have removed the windows, installed lead doors at a cost of several thousand dollars a piece, and built them as far from civilization as possible. If he really wanted to do it right, the guy with the long hair and tie laughed, he had to reconstruct the walls. Or, rather, he had to build another dry-wall on top of the other, so that the two never touched, and then carry out his experiments inside this smaller room, without any direct light or contact otherwise with the outside world. This, he did. And just to make sure, between the two walls he installed a set of early acoustic panels from the abandoned Black Arrow program, acquired through an ex-girlfriend at the British Defence Research Agency (which were just sitting in a warehouse in Belfordshire, anyway, and no one would really miss them). One eighth of an inch of this viscoelastic polymer was the equivalent of one foot of poured concrete. So he installed a foot of it. And then he was ready.

At first he just sat there. On the Sallomön chair he'd picked up at the Ikea for under twenty euros. When he realized it squeaked from the loose spindle on the back legs, he switched to the floor, which meant he also had to cut the legs off the piano. This was followed by a painstaking retuning of the strings. But it didn't work the way he had hoped. It just sounded like an out-of-tune piano. He thought maybe things were being thrown off by the clacking of the keys, or even the cottony tear as the mallets dismounted their wiry partners. So he re-designed each key to work on a system of well-greased pulleys instead of the squeaky wooden action levers, simultaneously removing all the black keys to prevent indirect friction and replacing the hammer and damper ends with hard rubber. The Sound Pressure Level Meter he had borrowed from the television station was still picking something up, though, and in the end he was forced to realize that the piano was an imprecise instrument, designed for making noise, not silence. No matter how much he tweaked and prodded the thing, he could never quite get it right. The meter still showed 8 dB. Quieter than ice melting and too low for him to hear, but not the mathematical silence he was searching for.

Reprogrammed electric keyboards were no more successful, once more arousing the needle of his meter. This time he could rule out any of the mechanics of the instrument. There were no moving parts. He'd even disconnected the fans. 8 dB. So he turned to the human voice, which initially failed due to improper training. He could not block the nasal twang of most of the singers in his own peer group, or the glossal gossiping of the amateur women's choir he approached through a friend at the Methodist Church. He approached the choral department at the university, which was pretty close but still tragically too novice. And finally he was forced to approach members of the London Opera Company. They wanted more money than he could afford, but by this point he was too close to abandon the project, so he pawned all of his instruments, maxed his line of credit, and crammed the singers into his room, rehearsing for weeks before they could manage to hit the notes exactly as he wanted.

And then he realized the problem was the sound of his own heartbeat.

As the end of the project drew nearer, Cohen's list kept growing. Unwilling to see the collection completed, he made requests for figures representing the actors themselves, half in costume, with Chewbacca's head replaced by a Han Solo head with hair extensions to resemble Peter Mayhew. They made two heads for Darth Vader (who was acted and voiced by different people). Then Cohen began compiling lists and photos of the stand-ins and the production crew, composer John Williams, the full F/X team, the casting company and the caterers, George Lucas himself, anything to prolong the thing that had begun to define him, to define both of them. More old figures – probably collector's items in their own right – were purchased and destroyed as additional fodder. Cohen's display room had to be expanded again by knocking out a second wall. But what did it matter? They were both happy. And when they'd run out of gaffers and grips, Cohen asked Chris Eaton to render his family: And be sure to include yourself.

This was when Chris Eaton began to realize that, when Cohen talked about *all of this*, he didn't just mean the project, he was actually referring to his entire estate: the house, the art, the horses, the moustaches. He wouldn't really get all of it, of course. Cohen's wife, though they rarely spoke any more, would be taken care of. And Ocean. But when all of this was done, he would never have to worry about anything again.

And by then he was just four figures from the end.

The easiest ones were of Cohen and himself. Cohen's wife was also amenable to the idea, but she would only let him work from old photos of her, as if this past woman was the only version of her that was really truly her. Ocean's reaction, however, was at best reluctant. By the time she was in her early-twenties, as might be expected growing up in the seventies and eighties, after Altamont, and surrounded by punk and extended Republicanism, Ocean had already begun insisting that people call her Trish. Up to the point that she was asked to do a sitting, Ocean/Trish had treated her father's little game with the same apathy with which she had showered all of his other little games before it. Being asked to take part was the last straw, and she pouted through the first session without saying a word. When she saw how much fun Chris Eaton and her father were having together, though, her mood changed, and at her second sitting, when Cohen was not present, she asked how he and her father had met (That figures, she said unintentionally, and they both laughed), what kind of family he came from, what sorts of things he and Cohen talked about while working on the collection, what he thought of bands he'd never heard of, and gradually worked her way to his accident, where he broke down in her arms reliving the day he learned he'd never walk again. They started having lunch together. Although she lived in her own apartment across town, she visited frequently. She even began acting as his model for his own project, creating an entire line of characters to reflect the dreams he was having, as a nurse, nun, teacher, actress, until she accused him of just trying to place her in sexual fantasy roles. He looked down at that, and they were both awkwardly silent. She turned away, coyly inquired about the logistics of sex in his condition, if he could still feel anything down there, and then looked back.

They made love on the floor.

And when Cohen walked in on them, he threw Chris Eaton out of his house, and vowed to destroy him.

***

Of course, none of that mattered any more. He had found the love of his life. None of it – not the end of the his perfect job, or the loss of such an enormous potential inheritance, or even the savagery of Cohen's public attacks on his skills and identity – could shake his happiness. He had learned that you can achieve dozens of other goals, but it's only in meeting the person you're meant for, in finding your other half, that you become who you really are, who you were really meant to be.

The next day, he swung by Trish's apartment and was confronted outside by security. After trying to explain things to them for nearly a half hour, one of the goons finally agreed to call up and she came downstairs to meet him in the lobby.

"You don't get it, do you?"

"..."

"Why would I share it with you if I could have it all to myself?"

And she turned around and re-entered the elevator.

His world came crashing down around him, standing around the coffee machine talking about microwaves with some of the secretarial pool, trying to get something through Brenda's thick skull, when they heard the hum and dismissed it as regular traffic from Reagan National, and the explosion's concussion blast ripped the room apart and the door of the microwave actually beat him to it.

There had been studies, he'd been saying. Russians who ingested microwaved foods showed a statistically higher incidence of stomach and intestinal cancers, he'd been saying. Ingestion of microwaved foods caused a higher percentage of cancerous cells in the blood serum, he'd been saying, when he could get a word in, as well as attacking the lymphatic system. Heating prepared meats sufficiently for human consumption – were they even listening? – led to the alarming creation of the cancer-causing agent d-nitrosodiethanolamine, not to mention significant decreases in the nutritional value of most foods. Then the hum outside the Pentagon got louder. And the Boeing 757 collapsed in on itself like sausage casings against the Pentagon's West Wall.

Brenda was the first to move. The force of the microwave door connecting with her jaw snapped her neck almost instantly. Her mandible and right maxilla were torn completely from her face, taking her right eye with them, the stench of her sinuses, rotten with cigarette smoke, splashed across the wall. Marcie (or was it Emily?) just seemed to drop to the floor, as if her soul had suddenly been ripped out through her hamstrings.

There was Marcie's/Emily's scream.

Then the cessation of Marcie's/Emily's scream because the force of the explosion had blown out his eardrums.

There was too much dust to know what was going on.

He couldn't move.

He was alone, pinned beneath several floors worth of rubble.

The light on the microwave – was that it? – kept going red, then black, and then stayed that way.

And he supposed there were good reasons for this: a good reason why he was there at the Pentagon: sent to repair some damage to an old lectern used occasionally by Republican Presidents when addressing matters of Defense to the entire nation; a good reason why he got stuck making small talk with those two cows Brenda and Marcie, whatever that was; and a good reason why he was even in Washington in the first place. But as good as those reasons were, he didn't feel like they were the result of anything he had done, decisions he had made. Julie had wanted to go back to school and complete her Biology degree, intent on enrolling in a dental program. And when he couldn't find work in his chosen field, he applied for this, despite no real experience in carpentry except a brief summer job that had ended in an injury, worker's compensation, and bad feelings all around, with a recommendation from his cousin who had already enlisted with the Army's White House Communications Agency:

> **Duty Title:** Carpenter; Cabinet Maker
> (Fabrication); Facility Manager
> **Rate:** None
> **Duties:** Carpenter/Cabinet Maker will
> be required to design, construct and
> repair Presidential and Vice-Presidential
> lecterns. Will design and build cases
> for both fixed and mobile secure and
> nonsecure electronic equipment. May
> design and build cases for unique ship-
> ping needs, and may be called upon
> to remodel office spaces, and maintain
> shop equipment.

It was like a dream, a figment of his imagination, like he was actually watching someone else's life unfold, perhaps in a movie, sitting in the audience and yelling at the screen with each of the hero's poor choices. It wasn't the life he would have chosen, was not real, an idea that was reinforced by weekly letters from his grandmother back home, with her strange habit of placing quotation marks almost randomly around some nouns and proper names:

Have you heard from your "sister" lately?

How is life in "Washington"?

Say hello to "Julie".

Coincidence? A coincidence involves two unrelated events that appear to be planned. But how many "unrelated events" does it take before a real pattern emerges? A purpose. Perhaps one of the more famous coincidences of American history was the death of Thomas Jefferson, not only on the 4th of July, but more specifically on the 50th anniversary of the Declaration of Independence, for which he wrote the original draft. And not only did Thomas Jefferson die on the 4th of July in 1826, but so did John Adams, under whom he had once served as Vice-President. The very same day! But September 11 would eventually go down as one of the most important "coincidences" in American history. Forget the initial speculations that the date was some link to the 9-1-1 emergency number. Consider instead that 9/11 was the day that Henry Hudson discovered Manhattan in 1609. On Sept 11, 1773, Benjamin Franklin wrote: *There has never been a good war, or a bad peace.* And on that day in 1777, General Washington fought and lost the battle of Brandywine, representing the second greatest number of Americans to lose their lives on U.S. soil as the result of an enemy attack.

Second only to September 11, 2001.

Within months after the 2001 disasters, US forces would mobilize to advance on Afghanistan. A half-year later, against the majority wishes of the rest of the world, they declared war on Iraq. And a year after the attacks, he would find a photo of a soldier posted over there with his name, trying to hoist a makeshift New Year's Eve ball up one of the communication towers at their base camp. Shortly after that, he would also discover, the soldier had disappeared. Missing in action, presumed dead. Through these links, these coincidences, he would start to see the bigger picture.

When they finally dug him out of the rubble, they told him he was lucky to have his offices in the third ring, or he never would have survived. As it was, he was the only one still alive in his department.

He thought to himself that it might have been better to have never been there at all.

The last thing he remembered was the face of Varda Chi, the junior Senator from California, bending over him like an angel, so beautiful and untouched, without even a speck of dust on her.

Lucky Varda.

Had the man at the collector's shop on South Broadway been more knowledgeable about these sorts of things, there probably would have been a sharp intake of breath on his part, and with one eye closed and the other tightly gripping the loupe, he might have turned to a shelf beneath the counter, beneath the displays of French *louis d'ors* and napoleons, crouched like an old woman raising her skirts to pee, and returned with a tome likely covered in dust and, if the cliché really called for it, cobwebs. A puff of air, a wave of the hand, and he would have had it open to page three hundred and fourteen, or more likely something like three hundred and sixty, then working back page by page, haunted by the image of the page in his memory but not certain of its exact whereabouts until the loupe blew it up before him. There it would be, a drawing of the coin Chris Eaton had found, with a short description of how Britain's King George III had used them as indicators of a person's worth, at least to him, bestowing them on people he wished to provide with protection, or privilege, or a message, such as the one he gave to his parliamentary emissary Sean Richard Vath (also known as Ricardo Vath, for his years in the Spanish military as a youth, training first at the *Colegio Real de Guardiamarinas*, then joining the campaign on Sicily in 1718, becoming a Knight of the Spanish Military [Order of Santiago] in 1737, and returning to Ireland as Min-

172

ister of Foreign Affairs), who brokered an end to the Seven Years War, after which Vath was made the official Ambassador to France; and further down the page, a list of other known owners including, most perplexingly, a Swiss pirate by the name of Aar, who was thought to have been given the coin unbeknownst to George by one of the king's favoured English noblemen, The Viscount of Rhode, who supposedly used Aar on the sly to increase his own wealth.

Most historians now surmise that Pirate Aar and Hon. Vsct. Rhode were more likely both Finnish (see the section on the Jokinens in Garwood's *The World of the Pirate*), possibly even related (ref. Ron Vaschat's *Pirate Horde*), and masters at changing their identity as it suited their needs; two sides of the same coin, so to speak. Both were arrested and interned in Kazan in the late-1760s for allegedly conspiring against Russia's presence in Poland. Yet at that point Rhode was claiming to be a Hungarian Prince named Benyovsky, of which, he was also fond of joking, there were already far too many. Princes, that is. The tiny country had had so many revolutions and upheavals that anyone could rightly attest to being descended from one of its victors. He heralded himself as a descendant of both the Revays and Urbanovskys; his presence in Poland, he assured the tribunal, was purely to seek out a long-lost family relation under the name Beniowski, who had apparently left him a large sum of money; he'd been told, after no small amount of rural bribery, that he might find this dead uncle in Smolensk. Perhaps it was true. Luckily for him, the similar linguistic roots of Hungarian and Finnish made the difference in his accent undetectable by the Russian soldiers who took him in. Less likely was Aar's story, claiming to be an Italian on holiday, giving his name as Arno and bragging that he'd never even heard of Poland. They were both supposed to stand trial as prisoners of war in the Fall of 1769, but as Austria swept into the Hungarian Szepes, attention was deferred from war to diplomacy, using Polish land as a form of political appeasement. Aar and Rhode managed to escape by land, spending several months as novices in Tibet before making off with: a gilt bronze lama; a Mongolian painting depicting the Buddha Shakyamuni flanked by two disciples; a bronze statuette of a rare standing Padmapani; and a pair of Tibetan wood carvings, one depicting the three deities of the lotus family and the other more abstract but meant to represent the space of time directly before the Buddha's birth in Lumbini. They hoped to sell these in Macau, though the wood pieces they'd taken mostly for personal aesthetic reasons. And in Macau, the pair learned to sail from Choi Tse-Ran (who took Chinese shipbuilding from the junk era into more elegant vessels more similar to the multi-masted American schooners), eventually hitting the high seas as rice merchants and settling in Madagascar, where Aar, pretending to be a French naturalist and sportsman by the name of Ruisseau, studying the effects of isolation on evolution (specifically how the island's early separation from the continent had preserved the lemur population), managed to practically exterminate said nuisance lemur population with a new breach-loading rifle prototype and subsequently spent some time as the island's elected tribal *Ampansacabe*, or King.

Rhode, perhaps more jealous than anything, stayed on the ship.

Bestowed with separate and conflicting opportunities, their paths diverged. Rhode settled in England, claiming to be of royal German lineage and a distant cousin to King George III himself. Not many believed him, but the only important one was George III, who was already quite far into his senility and was as likely to believe the tricky Finn was the King himself from the future. The elder Jokinen grabbed the King's ear by claiming to have solved the Longitude problem, which had been set by an Act of Parliament over half a century prior and came with a reward of twenty thousand pounds (worth well over two million today). The two of them made plans to set sail the next spring to test it, and they spent much of their time together setting and resetting the appropriate menu. George had recently purchased several new clocks and was under the delusion that he could, if he had them all perfectly synchronized, actually control time's flow, and he ordered Jokinen around the palace to adjust them to his needs: three seconds forward; one back; four forward on the John Arnold; one forward on the Donisthorp; five back on the double-pendulumed Janvier; nine on the balance-spring Salomon Coster. Though George forgot about the sailing trip by Winter's end, and Jokinen's device was found only to be accurate to a degree rather than the requisite two minutes, the King still bestowed upon him his latter days title, with a private estate near Bridgewater in Somerset, and they remained close friends until George mistook him for "his true wife" and declared Charlotte an impostor. Ruisseau, on the other hand, tried to obtain support from France and the Americans to use Madagascar as a base against England. And when that didn't work, he changed his name once more to Aar (from whose name we get the stereotypical pirate exclamation) and started robbing from all three.

It's unclear exactly when Rhode provided Aar with George's seal, but most often, it appears, Aar seems not to have required it, not even when the British man-of-war H M S Sackville, captained by Admiral A. Cheriston, had set a trap for him at the inlet of Chantie's Or. Despite all common sense, Aar and his men suddenly changed course and charted through the dangerous reefs rather than sail calmly into Cheriston's trap. Likewise, at the Battle of Flamborough Head, where Aar had briefly leased out his services to the Americans. His ship came under so much stress that it would completely fall apart two days later, but in the heat of the battle itself, when things seemed their worst and everyone thought he would finally surrender (that he *should* surrender), he called out that he had not yet begun to fight and captured the H M S Serapis as his own.

That was generally how the legends began, that the seal had other magical properties beyond royal protection, and could perhaps predict the future, were it ever presented with only two possible options. Aar was said to have consulted it on all matters in his life, from military tactics to what to eat for breakfast. Only once did Aar require the coin for the purpose that Rhode had set it, when the coin instructed him to sail once more into Chantie's Or, the gubernatorial home of Richard Avon. Despite threats of mutiny from his crew, despite the insanity of such an order, Aar didn't have much choice, anyway. The Chanti Rose (the new name he christened the Serapis) was practically rotting under their feet, breaking down on them at their moment of most needing, after a storm caught them by surprise near Bermuda, and the only light they could see was the beacon from Avon's topmost tower. That Aar had coincidentally decided to name his ship something so similar was not seen as a good sign, as many ships that were not named for places and people present at their launch were thought to be linked to the places they might go down.

Upon witnessing the seal with his own eyes, Avon reluctantly welcomed the pirate and his chief officers to dinner with his family, including his comely daughter, with whom Aar was instantly taken. After they had been shown to their rooms, Aar snuck back to the Governor's daughter, a temptation so great that he must have failed to consult the coin on it, and Aar was struck down by Avon himself *in flagrante delicto*. The coin was still in his pocket when his body was dumped from the parapets onto the rocks below, where it was eaten by a sea turtle, which was later caught by poachers while laying eggs in Costa Rica, and the coin began its tale anew. The meal is actually captured in a painting by the Italian Agostino Brunias, known mostly for his depiction of life in the surrounding islands, called *Richard Avon Eats* (1784), in which Avon is totally engrossed in his meal while the pirate and his daughter play footsies beneath the table, observed rather closely by a shocked slave who has bent down to retrieve a fallen shaker of salt.

Of course, the actual man at the coin dealership knew none of this, and both surfaces had worn so much that they were nearly smooth, so he shrugged, handed the coin back, and told him he was sorry, it looked like it was worthless.

***

He and Julie, it might have been said, were similarly on the rocks, by which one could interpret that the two were commonly taken to drink, except that, though true, Julie was more inclined to cheap wines from California than anything with ice, trying to look as though – through her unorthodox choices – she were trying to buck the establishment rather than just trying to establish the saving of a buck, and Chris was more partial to snobbish beers and drinks to which you'd never add more than a few drops of water. They were no longer getting along with any regularity, certainly nothing bordering on love, or even in the demilitarized zone of friendship or casual relations. They were having such fun throwing large dinner parties, however, that it was often difficult to notice the firm undercurrent of distrust, mild resentment and general boredom. Their guest lists, while not yet the veritable *Who's Who* of Denver, were often impressive in an underground art and media kind of way, at least on his side, including several painters who'd had their work shown outside the state, as well as one who'd even made a living out of selling his work at outsider art fairs until someone discovered his certificate from the Rocky Mountain College of Art + Design and he was banned from these events for life; a writer from abroad who'd had her work lauded fairly young, come here for the MFA program, then failed to produce anything else of note but remained continuously charming; people who wrote for the free Denver weekly, *Westword*, on subjects like music, movies, city politics and perverse sex, when not making unprofitable art of their own; and the indie banjo player who'd had a video on MTV2 and enjoyed much of that delightful buzz and hype without any of that horrible success; but there were also several of Julie's workmates, like the woman who'd started in advertising with her yet managed to become the creative director of her agency before turning thirty, on the strength of a campaign even Chris Eaton respected; someone Julie had gone to school with who had founded a running magazine for new mothers; and an Ecuadorian, also a workmate, who'd come to do her MBA at Daniels and then gotten married instead to a distant cousin of the McNichols family (for whom the arena in which the NHL franchise Avalanche and NBA Denver Nuggets played was named, and with whom he held a token management position). Then there was:

- a DJ they'd met through the banjo player, making a name for himself in clubs none of them had heard of, not that anyone cared for the details;
- the son of a left-leaning politician;
- a sommelier, who threw up all over the bathroom and successfully cleaned it up so they never noticed, until the next time they went for the lubricant under the sink, only to discover the mouldering facecloth he'd stashed behind the plumbing;
- and a portfolio manager, who was a friend of the Ecuadorian's husband, who came uninvited because he was visiting on business and who, when asked what he did, listed his full work title as Head of International Equity Portfolio Construction for the Colorado Association of Educators (CAE) Pension Plan, in charge of investing over seven billion dollars for the retirement of the state's teachers.

And when he heard this, the owner of the sports memorabilia store, who had arrived drunk, started into a tasteless joke about an investor with three girlfriends. And the Ecuadorian, who Chris felt might be flirting with him, turned away. The DJ, whose distant Great Aunt had recently passed away, and who had just inherited several thousand dollars, said he could use a few tips on what to do with it. And Julie who loved money but was still uncomfortable around it, made a joke about student loans. The sports memorabilia collector, after several attempts, finally hit his own punchline, just as the Ecuadorian's husband was trying to diffuse, for his friend, the assay at unpaid financial advice. And the Ecuadorian squeezed her husband's arm, distracting him momentarily and allowing the DJ to mention specific tech stocks. And he heard the portfolio manager say: Tech stocks are for amateurs. And he and the Ecuadorian's husband had a good laugh. And the collector said his stock in an online browser company was doing fine. And he heard the copywriter say: Gaming systems. That's where it's at. And someone else said: Have you heard about hard-disc storage? And he heard the portfolio manager say: Look, maybe you should just leave this sort of thing to the experts, at which the sensitive Ecuadorian tried to change the subject to Julie's cat, and eventually even that, too, turned into a confrontation, and he heard someone say: All they do is kill the birds. And he heard that same person later respond: But it's not like they're really wild animals, because they wouldn't really exist without human intervention, they're more like robots. Or weapons. And Julie decided to go to the kitchen. And he heard the portfolio manager whisper something to the Ecuadorian's husband. And finally he heard someone say: Bullshit, it's all bullshit, and realized it was himself.

What is, whispered the Ecuadorian to her husband. What is, said the Ecuadorian's husband, only louder. Oh, you know, Chris Eaton said. And finally the portfolio manager himself chimed in with: No, we don't, why don't you tell us. And it was obvious his back was up, which made Chris Eaton dig in even more, until the two of them had tightened their grips on their drinks, refusing to break eye contact. And Chris Eaton said what he said. And he heard the DJ laugh uncomfortably. And he heard Julie say: This is ridiculous. But the Ecuadorian seemed to be egging him on, smiling coyly at him when her husband wasn't looking, and so he continued, listening to the portfolio manager list off his credentials and, again, the seven billion dollars. And eventually the same challenge re-emerged: You do what you do and I'll just flip a coin for a month and we'll see who really deserves your salary. And they shook hands in the pretense of being gentlemen and everybody went home.

For the next month, despite the obvious outcomes to various friendships, they ran the experiment anyway. Like they were taking part in a high school economics class, each was given a hundred thousand virtual dollars to invest how he saw fit, and whoever had the most money on the first of November would be the winner. The coin never missed. And as word spread in their circle, the coin became more of a party focal point. An assistant to a city councilor with some favor in the mayor's office queried the coin (for this was how they referred to it now, not asking Chris Eaton to make his toss but "querying the coin") about a home she was considering purchasing. Should they purchase stocks in this Canadian gold claim in Borneo? Would the Avalanche win the Stanley Cup this year? And they continued to joke about its accuracy, even as they scribbled the predictions down in their notebooks and went home. One night, after showing the news anchor and her husband to the door, Julie said it had to stop. "I know," he said. "It's like I've stopped existing or something. The only reason they come now is for the coin. I could completely disappear, for all they care." And he was happy that she saw it the same way. But no, she didn't mean stopping entirely, just no longer giving it away for free. Did he realize how much those stocks were making people?

"But it's just a game," he said.

They merely asked for ten percent of the action, win or lose. And the weekends were thus transformed into old spiritualist-style séances, with the pretext of dinner all but forgotten and replaced with Chris Eaton seated behind their round dining room table with the coin in his outstretched palm.

Julie bought a new tablecloth.

* * *

With her marketing savvy, Julie was able to increase the circle of their influence, now attracting many of the local celebrities and sports heroes, politicians, and to make it all legit (because it was practically impossible at this point, despite having the mayor as a client, the chief of police and several judges, to remain under the radar), Chris wrote the Series 7, Series 63, 65 and 66 exams over the course of a week. Their multiple choice format meant he had nothing to study, just ask *Is it one of the first or last two answers?*, toss the coin, and then flip again over the two remaining choices. At this point they were even advising several members of the Avalanche, one of whom came with a collection of his own good luck charms with which to test him, as well as the Broncos' John Elway, a prominent folk singer seeking help with airplane purchases and the star of a successful television program who wanted to know if he should extend his contract for another two years or immediately make the move to film. They even began taking their own profit and investing it alongside their clients, doubling and trebling their take.

They were the talk of Denver. On weekends, their home was the place where everyone wanted to be invited. During the weekdays, however, they continued to grow apart, as though they were from completely different countries, with completely different cultures and languages, trying to explain to each other proper etiquette. He was feeling more and more separated from himself. He gave up painting. But since Julie was at work all day, he saw no reason to leave the house. And in the evenings, if he could think of no film to see, or overhyped concert to attend, and she had no pilates class, he would pretend to enjoy her TV forensics or medical drama, and then they would go to bed and fuck like they were strangers, except on the day that he called her Emily by mistake, wherever that came from, after which he made stronger efforts to make her feel special and loved.

One day he asked the coin – for at this point its power was undeniable, even to him – if they should split. It said no. He queried again. It said no. Again. No. In total, he flipped the coin twenty times, and each time it urged him to stay the course. Had he known the story of Aar, he would have known the coin had lost its magic, and was simply leading him to his end.

PART 7

The first time Chris Eaton really fell in love was after he'd moved back to the US, to New York City, which he chose mostly because he didn't know a soul there – he'd never been – and so it felt like a place he could start all over, be reborn, be someone else.

And within the first day of landing at JFK, with no more than half of the clothes he'd started with, the garbage bag he'd been forced to pack so hastily having ruptured in transit and the cardboard box that replaced it hobbling off the oversized luggage belt like a possum that had been struck by a car, the assistant manager/cashier/cow at the Tower Records in the Village was staring at the name on his credit card in disbelief and boring him with her *Amazing Stories of Retail*.

"Is that your name? Really?"

There he was, half-drunk, in banana-yellow short-shorts, his shirt tied up Daisy Duke-style, a black leather jacket that seemed to sweat more than he did, and a cardboard Burger King crown he'd mangled to read *Urge King*. And she wanted to know if he needed a job. Just because he shared a name with the person who'd quit the day before. The job didn't pay particularly well, at least on paper. And he disliked almost everyone he worked with. But for all her talk about names meaning something, he'd begun to believe it. Maybe he was meant to be here in this place. Maybe there was some destiny he'd been given by his parents at birth. Plus, all the cashiers had the authority to discount prices if the customer claimed it cost less down the street, so by memorizing the relative final costs with tax to the actual sticker price, he could tell the customer one total, then ring it through as something else and pocket the difference. This was good for an additional fifteen to thirty dollars per shift. And so long as his cash was off by no more than five dollars, no one asked questions. This meant, if he played his cards right, he could make another $4.50 per hour.

It was brilliant.

Then one day they showed him the video surveillance tapes and escorted him to the door without even a final paycheque. He took out two displays on the way out, and screamed at the door from the street about sexual discrimination.

And that's how he ended up working at Hollywood Montrose.

* * *

"I support the gays," Ernesto Monterossi would say. Like he was supporting the Army. Or a Presidential candidate. Or cystic fibrosis research. "My nephew's a gay. So I know how it is."

" . . . "

"You need a job?"

And just like that he was filing the nipples off mannequins that had gone out of fashion, for "one of the leading manufacturers of display-window mannequins in the country." Or so Ernesto liked to tell it. In reality, his set of leading manufacturers included the several top dozen. And even if he didn't count Pucci, or Cranston and Cymbalist in San Francisco, or Auton (the only major player in the UK), or Silvestri California (who was already becoming the behemoth of the synthetic clothes-monkey racket, buying up the competition instead of designing a better product), there were still a handful of companies right in New York City that probably didn't even know he existed. Montrose was that small. Of course, no one knew those other local shops existed, either, except maybe Ernesto. And every time one of them succumbed to a Silvestri bid, Ernesto – or Ernest, rather, as he preferred to be called – would make one of his rare appearances in the warehouse proper, peering over the tops of his Vuarnets as he rang the bell near the break table and made his important announcement. Congratulations, everyone, he would say. We just moved up one spot!

Ernest was well-acquainted with the story of Silvestri California because he was planning to do it in reverse. Serafino Silvestri was the son of the Italian sculptor, Talone Silvestri, best known for his proficiency in *papier maché*, a medium that had largely seen its peak in the late 1800s with works by the anonymous Chinese and Kashmiri masters, but also by the Russian greats like Lukutin and Korobov. Check out any thesis on *papier maché* and within the first few pages you are likely to find Lukutin classics, based on Russian folk tales, like *The Drunk Man in the Boat* (1894), or *The Great Green Belt* (1899; sometimes also referred to as *The Wall*, after which a British band had named their crucial 1980 album). By the time Lukutin's protégé Rudnitsky was done with the form, exhibiting his magnificently referential *Lukutin Accompanies Himself with Shadows* in Paris in 1916, everything was largely considered to have "been done." (This despite Rudnitsky himself having declared in his autobiography that "There is no progress in art, any more than there is progress in lovemaking. There are simply different positions whereby one can sit and look at it.") Born too late to really contribute to the glory days of the *papier maché* pantheon, the elder Silvestri was more of an ornamental frieze, never a pillar, but it was the muse that chose him, and not the other way around. So Talone labored away in poverty and obscurity, and sometimes now appears in the footnotes of *papier maché* research as the last heartbeat, the last blip, the last dying gasp, before the motion picture industry exploded and turned the art into a craft again, the walking undead of creative expression.

Talone's son, on the other hand, would be labelled the one who killed it. It was clear that young Serafino, even as a child, had inherited his father's solid jaw and plentiful salivation glands. They had to keep plastic sheets on the floors, he drooled so much. Newspapers needed to be read almost immediately or into his mouth they went. Serafino's mother tried to dissuade him from this path of disappointment and poverty by baking with coarser, whole grain flours, which were more difficult to convert into a suitable binding paste, but he merely developed more alternatives to bond the paper, using anything from cinnamon to mashed potatoes to his own belly button lint as the main ingredient. And perhaps because of these constraints, his work exceeded even that of his father. Perhaps they were even greater than those of Lukutin, not necessarily in beauty, because any claim like that would be ridiculous, but with such an intense devotion to realism that a candidate for California Governor – the actor, who should have really known better – was once embarrassed trying to kiss one of his *maché* babies, and the actress Chanti Rose wore one of his paper dresses to the Oscars at which she was *not* nominated (much to the surprise of most critics, who felt she was a shoe-in for her supporting turn in the film *Nicer Oaths*, about a young nun who falls in love with a blues guitarist). At his father's grave, Serafino placed a bouquet of paper flowers he'd created out of his father's own paste recipes, and no one could tell the difference until several days later, when they were the only ones not to lose their petals.

The movies were probably the only thing that kept the genius Serafino from eventually taking his own life. Unable to find work in his hometown of Salinas, he'd moved to Hollywood to live with some relatives, and had worked his way up to relative poverty in a boarding house called the San Bernardino Arms, rarely leaving his room. In fact, it was unclear how a big-time director like William Wyler would even have heard of him. But Hollywood was built on rumours and hearsay; you didn't truly know anything until you had heard it secondhand, or possibly third. So there you were. All Wyler needed were a couple of fake boulders and breastplates for his remake of *Ben Hur* (there's no way Heston would have been able to lift the real thing), which was so beneath Serafino as to be laughable. Boulders?! He was a genius! But the young Silvestri surprised everyone and accepted, recognizing the resources that he would be able to tap, and he eventually persuaded Wyler to let him construct almost everything else, including the arena, the chariots, and even the horses and lions. His work was so believable that animal rights activists are still claiming six horses died during the filming. In the famous chariot race, when the competitors round the first sharp turn, unbeknownst even to Wyler, Silvestri inserted a fake soldier.

Suddenly Silvestri was famous. He became rich, built himself a *papier maché* mansion, was seen at all the biggest parties. The legend of his skill grew and grew. There was even a rumor that he created little Ricky during his work on *I Love Lucy*, which was why the boy's acting was so wooden. When a famous actress fell ill during the shooting of her breakthrough film (he would never disclose who), he created a stand-in for several scenes.

Then word came down from the peak of the Chicago Sears tower. Young Alvah Roebuck and his partner were planning to branch out from their mail order business, with actual department stores across the country, where young housewives could see their new line of clothing up close and personal. But Roebuck's feminine tastes tended toward the more weak and helpless. He liked his women practically see-through, and found the European mannequins too husky for his new national ideal. Plus, they had more old catalogues than they knew what to do with, so...?

Silvestri, with dreams of creating people so real they might one day replace us, accepted.

Tragically, he died by choking on a significant wad of hundred dollar bills before the first model came off the assembly line. Some random stranger bought the business and kept the name.

* * *

Domenico Monterossi had only one son. Ernest was it. When he immigrated from the Northern Italian village of Cinque Terre in 1923, evading mandatory military duty under Mussolini, he had dreams of creating an electrical family dynasty. This was what America had promised him. Instead, his beloved Isabella amped out girl after girl, with only the third youngest child, Ernesto, to show for his troubles. And the little brat never did learn the difference between a volt and a watt, spending all of his time at the movies instead of apprenticing with his father where he should have been.

When America finally joined the Second World War, Domenico enlisted, a much older man, just so he could contribute like his nephews and brothers and cousins in the resistance back home. He never returned. Ernesto's mother pressured him to take things over, for his father's sake, but because he had built up a dream of celebrity for himself, he refused to be part of the laboring class, and instead decided there was more money to be made in creating cheaper parts for other electricians to purchase. He was right. And he eked out a decent living with his small stable of employees for several years.

Then one of Monterossi's technicians developed a urethane compound that could be color-infused. With the rise of interior design magazines, there was a higher demand for fixtures – particularly electrical outlets and light switches – that were more favorably delicate on the color spectrum. Traditional plastic fixtures were difficult to paint, so this new invention allowed all manner of new living environments. Within six months, Monterossi and Sons was the brand people asked for by name at their local hardware stores. Ernest was richer than he'd ever dreamed, and was able to buy new homes and automobiles for his mother and all his sisters, most of whom had already married and started having children of their own. By the time the competition caught up, the company still owned the patent on the process, and so he continued to make money even when consumers went elsewhere.

Ernest remained unsatisfied. How much talent or skill did it take to make plastic wall covers? But his schemes all seemed to fall back on him, like when he tried to take on the fashion industry, using this same color-infusion technology to create the first ethnic mannequins. He even changed the company name to Hollywood Montrose to sound more American, as many Italian companies were left floundering after the war. But before he could get them into market, Pucci launched a new test series of headless abstractions in Munich and Prague, enabling stores to avoid the whole race thing altogether while also not alienating their current Caucasian base. The same thing happened in the nineties, when he tried to create the sexiest mannequins on the market. Hence the reason why he needed Chris Eaton to help out. And then the young starlet Ema Hesire showed up at the coldest Oscar night on record and suddenly they were looking for ways to stick the nipples back on again.

This kind of cycle seemed to repeat itself indefinitely until Ernest, too, was also bought out by the behemoth Silvestri and went to work for the enemy.

* * *

Chris Eaton worked the nipple line with Ernest's nephew, Angelo, who was trying to get into gay porn, of which Ernest was in firm support. Finally, a Montrose in show business. Of course, Ernest had no idea about his stage name: Ian Dowd (although he'd also considered Phil Anders, which he considered too high brow, P. Hugh Birdie, which was too kiddie porn and too clever by half, and Dong Juan, which was far too ethnic, even if his skin was dark enough to pull it off). Angelo was working on a mockumentary-style film he made with some friends parodying Michael Moore's *Roger and Me*, called *Rogering Me*, which they managed to show once in a friend's apartment but couldn't convince anyone to distribute any more widely.

Angelo was a mooch, with no obligations to anyone or anything but his dream, and at first they just made out a couple of times after work. The last thing Chris Eaton wanted so soon after leaving Albert was a steady relationship. But there was something about the way Angelo spoke – and his belief in unattainable dreams, his faith – that had Chris Eaton completely transfixed. He was an enigma. He swirled his wine before drinking it but didn't even know what Brie was. Within a month, they had moved in together. He nearly came out to his parents.

Then, naturally, things turned sour. Chris Eaton became less comfortable with Angelo having sex with other people, and more resentful that he was the one paying the rent while Angelo lounged around in a bathrobe all day drinking. He was also beginning to worry that others were defining him by his relationship to Angelo, who was frequently opinionated in public. He tried to leave several times, but on each occasion, Angelo broke down crying, told him he'd change, and convinced him to stay. For the next month, everything was fine again. Good, even. And then they'd be on a subway platform screaming at each other.

In the final month of their relationship, after Chris Eaton would no longer lend him money for more film, Angelo began stealing from him. They often fought in public. Then, shortly after they split, Angelo was involved in a horrible bike accident, catching his wheel on an unseen chain while jumping a short flight of stairs in Central Park. His forward motion ripped him from his seat, but his pant leg became hooked on the bicycle's chain ring, thrashing him wildly, like a killer whale with a seal, and he came down hard on the railing and slipped into a coma. Chris Eaton made a special trip to the hospital to see him, just to verify that the story was true and not merely a way to get out of his debt. Then he left the city to start over back in St. Petersburg.

He started dating a city planner, and as far as she was concerned, the State of Maine should be shut down. It was a burden on the system. In a future without oil, it was crucial to base civilizations around the larger centres, more people packed into smaller spaces, to reduce any need for mechanical transport. Maine was too far away from any hubs and too far north to grow the crops it needed on its own, so rather than maintaining all those aging fishermen through social assistance and trade incentives, depleting one fish stock after another after another, it made more sense to move all of them to high-rise living in Boston. He was mildly offended, as he'd also been raised in a small town. But he'd also just come out of another relationship that had left him confused, and perhaps looking for fights.

When they met, the city planner was already living with another man. Chris Eaton knew about the other man, and the other man knew about him, and he knew that the other man *knew*, but it was unclear whether or not the other man knew that *he* knew about *him*. The other man did not like to have sex. The city planner, on the other hand, liked it very much, although she was not particularly good at it, or not very good at reciprocating, or perhaps both, not that Chris Eaton noticed anyway, unfamiliar as he was at that point with good sex or even the idea that there was anything more she could be doing.

Whether or not the other man knew that *he* knew was further confused when the city planner would invite Chris Eaton to their place. At the first invitation, he had assumed the other man *must* know that he knew, or that he would find out. But naturally these occasions only occurred when the other man was out, and on entering the apartment, Chris Eaton was surprised to find it lacking in any characteristics that were not hers. There were no men's boots in the foyer, no distinctive shaving supplies in the medicine cabinet, no dandruff shampoo. The cupboards contained no canned meat. Everything in the refrigerator was covered. In fact, he briefly wondered if there was no other man at all, that it was just some sort of tactic she used to increase devotion. Then gradually he began to assume that this must have been part of their deal, that the other man never wanted to meet the *other* men, and that he never wanted anyone to know that he was being cuckolded, even if it were by his choice. He also assumed, then, that the other man must *not* know that *he* already knew about *him*, unless all of this was just some strategy they had concocted to make Chris Eaton feel less uncomfortable. Or, he wondered again, there was no other man at all.

The only thing that gave it away was the CD collection, which easily went beyond any sorts of references she had previously made to music. She danced, when they were out, a lot, and to the same popular songs you couldn't escape on the radio but with extra bass. But the shelves in the apartment were full of bands and records he had never heard of, with a strong element, in particular, of punk (e.g., Richard Hell and the Voidoids, The Heroin Cats, Nina Hagan, The Slits...) and world music, including Victor Jara (arrested and shot shortly after the Chilean coup of September 11, 1973), Silvio Rodriguez's *Cisne Harto* (1978; an ode to nature, recorded while still in his optimist phase, in the same session that produced *Mujeres*), and Stina Verda's first CD, *Charo* (1980). On subsequent visits, Chris Eaton would listen to many other discs in the collection, but this last one was the recording he would always come back to, seemingly named after the Spanish flamenco star and sex symbol of the eighties, completely unaware that the passionate, self-assured voice was only nine years old.

***

It was likely because of this CD that he and the city planner took their first vacation together to Panama. She loved to travel. The other man, if he really existed, did not. Having never traveled to Central America before this, Chris Eaton and the city planner were unprepared for how hot it was. The room they slept in for the first few nights was an unventilated oven, with nothing but his grossly under-padded yet over-insulated Gore-Tex jacket as a pillow, and a few sheets of cardboard for a bed. Of course, their living situation was his own fault for not learning better Spanish before he left. When you're arranging accommodations with someone who has broken English at best, *furnished* and *furnace* can sound very similar. As soon as they stepped off the plane in the capital, he was struck first by the heat, like stuffing wet gym socks down his throat, and then by the throng of people wanting to do them a favour. The cabbies rushed to help with their bags, firing "Taxi?" and "Where going?" and he was so overwhelmed with their helpfulness that they left with the first one to wrest his backpack free.

The second thing that struck him was the poverty. After America's completion of the legendary Panama Canal, so many men had been left unemployed that it had created an entirely new class of financial barrenness. And he wondered what he could do to help.

For the city planner, the vacation was only marred by a film shoot in Bocas del Toro, which transformed their secluded paradise into a mini oasis of America. The production company was working on the final scenes of a horror/action/thriller called *Sloth vs. Manatee*, starring Ema Hesire and Ian Dowd, which would go on to be a cult hit, gross hundreds of millions of dollars, and actually start a sort of franchise. But in order to make the Panamanian beach look more exotic, they had brought in thirty mature palm trees from Hawaii and were in the process of reshaping the entire lay of the coast.

"*Hay las palmas en Panamá*," said one of the village elders. And the government's Tourism Minister, Ruben Blades (who'd also been given a minor role in the film), translated.

"Are you kidding me?" the production manager said as they started digging the holes. "Those things? The Western public expects a certain something from their paradises, and if they're really going to accept your beautiful country as their new vacation dream spot, then there's gotta be the right kind of palm trees…"

Blades translated back. The elder looked unimpressed.

But the Panamanian government wanted a piece of the action that Costa Rica had. And Cuba. So they stood back as the foreign palm trees were shipped through their famous canal (where several itinerant Eatons once came to dig, he noticed when he visited the locks at Miraflores), and some of the locals were even enlisted to help dig the holes. The beach was perfect. All it needed were those few extra touches to drive it home. So they tied old, dried-up coconuts to the branches of the palm trees, because no one would ever recognize a ripe, green one. They bleached full stretches of sand to make it whiter. They even re-landscaped several of the dunes so they could capture the right shots from the water, and extended the beachscape by hacking away at the mangrove stands that bracketed either end. After they had finished shooting, they restored the beach to its original shape. But without the proper shore grass holding it together, several of the dunes collapsed the next rainy season. The dens of the hermit crabs had been trampled so frequently, they packed their shells and never came back. With their main source of food used in campfires for the crew, the manatees did likewise. And you'd be lucky to spot one in Panama today.

Soon after they returned home, Chris Eaton suggested another trip – to Peru. But the city planner's horrific memories of Panama still needed time to wane, and the relationship soon ended.

* * *

Stina Verda, on the other hand, remained a lifelong obsession, Christina "Stina" Maria Rosita Verda, born in the US military hospital in the Canal Zone of Panama City in 1971, the daughter of a forbidden love between a Panamanian housekeeper and a Hispanic-American soldier. After the flag riots in the mid-sixties, where twenty-one locals and four soldiers were killed, tension remained high between Panamanians and the American military, and when it was discovered that Officer Verda had fathered a child with the woman, it was decided it would be safer for everyone concerned if they were sent back to America.

In Florida, little Stina showed an early showbiz bug doing celebrity impersonations, and was discovered by a producer named Luke Harmon while taking part in a talent show at a mall in Miami. The competition had strict rules that the age of all children involved should be over ten, but somehow eight-year-old Stina convinced her mother to lie for her, or her mother coaxed Stina into it, or perhaps her mother just didn't understand English very well, and before anyone could really stop it, she was gyrating across the stage in a sequined pant-suit, shaking her non-existent breasts at the audience and screeching *cuchi-cuchi* to beat the band. The Spanish musician and actress Charo was riding a second wave of popularity, appearing on such television hits as *The Love Boat* and most of the popular variety shows, including *Donny & Marie*, *The Captain and Tennille* and a short-lived show of her own called *Charo and Sevirat*, with the king of ventriloquism at the time, the Frenchman Camille Sevirat (still the record-holder of the most words thrown while drinking a glass of water), and Stina's performance, rather than shocking, was an immediate hit. Her re-production of Charo's guitar stylings was also spot-on, and her voice stopped Harmon in the middle of buying a Cabbage Patch kid for his niece.

By the age of nine, Stina Verda had her first hit song. Harmon re-leased it on his own label, and it attracted the attention of the head of Warner's Latin Music division, as well as the folks at Disney, spawn-ing both a television show and a larger recording contract. At eleven, she was the most popular Latin artist in America, and had the top-selling CD in most Spanish-speaking countries: a concept record called *Ven Hartar Sodica*. To celebrate her thirteenth birthday, she appeared with the real Charo on one of her last *Love Boat* appear-ances. Her third album swept the Grammy Awards.

At seventeen, she fell in love with her bass player, and much to the dismay of her parents, they became engaged.

At seventeen and four months, they broke up.

And just two weeks before her twenty-first birthday, she was found floating face down in the rooftop pool of the Hotel Montreal in Panama City.

***

The police investigation was conducted in both countries simultaneously. At first, most people assumed it to be some sort of drug overdose. She was, after all, a rock musician, thrown into fame so quickly and early, and stereotypes, as one of the detectives in the US told the press towards the end of the investigation, existed for a reason. Everyone was the same. Everyone had the same hopes and dreams, more or less. And everyone fell prey to one vice or another. It was only the state of the body – completely swollen from head to toe and covered in large red welts – that seemed to indicate foul play.

Within a few weeks of the scandal, most of Verda's albums were monopolizing the Billboard charts. By Christmas, her label had managed to cull together a box set of greatest hits and unreleased material – surely not the last of it – called *Archivador Estan*. A film of her life was supposedly in the works. The tabloids were covered with pictures of her last days, or shots of the hotel in which they had found her body, still covered in police tape and roses. Speculation was already circulating about who might be responsible. The welts and swelling would seem to have indicated a struggle of some sort, and there were traces of semen in and around her vagina. But there was also no internal tearing and her clothes were completely undamaged, which led police to suspect she must have known her assailant, and possibly even had consensual sex with the murderer directly before her death. Verda's lover, a part-time stuntman in Brazil, was brought in for questioning, but he had been out of the country shooting scenes for *Sloth vs. Manatee 3D*, so they turned their attention to her boyfriend, a Panamanian politician and the son of a past President, who was approached while leaving the legislative assembly and brought in publicly for official questioning. The Minister had recently been involved in a bribery scandal that had taken months of police work, only to be thrown out by the country's Supreme Court, so police commissioner Perlas Archipelago was particularly happy to have him in custody again, if only to return the favor of his national humiliation. The Minister refused to cooperate, claiming emotional brutality to accuse him of the mur-

196

der of the woman he loved. The sperm was a match, but his alibi was solid, and the American forensics experts who'd been flown in to help with the case acknowledged that the sample, if she had not douched since then, could have been there for days, and perhaps longer if she'd been underwater for very long, creating a seal to keep out the air.

In the US, meanwhile, investigators began building their case against Stina's manager. For so much of her career, she had been a minor, and so most of the profits from her royalties and performances, minus a generous allowance for her and her family, had been placed, on Harmon's advice, in an account that she would be able to access when she came of age. As the police delved further, however, they discovered Harmon had been embezzling funds for at least the last ten years and probably more, registering all of the songs in his own name and telling no one. They couldn't be sure if Stina had ever found out, but it could have explained why the Verdas had decided to fire Harmon, and would provide a fairly strong motive. When Harmon could not be found at his home, a massive manhunt was launched, and luckily for the humiliated Panamanian police, they were the ones who picked Harmon up trying to board a plane to Kuna Yala. At an unorthodox press conference, his lip split and left eye swollen tightly shut, Harmon confessed. Both countries rejoiced, but the Panamanians were particularly celebratory. It was like a soccer victory over the US, or at least a tie, and it was agreed, for national stability, that the trial should take place in Panama, but in the American-occupied zone so Harmon could also receive a fair trial as a US citizen. As the trial progressed, Harmon changed his story to say it had all been an accident. When asked why he was changing his story now, he said he was afraid. This wasn't his country. He didn't know what would happen to him. And when prosecutors drilled him about the events leading up to the murder, it became clear that he had no idea how Stina Verda had even died, had been in Panama merely on a scouting trip to find a replacement for his old star, and had only confessed after a thorough beating.

Two-and-a-half years later, with no new leads to go on, the case was officially closed.

When Chris Eaton's husband took a bath, the water was left with all sorts of organic detritus: body hair, toe jam, bits of skin he'd pumiced from around his ankles, circling around the edges of his legs like dust in the sunlight. The combination of his allergies and the hot water made his nose run, and he blew the snot out in hot, dirty clumps into his chest hair, a sound she could hear in the other room as she read her pulp novels in bed. When she witnessed it the first time, breaking his phlegmy sanctuary to pee, dropping her pants to the tiled floor and staring hard at the discoloured clots that decorated his chest like hardened cheese ends, she knew it had to be love because it didn't bother her in the least.

She wiped herself. Pulled her pants back on. And her smile stretched all the way from his side back to the bedroom.

A year passed. And then another. Was this what love was? A time machine that sprinted you into the future with each loving caress? She'd always thought of herself as solitary. After her last relationship, she said she'd never fall in love again, and spent the next three years cultivating a distinguished air of celibate spinsterhood, with only occasional carnal lapses, with a hospital intern, a scotch whiskey rep, and a professor of English, with whom she actually broke down and met twice, knowing he was married but saying nothing when he didn't volunteer the information. She took a trip to East Berlin shortly after The Wall came down, and afraid that if she attempted to remove any of the devalued currency from the former country that they would find some way to detain and torture her, she spent her last dollar on a dozen notebooks, some playing cards, a bottle opener, and several waxy sticks of plasticine in primary colors that transferred almost immediately to the hands of her nieces and nephews. One of the notebooks she used to keep a list of sexual positions she found in books like *The Kama Sutra*, or just on the online men's sites: *Union*

of the Cow, Union of the Elephant, The Position of Perfect Alignment.
Or *The Position of Andromache*, the traditional woman on top position, which somehow became connected with the wife of Hector
from the Trojan War, perhaps as a joke, as if, after Achilles had killed
him and let him lie outside the wall for days, maybe Andromache
stood at the wall and dreamed they might make love one last time.
Then there were the French positions, like *The Varlope, The Pompe,
The Brouette* and *The Jardinier*, which appeared to involve the man
entering the woman while she rested both hands on the ground, as
if she were a wheelbarrow, perhaps even walking around like that. It
was often hard to tell from the diagrams if any additional ambula-
tory movement were involved. She supposed there must be, at least
occasionally. The men she took home were unfortunately much less
imaginative, mostly trying unsuccessfully to guide her head down to
their crotch, a position she called *The Game Show Plunger*, or just
passing out on top of her, which she decided to name *The Position of
Thanatos* after the Greek God of Death.

Then she met Laurent, who was French but from Canada, so not
nearly as prissy. He spoke like a peasant farmer and was covered with
hair from head to toe. She'd arrived last on purpose at an improv class
she found mostly ridiculous but had attended because of a friend
who took four classes a week and dated interesting men who liked to
fence, or salsa dance, or pick their own fruit, who occasionally traveled by hopping trains or spontaneously slept on beaches in exotic
island countries, like the Martinique, or Greenland, with the latest
gadgets or completely off the grid, with waxed moustaches, or pubic
hair, or at least claimed such things. Once her friend had even dated
a man who balanced furniture as art, fitting a stack of end tables and
television remotes between the floor and ceiling of a semi-famous
London hotel lobby without a millimetre to spare, until he caught
wind of a furniture-balancing guru – indeed, an entire culture – in
Tibet, and he was thrown into complete despair.

He had led such an interesting life, gestating for his first sixteen years in a small Quebecois highway town, with nothing but a hockey rink, strip club, motel and gas station. At sixteen, he was selected to play in the Quebec Major Junior Hockey Association in Chicoutimi, New Brunswick. But then he failed to make the Canadian National team and defected to play for England, where his mother's father was from, in the C league of international play. Before Laurent arrived, it had been a team comprised mostly of weekend recreationalists. Their star player ran a chip truck in Sheffield and had borrowed his skates from a brother-in-law (whose ankles had become too fat to wear them himself); he was the second line's left wing, although they had never come across anyone before Laurent who actually shot left, most of them having been raised to play on a pitch, not a rink. In the two years Laurent played for them, the team never managed to win a game, but he did get to see a lot of the world, and faking a knee injury and a concussion after two years of star worship for his occasional goals, it was easy to find a cushy job in London, reading magazines for an agent that represented dozens of paparazzi, searching for un-licensed usage and passing the examples on to the litigation depart-ment. From there he got a job watching TV, in a similar capacity to the magazine position, but for a marketing research firm, locked in a room with nine television screens (a number they had arrived at, through further research, that was the most one person could ab-sorb at once without missing anything), scanning for specific trends in news coverage and writing a short précis of each news feature and talk-show theme, from climate change and gas prices to celebrity teen pregnancies, tide levels, the lunar perigee, whale beachings...

After two years in a low-rise apartment infested with mice, they bought a home infested with ants, with several flights of steps that were either too short or too long and never just right. The back drain-pipe had been installed without consideration for how the rain would pool against the side of the building. Similarly, the end drainage on their bathtub wasn't actually connected to the pipes but just ran into the space between floors and left a browny-orange ring on the ceiling in the living room. The rain gutters surely needed repair. There was a pipe sticking up in the middle of their front lawn, and one day she kicked it and it broke. She had no idea what it was even for, and covered it with a brick for two years before asking anyone.

The previous owners had transformed the basement into an apartment for an aging poet who had apparently died there, presumably from mould inhalation. Air, musty from water leaking down an unused chimney through the shared wall of the duplex, hung in all the rooms; and sawing a hole through the drywall with a nail file to examine the extent of the damage, she discovered, directly beneath one of the heating vents, the secret deposit of allergy medication and other assorted paraphernalia of loneliness: empty canisters of fluoxetine, fluvoxamine, citalopram and nefazodone; phenelzine, Zoloft and another where the name had faded to illegibility; some utility bills, snug in their elastic cradle; a loonie; several cans of beer, uncrushed; three more, crushed; a toy train; two 1.5 L bottles of cheap rosé; a half-dozen airplane bottles of a Canadian rye whisky called Canadian Club; several chocolate bar wrappers, including a Mounds, Big Turk and Milky Way; and a dead bird. The prescriptions had sometimes been written only days apart. When they discovered the mould, they scooped out handfuls of the sodden pressboard like hunks of diseased lungs, protected by only the thinnest of paper masks, cursing idiocy and laughing in deep gasps. Then they read the articles online about mould toxicity. About immune system abnormalities and brain damage. And about bleeding lung disease, which seemed to be such a threat to youth in Cleveland specifically. The contractors' estimates ranged anywhere from $600 to $30,000, depending on whether or not they wanted to excavate, which would also involve demolishing and replacing the deck. The estimates were hand-written on the backs of bill envelopes, or on carefully designed checklists, or were drafted on word processing programs by secretaries and then delivered by mail. Chris Eaton and Laurent decided to wait and see what happened, as this option really involved not deciding at all. But it only led to more stress, checking the basement hygrometer twice daily for what they thought would be tell-tale indications of something more insidious, something they could not see, something behind other walls. The back-story. They bought a 30-pint capacity dehumidifier, afraid of being ripped off, figuring the 65-pint dehumidifier was more than they would ever need, and then regretted it. That fall, she was down on all fours under the deck, fixing the grading around the foundation with clay she'd stolen from a nearby excavation site, covering it all with construction-grade 3-ft laminated plastic sheeting that the neighborhood cats would puncture in weeks, come the next spring thaw.

He met Chanté on his first mission to Haiti, a two-week trip he organized for two-dozen Christians to teach the local drug farmers about proper tilling, better irrigation and other potential cash crops their neighbours were cultivating, like coffee, sugar and cocoa. In 1986, after twenty-nine years of dictatorial rule (fourteen by his father and fifteen by himself), Baby Doc Duvalier decided it was as good a time as any to pass the torch, so to speak, before the locals burned him alive in his home, and the US military came in to clean up the mess. The public plan was to re-establish democracy and economic development in the region, to set the stage for elections and be out in two years. But truthfully they were mainly using the island as a foothold for *la Service d'Intelligence Nationale* (appropriately, s.i.n.), taking on the Colombians in one of the greatest anti-narcotics operations in the history of Central America.

After witnessing such abject poverty in Panama, Chris Eaton thought this was how he could make a difference. Everyone else in the world had it so much worse than they did, couldn't even afford to have hopes and dreams, unless you counted hoping for fresh water, or to not get eaten by wild animals, or for love, would never have a nice home or a car, would never taste a prime cut of steak, would never become famous. Of course, he had no idea that the same advice to grow breakfast beverage staples was being given to every developing Third World country, and the sudden abundance of these once-luxury items resulted in a global price collapse. Peasants in most other countries turned back to drugs. But with the new international anti-drug force in place, peasants in Haiti looked to forestry, not for the potentially rich income of endangered lumbers, but as charcoal for their own personal heat and energy. He had also not planned on the airline losing half of their luggage, misplaced during the transfer in Georgia. Most of it never even arrived in Haiti, largely because the airline went out of business three days after their arrival. And he quickly found that most of his time was spent either trying to find people clothes or locating another airline that could take them back to America.

Thank God for Chanté, who always brought his silverware wrapped in paper napkins and whose Creole French sailed past him more often than he acknowledged. Every night he hid from the others' complaints in her restaurant, eating fried chicken and rice and what would be the last Haitian plantains before the Dominicans eventually underpriced them out of business. And every night she would astound him with how useless his French lessons had been growing up. He was mesmerized by her. She wore her hair constantly in curlers. She'd never seen a movie. And by the end of the two weeks, forced to wear mu-mus Chanté lent him from her mother, he discovered that no one had anything but good things to say about the experience. Two couples had even fallen in love. The rest had found more self-worth.

When he went back home, Chanté gave him a sculpture her father had made of a tiny black boat, so crude it was barely recognizable as such, to symbolize the distance that their affection could cross in it. It was made from cocobolo, a wood that smells like roses when cut, and is so dense it will not float on water.

The business card that came with it had this further description on the back:

...which was when he met and fell in love with Jules, and had to think about finally telling his father.

Her father threw a party. To celebrate his retirement, his new cabin, just to throw a fucking party, Jesus, why don't you just get down here already, I never get to see you. Her father never used to swear. But one time, when she and her sister were visiting for Christmas, she mistakenly rented a film about reluctant British gangsters – mechanics and other down-to-earth types (like her father, which is why she rented it) who naturally turn to organized crime when they lose their own livelihood – who screw up a job for the biggest boss and have to recruit a bunch of other fuckups to make it right, and when her sister arrived partway through the barrage of obscenities and asked her parents what they thought of it, they said "great fucking movie" and "fucking awesome," and when she laughed at them, the floodgates were open from then on. That was before her mother died of breast cancer, in her early-fifties, and her father threw himself into planning for his retirement, with a lump of sorrow in his throat so large that it sometimes made it difficult to fit through the massive double doors to his job at Stoic Heran Tool and Die, which despite popular assumptions (which was not helped in the least by the accompanying bird logo), was not merely the result of an overzealous and under-educated sign maker, but was, in fact, more uninterestingly named for its founder, Patric Heran, an Anglo-Norman name derived from the old English *heiroun*, a word that meant heron but otherwise had nothing to do with the bird at all.

It was a name that nearly disappeared entirely a century before old man Heran was even born. When Heran's great-grandfather, James, first arrived at Castle Garden in the New World in the mid-1800s, he was asked his name, occupation and the amount of money he was carrying on him, and since he had neither of the latter two, having never been much good at anything specific in the second category and having lost what he had of the third category playing dice with the Irish thugs on the voyage over, he was not particularly distressed when the overworked state processors mistook him as part of his new group of "friends" and issued him papers under the Irish spell-ing of Haran, which he promptly altered one more time once he was through by adding an additional O' to the front. If he'd learned any-thing on his trip, besides never to gamble again, it was that the Irish were already overrunning the place, representing more than half of US immigration at the time, and had placed themselves in so many supervisory labour positions that finding work in that sector would be easier this way. Besides, he'd come to America in the first place to escape the influence of his own family, so starting all over with a new nationality seemed fitting.

That was how Jimmy O'Haran started west, or more accurately, for The West, which would keep moving away from him and his de-scendants each time they drew close, like a pot of gold at the end of a rainbow, following the sounds of Irish lilts from labour gang to la-bour gang, hefting a pick and shovel and laying the infrastructure for the nation. He was quiet, mostly to hide his poorly mimicked accent, but this was seen as an asset by most businessmen and contractors, as the country was expanding at such an alarming rate, and there was money to be made, the contractors told them, if for a moment they could all just forget who they were (implying the different nationalities and religions that would have been fighting back in Europe but really meaning the people who would be working and the people who would be making all the money), and put their nose to the grindstone to make the country work. O'Haran bought it, hook, line and sinker. At least he wasn't working at his father's pencil factory any more, wasn't part of that new British nouveau riche. After toiling for more than a year on The Pennsylvania Main Line Canal, he was discovered by another man named O'Haran (presumably his actual name) who told him of some work in South Carolina, connecting a railway to Memphis, Tennessee, that would pay near double what he was currently making, where he probably would have stayed were it not for the outbreak of The Civil War.

***

Whatever part Jimmy O'Haran played in the war is uncertain but easy to surmise as he was, like most Southerners, disinclined to discuss it and, like most cowards, disinclined to fight. Likely as not, he faked an injury. Or judging by where he eventually ended up, he put his newly acquired brogue to good use and won the heart of some defenseless widow, a dry-innard woman who snuck meals and other treats to him in her horse barn until the fighting was over. In the spring of 1865, April 9, the very day Lee surrendered to Grant, the city hall in New Orleans contains a record of the marriage of "the widow Hibbard," whose deceased husband had run a moderately successful business manufacturing blackboard chalk, to one Jimmy O'Hara, which we can presume to not be the result of a typo this time but part of James's final step in adopting his Irish alter ego.

Of course the first irony was that, through this single act of integration – in the manufacture of writing implements, no less – James became everything that he had tried to escape in the first place. The second was that the widow weren't so dry after all, the doctor scraping out a single son they named Carey, and the Heran curse of duplicating the previous generation continued without abate, each new brood forging a new path only to end up in exactly the same place, personally if not geographically. True to form, Carey O'Hara changed his own name back to Charles Heran and headed just south of Dallas to work for the Corsicana Oil Development Company under John Galey. An avid, self-taught, amateur geologist, Charles was convinced of two things. The first: salt and oil were inextricably tied; where you found one you would find the other (a view shared by other so-called lunatics of the period like Patillo Higgins and E. I. Stronach). And the second: salt, rather than oil, was the fuel of the future.

This assumption was not as far-fetched as it might seem today, or rather, no more far fetched than using oil, equally ridiculed at the time, as up to that point oil had only been used for lamps and lubrication. Until the Industrial Revolution and the internal combustion engine, ground salt had been hard to come by. It was one of the more dangerous and expensive substances to get out of the earth. In Rome, they used prisoners as slaves to extract it. So did the Nazis. Charles's theories: once it could be removed more easily, the geothermal heat could be captured from the salt domes and used for fuel; or by over-salinating water one could extract the hydrogen from it and have it burn freely; molten salt reactors. But when the Spindeltop gusher began producing more than a hundred thousand barrels of oil per day, and the population grew from ten thousand to fifty thousand almost over night, everyone and their dog erected another derrick, and any ideas of extracting the salt from the dome over it had to be abandoned. Like his father he turned to gambling, coupled with drinking this time, and whoring.

Among the various progeny he likely sired, the one with his name continued west to Arizona, became a farmer and married an Evangelical Lutheran. Gradine Heran would become one of the initial founders of the state's Anti-Saloon League, and thus one of the leading supporters of the eighteenth amendment for national prohibition in 1919. Most citizens assumed prohibition would decrease crime and violence while improving overall health and morality, but this was far from the case. Illegal stills popped up in every second basement and back lot. Contraband moonshine, which was far from regulated, often contained things like creosote, or embalming fluid, resulting in frequent blindness and paralysis. And perhaps strangest of all, the theft of bees, whose honey was needed to kickstart the fermentation process, became rampant. Without a large percentage of their pollinators, crops began to suffer. Charles lost almost everything he had. And while Gradine welcomed God's test, Charles began to lobby for changes. When it came time to repeal, three quarters of Arizonians voted in favor of this amendment, too. Gradine never spoke directly to her husband again. Charles started drinking, and became one of the state's most popular politicians.

Naturally, the greatest problem facing their son Patric in his earliest years, as well as those years in the middle, the twilight, and basically right up until the end, was whether he would be shaped to a larger degree by the prudish determination of his mother or his father's clandestine addiction to everything bacchanalian. But rather than choose a side, he shunned decisions and emotions altogether, and earned the nickname Stoic for the rest of his life. Even after his tool-and-die company became so successful during the forties, affording him a much larger home, a membership at the most prestigious golf and country club, cars for all of his daughters on their sixteenth birthdays, Stoic Heran seemed to take little pleasure in it. Success, to him, was just another aspect of life, with no more celebration to be taken from it, or time taken to dwell on it, than from failure, or luck, or breakfast, or a daily bowel movement. Each moment of every day was just one tic closer to the end, when he might finally let everything loose and really enjoy himself in the afterlife, like one of his employees might count the seconds in front of his machine, longing for the weekend, rather than thinking about the other able-bodied Americans who were, at that very same second, perishing in a trench in France, or perhaps wishing they were. Life was the job; Heaven was the reward. And like a job, he felt no need to be good or pious or even particularly pleasant to people, drinking excessively *and* judging others for it. He merely had to put in the time until he could punch his card and relax, having his feet massaged all day by the hands of the sinners.

That was how Patric Heran saw Heaven: a place where the workers were finally able to reap the benefits of their labor, as he imagined his great-grandfather, the last truly great laborer in the family before himself, being waited on, foot and hand, by the politicians that had made his life hell to begin with. Chris Eaton's idea of Heaven was a sort of nothingness, without weight or mass or appearance or idiocy. Chris Eaton's father, who worked for Stoic Heran for nigh on thirty-five years, giving up most of his life along with his right index finger, his idea of Heaven was a cabin in the wilderness, with wood in the stove and an outhouse in the back, on a pond or a lake, or maybe just a mountain stream, but definitely with water, a lot like Thoreau's heaven but without his mother stopping by to cut his hair or with the occasional pie, with enough distance between himself and the nearest neighbour that he could have his legs crushed beneath a fallen tree and never be able to scream for help. By the time Chris Eaton's father got the idea for this perfect retirement in his head, perhaps coinciding with the third anniversary of his wife's death and perhaps not, he had already spent more than half his life making machines for Heran, machines that made machines that, in his case, went on to make automobiles, blenders, computers, children's toys, seltzer bottles, Frisbees, an entire assortment of doodads, gizmos, farkles and widgets, thingamabobs, thingamajiggers, and even a third generation of machines that were supposed to manufacture – unbeknownst to the elder Eaton, who could have cared less if the end product of his labour ended up bombing the living shit out of Afghanistan and Iraq – more efficient home HVAC systems that would have saved their owners (plus the government, tax payers, you name it) close to thirty-six percent off the day's energy costs, had they not gotten caught up in a lot of union red tape. Worried that they might also last longer and thereby eventually reduce the need for future units, the systems ended up rusting at the back of one of the waterfront warehouses in Brooklyn that most locals assumed were actually just fronts for strategic defense missile silos, until several blocks of them were destroyed in a raging fire that sent plumes of acrid bromium biocide smoke into Manhattan.

City life had never been her father's bag. The air was bad. It was too loud. He was also *an idealist*, which was sort of a fancy word he used in place of *anti-social*. So as soon as he had managed to save five thousand dollars, he bought several acres up north, near the town of Pine, built a fence out of stones around the entire perimetre (an undertaking of approximately two-and-a-half years, in and of itself), and started building his dream cabin.

He built the whole thing with his own bare hands, too, even drew up the plans and, for a small cash fee, convinced a certified architect who had fallen on hard times to claim he had legally authored them, cleared the site of trees and large rocks and purchased a four-wheel all-terrain vehicle and a length of chain to drag them to the nearby escarpment. The soil was highly acidic from decades, if not centuries, of human neglect. The tree canopy created so much shade that, even in Arizona, annual rainfalls nearly always exceeded their own evapotranspiration, depleting the natural calcium, magnesium and potassium deposits and replacing them with iron and aluminum, which was great for blueberries and strawberries, maybe potatoes, but it also meant he had to make sure to grade the land to guide water away from the house instead of into his foundation. The night he finished laying the roof, he slept under it.

His daughters couldn't understand why he'd spend so much time working on something like this when, at this point, due to powerful union lobbying of the tool-and-die industry, he could easily afford to hire professional contractors to complete it in a month. Then he could just enjoy it, retire and move up there for good, just like he'd always wanted. But that, for him, would have been cheating. He had set out to do it himself, and that was how he was going to finish it. Anything else just wouldn't be as satisfying. And two years later, he dug the well, and the hole for the sewage tank, just like they would have done it in the old days, with a pick, shovel and occasional dynamite.

And he looked at what he had done and smiled.

* * *

Then Chris Eaton's father took ill. He came back from the bar one night with his breath crackling like playing cards in his bike spokes. Nothing major; in the morning, it was gone. But a few days later, he collapsed climbing the stairs to the observation floor at the machinery. He had severe chest pain that was initially thought to be a mild arrhythmia but then was rediagnosed by a doctor independent from the company as a mild pneumonia due to an additional mild fever. Patric Heran called Chris Eaton directly and she grabbed the first flight she could find, told Julian she'd be back soon, that her father just needed someone to look after him until the fever broke, and they agreed to consummate their relationship on her return. Her sister had said she'd pick her up at the airport but then cancelled at the last moment, saying she couldn't get away from New York right now, so she grabbed a cab directly to the hospital and spent at least a half hour being reassured by the attending physician – they weren't sure, to be honest, the chest x-rays looked completely normal – then sat with her father until he fell asleep again. She went to the lobby and bought a cola, waited another hour or more while watching television, then called her sister, said everything seemed fine, everything was looking up, and when there was a pause at the other end, added that there probably wasn't any need for her to be there after all. Thank God, she said.

She returned to her childhood home, telephoned St. Hecarion, said many of the same things but with more technical details, and assured them she'd only be gone for a few days, the rest of the week at the max, and they told her to take her time, to make sure her father was doing alright, that in the interim some of the nurses could bring toys to the children's rooms instead. The important thing was her father's health.

Then she called Julian, said many of the same things but with fewer lies, then told him that she missed him, that she hadn't realized how much strength she got from him, that she wasn't a whole person without him. She wanted him to touch her, to lie down beneath him and have him enter her slowly, so she could savour every second, and while she told him, she reached down to touch herself for the first time, and if she wasn't already wet, she was pretty close, so she told him that, too. She wanted to grab his cock, she said, then felt silly, but she could hear his breathing getting heavier on the other end so she kept going, with more clichés and more inner humiliation, more stuffing and filling and hardness and good, until she couldn't really touch herself any more. Then she told him she was tired, hung up, and for several hours tried to fall asleep.

* * *

By the end of the week, her father was definitely not okay. His breathing was getting marginally better, but increased head pain and dizziness seemed to indicate some sort of tumor. X-rays provided the doctors with clear evidence of brain swelling, but no one could tell them why. To be safe, they placed him on a program of Mannitol and Dexamethasone, and hooked him up to a ventilator to increase his breathing rate and capacity. If the swelling continued, they said, they'd want to explore the option of stereotactic radiosurgery, resisting the third option as long as possible to remove one of the occipital lobes. She called her sister again. Another week, she said. No problem, St. Hecarion said. That sounds about right, Julian said. Seems like you're in good hands, Julian said.

I still can't make it, her sister said. People are coming to see the house on Tuesday.

＊＊＊

He started coughing things up. Dark things. He couldn't eat. Or didn't want to. The top respiratory specialist in Los Angeles was not answering their calls so they sent samples along with vials of his blood and urine to Dallas. She said she knew someone in Houston, but they still sent it to Dallas. Her sister wanted to know if they were doing everything they could. Her sister wanted to know if the doctors seemed competent. To her, they did not seem competent. Chris Eaton wanted to hang up. At St. Hecarion, they were now getting concerned, not that they couldn't hold the job for her but that, if it continued much longer, she might have to take unpaid compassionate leave. She said she understood. The specialist who was not in Houston said he had performed an immunoassay and a polymerase chain reaction on her father's blood and discovered several antigens that concerned him. He was concerned. So he was testing the phlegm for traces of spores. The results ended up inconclusive, but indicative enough to warrant, he felt, a partial lung biopsy. She started to call her sister, then called Julian instead. He said he wanted to hold her. He said he wanted to help her. He said he felt powerless. She told him she loved him and he told her to hurry home.

＊＊＊

Her sister wanted to know why she wasn't consulted on the biopsy option. Her sister wanted to know why this was the first she was hearing about blasted psychosis. Blastomycosis, Chris Eaton corrected her. Whatever, she said, what are we going to *do*? The case was severe, and could take weeks or months to properly fight, a fungal infection that he had likely contracted when disturbing the soil to dig his well – the final step to his retirement – and while it had stayed fairly dormant throughout the cold, dry winter, the damp spring had caused the infestation to multiply and spread through his blood and lymphatics to his brain. The specialist who was not from Houston said it was common in AIDS patients, then waited for her to respond. The doctor who was from Phoenix nodded. She said, Are you saying my father has AIDS? And they both said no together, no, they just wanted her to realize the severity of the situation. So they said AIDS. She said she understood, to get them to stop talking. They wanted to place him immediately on an oral treatment of Itraconazole, but the pills were huge and difficult to swallow, and several hours after the first dose, her father couldn't stop vomiting. His urine had grown dark and pungent, and the doctors grew even more concerned over his dehydration than the original fungus. So they switched him to the more controversial Ketoconazole, which seemed to fair much better. By the fifth dose, it already seemed clear he was getting better. He was laughing and joking and able to make light of the fact that he was basically eating the same stuff they put in anti-dandruff shampoo. But the doctors warned that the increased joviality might actually just be a side effect of the medication, which was also occasionally used to fight depression, and that the full treatment could take months. Julian tried to distract her with stories of life in Houston. He'd gone to a party at Carol's and everyone was asking about her. The party was a lot of fun, he said. Carol made some spectacular hors d'oeuvres and they played a game all night where everyone had to guess the identity of everyone else just by looking at them, "murdering" or "lynching" someone by turns, and he and Carol were always killed early so spent most of their time talking to each other in the kitchen. It went way too late, too. Before they knew it, it was four in the morning, but poor thing, he stayed and helped her do the dishes before heading home, unlike all those other ingrates.

The connection was bad and made Julian sound far away, or like he was buried beneath Chris Eaton's house, trapped there and muffledly calling for help.

* * *

She hadn't been working for two months. She called her sister. Dad was doing better, how was the East Coast, had she managed to sell the house yet? No, her sister replied, and the stress of it was really starting to get to her. There weren't enough hours in a day. Chris Eaton felt uncomfortable asking her about money.

Stoic Heran called and asked if there was anything he could do, buy her groceries, take some more shifts sitting with her dad at the hospital. He'd been dropping in on her father more and more often, and every few days they would pass each other in the hallway. And then she would see a woman she thought was his wife looking at magazines in the gift shop, or waiting outside in the car, as if she were afraid of sick people.

And then she called the elementary school where her mother used to teach before the cancer, spoke to the principal, who had always liked her mother, it was so sad to lose her as part of the team. To be honest, there wasn't a whole lot she could do, they had a long list of dependable supply teachers, but if she didn't mind overseeing gym...

* * *

Her father started vomiting again. Another bad reaction to the Ketoconazole. The dehydration was so severe he could barely lift himself up to talk to her, just lay there in bed with his mouth hanging open, trying to swallow. They switched him to an intravenous treatment of Amphotericin B, which made him delusional, to the point that he didn't even recognize her and once, when she was the only one in the room, he told her it was so long since he'd been with a woman and

215

would she be a dear nurse and help him out manually. She cried on the phone with Julian but couldn't tell him about it. I'm sorry, I have to go, he said. There's someone at the door.

* * *

Stoic dropped by with another meal and stayed to eat it with her. She asked him why his wife was afraid to go into the hospital, and he said he wasn't sure what she was talking about.

She called Julian and the connection was bad again. Where are you, she said. Just out.

* * *

It sounds like you're at a party.

A bus just drove by, he said.

* * *

I could really use another week of work, Mrs. C.

I'll see what I can do, she said.

* * *

Another month went by. Her father was getting better, to be sure, but the doctors still weren't sure what was a result of the original illness and what was merely a side effect of the medication. I'm sure you can see how difficult this might be, the doctor's assistant – also from Phoenix, but not originally – said. Treatments like this can be highly toxic. It's not easy.

He broke his hip tripping over a dodgeball, her principal said. We could really use you for the rest of the year, at the very least.

I'm sure you understand our dilemma, St. Hecarion said. Good luck in all of your future endeavors.

216

This has been so hard on both of us, her sister said.

I'm sorry, Julian said.

Neither of us meant for this to happen, he said.

I'm sorry.

* * *

Three weeks later, the doctors said the infection was gone. Within a week of being released from the hospital, however, Chris Eaton's father died of severe nephrotoxicity and acute liver failure. She was so alone. And the loneliness felt like a hole she had to fill however she could.

The romance novels she wrote were based on the idea of an innate emotional justice, the notion that good people in the world were rewarded and evil people were punished. For example, in a historical romance like her own *Crystal Angel*, what they called a *yearn and learn* in the industry, the lovers who risked and struggled for each other and their relationship were rewarded with emotional justice and unconditional love. Her hero was a government bounty hunter in the frontier territory of Colorado in 1868. Her heroine went dressed as a nun. And she'd literally embodied this sense of right and wrong by writing the point of view of a guardian angel, which originally had taken the shape of a watchful grey fog but had later been altered by her editor to be more like ice. But was that the proper arc of life? Was that how we could all expect to live? Where did that place all the other stories? The ones with people who weren't perfect? The ones with their beautiful endings of death and disaster? Was there anything more romantic than death, especially when it kept two lovers apart? That was simply the way things happened sometimes.

The Prince Charming she eventually ended up marrying wasn't even a cowboy, or a burly gardener, or even a stockbroker with a passion for painting. He was a crop insurance adjustor for an agency based in Saskatchewan but covering large portions of the American Midwest like Wisconsin, specializing in grain varieties not traditionally covered by core multi-peril crop insurance, like red clover, borage, rye grass, hemp and millet. His name was Jones (the name she would publish under), with hair as black as charred meat, and a bottom lip you could swing off. She loved him despite the fact that he ate most things with his hands. His favorite thing to do was watch tennis on television. He could spend hours talking about the potential risk of an early frost to Wisconsin millet crops. Ascochyta-resistant chickpeas, were they possible? And sometimes, after a night of drinking, he would get up and pee in the corner of the room or, if he made it to the washroom, on the bathroom scale.

He was the one who sat by her – or near her, rather, playing *Risk* with strangers online – as she marked her territory around the dining room, was her moral support, as she worked, scattering gnawed pencils and shavings around the couch. She found the idea of writing a novel with pad and pencil suitably romantic, feeling it connected her with the writers of the past, at least those who wrote between the decline of quill and ink and the ascension of the typewriter in the late nineteenth century. She tried a typewriter for a short time, but it jammed so frequently, and changing the ribbons left her fingertips in a constant blackened state. Plus, it made her feel like a man, like someone writing stiff, logical, hard-boiled detective novels rather than something of real personal value. Her longhand was also so abysmal, more like letters dying of some debilitating disease than the words that are actually coming to life within them, so she never had to fear anyone else reading the text until it was done, not that her husband would ever present such a threat.

It was ironic, she supposed, to be inventing tragic flaws when her husband was such a wayward home for them. Why would anyone want to overcome these things? Why not embrace them? But her editor would never let it pass. There had to be a single obstacle of character. Someone had to improve. Then her husband leaned back, placed his head in his hands and whispered a single word, *Indonesia*, which set her off on so many tangents she could barely sit still. *Tunisia, Silesia, Dyonisia, amnesia*... Its opposite, *hypermnesia*? Perhaps. *Amnesia* had been done to death, obviously: man meets woman; man gets in car accident and can no longer remember who she is; woman must make him fall in love with her all over again. But *hypermnesia*? A character who remembers everything? Including things he has not lived? It was like tapping into a group consciousness, what's the word, existing in such a state of constant sadness at remembering things like Hiroshima, the concentration camps, Lady Diana's death, what's the word, *telaesthesia*? There was promise there. *Analgesia*: same man gets in car accident and she must nurse him back to health until he can walk again, or with a heart so broken that only drugs can mask the pain. *Ecclesia*, she's done that already. And *framboesia* was a possibility, set the story somewhere tropical and let the environment wreak its own havoc; but with symptoms so close to syphilis it was, perhaps, not very appropriate for a romance.

Even the way they met would not have been considered romantic to anyone other than herself, living down the street from each other that whole time? She and her husband should even have been in the same class during their final year of high school, an advanced curriculum they introduced to allow the smarter kids to graduate a year earlier, but she got pneumonia at the beginning of Grade Eleven, and was unable to keep up from home, so they held her back. She attended the local state college for a standard BA. He went to the University of Missouri to do a BSc in Agricultural Economics. After they had both graduated from university (at the end of the summer, he was essentially drafted into the insurance business by an uncle and whisked off to Necedah to learn the ins and outs of seeding, water management and crop chemical application, while she was three hours away in Milwaukee trying unsuccessfully to become the *Journal Sentinel*'s book reviewer), their mothers made them go out on one date. They were engaged within a year.

She still has the ticket stub.

After their wedding, before political upheaval transformed the region, they honeymooned all through Central America, snorkelling in both oceans and hiding in the shrubs in fear one night as they watched a group of poachers dig thousands of turtle eggs from the sand in what they thought was a private, secluded cove. On a hike through the mountains of Costa Rica, they nearly spotted a quetzal, although really all they saw was an eruption in the foliage around them and brief flash of colour before it disappeared.

On one of their last days before their planned return to the UK, they ate undercooked burgers and yucca fries at a barbecue stand in Panama City. As the city was already a global banking centre, most shrewd businessmen spoke near-fluent English, and while she was in the washroom, Walter struck up a match (for a cigar) and a conversation with the stand's owner, who as a younger man had made his fortune selling propane and propane barbecues in America. The first propane had become commercially available there in 1922, and backed by multiple articles in the *New York Times*, its popularity grew almost exponentially. Within five years, sales were in the millions of gallons. Within ten, it had topped fifty million. But it was the creation of the railroad tank car in the thirties that allowed this man to make his fortune and return to Panama as part of the new upper class. Transportation was the secret. It didn't matter what the cargo was, everyone had to get something somewhere, particularly in America after the Second World War, when the whole country just felt the inexplicable need to keep moving around, as if dodging bullets in the trenches had become a frame of mind.

The more they talked, the more Walter began to see the advantages of the transportation business in general. Private combustion engine automobiles were catching on like the plague, and there was certainly more than enough need for cartage in the more removed areas of America that the regular rail lines could not service. Plus, the U.S. federal government had budgeted over $81 million for the improvement of cross-country highways and interstates, which would practically act as a subsidy for a new business like his. By the time they had reached the end of their honeymoon, Walter had already made some calls to banks in the UK and the States, an old friend in Sheffield he thought might be interested in a potential partnership, a few manufacturing companies, immigration lawyers. They could buy a respectable fleet of used, gas-powered flatbeds in New England and specialize more in the short-haul business rather than compete with the big boys who had sprung up during the war effort. They could call the company C A R K, after the Imperial unit of measure equaling three to four hundred-weight but also after its more popular usage which meant simply "a burden," as well as being a town near his birthplace in Grange-over-Sands in Cumbria, and they could start by delivering produce from local farmers to the new supermarkets for resale.

He even spent two weeks in Massachusetts scouting the region. But very quickly the local pronunciation of the name – and the ridicule that would have grown with it – drove him insane, and he tossed it all and went back to being an insurance adjustor in England.

Back in the UK, she returned to her Master's thesis, through the University of Lincolnshire and Humberside, studying packaging literacy in America and the UK after the First World War. In the early-1900s, the American Food and Drug Administration began cracking down on pharmaceuticals to remove false claims from packaging. It was in the fundamental rights of every man, woman and child, President Roosevelt himself declared before Congress on June 30, 1906, to know exactly what was going into their bodies. Congress agreed. (In fact, they took Coca-Cola to court over it, accusing the soft drink manufacturer of false advertising because the product contained neither coca nor cola, and also had way too much caffeine. In *The United States vs. Forty Barrels and Twenty Kegs of Coca-Cola*, the Supreme

221

Court eventually decided Coke had the right to add as much caffeine as it saw fit, but not before the fledgling company ran out of money and had to settle out of court by agreeing to lower the amount, anyway.) The pharmaceutical companies fired back by using names no regular person would ever understand.

Of course, the upshot was that people did eventually learn to understand them. Especially when they were also forced to introduce the number of calories. Today her paper would have been even more fascinating, as literacy levels have significantly climbed in the past ten years. It took a bit longer, but people finally began to realize that monosodium glutamate was the same thing as the MSG they'd been warned about at Chinese food restaurants for so many years. Then they realized it was a kind of salt. It became apparent that something as innocent as corn sugar, found in most pre-packaged foods, could be contributing to increased obesity levels. And with the proliferation of organics in most of the big chain stores, and a trend towards more local produce, some food producers had begun adding information that was not yet required by national food and drug acts, leading the way in furthering the language, creating certification boards to indicate lower levels of pesticides or bovine growth hormone, or listing locations where the ingredients were grown and harvested. One company from Sheffield was even printing the distances that each ingredient had to travel, placing an entirely new focus on the carbon and energy cost of the food we eat. The small paragraph on the back of a frozen lasagna is now like the shortest of short stories.

Laurent traveled on business. And she always found it hard to sleep when he wasn't around. Sometimes she felt like every sleepless night she'd ever had, even before they met, was because he was awake somewhere else in the world, and her body wanted to be awake for that too. In his absence she crawled around the house on all fours, picturing how their children might injure themselves: split lips on table corners, hanged on the cords from blinds, electrocuted by dangling stereo wires. And when he returned they talked about it, and he agreed that it might not be the perfect time but what time would ever be perfect? So she took notes of when she figured she'd be ovulating and even started eating lots of folic acid supplements because she'd read on the Internet that it would help prevent birth defects, like being born with an incomplete spine or thinner skin around the neck. But nothing seemed to work. And after four months, she began to worry that being on the pill for so long had made her infertile. She'd been on it since she was fourteen, when her doctor prescribed it for monthly pains that kept her from going to school. (Now, off the pill again, her periods were so strong that she was throwing up from the pain, unable to sit still or move around, or even lie down and cry softly.) Her doctor tested her blood for LH, FSH, estradiol and testosterone. Also CA-125. And she recommended an ultrasound, just to make sure.

The technician said, "You're not a virgin, are you?"

"I'm married." Her feet were already up in the stirrups and she had to strain her neck to see anyone.

The technician said, "I never assume any more." The chemicals they rubbed on her stomach were cold and smelled like glue. "Once, I tested a woman who was thirty-five. I didn't ask, and it was horrible."

She had trouble imagining this as the transducer was inserted.

Two weeks later, the tests revealed she had developed cysts on her ovaries. Apparently one was the size of a golf ball, on a part of her body that was only the size of an almond, which made her consider if it were the cyst that developed the ovary or the other way around. It didn't necessarily mean anything, the doctor tried to reassure her. Ovarian cysts were a natural bodily function. It was how the ovary actually released the egg in the first place. Sometimes these cysts would even remain for a short time. Mostly they went away on their own. And so she spent a month crying softly on the edge of the bathtub, afraid to tell him, afraid to say it out loud because somehow that might make it come true. She hadn't even wanted to ask the doctor about it, to take it seriously in any way, because she didn't want to hear her say that she wouldn't be able to have kids. It obviously meant so much to Laurent. To her.

And when they re-tested a month later: nothing to worry about, the cysts were gone.

And at last they had a baby. At the time, he was in love all over again, and the city planner had either abandoned the other man or the pretense of the other man and they had moved in together, whereby he had the opportunity to see what was hers and what had once belonged to the other man. The Verda CD was gone. But she claimed that was only because it had been stolen from her car on a trip to Miami. He attended several of the appointments with the midwife, even though it terrified him to put the trust of his unborn child into the hands of this woman who didn't even wear a stethoscope, or carry popsicle sticks in her pocket. She just stared at the centre of his forehead as she spoke, almost as if he weren't even there and she were just practicing, speaking in a tone so soothing he could never pay attention to the words. At nine weeks and five days, he heard the heartbeat, like galloping horses, and nearly cried. And he was present for the birth, although he nearly missed it when the nurse told him to get something to eat, that it would be some time before the baby actually showed itself and he should save his own energy. When he returned, with the sounds of the Super Bowl half-time show spilling from a television in the lounge, she'd suddenly gone from two centimetres dilated to one centimetre short of pushing, her arms around the midwife's neck, who appeared to be helping her back into the bed as if she'd fallen out of it. "Everything's gone wrong," she cried to him. And he wondered: Where are the doctors? And: Is there a button to press that will call the doctors? And also: Should he go into the hallway and call the doctors? And the midwife tried to stay calm, but it was clear that she didn't have enough hands for this. Or a stethoscope. She called her back-up, trying to speak softly. "Well, how soon can you make it, then?" he heard her say. And also: "Well, go as fast as you can." Taking her cues, he told the city planner not to push. It was too early. And she said, "Not gonna push." But as she said no, she was nodding yes. And Chris Eaton said, "This is it, lover. This is what we've been waiting for. This little baby. Nine months of waiting. We can wait another while longer."

And once again she said, "Not gonna push." Again, nodding yes.

At first, the most difficult thing was just staying awake, and for nearly two months, he just held the boy as close as he could, often falling asleep with his son on his chest. The first time the boy reached for him, he nearly cried again.

Then he began to worry: about the baby's development, that maybe he should be reading to him more, setting the stage for him to be literate before he entered the Florida school system. The boy began laughing, and walking, and looking so much like his mother that spending time with him was, for Chris Eaton, a double kind of joy.

He had never realized it before, but this was all he had ever wanted. He considered putting off the campaign until the next election. He was so happy.

And then he blinked.

PART 8

Chris Eaton was not hurt. He was not even emotionally distressed, particularly. He simply felt disassociated from himself, from the rest of the world, as if perhaps he had even died in the accident, and now he was simply witnessing the rest of his life through the eyes of his ghost, or worse, some stranger. Every inconsiderable thing he did in the course of a day, from cutting his eggs to wiping his ass to counting his change for the bus, none of it seemed real. Even when he spoke to Julie about it, he got caught up in listening to the specific words, and mere seconds after they had left his mouth he was already trying to understand what they were saying, most times second-guessing them, realizing immediately that he was lying, or maybe, at best, that the words this man had chosen had been selected so poorly, that they didn't even come close to what was going on inside of *himself*, this confusion and distance between his thoughts and actions, and maybe, and this is where the real problem lay, was that, even in try-ing to understand it, he was being so hypocritical, because really, he didn't feel like the words were even coming from himself, so that most times he would just trail off in mid-sentence without having made his point.

He felt no real stakes in his own life, as though his own existence was nothing more than a movie. Or like he was reading a book. A bad one.

Archie Nots, the lawyer who had approached him about the accident, said that was good enough. Chris Eaton felt uncomfortable about it. But Julie assured him that this was for the best. He needed help. More than she could offer. They couldn't afford to live without it. Without something.

Why, he asked.

Why what?

Why did he need help?

* * *

They kept a close watch over him in the weeks following the Pentagon attack. Security was tight. As the only survivor in the area of the impact, he'd become a bit of a celebrity. People were talking about miracles. And so his room at the George Washington University Hospital was made completely off limits to everyone except his medical attendants, his wife, and the occasional agent in black suit and sunglasses.

There was nothing wrong with him. Not even the excessive dust inhalation seemed to have affected his lungs. Yet he seemed reluctant to speak to anyone about what had happened. He responded physically to all of his examiners with utmost respect and immediacy, but when asked direct questions, he remained silent. Only when they left him alone with Julie did he confide in her that he wasn't sure why he was there. He couldn't remember what had happened, could only recall going to work like any other day, taking a nap in the storage closet, and then waking up here. His body was sore. He wanted a beer.

But he would talk to no one else, would trust no one else. They were out to get him, he said, and he wasn't even sure who yet, but someone. Them. He had developed some outlandish conspiracy theories, many of which were based around the numbers 9 and 11. Not only did the Twin Towers stand like an enormous 11 over the New York skyline, and the first plane to hit them was Flight 11, but New York was also the 11th state to be added to the union. The words

New York City, *The Pentagon* and *Afghanistan* were all comprised of 11 letters. Likewise the name Ramzi Yousef, who had masterminded the 1993 W T C bombing. Flight 11 had 11 crew members; and 92 passengers (9 + 2 = 11). Flight 93 had 38, which also adds up to 11. The number of passengers on Flight 175? 56. The total number of people on the same planes including crew members? 81, 45 and 65.

The date of the attack: 9/11; 9 + 1 + 1 = 11

9/11 is the 254th day of the year: 2 + 5 + 4 = 11

The number of days remaining in the year after 9/11: 111 days.

The winning numbers in the New York State lottery that day? 9-1-1.

It seemed too ridiculous and random, and yet all these connections had to mean something. And the more he looked into it, the more meaning it seemed to take on. He became equally concerned with the numbers 7 and 15, and the Lincoln and Kennedy assassinations. The names Lincoln and Kennedy both have 7 letters in their names. Both men were elected exactly one hundred years apart, and were both assassinated on Fridays, by gunshot, while seated beside their wives. Lincoln was shot in Box 7 at Ford's Kennedy Theatre; Kennedy, in the 7th car in a convoy of Ford Lincoln Continentals. Both were succeeded by men named Johnson, a name that also has 7 letters.

On the side of evil, both assassins had 15 letters in their names, split into three words. His name – Chris Avard Eaton – was actually the same, which perhaps put him on the wrong side, too. Booth shot Lincoln in a theatre and hid in a warehouse; Oswald shot Kennedy from a warehouse and hid in a theatre.

Both were originally detained by men named Baker.

Both failed to make it to trial, killed by a single shot from a Colt revolver.

He'd also become convinced that the true cause of the Iraq War was salt.

* * *

About a hundred years ago (he told Julie the next time they were alone), with the production shift from primitive solar evaporation to deep rock mining, global salt prices had unexpectedly plummeted. Global warming had likewise threatened the winter road-salt market, and it had become necessary to devise more and more ways to use the world's only edible mineral. Luckily – if you believed in luck – there was Sir Humphry Davy, a known Freemason and, in fact, the son of a suspected founding member of the English branch of the Illuminati. A century earlier, building on the research started by other members of his order (the Bulgarian and Spanish scientists, respectively, Christo and Varea), Davy had perfected a process for splitting the salt compound into its two basic elements, sodium and chlorine, but at the time the only reason for working on this was to supply the explosives used by groups like Christo's displaced Bulgarians, who were attempting to retain freedom under their Turkish oppressors by roaming the Balkan Peninsula as armed *kurdjalii*, as well as Varea's many sons and nephews in the Peninsula War for Spanish Independence against Napoleon. For decades the Illuminati used their processes solely for terrorist warfare; but as time wore on, and empires were overthrown in France, Spain, and even Bulgaria (with the 1876 uprising and massacre, and the subsequent Russo-Turkish War), the secret society's salt producers were left with businesses that were becoming increasingly obsolete. And in a world where money was becoming the weapon rather than the stepping stone to purchase or produce other weapons, what was a secret society to do?

In the early-1900s, therefore, the Illuminati set their members to creating more and more uses for the salt and its basic components. Gradually implementing its New World Order through scientific discovery, it took salt from the curing and preserving of meats and fish to much broader application: the production of cleaning products and bleaches; for use in making certain dyes; glazing pottery; as a natural remedy for sore throats; the creation of high-powered magnifying lenses for microscopes; in the production of ink; mining silver; refining oil; fertilizers, insecticides and medications; cosmetics; plastic and polyester; rayon; P V C pipes, cellphones and flat screen TVs; and as the environment became more of a political issue, using salt in solar panels for producing electricity, as well as greenhouse gas sequestration. By the sixties, they'd made salt the leading ingredient in about ninety-five percent of the world's chemical processes. Even after the Cold War, when the U.S. and Russia began dismantling their nuclear arsenals, they discovered they could dispose of the dangerous materials in a more environmental way by dropping them into pits of molten salt.

Perhaps the most ingenious idea, however, was created by the German novelist and food writer Tonia Hersc, who was likely one of the first women let into the group despite the Illuminati being supposedly pro-feminist from their outset, almost immediately before the First World War.

* * *

Hersc had grown up in the Lower Saxony region of Germany in the late-1800s, the only child to a father who owned several potash mines and refineries, a man who was both thick and watery at the same time. How he had come to be part of the Illuminati was a problem facing the entire organization, with inheritance of invitation outrunning inheritance of brilliance. It was her grandfather, Jeorg Hersc, who was the true member of the order, a man of unparalleled thinking who had written several books of poetry (including *Du Hasst*, 1836) and existentialist philosophy (*Stille Nicht*, 1845) while also mastering the field of geology and discovering massive deposits of potassium carbonate in the area he eventually settled. Her father, who wasn't even worth naming, was not even a real businessman, not in the best sense of the word. He was more like a placeholder, someone to be called at meetings until someone better emerged to really answer to it. Tonia ran away from home when she was fourteen, somehow making it to

Paris on nothing more than the change and jewelry she'd stolen from her parents' dresser on the way out the door. There she lived on the streets for several years until a young dressmaker near the *Opéra Garnier*, named Jules-Joseph Villars, spotted her and hired her to stand as his living window mannequin, a marketing trick that built his business for several years. By day, she walked around a tiny glass box; at night, she slept on a pile of discarded material shards in the back. She was barely a real person – just the idea of a person that Villars would create to entice his customers. She also began to fall for Villars, and on top of her nine hours of daily prancing and primping, she began to cook his meals. The daughter of a rich mine owner, she had never made a dish in her life, but she asked the women at the markets how best to prepare food that might win a man's heart, and they took her aside and whispered to her all of their secrets.

She was a natural. And soon *Le Boutique Villars* was known as much for its fashion and its living mannequin as it was for the smells that held and caressed every nook and corner of the shop. They began selling soup on the side, then pastries, and eventually full lunches, until one day she had the pleasure – or would have had the pleasure, had she know who he was at the time – of serving Auguste Escoffier before he took off for London. He offered her a job in one of his kitchens in Cannes, first at the *entremetier* station and then as chief *Saucier*, after which she quit because making food for strangers was not the same as making food with love. She discovered, however, that what she loved about food was not the preparation of it but the consumption. Under Escoffier, she was exposed to some of the best food in the world and, with her famous first review for Michelin, which contained the line, "A meal that doesn't end with cheese is like making love to a beautiful woman with only one eye," Tonia Hersc began her food writing career.

Meanwhile, she and Villars were married. On their honeymoon, they attended the Frankfurt Automobile Show, and Jules-Joseph was struck particularly by the new portion dedicated to aircraft. Over a

Wednesday and a Thursday, Villars barely wanted to leave the grounds, able to stand inside an early Zeppelin prototype, run his hand along the French *Bleriot IX* (which never really achieved sustained flight and would only have been of use as a little island hopper, if one could nail the accuracy needed to hit each island), and admire the workmanship of the German *Etrich Taube*, which was built to resemble a giant dove from below. Villars was transfixed and mesmerized by these flying vessels, insisting they skip Berlin entirely and remain for the stunt show on the weekend, where two early Aviatiks clipped wings during a simple demonstration of side-by-side maneuvers, and they witnessed both pilots plunging to their deaths. He was visibly distressed, insisting again that they end the honeymoon immediately and return to Paris. He was quiet for weeks, would not even open the shop when she went back to Cannes to work at the restaurant. He sent her telegrams and letters full of increasing sadness and loss, despair, unable to shake the visual of those falling men, wondering what they must have felt as they struck the ground. When she returned for her next visit, the boutique was covered in large swaths of silk, and she was happy to see him working again. But on returning to Cannes, she heard the news reports about the man who was intending to jump from the Eiffel Tower to test his new frameless parachute suit, and she knew this happy part of her life was over. The autopsy revealed that Jules-Joseph had died from a heart attack during his fall.

***

Hersc begged Escoffier's forgiveness, quit the restaurant, and swore to never leave another lover's side again, of which she would have many, including: her second husband, the dashing foreign news correspondent from England, Chauncey Ackart; a stunt driver of motorcars; Tour de France winner Henri Pélissier; Paris-Brest winner Charles Terront; *Vélo* editor Henri Desgrange; Paris's *prévôt des tromptemps*; and almost immediately on returning to Paris, a torrid affair with the married chemist-in-exile, Luis Petrousa, from whom she would pick up a thing or two, not counting the mild case of gonorrhea. Before her death in 1938, she would write several dozen books of poetry and fiction, although only one is widely known outside of France, called *Frou-Frou* (1944), about a young French street urchin based on herself (Frou-Frou was the name she had given herself when she had first arrived in the capital), who is hired to clear tables at a ritzy hotel, and her relationship with the cultured and moustachioed *maître d'* who realizes he is in love with her. *Frou-Frou* was later made into an unsuccessful film, an even less successful Broadway musical, and despite all of this, into an updated television series renamed, for some uncertain reason, *Lou-Lou*. She would also publish scads of cookbooks, written under various pseudonyms, as well as two books under her own name on the lost city of Atlantis, in which she was a firm believer. The first of those cookbooks, *Pains d'Amour Perdu* (published by Berowne and Dumaine in 1910), inevitably caught the attention of the city's elected prince of gastronomy, Curnonsky, who tapped her to write for the fledgling Michelin Red Guide, as well as vouching for her at *Le Journal*. It was then – now writing mostly under the name Tatienne Villars – that she began to be followed, and not merely as a journalist. Curnonsky told her not to worry, that it was probably someone from *Le Temps*. The importance of good food in France had reached such a zenith that both papers wanted to know who the other would be reviewing, so there were often men in long coats following him. And she believed him until the night she came home to discover that her apartment had been completely overturned, with two men standing at the foot of her bed holding the shreds of Jules-Joseph's failed parachute.

***

They'd been searching for her for some time, but she'd been hiding under so many assumed names that it had taken them some time to verify it was her. It wasn't until they found the locket she had stolen from her mother (which had proven too sentimental an object to sell) that they knew for sure. Her father was dead, they said. Her mother was useless. Her father's business – her business now, she realized – was failing. And thus the Illuminati had finally come looking for her. The order had always assumed her father would sire another child, but her mother proved to be more than useless, she was also barren – a complication arising from Tonia's own birth. These things normally passed from father to son, but as the only child of the Hersc they would no longer even name, they extended invitation to her. Many of their best people, they assured her, were working on the salt problem as they spoke, but they understood she was working with Petrousa, by which she could tell they meant screwing but their point was made.

She agreed, not out of any filial obligation or Illuminatic gratitude but because the entire economic structure on which her grandfather Jeorg Hersc's ideals had rested was in peril. She first approached the problem as all the others had, on primarily a volume level, trying to devise procedures that might involve as much salt as possible with each use. Petrousa didn't even ask why, just threw himself into the game of it, and tried combining various amounts of the separated chlorine with crude oil, hoping to invent some sort of polymer for use in making giant rubberized balloons for gigantic, cruiseship-style flying dirigibles, like the German Zeppelins but more on the scale of the Titanic. He accidentally exposed the experiment to too much sunlight, however, and the substance hardened into a useless white solid inside his flasks. After that, he threw himself into one of his legendary pouts and refused to help any more. But even if he had succeeded, Hersc considered, while the amount of salt per project would be large, how much call would there really be for so many flying cities. Even if she could just find a way to get every person in the world to use a little bit, on a regular basis, she might solve the problem in one go.

Then, through a series of columns published over the war (one of many efforts by the paper to put some joy in people's lives), Hersc published countless recipes that she had altered to include a pinch here and a dash there. Sometimes she used the war as a reason, citing properties in salt that could boost the body's perceived caloric intake, or allow the body to retain more water, as both malnutrition and dehydration were an initial concern. But as the war ended and a new cultural boom came to France, she shifted her message to that of taste. Tatienne Villars had already gained such prestige for her scathing critiques ("This new habit of beating eggs rather than whisking is like combing your hair with a rake") that everyone began to listen. Salt, she said, was a flavor enhancer. Everyone had agreed with Curnonsky when he said: Good cooking is when things taste of what they are. Now she was saying that salt made things taste like what they were, only more so. Much like The Emperor's New Clothes, even the top chefs began to believe her, to notice the difference for themselves and to repeat her aphorisms at dinner parties and in cafés. From the top restaurants, it spread to the general population of rural France and then, because French cuisine had become the *de rigueur* fine-dining choice across the globe, to the rest of Europe and North America. Hemingway wrote an essay for *The Toronto Star* about it, which was summarily picked up through the Associated Press by everyone from *The New York Times* weekend edition to *The Washington Post*. By the mid-twenties, you'd have been hard-pressed to find a new cookbook or revised edition of an old one without salt in most recipes. By the fifties, salt was just a given, and a major cash business. Why did the terrorists attack the U.S. in 2001 in the first place? Because it was the wealthiest nation on Earth, and the leading producer of salt. And why attack Iraq in response? Anyone who claims the reason is oil is simply short-sighted. It just happens that salt domes were created in the same cataclysmic events that rendered organic materials into petroleum. In fact, these salt domes were what enabled the oil to develop, acting as a barrier to keep the oil from dissipating. Why else do you think Iraq is such a desert? The oil just helps us know where the salt is.

Before companies like Cargill and Morton and Sifto made the

process of ingesting salt much more convenient, our prehistoric ancestors used to get it from the animals we ate. Apparently, the animals we eat today aren't nearly as kind to us. Every cookbook Chris Eaton could get his hands on – and, in the beginning, they were only too accommodating towards a hero like him – seemed to back him up. He was getting overly excited. If you check out any toxicity site, it lists sodium chloride (i.e., salt) on par with PCBs. The body recognizes sodium chloride as a poison and goes to work quickly to eliminate it. This cleansing process causes an overburden on our organs. When we consume table salt, our bodies must dilute it by twenty-three times the amount of cell water to neutralize it. Our bodies then retain water, causing edema and, later, cellulite from the excess fluid in the body tissue. Iodine was originally discovered by one of Napoleon's chemists trying to make gunpowder out of seaweed, and they started adding it to salt in the early-1900s, theoretically to prevent goiters. Significant amounts of iodine can contribute to hypothyroidism.

Some table salts even include aluminum hydroxide, for easier pouring, which is a known cause of Alzheimer's.

"Did you know that our ancestors of six to eight thousand years ago didn't suffer from any of the debilitating diseases we have today?" Chris Eaton was surrounded by doctors at this point, and not the ones who fix your body, just your head. "Who knows? It might even be the cause of cancer. This salt is changing us. Into something we were never meant to be. The body does need sodium to live, but studies have shown all you need is about five hundred milligrams per day. Most people are consuming over six thousand! They're trying to kill us… I think… or at least dumb us down…"

"And what proof do you have of this, Mr. Eaton? What makes you think there's someone out to get you?"

"Who needs proof when you have facts?"

And they suggested he take some time off.

* * *

The doctors figured his delusions had been brought about by the incident. It was a fairly natural reaction, they said, for the brain to try to make sense of something so nonsensical. Likely there was already something inside of him before the accident, they said, something about who he was, perhaps genetic or perhaps the result of some random coincidence, that was already making him feel confused and unsure about himself, that he felt directly connected to things the rest of us might ignore, or might associate with fate, or religion, or chance, and he had no way to make the logical leap to those connections until the proverbial pin dropped on this whole salt thing. Somehow, the stress and trauma of the situation had brought a jarring realization to his brain, and no matter how ridiculous it seemed to anyone on the outside, this was how his brain had fixed itself, so no amount of logic was likely to convince him otherwise.

The iloperidone helped, but mostly it left him dizzy and sleepy. And his dreams were always of other people. The real remedy came from Julia falling ill. She collapsed while waiting for the bus to school, and the next driver on the scene called for an ambulance. She felt fine, she said to him, embarrassed. Really, she told the paramedic, there's no need for all this. I'm not even sure why I'm here, she said to the doctor on duty. And by the time Chris Eaton reached the hospital, the doctor was saying it was nothing a good birth wouldn't fix. They'd been so crushed by the late miscarriage in their first pregnancy that they'd found it difficult to resume a healthy sex life, and this news came as a surprise. But it also gave Chris Eaton a new focus. He had learned a thing or two about carpentry while working at the Pentagon, and while Nots's injury lawsuit was ramping up, he put that to use redecorating his office into a baby's room, building a crib from scratch, as well as a high chair and several simple toys, from a duck to a boat to a small bike and tennis racket. In the face of this new life they were creating, the strange connections he'd been making before seemed to disappear, or become less important to him. Besides, there was an all-important piece missing, like a jigsaw puzzle without a box to compare, and the section in the middle was impossible to complete. Who stood to really benefit from the 9/11 attacks? Who was pushing the buttons in America? Who was his fabled Illuminati ringleader? None of it made sense any more.

One night, with Julie hugging him from behind, the baby kicked so hard he could feel it against his back. When he put his face against her belly and spoke gently, there was always a reciprocal tap. He forgot about the Pentagon and the salt and all the numbers. There were bad days, naturally, but mostly he thought how nice it would be to finally return to work like he used to. Would he still have a job at the Pentagon after all this? He wasn't sure.

Then, when the doctors felt it was safe, Julie showed him some research of her own. There was no Tonia Hersc, never had been. She'd found some of the cookbook titles he had told her, but none of them were by Tatienne Villars. *Le Journal* had no record of her. There had never been a poet and miner named Jeorg Hersc, only a soldier in the Seven Years War. No Humphry Davy. Hemingway was real, of course, and Petrousa. But Petrousa had never left his native Greece to live in France. And the winner of the first Paris-Brest race was not named Charles Terront but Charles Thery. Chris Eaton stared at her for a moment. Then his face softened, and he thanked her. It was all starting to make so much more sense.

"I love you," he said, and pretended to fall sleep.

* * *

The settlement wasn't enough to support them forever, but was enough to allow them to spend a few years with their child before either would have to return to work. Julie wanted to put it all behind her, anyway. This would let them start over and forget this whole thing ever happened. But he couldn't forget. Before the government lawyers came back with their last offer, they delivered a big speech to him about how they understood what he was going through, and that, as the only survivor of that section of the Pentagon crash, they knew he was important to the American people at this moment, and that they wanted to make sure that he was treated fairly. They wanted to make sure it was not unjust. And Chris Eaton paused, then leaned over to Archie and Julie and whispered something they could not hear. They asked him to speak up.

"What do you mean," he repeated. "I was the only survivor?"

And the next day the lawyers came back with a deal.

***

After the next elections, Senator Chi left her position in California to take over as Secretary of Health and Human Services. The product of a Jewish mother and Chinese father, raised partly in Asia, with a PhD in biology, and one of the most popular public officials the West Coast had ever produced, not even the opposition could argue against her appointment. She could converse easily with the Chinese scientists about the burgeoning avian and swine flu problems they were having. She gave a speech about it to Congress. It was only a matter of time, she said, until one of these flu viruses became capable of human-to-human transmission and the next pandemic would sweep the world. Then, an entire island of aboriginal people fell ill in Central America with "a respiratory illness of unknown provenance." Cuba ceased letting people in or out of the country but would not say why. In Mexico, a battery manufacturer had to shut down production when no one showed up for work. The first US case happened in California with a nine-year-old girl who could not be named in news reports. A young hockey player in Canada had died on a weekend trip only hours after contracting a fever. Agents from the American Centers for Disease Control were dispatched to all locations. Less than three weeks later, there were confirmed cases in Spain and Scotland. In Wales, Israel, and New Zealand. What did it mean, Chris Eaton wondered. What were the links? Austria and Germany. Ireland, the

Netherlands and Switzerland. Several more in Canada. Three hundred and fourteen people placed under quarantine in China. Multiple cases in California and Texas. In fact, an entire school district in Texas was shut down for a week, from what later ended up being a false alarm, but there was increased pressure on the CDC and Senator Chi to introduce a nationwide vaccination program. But not until the illnesses of celebrities like Ani Torches, Rich Gannon and Ian Dowd put a very public face on it did they start rolling things out.

Near the end of Julie's second trimester, in her twenty-fourth week, the government decided the disease was reaching epidemic proportions and that it would be best to vaccinate the entire population, with the highest risk groups including the obese, those with heart disease, people with diabetes, asthma or kidney disease, people with AIDS and pregnant women going first. It was also initially suggested that pregnant women get a special non-adjuvant shot, but the supply of that one was quickly exhausted, and their midwife recommended she get the full adjuvant shot, anyway. Chris Eaton was fairly adamant against it. Something was wrong, he said. He didn't want to go into too many details, however, because he and Julie were doing so well. She agreed without too much argument.

Julie's midwife, however, was also worried, but for different reasons. They were already running out of the vaccine in California. There was talk of a major blunder by the government, and she wanted to make sure Julie was protected before the shit really hit the fan. On her recommendation, Julie got the shot on the Friday. All weekend she had to resist jokes about not being able to lift her arms. On the Tuesday, she came down with mild, flu-like symptoms, which was to be expected, coughing, exhausted and achy but with a body temperature barely peaking over a hundred. Nothing serious. Their doctor diagnosed her with a mild sinus infection and prescribed an antibiotic. A week later, her lungs were full of fluid and they had to rush her to the hospital. Her blood oxygen levels had fallen below seventy and she was delirious, resisting all attempts to intubate, so they had to strap her down until they could purposefully sedate her into a paralytic coma. Her kidneys went first and her lungs, under constant pressure from the ventilator, were close behind, collapsing twice during the third week and blowing her up like a balloon. She looked like she weighed four hundred pounds, and stretch marks covered her body from her face and neck to her ankles.

Chris Eaton was told he might have to decide between saving her and saving the baby, and he told them to save her at all costs. They could always make another baby. But there was only one her.

After five weeks, while still in the coma, Julie's lungs collapsed for the third time, and the baby's fetal heart rate plummeted. With all choices now removed, Chris Eaton's son was delivered by Caesarean after only twenty-nine weeks in the womb. His hands were so tiny and perfect, but his own airways were too blocked to admit a breathing tube, a side-effect of the drugs they'd been using to keep Julie alive. He lived only nine minutes and made only one sustained monosyllabic sound. Julie died the next morning.

Her grandfather died shortly after turning eighty, asleep in his bed, with his toupée on the nightstand and the bedroom door locked tightly against "the children." This was despite the fact that they'd all grown up and moved out and had children of their own, from whom they likely kept their own secrets. It was only from the mortician that they would discover his baldness, when he rushed from the embalming room to meet them, and their father's scalp was dangling from his wrist, the ample bangs caught in the pin of his heirloom watch, when he reached to shake their hands.

It's surely from her grandfather that Chris Eaton has adopted the need for routine. On that last night, he did the same things he did on every night of his life since he'd married her grandmother, performing the same ritual for the past fifty-four years, nearly nineteen and a half thousand times, minus his six months of service in World War II, the occasional business trip, the nights he camped with the boys in the back yard and taught them to tie knots, the evenings before her grandmother's birthdays when he feigned insomnia so he could set up his surprise for her in the morning, the few nights after he had had his first heart attack and was recuperating in hospital from his "routine" bypass surgery (he'd performed the first one in North Carolina himself, in 1953, when the chances of survival had been estimated much lower), the nights she had spent with her daughter-in-law when all of her kids fell ill at the same time, and his thrice-yearly fishing trips with their eldest son (her father). They watched the news together, drank a cup of lemon tea, brushed their teeth, complained about immigration, changed into their pajamas and he gave one final rant on the health detriments of drinking milk past childhood before turning out the light.

When her grandmother woke up the next morning, she discovered he'd stopped breathing.

"I can't think of anything sadder than waking up one morning and realizing the person you love most in the world no longer exists. That he's passed away when you weren't even paying attention."

But, of course, the more she thought about it, the more it seemed like the best way to go, so peacefully that he didn't even wake her up. And the last thing they did was follow the rule they set up on the first night of their honeymoon: to never go to sleep without a kiss on the lips. "Honestly, I don't know how long it would take me to go pick up that phone and call the hospital. You know? Knowing that was the last time I'd ever get to lie there with you again…"

She and Laurent had still not succeeded in getting pregnant. Plus recently she had started throwing up for no apparent reason. She would be fine, sitting at the computer in her underwear, when her entire mid-section seized up, and a violent thrust of nausea swept everything up into her chest. She ran to the washroom, threw up (four dry heaves and one shot of syrupy bile), and then curled up on the couch to wait for him to come home. Her doctor assured her it was still probably nothing, maybe just stress, which she'd been under a lot lately with the death of her father, but she also recommended another ultrasound and a stomach x-ray just to make sure.

This time the ultrasound technician said, "I use a condom."

"What?"

"On the instrument. For your protection."

But what was she being protected from? Wasn't the problem already inside her? Why hadn't they used it last time? The technician covered the condom and transducer with more Vaseline and pushed it inside her. Chris Eaton took deep breaths and held them, rolled on to her side, returned to her back, then walked down the hallway to wait outside the x-ray room. "Drink this fast," the x-ray technician said with the lights out. She sucked the chalky paste through a straw, which tasted vaguely like medicine she used to take as a child, and five minutes later she was done.

They told her to drink lots of water. What they didn't tell her was that her bowel movements for the next few days would come out completely white; mushy albino turds that only reinforced her fear that she was suffering from some kind of stomach or bowel cancer.

Nevertheless, the tests came back fine. She had a slightly herniated esophagus, which might explain the nausea, but her previous cysts had not returned. And nothing seemed to have spread to her uterus or colon, which had eventually taken the life of both her mother and grandmother. They were so relieved. They celebrated at their favorite restaurant. They bought a new crib and screwed on the floor next to it. But then that relief faded and again, they stopped having sex. It was the summer and they'd decided to save energy by dumping the air conditioner. And in the early days of July, they slid across each other like melting icebergs, falling with large splashes when they got out of bed in the morning for work. Once, she tried rubbing his leg under the restaurant table, sliding higher, and he pulled away. For a while, she even suspected he was having an affair. Then, she walked in on him while he was fondling himself in the washroom, and he let her feel the lump for herself.

The doctors said that testicular cancer was actually more common than breast cancer. Highly treatable. Low risk. Near a hundred per cent success rate. (These were terms they actually used. They said them almost without thinking. At any treatment facility, the most commonly used tool is vocabulary.) On closer inspection, however, his lump had already metastasized into his retroperitoneal lymph nodes, so they admitted him to the hospital immediately, removed the left testis and lymph node through an incision in the groin, then set him up for four rounds of BEP chemotherapy, which made all the hair on his body fall out until his skin seemed somehow unfamiliar to her, like some kind of beached whale on the couch watching illegally downloaded episodes of British sitcoms. Occasionally he would even leaf through a novel or two, and before all expectations, he was back at work. He was a real fighter, the doctor said. A real fighter. And no worries, they should still be able to have those kids they wanted, one testicle should handle the job nicely on its own. They weren't entirely out of the woods, of course, but the first monthly tests came back clean. It looked like they had managed to get the whole thing.

Then, in the second month following the surgery, they discovered increased levels of neuron-specific enolase and human chorionic gonadotropin in his blood, and the CT scans confirmed that the cancer had spread to his left lung and a portion of his pectoral muscle.

Another operation.

Another strong recovery.

Three months after that, he started getting his own stomach pain.

She kissed him before he went to sleep.

They fell in love. They got married. And after a four-year residency in the colorectal unit of the Cleveland Clinic, she left the practical field to teach in the new Associate Degree Nursing Program at Hartnell College back in Salinas, California, introducing the first courses for enterostomal therapy in the state. Her husband, who was a distant cousin of the Kroger family, sold his father's store to the grocery magnate in the funeral home parking lot, and spent most of the mid-sixties in Ohio with a hefty salary and not much to do but golf and put on weight. But those years were also some of Kroger's finest, increasing their annual sales by another billion, so he was able to land another cushy job as Director of West Coast Marketing for Dole Food Company, Inc., where his greatest challenge was convincing a fast food nation that it was important to eat something besides processed meat and the occasional cheese slice. He helped initiate the national "5 A Day" program, aimed theoretically at curbing the rise of American obesity but really designed to launch more Dole products off the shelves. Before long, Chris Eaton had been appointed Director of the program, and was becoming heavily sought-after as a guest lecturer, across California and the rest of the country, on the importance of nursing in the nation's failing healthcare plan.

She received the Erica Harden Excellence in Teaching Award.

She held an executive position briefly with the American Nurses Association.

In her late-fifties, she even picked up the guitar again.

Then, after she retired in 2000 after thirty-two years, she and her husband took a trip to Washington State. They'd taken a short hike from the Illahee Park ranger station to the fishing dock on Puget Sound, intrigued by the half-dozen Vietnamese casting out at low tide. "What are we hoping for?" her husband asked jokingly, winded from the five-minute downhill trek. And one of the women, in a t-shirt that read *Hockey is my life*, showed him her overflowing bucket of squid.

"I only catch three," laughed another elderly woman without taking her eyes from the water. "She the Squid Queen!"

"You can fish for squid?" He was amazed. He pushed his finger against the squid's gelatinous shell. His eyes were like smoky forests. Or tropical storms. Clouded and wet.

"I eat whole thing. But my husband, he American. He no eat head. Only calamari."

They watched the women fish for at least a half hour, under her husband's assertion they'd see at least one catch. They'd walked past a state park information sign that said Puget Sound was home to the largest octopuses in the world, and so the potential for action was definitely there ("The age-old struggle between Vietnamese women and octopi," he chuckled). Her husband sat down on the end of the ramp and fanned himself with his hat. He was sweating more than normally. They caught nothing. Every ten minutes, they'd also retrieve an empty crab trap from the bottom, completely unaware of the dozens of crab perched on the dock's legs directly behind them, just below the surface of the water.

The next morning she called the ambulance when she couldn't wake him. His blood pressure had risen to an astonishing level, and the doctors in Seattle were unsure of how to proceed. Coronary stents relieved some of the stress on his heart, and his blood pressure returned to normal for a few days. He was sitting up in bed and laughing ("Whoo, that was a close one!"). He was even deemed healthy enough to return to Salinas. But then another artery system gave up on him, this time closer to the brain, and they rushed him to Oakland where a circulatory specialist was flown in to help.

That's where he died, and the plague began.

He began to think that he'd made all the wrong choices in life. How else could one explain it? From childhood's hour, he felt, he dreamt, that he had not been as others were, that he was drawn, from every depth of good and ill, towards some mystery that he could not quite reach. Or rather, he had always thought he was being pulled towards some greater destiny, and in his mind's eye, from that same hour of infancy, he had always imagined himself to be sure what that destiny was. He was going to be a famous musician. He had told his mother so. But then he often questioned it, often wondered what it might be like, if maybe he might have been happier, or even as content, if he weren't so driven. He even quit on several occasions (the longest stretch, back when he left Strange Brew: nearly two years without even picking up his guitar; the shortest: one night while he was passed out on his bass player's couch), but he was always lured back, like a fish on a line, whether by a North American tour, the chance to open for one of his idols, the offer to perform as part of the house band for Breakfast Television, an invitation to collaborate with a Baroque orchestra, or some form of guilt or obligation to one of his bandmates, who had given up a great job for this, always having his decisions made for him, by his art, an experience with which he imagined his hero, Hornet Cisa, must have been similarly well acquainted.

Hornet Cisa was one of the most popular and most decorated athletes in British history, winning championships both at home and internationally. He was on record as being the favourite athlete of Queen Elizabeth herself, not to mention Prime Minister Callaghan, and his matches against top challengers regularly drew upwards of eighteen million viewers. There was even talk of a children's television show using Hornet Cisa as a character, until the events of the early-eighties changed everything, and he was basically forced to leave the country.

From Hornet (a.k.a. Shirley) Cisa's childhood hour, he was obviously destined for greatness on the sporting field. His father, who would have made a name for himself in the sport of fell running if people in that sport did such things, took one look at the boy's feet and declared him the second coming of Dixie Dean or Ten Goal Payne. His mother, meanwhile, was not a sportsman herself, and had always prayed for a girl to keep her company when her husband was off competing, so she named the boy Shirley anyway and signed him up for things like dance classes and gymnastics. This resulted in an educational tug-o-war that existed throughout Cisa's youth, as his mother and father alternately signed him up for rugby, swimming, rowing, knitting, etc. For many years he excelled at all of them, threatening or even breaking records set by boys twice his age. To the horror of his father, however, his main love was gymnastics, to which his long, lean body was particularly adept.

Already a bit of a local celebrity at the age of ten, towering over the other boys in his under-12 leagues, Shirley Cisa's path in life seemed set. Perhaps it was. Spotted by a scout named Ian Chevston-Darra, he became the youngest boy ever drafted by Tottenham Hotspur, and was whisked away from his parents to train with the team outside London. With Chevston-Darra also taking on the job of managing Cisa's career, the boy was soon seen on the covers of all of the big national publications, usually in some sort of amusing combination of sports, like kicking a soccer ball while doing the rings, in the water pushing his rowing shell, or executing a vault over a real horse. It was generally felt that when he was old enough he might go to that year's Olympics and take home multiple gold in multiple sports. Some people had bets on Mexico in '68. Some even joked that the country could save money by just sending Cisa as the entire team.

Then, at the age of fourteen, he hit a growth spurt. At fifteen, he hit another one. By eighteen, it was generally accepted that he would keep growing forever. Without an ounce of fat on his body, he was becoming too heavy to ride a horse, too heavy to row, probably too heavy to swim. Tottenham's coach, the Armenian T. C. Herosian, came to Chevston-Darra and suggested Cisa might now be too tall for the quick stops and starts of football. And although his tumbling floor routine was a gorgeous thing to behold, the British squad was afraid that he didn't have the right body type to achieve top style points at an Olympic level any more, and they cut him with only a year to go until Mexico.

Naturally, this came as a blow to both Cisa and his manager, who by this time had quit his job with the Spurs to guide Shirley's career full time. The Olympics had held the lucrative promise of multiple advertising and sponsorship deals, enough for them both to live comfortably for at least the next ten years with proper re-investment, probably longer. But nothing, as yet, had been signed. Trying to capitalize on his monstrous size, and desperate to regroup for the '72 Games in Munich, Chevston-Darra started Cisa in a new sport called powerlifting. Similar to classical weightlifting, it involved the movement of heavier and heavier objects, but rather than jerking the dumbbell over one's head, it involved shorter displays of strength, like the bench press and squats. And despite it being less regulated, and largely looked down upon by traditionalists and Eastern Bloc countries, it was gaining rapid popularity in the West, where the IOC hoped to increase viewership. They were interested in heroes, they told Cisa when he gave a display for them in Lausanne. But apparently not interested enough to include it in Munich, caving to Eastern pressure and rejecting a combined bid from Great Britain and the United States for its inclusion. In any case, Cisa would not have been able to compete, having torn his right pectoral muscle trying to bench 300 kg, which put an end to his powerlifting as well.

The only thing left for him after that was professional wrestling, which at the very least had started gaining audiences through a weekly television broadcast called *World of Sport*. And this was where Shirley Cisa would finally find his true fame, as The Hornet, in his trademark black-and-yellow-striped unitard, eventually holding both the regular British Wrestling Federation (BWF) and BWF Intercontinental Championship belts at the same time, as well as briefly sitting as the reigning champ of the American Wrestling Association (AWA) under the name Inert Chaos, leader of an elite team of international heels known as The Antihero Corps. His matches against top challengers like Bert Assirati, Rich A. "Horseface" Stone, Big Daddy and Giant Haystacks (who would also go on to fight in the American World Championship Wrestling [WCW]) were some of the biggest sporting events of the seventies, hands down. His move to the U.S. was noted by North American fans as one of the main causes of the brief resurgence of the AWA. But his wrestling career ended abruptly on April 9, 1986, the day he made the move that also destroyed the career of the young Sean Hicort.

***

Of course, he nearly ended his own career about a year-and-a-half into it. Due to his size (finally settling in at six-foot-nine with a 72-inch chest and 27-inch biceps), the British Federation had set him up from the beginning as a bruiser and a loser. To witness the fall of something so huge and magnificent: it could have made him a solid attraction for decades. But he was also a wrestler's wrestler, capitalizing on his gymnastics background to pull off some of the most impressive moves in BWF history, including a mind-bending 630 Senton Splash before losing to Bert Assirati on that man's route to his first championship crown. He was also getting to be known as a bit of a loose cannon, exemplified in spectacular fights like his '71 match against Killer Karlson (a.k.a. Göran Carlson, but the Federation promoters felt the K would look more menacing and a first name that was ostensibly pronounced *urine* definitely had to go), in which, rumor has it, he was supposed to have lost but instead broke a startled Karlson's arm and forced the crying man to submit. The crowd, who had come to expect The Hornet to lose, leapt to their feet in a standing ovation, while behind the scenes Chevston-Darra was able to successfully run damage control to the point where they were not sued by the BWF or Karlson's team. Miraculously, C-D was able to convince the writers to spin this in a way – "Hornet Cisa starts winning?! It's the sports story of the year!" – finally giving The Hornet a shot at the belt against current champ Charles Windsor. After a year of solid jobbing to men with half his skill, even if he were to lose once again, this would still be a coup.

With this small taste of success, however, Cisa let himself go. Suddenly, the tables were turned, and other men were jobbing for him, making sure he looked good before his title match with Windsor. So he stopped working out. He took up drinking and carousing. In fact, one of his favorite things to do before the press caught wind and started writing stories about it was to go out on the town with a friend from his weightlifting days, Precious Mackenzie, a black South African who was only 4' 11" but who had recently won the under-62 kg weight division at the Commonwealth Games in Jamaica. Cisa would quiet the bar by waving his arms, then boisterously claim that he could and would lift the tiny man over his head "if one of you will give us free beer all night." Inevitably, due to his renewed celebrity, someone would recognize him as Hornet Cisa, laugh out loud, and say, "I was there when you tossed The Blonde Adonis out of the ring!", then point at Precious and say, "If *he* can lift *you*, I'll buy you both dinner, too," and the two of them would then polish off a keg between them.

Pulling this trick almost nightly in the weeks leading up to the match, Cisa gained nearly twenty-five pounds. Cisa invited the press to watch him train, but he forgot the arranged time, and the photo on the cover of *The Guardian* showed Cisa passed out drunk in the corner of the weight room. Chevston-Darra was nowhere to be found. Cisa was surly. His skin had begun to yellow, and it hung off him like a blouse. Charles Windsor (a.k.a. The Prince of Wails) was conversely good-looking and charismatic, and according to Windsor's later biography, *The Windsor Knot: Charles Windsor's Stranglehold on the BWF*, Cisa's pulse was measured at the pre-match weigh-in at more than twice its normal rate. The doctors nearly called it right there, but with so many rabid fans already in the stadium, they figured this might be more dangerous to Cisa than just letting him fight.

Cisa knew the game. He had agreed to lose the match around the sixteen-minute mark, and in return they would create a ridiculous Intercontinental title for him to win in the future. So why bother putting too much into it? He and Windsor had little respect for each other. He considered Windsor a pretty boy without talent and had no interest in making him look good. Windsor, who really did have some nobility in him, found Cisa's rebellion crass and classless, and had decided to take this opportunity to not only beat The Hornet, but to make sure Cisa knew who was really in control here. Throughout the match, The Prince taunted him, quietly bragging about how he owned him, calling him fat, lazy, impotent, homosexual. In the opening speeches, Windsor repeatedly referred to The Hornet by his given name, and this continued throughout the match, with The Prince bellowing "Come and get it, Shirley!" or "Who's your big daddy, Shirley?" from across the ring. At sixteen minutes, Cisa refused to be pinned, breaking The Prince's signature move and applying one of his own called The European Sting, pressing his chin into Windsor's back and pulling back on both arms. It seemed to most people in attendance that this was the end of The Prince's reign. But Cisa seemed to navigate him closer to the ropes on purpose, and Windsor was able to get a foot on them and have the clutch broken. With punishing hold after punishing hold, Cisa prolonged the match for an additional thirty-eight minutes, shouting "What's my name?! What's my name?!" until The Prince's eyes were nearly swollen shut and his body could barely move.

Then, just as suddenly, Hornet Cisa slipped awkwardly on some of Windsor's blood, hit his head on the mat and The Prince was able to crawl to his comatose body and pin him.

Some say they could see Cisa grinning as he was carried from the arena on a stretcher. The Prince, hugging the title belt to his hip, was booed all the way to the dressing room. Within the next six months, The Hornet had claimed his promised inaugural Intercontinental Championship as well as the BWF Championship, both of which he held for the next eleven years.

* * *

Although The Hornet was definitely the king of the BWF in the seventies, professional wrestling in the UK was still a fairly marginal arena, nothing like the American wrestling spotlight that would emerge in the mid-eighties. It was difficult at the best of times to make ends meet, and most of the men had to find second jobs during the week.

While becoming a bouncer or bodyguard seemed an obvious choice, it was incredible how many drunks wanted to pick fights with them, already claiming that the events were staged and that they weren't nearly as strong as they looked. So several of the top stars found work in the trucking and oil industries or stocking shelves on night shifts. Taking a different tack, The Hornet joined the British National Service, which mostly just involved reporting to the base on a regular basis for basic training (which helped him keep in shape, anyway), and possibly stacking sand bags along the River Don during flood season.

Unfortunately for him, far across the world, Argentina was going through a similar economic crisis. Its citizens were growing restless, and tended to turn their frustration on the military dictatorship they felt was living large while they starved. To distract them with national pride, the Argentine leader, General Leopoldo Galtieri, sent mercenaries disguised as scrap metal merchants to raise their flag on South Georgia, a practically uninhabited and entirely inhospitable island Argentina had theoretically claimed around 1926 but was still occupied, inasmuch as a few Antarctic scientists and support staff could be considered a true occupation, by Britain. A terse radio transmission from the UK kindly urged an Argentinean apology and retreat. Instead, Galtieri ordered his men into the Falkland Islands, too.

Suddenly, England was at war. Cisa, despite making his living as a fighter, was a pacifist, and even while signing his enlistment papers had assumed he would never find himself in this worst-case scenario. He prayed, due to the islands' remote location, that the battle would be purely aerial, that they would merely drop a few bombs on the South Americans and everything would just fall into place. But when that strategy failed and the Argentineans managed to sink the HMS Sheffield, the British called in the infantry. Cisa went AWOL, turning up a few weeks later at the home of an ex-girlfriend. He was found guilty of a felony against the state and sentenced to five years in prison.

By the time he was eventually released on good behavior, fans in the UK would no longer accept him. The press had not been kind. Even his manager dumped him the moment he shirked his national duty. Besides, the popularity of British wrestling had been on such a steady decline in his absence – *World of Sports* had been cancelled the year before Cisa's parole – so there wasn't much to even come back to. Due to some connections with another ex-wrestler, he got some work moving barrels of oil at a refinery in Pembrokeshire, Wales, and would subsidize his income by lifting unused coking pots over his head for tips.

Then one day he received a phone call from the United States. The AWA, who had recently come under new promotional management and had already given a break to his friend Haystacks, were losing the ratings game to the fledgling World Wrestling Federation (WWF) and had to come up with some new tactics to save face. First and foremost, they told him, they needed to create a champion that was not the son of the Association's old owner; someone with real skill and presence, unlike the muscle-bound goons they had now, someone who people could look up to, someone kids would want to grow up to be. Would he be interested in helping make this happen? Yes, he said, yes he would. Then he should get on the next plane to New York (or rather the first truck to Praa Sands, take the bus to Penzance, travel by rail to Plymouth Station, walk two minutes past the Stone Chair – just one of Plymouth's twenty war memorials, on which Sir Francis Drake sits, a small silver spoon dangling from his right thumb and index finger, his left hand over his face, bereaving the fact that he could only plunder all of the gold from the Spanish in Panama but had to leave the silver behind because it was too heavy – to the city centre for another bus to Heathrow's central bus station and then another three or four minutes on the underground, and *then* a plane) and they'd get started right away.

He did.

When they greeted him at JFK, they all realized their miscommunication. The AWA's head writer, a rake-thin man who had once wrestled under the names Chase and Nitro and who had been hired by the Association's new owners to save the franchise, had no intention of making Hornet Cisa his new hero. No, they already had someone in mind for that: a young unknown by the name of Sean Hicort. Cisa's role was to help them create a scenario whereby Hicort's introduction would be more believable and embraced, as though his arrival in the AWA, and perhaps the entire world of professional wrestling, were to come as some sort of deliverance; an emancipation, if you will. Capitalizing on the incident with Killer Karlson and his broken arm, as well as Cisa's several years in prison, they wanted to turn him into the biggest heel the world had ever seen, named Inert Chaos because he was unpredictable and, due to his size, nearly impossible to move. They would make him unbeatable. He and his minions, dubbed The Antihero Corps, would take control of every aspect of the AWA, from owning every belt to the intimidation of Association management. Inert Chaos would be the one who decided who fought whom. Inert Chaos would be the one to impose penalties and sanctions – or more importantly not impose them – on dirty play. In short, they would make Inert Chaos the most feared and hated man in the world. So when Hicort did finally defeat him, overcoming all odds and restoring order to the world, they could ride the wave of his popularity for years.

As he had done so many times in the past, Shirley Cisa did as he was told. Both characters were introduced in St. Petersburg, Florida. They played up Cisa's release from jail, tugging him to the ring in chains, like a reluctant King Kong. A countdown was started. A bell went off. His chains fell to the mat. And he stood motionless in the centre of the ring as the unknown Hicort tried to haul him down. Cisa didn't even fight back, just stood there, suddenly wondering what he'd gotten himself into. Even at the point when he was supposed to pin Hicort, setting up this ultimate rivalry for its ultimate ending six months later, he remained still. Sean Hicort, immature, full of testosterone and frustrated, decided to break with the plan and try pinning Cisa instead, and when that didn't work he walked around the big Brit yelling at him. The crowd, having been prepped for explosive violence, began to boo. The referee looked to the sidelines for guidance only to receive a shrug. People started throwing popcorn at them, then programs, then drinks. And just as the referee was about to call it, a muscle finally rippled in Inert Chaos's back, and he broke Hicort's nose so violently that several people in the front row went home with the trophy of fresh blood. Breaking the referee's nose, too, Cisa then left the ring.

Over the next six months, as heels of every foreign nationality joined The Antihero Corps, Cisa's new legend continued to grow. In Cincinnati, people claimed he forced Louden Swain, The King of Pain, to submit, and then snapped Swain's pinky finger just for fun. At a draw in Salinas, California, Cisa dislocated Randy Robinson's shoulder with a splash off the top ropes while he was still lying face-down on the concrete. According to rumour, Inert Chaos left a trail of broken bodies behind him. And rather than dispel any of this, because it was definitely all good for press, the AWA had various wrestlers play with splints on their hands, or with complicated wraps, faking injuries to play it all up. Leon "The Lion" Leone, a very popular face at the time, was even removed from a bill in Pittsburgh at the last moment with an announcement that Chaos had smashed into his dressing room before the match and broken three of his ribs.

Then, at a marquee event at Madison Square Gardens, Hicort returned, his nose totally healed, and declared himself the Association's new sheriff. He was taking the law into his own hands. He renamed himself The Supreme Hicort and became a constant presence at all matches, often thundering into one at midpoint to rescue a belt for Good. It worked. Crowds continued to grow. By the next spring, Hicort had managed to defeat – not in any sanctioned matches, of course, because Inert Chaos would not allow him to fight, so he had to supposedly sneak past security at each arena, sometimes tearing his disguise from himself as he sprang from a wheelchair in the audience – every member of The Antihero Corps, until not even Inert Chaos could refuse the call of Hicort's challenges. The match was set for April 9, 1986.

**

Many times between that day and the fight, Shirley Cisa thought about calling it off. He thought about the freedom. He thought about waking up without cuts and bruises all over his body. He thought about losing some weight and maybe even becoming attractive to the opposite sex again, instead of just being feared. He thought about maybe entering a bar and having the staff know what he wanted, not because he was a celebrity but because he was a regular. He was their friend. Shirley Cisa thought about the money. He thought about, or tried to think about, things in his life, as a child, that he had wanted more than anything: toys, to live in a castle, a sibling to boss around, a pet. Then Shirley Cisa thought about his parents, how he had already disappointed them. He thought about Chevston-Darra and he thought about his fans.

Alone in his apartment, surely overlooking something spectacular, Shirley Cisa thought about a writing assignment he'd been given in the fifth grade. He'd been a handful to say the least, always acting out, telling jokes, talking back. And then his teacher had asked his entire class to write a story. Write a story about something strange that happened on the way home from school, she said. Write about whatever you want. And no one had ever read it. He thought about the aptitude tests they'd taken in grade seven that said he might be best suited as an astronaut or a waiter and he thought about how it might have been nice to have been either.

Hornet Cisa thought long and he thought hard, over breakfast and lunch, and midday snacks and then dinner, about his life. He thought about how he'd never made a real decision, not one real decision in his life. And he thought about how he'd never been happy. Happy for other people, sure, but never happy for himself. And finally he decided, when the day came, that he would not fight. There were contracts that could ruin him financially, but he didn't care. He would not fight. He could not win. Because even if he *won* he did not win. He and Sean Hicort were not enemies. They were the same. The exact same person. Even their names were just anagrams of one another. He was just wrestling his own inner demons. He decided he would walk away and never wrestle again. He decided he would no longer allow others to make decisions for him. And he decided, from that day forward, that he would be the one to shape his own life. It would be like his birthday. He felt like an entirely new person.

Meanwhile, outside his apartment with the spectacular view, the excitement and expectation of the fight continued to build. Ads ran on every network and huge billboards with his face were erected overlooking New York and Los Angeles. He refused to give any more interviews and no one cared because they'd essentially invented him anyway. He was a legend now and could thus be written about without facts or concern over contradictions. The arena sold out a month before the date and people slept with their tickets beneath their pillows, dreaming.

Then the day came. The lead-off matches of that evening were booed from start to finish. The crowd in Los Angeles was there for the main attraction. For blood. Outside the stadium, hawkers had sold fake vials of it, along with mock casts and slings commemorating some of Inert Chaos's more famous fights. Inside, the AWA had hired actors to dress as paramedics, making violence seem more likely, and had provided the front row seats with sheets of plastic to put across their laps. The audience was also filled with countless cowboy hats and deputy sheriff badges, not to mention thousands of Supreme Hicort-branded gavels: what proved to be an unfortunate promotion device given to the first fans to arrive. The first was launched at the ring during the second bout between a young Terry Bollea and The Cuban Assassin, and by the fourth match-up, a full-blown riot forced the promoters to shut off the lights and call in the police. The rest of the bill, including Cisa's fight with Hicort, was cancelled. In the chaos, someone ran off with the money from the box office. And months later, once everything had settled, the courts ordered the promoters to pay everyone back. The AWA declared bankruptcy, and without a supreme enemy to defeat, Hicort's own coltish legend faltered in the gates. When everyone eventually jumped ship to the WWF, the Supreme Hicort was not made an offer, and he disappeared from the wrestling radar entirely.

* * *

After that day:

- Sean Hicort (whose real name wasn't even Hicort but Smith) made several attempts at acting, insisting that his agent only seek out serious roles but only landing two credited parts as *Thug #1* and *Goon at Bar with Bat*.
- The man formally known as Nitro disappeared, and was not heard of again until police tracked him down to his hometown of East Chariston, Kentucky, where he incorrectly surmised no one would rat him out for his sudden financial good luck. The final showdown with police resulted in two deaths, one of which was his own.
- When the Berlin Wall fell in late-1989, T. C. Herosian saw the opportunity of a free Armenia and returned to his home an hour south of Yerevan to enlist in the New Armenian Army. He was killed no more than a year later, one of only five Armenian casualties in a bloody shootout with Soviet Internal Security Forces at the Yerevan train station.
- After retiring from wrestling management, Ian Chevston-Darra left the UK and moved to Canada, where he began recruiting for the men's national soccer team and

helped them qualify for the 1986 World Cup. He then settled in Alaska, where he took up dogsledding, until he fell asleep in the middle of the Iditarod, and the sub-zero temperatures froze the glass of his goggles to one of his eyes, partially blinding himself on one side when they were hastily torn away. It was perhaps the greatest testament to his skills as an agent that he was then able to turn this feat of ineptitude into a sponsorship from a rifle sights company called Aarhos & de Vart Inc., based in Odense, Denmark, with the campaign slogan *En øje nemlig en øje*.

- Shirley Cisa retired from wrestling for good, suffered a stroke in 1993 and died several years later. A full obituary was run in the December 6th issue of *The London Times*.

His dreams had become even more troubled. He dreamed about failure and death. He dreamed about war. He dreamed that every relationship was measured by the finite number of times a couple can willingly have sex, and when that odometer finally clicked over, someone snapped out of it. And he didn't want it to happen this time. Everything was so perfect. He wanted everything to stay the same.

He dreamed that he was able to make time stand still. And the stillness was so beautiful that he didn't notice how it was affecting her.

He dreamed they took on the care of a farmstead in Cape Rosier, near North Hadvat, a museum of sorts, dedicated to living without electricity or running water or leisure. And he dreamed of a grey fog that settled over their pastoral home like a force shield, until not even the passing of time could enter. It was a fortress, sealed off entirely from the outside world, impermeable and impenetrable, save for a tiny undetectable hole that let the remaining time leak out. And it leaked out slowly, with a hiss, and they were drawn further and further from the present reality.

He dreamed their love was perfect, and so was unaware, as they both were of the time hole, of how miserable she was, untouched for so long, feeling unwanted and unwantable, rolling over at night to cuddle him and being greeted by a gritty tension, his simmering fear that she would want to make love to him again and the perfection would be over. He was unaware of how he was treating her unfairly, simply because he was tired, or hungry, or sought ridiculous things, and he dreamed that the farm took on her blossoming state of depression. Their crops failed. Their animals faltered. There were rumors of bandits. One night, he was sure he heard someone out rustling in the garden. He'd found a small squadron of foil plates in a drawer in the kitchen, and rather than tossing them out in disgust, he strung them up around the garden's periphery. He wasn't entirely clear if this went against the rules, but he was pretty sure that tossing them in a landfill would be worse. He kept his gun close to the bed and lay awake holding his breath so he might hear the sound again.

Other times he would dream about the accident, about his collapsed lung, the fractured facial bones, his shoulder, how most of his ribs were broken at least once, the doctors inserting a tracheotomy tube to help his lungs heal, and various other tubes for feeding, draining, inspecting, other things, immersing him in a huge tube of thick liquid to control the swelling, which the doctors seemed quite happy with despite it taking four days for the swelling to go down so they could actually operate, fusing his spinal chord with metal bars, a bone graft at the point of injury, a twenty pound halo attached to his skull in the hopes that the first two vertebrae might recover, and still, even after being confined to his bed for over a month, he was the only patient in the ward who could feed himself, bathe himself, dress himself and wipe his own ass.

He dreamed about being able to walk, of more operations, with more tubes that weren't inserted into his regular orifices but jabbed directly into his legs; when he rolled over in his sleep, they would catch on the side railing and be torn out. He dreamed of being able to feel again.

And Chris Eaton thought about his life, and the goals that he had set for himself as a teenager, the goals he had told his friends about, including the names he planned to give his children, so there was no way he could back down from them, even after the crash. He dreamed of the crash. He dreamed he was dead. And the rest of his life was just dreams. And the dreams had dreams. And the dreams of his dreams also had dreams. And still he was unable to attain those goals. All of his time was spent chasing those goals. And if he managed to hook one and reel it in, it was just replaced by another, so that he was never happy, never even hopeful. It wouldn't even have mattered if his goals had been different, because then only the specifics would be changed, and the seeking would still sit haughtily at his side, like a jealous friend or even worse, on his chest, until he could no longer breathe. Like he was drowning.

He came across another Chris Eaton in the newspaper. In the morning. After his run and before breakfast. Still sweating despite the shower and five minutes of aiming his pits at the air conditioner, despite the fact that the temperature rarely got above twenty-four degrees centigrade in this place, despite walking most of the way today because of the clicking in his left knee. *The Financial Times* featured an article on Multimedia Messaging on mobile phones. *The Wall Street Journal*, with its new colour look, was covering the investigation and guilty plea of Arthur Andersen's David Duncan, the top accountant overseeing the Enron fiasco, none of which could be good for anyone in his line of business. He had to read those for work. But he also got *The Examiner*, *The Courier*, *The Manx Independent* – the locals. It was his way of integrating. The more he knew about the place, the more he could contribute to the coffee talk at work and the sooner he'd be accepted. But there he was reading a story about a young boy from Amherst, New Hampshire. In America. His brother had been killed recently in Fallujah while escorting private contractors to a demolished power plant. Iraqi citizens had dragged his body through the streets and strung him up from a bridge rail over the Euphrates. Just as the first grenade had ripped his brother's feet to shreds beneath their s u v, this American boy – the one the article was really about (news is never news without hope, particularly during a war) – had kicked a record fifth field goal against his school's crosstown rivals at Pelham. In the type of ceremony one would only see in America (they had symbolism down to a science over there, had practically replaced truth with it), they had buried the game ball the next week in the end zone.

The American boy was also named Chris Eaton. He smiled at the coincidence. What was it like to be a child? He could barely remember. They seemed so hideous and menacing when he saw them on the street, throwing tantrums in grocery stores, at the beach, their chests immeasurably frail and emaciated, and their arms projecting forward like the wings of bats. Arms that whipped around like they were full of bees. Fingers you could practically see through. Always crouching, hugging themselves. They could barely stop touching themselves, these kids. Even his days studying law at Birmingham, where he likewise couldn't stop touching himself, seemed so far away. Or the several years he spent working in London and Gibraltar before moving here to the Isle of Man in 1991 to set up an office responsible for the offshore tax operations for businesses in London, Dublin, Lisbon and the Virgin Islands. Thirteen years and the locals still considered him a *comeover*. From *across*. He and his wife. It was the nature of small communities. There were some bloodlines, like the Callows and Kerruishes, that went back centuries. His own children would probably still be considered outsiders, if he even still planned to have them. His wife. He could barely even remember what had made him fall in love with her in the first place. But being a stranger to his co-workers and his wife was nowhere near as unsettling as being a stranger to himself. And if he couldn't remember why he ever loved her, how could he ever hope to remember the person he apparently used to be, the one who might have made that decision to marry her in the first place? They say that the cells of the body are constantly regenerating, and that we are a completely new person every seven to nine years. If that were true, was there really anything that connected him to those past versions of himself any more than to this adolescent child in an Associated Press leftover from across the pond?

* * *

On the date of his birthday, the news was consumed by the story of Julie Eaton. No relation. Nearly a month earlier, on March fourteenth (or perhaps fifteenth), which placed his birthday, the first big news day, twenty-six (-five?) days later, the aforementioned Julie Eaton had received her bank statement detailing her month's transactions and found them to be misrepresented in a most unfortunate way, with fees equaling three and five pounds, respectively, on the eighth and ninth, and yes, as she looked more closely, another on the seventh, for an incredible nine pounds. She decided to complain about it. For weeks she seethed about it to her husband (not Chris Eaton), whose allergies dried his eyes out so significantly that it gave his indifferent glances the illusion of interested stares, which was his curse. For over twenty-one days, she poured out to those thirsty eyes in increasing detail, reliving those three days as if they – the Isle of Man Bank had suddenly become a "they" – had been stalking her for months in order to determine the times when she would have been least likely to notice their subterfuge, gradually pinpointing her exact space in the world when the transactions would have gone through, like the day she must have been at tea with the ladies, or waiting in line at the grocery, until he could stand it no longer and left her a note softly urging her to take it up with someone at their branch.

And so it was, on Chris Eaton's birthday, a Friday, at 10:04 AM, which Julie Eaton thought might beat the rush but also would not leave her seeming desperate, or petty, rather, arguing about seventeen pounds with an undereducated and underpaid teller in her genuine red-striped Chanel jacket (with matching skirt) and replica jewelry (the genuine items located in a safety deposit box somewhere below them), that Julie Eaton entered the Isle of Man Bank in Prospect Hill, followed closely by Per-Arvid Thorsen, in a green-striped replica Abibas hoodie and, hidden in a paper bag in the front pocket, a genuine EM-GE .22-caliber WWII-era starter pistol.

* * *

When Per-Arvid was fourteen in Denmark, he came home from swim class and dropped his gym bag behind the laundry room door. Dinner was pasta with chopped hot dogs, one of his favourites, life was good. But when his father eagled the boy's bloodshot eyes across the dinner table, the result of overzealous pool chlorination, he accused him of smoking pot, and Per-Arvid's mother briefly left the room. With the skin under his left eye split open by his father's wedding ring, Per-Arvid walked to the home of another boy on his team and they immediately took him in. That night, the man he thought was the other boy's father offered him his first joint.

The other boy's "parents" – his mother and her boyfriend – essentially adopted him, with both parties agreeing to say nothing to the authorities, and provided him with the first loving family he had ever had. They fed and housed him and bought him new clothes. They had everything he could ever want, including the latest gaming consoles, and the largest TV. He was happy. He respected them. For the first time in his life, he felt like he was really himself. Within a few months, he was helping his new parents out by making parcel drops and even selling directly to the other kids at his school. They loved him, they said. He was entrusted with storing most of the merchandise in his room, under his bed and in his closet, along with a small handful of semi-automatic weapons. He bragged about this much too often to the other kids, but curiously, he was first arrested for something completely unrelated, trying to saw the head off the large plastic Ronald McDonald on the bench outside the first restaurant in Odense. Because he was a minor, the police basically just threatened to tell his parents, but when he took them home to his new family they discovered everything. His new mother and father, who were well-represented legally, claimed to know nothing and successfully set him up for the fall.

In juvenile lock-up, he learned electronics, and was beaten by the other boys fairly repeatedly, but eventually found some solace in the establishment's boxing programme; not as a fighter, for he surely would have been pummeled even more, he was so much smaller than anyone else in his block, but as a referee. This did not earn respect from the other boys so much as concern, in that anything could get him to unfairly influence a fight. When he was released, he continued to oversee bouts with the Craidan Club in his hometown of Osterhav, near Odense, which was how the starter pistol ended up in his possession, if not how it ended up with him at the bank, on the floor, at the feet of the young security guard, Jem Kelly.

***

Jenken "Jemmy Jem" Kelly – unlike Per-Arvid, who had come to the Isle of Man in the nineties as a gaffer, and then, when the global economy began to tank and both the Irish and British governments began to offer filmmakers greater incentives to shoot films featuring England and Ireland at home, had gotten mixed up with the wrong crowd yet again and begun to oversee illegal Loaghtan sheep fights – was Manx born and raised. He'd never been to a sheep fight, and quite likely didn't even know they existed, so underground was this particular culture, but had, while recently out of high school, gone drinking with some other kids from school, consumed a bit too much, and participated in the brutal beating of a British tourist on The Strand, shattering his eye socket, breaking his nose, jaw and ribs, and collapsing one of his lungs, as Jem later read in the newspaper. Jem was never connected to the beating, but was so shaken and affected by it that he dropped out of classes at the International Business School, spent two years working at a car rental depot, and after speaking with some of the mall security guards, decided to go for a month to London (the only time he'd ever spent off-island) to complete his SIA training. It wasn't supposed to be his shift the day Julie Eaton came in to give a piece of her mind. He had begged his co-worker to switch shifts with him because he needed some extra money to impress one of the tellers, Agneish Lobb, by inviting her out to The King Edward Bay Golf and Country Club. And this was why Agneish was talking to him at the exact moment that Per-Arvid dropped the metal cashbox he'd brought for the teller to insert the ten thousand Manx pounds he'd been hoping to steal with little-to-no fuss, reaching back into his front pouch for reassurance and mistakenly pushing the bagged starter pistol out the other side.

* * *

Clearly to everyone but young, delusional Jem, Ms. Lobb was spoken for, with an unimaginative white gold band on her left ring finger. She was also in the earlier stages of pregnancy, although she had yet to announce it publicly because the branch was not as busy as it had been, and most of the other tellers had completed more training than she had, and she thought she might lose her job if they knew. Nor had she broken the news to her partner, because the child wasn't his. Instead of falling in love and marrying her high school sweetheart, Agneish Lobb had done the reverse, getting engaged at the prom, registering at the Selfridge's, inviting about a hundred immediate family members, and another hundred friends besides, honeymooning in the Maldives, and then falling in love with someone else, a man who had sent her a Nigerian lottery email. She was wise to this trick. She'd been told about it at work by someone who'd read an article in the newspaper. So she replied as a joke, to string the man along as he so obviously had planned to do to her. It would be her little revenge on the world. *This is exciting*, she replied. *I've never won anything before. How do I collect my winnings?* She wasn't about to fall for the trick of providing him with her bank information. She was smarter than that. She would meet him instead. And when he replied to tell her of the ease of a simple bank transfer, she wrote that *I've always dreamed of receiving one of those large novelty cheques*, and *Where can I meet you?*, planning to observe him from the other end of the café, or train station, then snap his picture from afar and maybe stick it on her fridge.

One thing led to another, and when she discovered she was pregnant with the man's baby, she committed her first felony. The Nigerian – he was obviously not Nigerian, born and raised in Sheffield by a waitress and the television – convinced her that no one would notice if she were to shave pennies off the deposits of each person who came to her in the course of a day, then making another lump sum deposit at the day's end to make sure her till balanced out. She was good with numbers like that, able to keep track of this daily tally in her head, and before long, when no one seemed to notice, she became further emboldened and began introducing what appeared to be random user fees, once again shifting all of this money to an account in the Nigerian's name – her own name, he suggested, would arouse too much suspicion – where he could then make honest withdrawals and stash the money in cash back at his apartment. She also transferred everything she thought she could get away with from her own joint accounts. They were sure they were going to get away with it, too. They'd already bought the plane tickets to Panama and were merely waiting for one more week of revenue before making the clean break. When the bag with the pistol fell in front of her, she smiled in that way that only bank tellers can, or flight attendants, or anyone in the service industry who has to wear a suit. Or someone newly in love who feels they have nothing to lose. And she reached down to pick it up.

* * *

At least that was how Chris Eaton imagined it as he watched the story develop on the news, marveling at the attachment he felt to the woman who merely shared his last name. He wondered how all those people came to be in that same place at that same time; like the parking cop across the street when the gun went off, a man by the name of Wilmot Kelly (no relation to Jemmy, which was not nearly as coincidental as Chris Eaton and this woman since there were as many Kellys as mosquitoes over there), who had no doubt been referred to the job by the family's obligatorily boring uncle, one who likely bragged at family gatherings about the freedom of his job, and how he got to work outside, and young Wilmot was the only one who decided to listen, so that, ten years later, he was dropping behind the nearest vehicle for cover, the crest of his hat peeking over the hood when Thorsen glanced out the window, convincing the Dane he was surrounded; or the primary school teacher, in the bank only because his mortgage was coming up for renewal so he'd taken the day off for some hard wrangling, who tried to yell some sense into Young Jem, now all but useless over the prone body of the adulteress Agneish Lobb, instead breaking Thorsen out of his own shock long enough to kabonk the security guard behind the ear with his empty cash box and secure another weapon; the Chief Inspector, reliving his father's life to the note; or the negotiator; or any one of the dozen remaining employees and clients he convinced Thorsen to release, because the bank robber couldn't possibly keep track of them all; as if they were all merely random particles bouncing around, their lives being constantly redirected by contact with other random particles until they all met in this one fatal reaction; as if that moment were the one moment for which they would always be remembered, that everything so far had just been leading up to this.

It was the pistol, though, that Chris Eaton thought about most. In one of the electives he had taken at college, he could recall studying a Spanish entomologist who had, for a time, due to his other research on mythic bugs in Guatemala, lived for several years among an indigenous South American people called the Itza. Though it was not his prime objective, the entomologist documented his observations of the Itza in great detail, especially their peculiar interactions with inanimate objects that he described as "like those of friends and enemies," including the story of one particular savage, named Ieao (they had no consonants in their language, reserving the tongue for bizarre feats of strength and communicating solely through variation in the duration of mouth shapes), whose mother had supposedly died during childbirth – among the Itza, a crime on the child's head – and he had imprinted himself on the burlap sack in which he was carried to the elders for judgment. Now an elder himself, he had spent all of his adult life caring for the well-being of this sack, with all the respect due to one's mother, as laid out in the tribe's matriarchal culture, and while it was considered a village tragedy that she managed to outlive her son, once the old man was put to rest, the burlap sack showed near-instant deterioration and fell completely apart within two weeks.

Here was an inanimate tool that had as large a role to play in this bank tragedy as any of the humans involved, manufactured in Germany in 1934 by Moritz & Gerstenberger, used at the Olympic level the year Per-Arvid was chosen to represent his country as a referee, stored in a box of mementoes for years, and then, after getting caught trying to fix a sheep fight or two, brought to a friend who had attempted to modify the innocent sporting tool for him into a working firearm – an experiment that failed miserably as Agneish Lobb tightened her grip around the paper bag in fear, easily recognizing the shape inside, and it went off in her hands like a grenade.

***

It suddenly struck Chris Eaton that everything he was disgusted him. He did not want to be British. Or white. Or middle-aged. Or a man. He did not want to be married to a beautiful wife, or wealthy, no matter what perks this afforded him. He did not want to have people look up to him, and be responsible for those people. He did not want to be *here*.

He also, to some extent, did not *not* want to be those things. He was quite certain others would look on his lot with envy. It just made him sick, to think that he would wake up every morning and it would always be the same, that he would be himself by default, until he died, because of decisions and actions that he or someone else had already made, as inconsequential as they might have seemed at that moment, and none of it could ever be undone.

The question: What was that one thing he had done to set himself on this path?

And also: What was he going to do about it?

He ran for the school board. He ran for sheriff. He ran for Council. He ran for Senate. He ran as a Republican. He ran as a Democrat. He ran on a platform of smaller class sizes, more school funding and regular meetings with neighbourhood leaders to create a better state-backed prescription drug plan. He positioned himself as "the Green choice" (a double entendre he pushed about being environmentally friendly as well as new to the scene). Hilariously, for his Senate campaign song, he chose a tune by Stina Verda.

From what Chris Eaton could tell, his namesake was a natural. He was charming. People wanted to like him. During the debate at the Suncoast Tiger Bay Club, he followed the Libertarian candidate with this quip: "It's hard to follow a guy who's going to abolish taxes. You win." And he had them in the palm of his hand. He would eventually be backed by the *St. Petersburg Times*, the PCTA-PESPA (the Pinel-

272

las Classroom Teachers Association – Pinellas Educational Support Professional Association), and the Sierra Club.

But of course, he also had only $26,694 in campaign dollars to spend, compared to the incumbent's $223,892, which meant he was fighting TV spots with appearances at the mall, and the only real opportunity he had to shine was at further debates, most of which his opponent just declined to attend. When Chris Eaton seemed to have the man cornered on the subject of his part in relaxing State environmental laws to allow tainted water to be pumped into Florida's underground aquifer, the Republican openly questioned whether Eaton had been around for the primaries, when he'd been forced to defend the same left-wing theories of water contamination against another unsuccessful usurper.

"Same tune, different singer," the incumbent rustled from his podium. "But what should I expect when I'm running against a political opponent who changed his party three times!"

He decided to take a trip. At this point in his life, he was still highly sought after for various fishing shows, not as the host, which would have taken much more conviction, not to mention a full set of teeth, but as the behind-the-scenes consultant who made sure the fish would be caught. He was skilled. He had a connection with the fish, everyone said, that nearly guaranteed a catch; that went beyond that of hunter and prey; that was almost familial; that bordered on the mystical; that no one could explain; which entirely outweighed his increasingly difficult personality. On the road, away from Julie and his daily routines and consuming massive amounts of alcohol, he had trouble sleeping, aggravated often by the remoteness of their shoots, which forced several of the crew to share rooms, or even bunks, in rustic log cabins, and suddenly to his ears, the sound of his own breathing was like a passing train, forcing him to lie as still as possible, so obsessed with quieting and slowing down his breathing that he couldn't relax, eventually becoming so frustrated that he would rise to make coffee, sighing loudly until the rest of them woke and they could start working. Unfortunately, his moods had their own gravitational pulls, sucking the rest of them into states of total inactivity and loss of will, including – it seemed – the fish, until whole days could be wasted in places so beautiful he might otherwise cry. And while most people would travel to such places and return to their families or girlfriends with an indigenous craft or a remarkable stone, or even a hastily nabbed shot glass or discount chocolate from the airport, the others often returned to their home countries wondering if the trip had even happened, the work complete but nothing to really show for it, no memories, no sense of accomplishment, nothing that had changed them for the better or worse.

After the shoots, and away from the pressure of competing with the host, he would be sociable again, and even fun, and they would hit the local establishments and he would apologize for his behaviour and buy a round or two to make up for it. He was funny and charming; well-travelled; and he told good stories, often related to the area in which they were shooting, like the story of Johann Beringer, which he told often, for whatever reason.

***

Johann Bartholomeus Adam Beringer had also taken many trips. At the time of his death he was perhaps one of the most travelled men on the planet. Born in 1667 in the town of Würzburg, Bavaria, Beringer showed a natural early interest in geography. His father, also Johann Beringer, was an apprentice cartographer under the Dutch master Sorric van de Haat with the v o c (or, Vereenigde Oostindische Compagnie), who had recently managed to establish a base camp at the Cape of Good Hope in order to facilitate their expanding spice trade, and while Beringer the Younger was much, much too young to come on any of those voyages, his father promised to take him to Egypt as a cabin boy when he was thirteen, and brought him maps from the various places he'd explored, including: Morocco; Madagascar; the African kingdoms of Kongo, Mutapa, Baguirmi and Lunda; an entire atlas of the continent that he received on his twelfth birthday; and several maps that the elder Beringer had merely invented for his son's amusement, such as a map of the routes to Atlantis, and his map of Heaven (*Accurata Coelum Tabula*; 1674), with directions from its candied Pearly Gates through several layers of ecstasy and bliss, including a peppermint stick forest and molasses swamp.

Because of this playfulness, as well as Beringer's penchant for both artistic ornamentation (maps that resembled crouching tigers, or mermaid tails, or that were meant to be more of riddles than any sort of accurate topological renderings) and horrible mistakes of judgment (his larger *Mappe of Afrika* famously connected The Nile and the Congo at the same source), Beringer's lifework became something of a celebrated oddity, particularly within the literary crowd. He probably would have sunk completely into obscurity were it not for Jules Verne and The Austro-Prussian War of 1866. Prussia's Chancellor, Otto von Bismarck, had made a deal with Louis Napoleon iii to stay out of the "familial" conflict, and once Bavaria was safely under Prussian influence, Bismarck made a gift of Beringer's puzzle maps to the riddle-raptured Frenchman. Louis Nap was so taken with them that he often displayed them at functions, inviting his guests to try their hand at *Tabula Incontinens*, which sometimes appeared to contain fifty-seven countries and other times sixty-one, or the *Isla Nubilar*, which upside-down looked like a beautiful young woman. Verne, who had become a fairly major celebrity as a result of his serialized work and could often be found holding court at Versailles, became particularly obsessed. Working from copies he scribbled when no one was looking, Verne first incorporated a Beringer map into *Ton Chariot Sphere*, his 1870 novel that experimented with second-person point of view about a fantastic orbital time machine that travels back to the earliest seconds of the universe, which was part of his Extraordinary Voyages series. When he published *L'Île*

Mystérieuse five years later, Verne was similarly unapologetic about its resemblance to Beringer's Madagascar as a prowling octopus. He even shared some of his reproductions with Robert Louis Stevenson, who saw Beringer's Kukuanaland on a visit to Verne's summer home in Nice and began work immediately on what would become *Treasure Island* (1883).

In his final years, after an attempt on his life, Verne became less interested in fiction, seeking out as many Beringer originals as possible. He'd already snatched up Napoleon's collection after the emperor's deportation, and so his next step was to approach the voc, where he spent months poring through the company's archives. Miraculously to him, Verne uncovered several dozen pieces that had gone straight to the vaults, so lacking in accuracy that they were apparently nearly destroyed, and convinced the current librarian to let him add them to the show he was planning to curate for the 1900 World Expo in Paris. The show was a bomb, failing to attract any more people than the unfinished Métro, but Verne remained undaunted, and spent the last five years of his life financing tours of the maps around Europe, even bequeathing a considerable amount of his fortune to their preservation and continued showings after his death. This is how, in Berlin in 1918, the young Austrian Raoul Hausmann attended the opening of the Beringer display at Herwarth Walden's *Der Sturm* gallery (he was renting the apartment directly above it). Hausmann was so enthralled he began producing poetic maps of his own, built entirely of manipulated typography, in the studio of his friend Erich Heckel. Along with Heckel and his mistress Hannah Höch, Hausmann launched the failed Kartist movement before joining the Berlin Dadaists, presenting one of his maps at the inaugural Berlin Club Dada. It was criticized roughly by the visiting Huelsenbeck – and even Höch – as too pretty, and eventually these morphed into his "phonemes," or poster poems, including *enscatohri* (1920), which Kurt Schwitters claimed was a direct influence on his seminal *Ursonate* (1922–32). Jorge Luis Borges, having spent all of his teenage years in Europe, tried several times to arrange a showing of Beringer's maps in Buenos Aires, but was unable because of the country's various fascist governments, towards which the largely Jewish Dadaists had always been opposed. Nevertheless, Borges wrote a piece called "Beringer's Library," included in *The Garden of Forking Paths* (1941), which amounted to an exhaustive list of his most outlandish pieces, real and imagined, most of which are actually the titles of poems by Borges's childhood friend, Sancho Rieta. In the 70s, after his country's civil war, the prized Nigerian author Thrinropo Sachete used Beringer's faulty African Congo/Nile map as the basis for his parable of corruption and AIDS in Western Africa, in which the entire region becomes separated from the rest of the continent, drifts into the Atlantic, and the rest of the continent rejoices. And most recently there is Artonio Phere's *Chatvard* (2007), where Italy's controversial *enfant terrible* uses maps of Beringer's home country in a novel about a futuristic totalitarian state where political correctness and fear of allergies is taken to its next logical step, building on the banning of smoking, peanuts and perfumes to include soap and even pets, until the simple act of bathing or owning a cat is punishable by death, and "a group of morons," as he puts it, "sets off to find a place where all morons and their crutches can live in peace."

Even before all of this, the younger Beringer viewed his father like a god, and wanted nothing more than to grow up like him, mated to the high seas. On the nights when he happened to be home in Würzburg, which were often six months apart, Beringer Senior would quiz his son on the nations of Africa, including the names of various gulfs, capes and inlets, the largest sources of coal and salt, where to avoid mermaids, and the best places to catch dragons. But on the eve of his thirteenth birthday, news arrived of a storm off the coast of Senegambia. The representative from the VOC said his father's ship had struck a reef and everyone was lost. But young Beringer knew from his maps that the more probable cause was that they'd sailed too close to the valley of the giant squid.

***

Without her husband's financial support (the V O C initially provided her with a meagre pension, but after the first several years, the packages stopped arriving and she had no way with which to reach them for clarification or appeal), Beringer's mother did her best to raise the boy on her own, cleaning homes for some of the professors at the town's university. When he was old enough, Beringer attended the school, on a scholarship provided by one of those professors who had taken note of the particular skills possessed by both son and mother, and before long Beringer had a new mentor and a new father. It was also at the university that he met Rio Schaaten, an American of all things, if it was suitable to call anyone an American yet, whose father had made a fortune as a coffee and cotton merchant in the prosperous, Atlantic Triangle between Europe, Africa and the New World. After eighteen years of doing all of his business with her at his side, Emil Schaaten had brought his daughter to Würzburg to nurture her artistic side under Richter Söph, one of the masters of the Wessobrunner School of stucco work that would dominate European ornamentation for the next hundred years or so. And Rio, who had spent so much of her youth travelling the world, wherever her father happened to be posted at the time, had never had a chance to make real friends in Philadelphia, or Amsterdam, or Frankfurt, so the attention of a naïve Bavarian with a view of the world so rural and unsophisticated enabled her to quickly develop – towards Beringer, of all people – feelings akin to affection.

Needless to say, Beringer was instantly smitten. Rio had already seen so much of the world, Beringer felt like a child in her presence: ascending the pyramids, dining with cannibals, even dancing with France's latest President. Even if she hadn't also been spectacularly beautiful, the subject of paintings by everyone from Murillo, when she was just a young child, to a portrait at seventeen by Rathniesco that had been condemned by the Church as bordering on pornographic, she still would have embodied all that he wanted in the world. Even her name was exotic, christened after a river in the Americas, though it was uncertain which one because either she or her father preferred to keep it a mystery. Beringer preferred to think of it as the Rio de la Plata, which was the deepest; or sometimes he fancied it as the Rio Atrato, because it was the most fiercely determined; either way, it was wonderful to think about.

Naturally, part of the appeal for Beringer was also her father's occupation and financial status. On the first of two occasions that Schaaten returned to Würzburg to visit his daughter in that four-year period, Beringer cornered the trader with questions about trade winds, nautical customs and kraken. Schaaten, who was hoping to hitch his daughter to a Bavarian prince but was beginning to think Beringer was the best opportunity he was likely to get, and having consumed too much alcohol, let it slip that Beringer should accompany him on a future expedition. On the second trip, Schaaten was barely off the train before Beringer was asking for Rio's hand in marriage, already dreaming of the three of them on the high seas.

The wedding, Rio insisted, should be in Würzburg. She'd finally made some friends, she claimed, and it was more important to her than anything else that they *all* be in attendance. No matter, Beringer thought. He'd been hoping to marry in some place more exotic, surrounded by naked children and topless tribeswomen, but he could wait until the honeymoon. And certainly Schaaten would provide them with a handsome gift with which to see the world. Rio's best friend was Amalia Pachelbel, daughter of the German composer, and she whisked Rio off to her home in Nuremberg to get ready, pampering her with every spa treatment imaginable and leaving Beringer to complete the final preparations on his own.

The day of the wedding was perfect. The sun broke spectacularly over Mt. Eibelstadt. Rio was rested and beautiful in a long, green gown, her hair up in a chaste, white headdress. Nothing could ruin things for Beringer at this point, so close to the ocean now – at least in his mind – that he could taste the salt on the air. The service was held in the university's chapel, with the reception near their home in the country. Emil Schaaten brought cherries from Spain and oranges from Southeast Asia, but they also received many other gifts, including a lovely gilt mirror from the university depicting scenes from the Passion of Christ, a chandelier, a tiny statue of Saint Margaret for fertility (from Beringer's mother), a small dog, and a pair of nondescript clogs from Amalia, in which she proposed Rio might try her hand at gardening. Amalia's father composed a song for the occasion. Amalia, fittingly, caught the bouquet.

What happened next would never be clear to Beringer. One moment everything was perfect, and then his world was being pulled out from beneath him again, Amalia consoling Rio as her father stormed from the tent, claiming to have disowned her. Beringer ran after him. But Schaaten was tight-lipped, saying he should ask his wife. Then he laughed. Rio would likewise disclose nothing, and when Beringer pleaded for her to patch things up (Did she understand how little he made?!), she said, What need do we have for money? Don't we have a home? Don't we have love? And what could he say to that? As Schaaten's carriage lurched out of town towards Amsterdam, Beringer was forced to acknowledge that he was stuck in Würzburg forever.

Had he not discovered the fossils near Mt. Eibelstadt, it's likely that his life would have remained entirely meaningless.

* * *

A short time later, Amalia moved into the shed behind their home. The composer's daughter had come to Würzburg to study watercolours, but had then discovered the genre paintings of the Dutch masters and, swept away by the Baroque fascination with the mundane, she began experimenting with media that were progressively more "of the people," eventually settling on knitting. She was not particularly adept, and proceeded at an astonishingly slow pace, working on the same pair of socks for what seemed to Beringer as an eternity and a day. But her book of patterns was the first of its kind, and while far from a commercial success – knitting had yet to catch on with the upper class, and the farmers' wives were far from needing patterns – it did begin to gain her the recognition she was seeking. Besides, her new philosophy also meant a complete rejection of all financial luxuries, living like a peasant by squatting on Beringer's land and joining them for meals. Whenever Beringer brought it up, she scoffed about his ego.

As Beringer's need to travel increased, things between him and his wife grew steadily worse. If she got a job, he said, they might be able to scrape enough together to take a proper honeymoon. But shortly after Amalia's arrival, Rio decided she was going to be a poet. Travel? Travelling was for the dull and crass. Travelling was like daydreaming for people without imagination. All Rio needed was right here, to be close to the land and the beasts of the land, and the German peasantry who knew more about what it was like to be alive, and to know who they were, than just about anyone. She liked to sit in the shade beneath a blossoming fig tree and watch them toil in the dirt, the sweat from their brows feeding the seeds of truth beneath them. The fact that none of them would be able to read her work made it even more real for her.

She also didn't take to his suggestion she might tidy up the house now and then, accusing him of belittling her new job, and he was forced to use more of his meagre stipend to hire a maid. This meant Beringer had to give up his office in town and both of them had to work from home (three if you counted Amalia), which seemed to put an even greater strain on their relationship.

It also meant that he was home the day the young child showed up on his doorstep with the "formed stone."

The idea of fossils had fascinated Beringer for some time, and he'd bored Rio and Amalia almost nightly with his talk of the mastodon bone they'd uncovered in Argyll, Scotland, fetched from the muck of a sheep farm by a Shetland Collie; or in Jemeppe-sur-Meuse, near Liege in Belgium, where a man operating one of the first steam engines fell down a well to find himself in the belly of a monster, like Jonah or Pinocchio, encased in a magnificent ribcage. The world is changing, he said through a mouthful of potatoes. We are changing. And Rio just yawned, while Amalia may have looked up from her socks. The truth doesn't change, one of them said.

But what was the truth? The most common belief was that the bones represented tribes of giant men, Goliaths, like the one slain by David. The local priests displayed them to their congregations as battle trophies, the scars of a world brought low by evil and mended by the steady hand of God. And the townsfolk ate it up. But children still slept uneasily, their untainted imaginations allowing room for things like monsters. And Beringer slept like a baby, dreaming of his father's dragons.

Needless to say, Beringer had never dreamed of finding any fossils here. He demanded to know where the boy had found it, ordered the child to take him there immediately. And by the end of the afternoon, the two of them had uncovered three more prime specimens: one with an image of the sun and two others with what appeared to be winged worms. The next Monday, he went back to the beach and discovered another five stones. On Tuesday, another three. And by Friday he was actually becoming quite good at it. He couldn't believe his luck. Sometimes they weren't even partially submerged in dirt, these things, these formed stones. They were just lying there, on a rock, on the bleached branch of a dying tree, or on top of another formed stone, not even trying. It was astounding no one had ever discovered them before. He spent weeks at it, months, more than a year. There was rarely a day when he didn't return home, exhausted at the end of a hard day's work, with at least a half-dozen more in hand, to find Rio and Amalia doing nothing as usual, and the result was *Lithographiae Wirceburgensis* (1726), the most comprehensive text on fossils to that date, with paleontological theories – although the word paleontology did not yet exist – that would lead to the extinction theories and comparative anatomy work of Georges Cuvier, but also, unlike most fossil work of the period, eschewed debates about religion in favour of mythology. Here was the proof, he said, of dragons, not to mention centaurs, and gryphons, and mermaids, and even an eye of the beholder. And Beringer's populist approach meant that it became the best-selling book on such things until Darwin's *On the Origin of the Species* over a hundred years later. It was his masterpiece. He was an instant celebrity, selling enough copies to buy another home, keep the maid on full time and allow Rio and Amalia to live in increasing states of leisure. He was also invited to speak as far afield as Oxford. But he refused. There were still so many stones to study, so much truth to uncover. And he immediately began working on the sequel, so good at locating them now that he barely had to look, transforming the entire world, or at least the way people saw it, from the little town of Würzburg.

Don't you worry about God?, Amalia said to him one evening as he was making them dinner. Aren't you concerned that God will punish you for ratting him out? And when he replied with logic, she just laughed and glanced knowingly at Rio.

Who do you think you are?, she said. And he went back to chopping the parsnips for the roast.

But he knew who he was. He was Johann Beringer, son of Johann Beringer. Johann Beringer, who had slipped through childhood like a drop of water, barely detectable among the other children as one who would rock the foundations of their understanding of life, now entering their collective consciousness like a grim reaper, gathering their faith to his emaciated ribcage and crushing it ever so slightly, with a beard like welded bees, like Greek ornature, barely moving, not even when he spoke. He was Johann Beringer, the father of dragons, the most famous geologist and de facto historian of his time, who had retraced the maps of Europe, who had crept into their minds like a colony of giant insects and set up nest, who was about to be remarried, as was right and fitting, to the rest of the world, and as he discovered several days later, the proud victim of a horrible ruse, as Beringer's flaking hand flipped the stone bearing a smiley face and his own name.

And he rushed back home to find Rio in bed with Amalia, the two of them painting stones they'd dug out of his garden.

* * *

It wasn't enough to make him a cuckold, they had to make him a laughing stock. And Beringer spent the rest of his life circling the globe in search of every single copy of his book his publisher had ever sold so he could destroy them. In 2000, Chris Eaton discovered a ninth edition as part of a book-by-book auction of the library of an eccentric Welshman who, although he had died decades earlier, it had taken this long merely to sort through and catalogue his entire collection. Chris Eaton had flown to London to be at Christie's when it all came down, where he managed to snatch it up for next to nothing, as other collectors were more interested in the complete works of Henri-Louis Duhamel du Monceau, including one of his earliest, *Traite de chapon hors var* (1737), on the particular castration techniques of Bresse roosters outside of Provence and the Riviera, written before he was contracted to investigate a disease that was destroying the saffron plant in Gatinais and he began devoting his life entirely to subjects of agronomy and silviculture; other early texts in the lot covered botany and agriculture by Theophrastus and Aristotle, Dīnawarī, Aria von Crestahd and Aimé Bonpland; and the star of the show, an original double-elephant folio of Audubon's *Birds of America*.

It was one of two books that Julie found on Chris Eaton's desk when she came to find him for breakfast and discovered he was gone.

When her husband died, it was like nothing she had ever been forced to deal with. She'd seen death before. Starting with her grandparents, and then her parents, and then her husband's mother and grandfather. But even before that, before them, there was the man named Jeffrey Miller, who she saw hit by a car outside La Cave, run over on purpose after an argument inside the venue over a girl, perhaps even her or, depending on which political spectrum of newspaper you happened to read, over who had won the televised town hall debate over Vietnam, the new Republican Governor of California or the new Democratic Senator from New York, or if you were into politics of a different sort, over which band was going to have the greater longevity, The Velvet Underground or The Heroin Cats. And then, naturally, since she'd been a nurse long before everyone in California started dying, there were countless patients, dying left-and-right, up-and-down and side-to-side, from simple intestinal obstructions to things that sounded like Dr. Seuss animals (gangrenous gut, fibrous stricture, pyloric stenosis), or even simple errors by surgeons, perforating a colon while sewing someone up or, depending on your susceptibility to conspiracy theories, closing up the wound with a watch inside, or a fishing lure, or an after-dinner mint. People died as they were being admitted on the gurney, in the operating room, as they were leaving. Once, she came into a room and it was clear that the man on the bed was just moments away. He'd been so close for weeks, suffering from an ailment no one could identify, and though both of his children lived in the city, neither had ever come to visit. It was near the beginning of her rounds and she knew she was in for a long day, so she turned around immediately and left. But in the hallway she was struck with a bout of conscience, that it was wrong for someone to die alone. So she returned to his side and didn't say anything, just stood in the room until she could no longer hear him breathing, then pulled up the sheet, made a note on his chart and left for her next patient.

For days after the virus first broke out, the news reporters talked about it pretty non-stop. There were profiles on the initial victims, stories on whether or not health insurance providers would cover

285

medical expenses, whether or not they could survive financially if they did, who cared whether the insurance companies survived or not. They also focused on the growing list of celebrity illnesses, with shots of a sallow film star apparently trying to drown himself in The Chester and Portia Havro Memorial Fountain in downtown Los Angeles, which was used in many films including *Pretty Woman*. Because it was *him*, people initially assumed the virus was sexually transmitted, a gay disease, but after Oakland Raiders hero Rich Gannon was admitted to hospital with pains at his sides below the ribcage and a headache, only to die five days later, the director for the Centers for Disease Control (CDC) enforced a mandatory call for all Californians to be immunized. Less than three weeks later, they'd completely run out of vaccine. Aventis and Chadarro, the two pharmaceutical companies who were licensed to manufacture it, issued quick press releases deflecting any blame from their decision to produce fewer doses this year because of the significant waste in expired stocks from the previous year, but added that there should be enough vaccine for everyone in the closets and cupboards of hospitals and general practitioners across the country. Even with the urging of the CDC and the White House, several states refused to comply. After all, it took six months to produce vaccines in numbers like this. What if the disease were to spread? Would they be saving the citizens of California only to damn themselves?

Thank goodness she had her children for support. And her sister. And all of her husband's friends. He'd had so many friends. He was very popular. In fact, he had more friends than she had even met, like the ones he had for dinner parties when she was away on speaking engagements, or who accompanied him to movies, which she despised, or with whom he went fishing. Several of them even offered to help write his obituary for the local paper, but Chris Eaton insisted on doing this herself. There were so many accomplishments to choose from, so many acts of wonder, so many stories she could tell, and she wanted to include them all, as if missing one detail might make him seem like less of a human being. But after sleeping on it, she suddenly felt very protective, and anxious, and mad, that someone's life could be so easily reduced to a list of dates and names, like the accounting ledger at his first store, or the back of a library book. Plus, would anyone really understand, anyway? They had shared so many private things, how could they possibly make sense to another living person? Would people understand, for example, their joke about buying the abandoned old hotel in the middle of nowhere and populating it with children, naming them not after family ancestors but with numbers and letters, randomly selected by choosing the license plate of the next car to drive through? She wanted no room for error so she began to cut, as if all of these memories were hers alone and she were suddenly unwilling to share them, not even with friends and family, especially the most private ones, like how they'd never used each other's name in public, just called one another lover; the things that made him cry; and where he liked to be touched; savoring each memory like chocolate on her tongue, for a moment, then striking it from the document she had created, hoping to settle on the one remaining truth that would perfectly capture the whole, until all that remained was one line: *He was my husband.* As if all that mattered with him was how he was related to her. As though, if they had never met, that his life and his dreams and his achievements would have meant nothing. And it made her feel selfish to write it. Here, she thought, was the most important man to have ever lived. Here was the person with whom she had shared everything. And all she could do was reduce him to a possession. As if the story had never been about them at all but only about her, lying to herself for years that they had completed each other when all he did was give her someone to feel loved.

Though sadly perhaps, when she considered how he had worked to support her while she pursued her music, then moved back to California with her for her new job, and eventually dropped his own career because she thought their kids needed a parent at home, she realized this may have always been true.

Sometimes the city planner would come home from work and work some more, and later she'd crawl into bed after Chris Eaton had already gone to sleep and try to wake him up by touching him. Once his eyes were open she would roll on top of him and put her arms around his neck. But he would say he was too tired, night after night, until he felt as though he were letting her down, not wanting to let her down, not wanting to say no but also unable to switch between roles of father and lover, so just the proximity of her would cause him to uncontrollably tense up, and gradually his stiffness turned her off so much that she stopped trying.

One night she started crying. It wasn't enough for her, she said, to be just the boy's mother. She needed to be a lover, too, she said. She needed to feel loved. It hadn't been like this before, she said. He said he would try. But he couldn't quite wrap his head around it. And eventually she left him, taking their son with her.

She woke up in the hospital and reached immediately for her children. They were not there. No matter what happened later in life, it all came back to this, with Walter telling some boring story to the kids about Loch Ness, or Ogopogo – which was far away in Canada but had somehow struck on the same gimmick for drawing tourists – neither eye on the road; the youngest, Dorothy, in her lap; the other two fighting over some travel books in the back that used invisible ink to reveal secret messages and jokes, no clue that more than half of the car had only a few more seconds left to live.

There was the car crash, with the sound like her children being shot in the back seat and her body going so rigid she couldn't turn quickly enough to see what was happening. Sometimes she remembered it one way. Other times, another. But every time as her forehead connected with the dash, the occipital nerves went to the muscles for comfort and the muscles, unaware of their own strength, hugged too hard. She felt like she was growing horns, that there were fires behind her eyes.

And everything changed. It was as if she were suddenly someone else. Some other Chris Eaton. And the people who came to visit her, whom she knew to be well-meaning, only served to remind her of that life she no longer had. So she asked the nurses to tell visitors she was sleeping. Indeed, she spent most of her time with her eyes closed, but also humming softly to herself, in an effort to shut out the beeping machine, and the IV tube, and the flowers, and the lack of mirrors, dismantling the "reality" of it piece by piece until she was just lying there in the darkness, the silence, the emptiness, which took years to perfect and several books on yoga and Sufism and brain waves and quantum physics before she could do it without crying. Of course, it wasn't the emptiness she was looking for but something else. Something from her past. Those perfect moments right before the crash. Neutralizing the present just seemed the first step because it had such a firm grip on her. Then she might go anywhere. Along with most of her face, the accident seemed to have shattered the linearity of her past. And sometimes, even thirty years later, her husband and children would be alive again, sitting beside her, perhaps even driving in the car, and then, again, they were gone.

It took very little time for the sickness to spread from its original epicentres in Oakland and San Diego, where it was thought to have crossed the border from Mexico until they narrowed it down to a flight from Central America. When cases started popping up in Washington and Oregon, the White House shut down all travel to and from the West Coast. Anyone approaching the border into Arizona, Nevada or Idaho was to be shot.

When things became more desperate, intrepid business people started selling flu shots on the street for thirty dollars a pop. The injections were nothing more than a saline solution. But by this point the local police constabularies had other things to worry about. Or, as was the case in most communities, the police were either too sick, had walled themselves up in their bomb shelters to wait everything out or they had joined the millions of others crawling past and over the long lines of gridlocked cars on their way to the border.

If one person's ability to monopolize on another's misfortune and gullibility was not unimaginable enough, how those crooks intended to get the money out of California was an even larger mystery.

The main thing she had hoped her children would learn from her was to make room for people on the sidewalk, to be aware of other people in general, to be conscious of others in need and to serve them, in whatever way they could. This would be good. She had hoped, in general, that they would learn to be good people, but more specifically that they would learn to hold doors, and offer seats, to love in the face of hate and have patience in the face of ignorance, to understand their own feelings, to share them, to be liked, but only for being themselves and not for doing things against their nature because they thought it would make them liked, to not make the same mistakes she did, to learn from her mistakes, to love, to accept being loved, to accept not being loved, if that were the case, to respect a hot stove, to admire a lit candle, to properly cleanse and protect their skin, using a light moisturizer when needed, to enjoy healthy food and exercise, to understand the value of money, right from wrong, not to sacrifice long-term gain for immediate gratification, but to also stop and smell the flowers occasionally, knowing all choices have repercussions, and all decisions have consequences, this, that, infinity, to remember all the math shortcuts, and that math is important, to love reading, to read "good" books and not just that nonsense that everyone else reads, to read philosophy, like Goethe, or Voltaire, to enjoy music, and to enjoy making it, but also not to try so hard to be different, because they'd be happier without the struggle of trying to be unique and accepted at the same time, better to be the same as everyone else.

Of course, it is with death that all learning comes most difficult.

Autopsies – in the beginning, when time could be found to actually perform autopsies – showed a peculiar growth in the back of the nasal passage, effectively closing off access to the pharynx (which explained the difficulty patients had with breathing) and creating a useless u-tube nostril that examiners were sure would even prohibit smell. This could have explained the patients' ability to eat – and sudden attraction to – things we would mostly find distasteful, like flies and silverfish. Their eyes were so vacant, reacting to only the shiniest stimuli. So she shook her keys in front of them and tried to at least keep them entertained. They were so much more mobile than her husband had been, especially when they were first admitted. At that point, they were really only suffering from dry skin, which began in small, itchy patches but spread quickly to cover most of the epidermis. It almost seemed like they were allergic to the air, as if the air itself were making them dehydrate so quickly. After a few days, which was generally the point where patients were actually admitted, the skin began to develop rough shingles or scales, hard to the touch and yet oozing an oily mucus that made the surface extremely slippery. No treatment, including healthy doses of antibiotics and flat soda, seemed to work. In fact, the antibiotics only seemed to induce extreme weight gain, which was even more strange when you considered how little they were keeping down. Even the children were clocking in at over two hundred pounds, floundering about their beds like injured seals, staring at her with a directionless, all-encompassing ambivalence, bottom jaws pawing helplessly at the air, eyes swollen out of their sockets like straight-legged kneecaps, held down with nylon straps so they wouldn't pop a seizure and flop onto the floor. No one had cleaned the floor in weeks. No one had done laundry, either, and the sheets were crusted and glistening with an iridescence that would have been quite beautiful, given other circumstances, as their situations worsened, the scales progressively taking over, until the only thing she could do was try to ease the pain by rubbing them with water. At first, with such severe dehydration, the doctors were concerned that too much water ingested directly through the mouth might induce more vomiting and actually be counterproductive, so everyone was placed on an electrolyte IV in priority of severity. All faucets in room bathrooms were turned off to remove the temptation. Then she found one of the children lapping frantically from the toilet, her face practically buried in it. After that, she fetched it for them by the pitcher and they gulped it down like flies.

It appeared to help.

The same child died two days later, tossing so violently on her bed that they had to strap her down, her jaw gone slack and her throat and chest heaving with exertion. Her eyes veered towards the outside as if she were trying to see behind her. Like a gecko. And she never made a sound. Not even a whimper.

By the end of the third week, the whole hospital was a graveyard of sound.

No one even bothered to cry. Or pray.

When we grow older, we become more sentimental, more challenged by artistic depictions of death, depravity, travesty, tragedy, horror, sadness. As children, death is something we don't even understand, something we watch like a ceiling fan then forget, something we long to put in our mouths. As adolescents, we are trained to be more cynical. Awkwardness teaches us to laugh at these things. But as we grow older, we become more affected, by these films, these stories, because our experience has shown them to be true. All of them. Each horrible event in our lives makes us realize that anything is possible.

Probable.

Has actually happened.

Is actually happening.

In fact, perhaps our imaginations are just a link to a collective unconscious, so that the thoughts we happen to stumble across while holding the hand of a dying lover, or staggering from the cafeteria to the bathroom, or tossing spoiled food into the furnace room because there's nowhere else for it to go and throwing it outside just attracts more wild animals and looters, are really just pinhole exposures into actual events somewhere else on the planet.

Stylized. Washed out. Blurred at the edges.

She hadn't eaten in days, perhaps even a week. The food in the cafeteria had gone bad two days after the power went out. Then someone broke in at night and ransacked the candy bar dispenser. Then there was no one. And she began tugging an IV drip from room to room because it was the only thing that hadn't yet gone bad.

She knows she, too, will soon die. Soon they are all going to die. It's only a matter of time. Of course, the other thing about growing older is that you stop being afraid of these things. Because you know they are inevitable. Because you have already experienced everything there is to experience and there is nothing worse than the boredom that accompanies that. When you're young, you can't imagine death. It's only when you start to accumulate things, or fall in love, that you start to fear it. They are replaced by new fears: having people discover that you're essentially deaf, and going blind in one eye, and often forget what day it is; that you have several cases of light beer hidden under your bed because they help with digestion, purchased by one of the triplets down the lane who is no longer a child but has a child of her own; or that you sometimes wake up in the middle of the night to discover you're standing in the middle of the hallway, or the driveway, or even worse decked out in front of the television because that's how you spend most of your daily hours too.

But still you fight on. Because that's what life is: an accumulation of fear. Or rather, even: constant fear, reminding you at every moment of your life and love and unattained desires. And with the joy of each new love comes more fear. With each false love: fear of it being false. With true love: fear of the truth, that all life ends and this particular life may end before does your love. You ignore these other lesser fears because they are mere reminders that you are alive and that, one day, you may also love. Like someone pinching you to prove you are not dreaming, or a bedside alarm that will not expire. You persevere.

But then all the things you ever loved are gone, and in the vacuum of their rending, all your real reasons for living disappear.

Did she have regrets? Would she have passed up love, and the birth of her children, if only to avoid everything that came after? Before Walter, she'd been happy to be alone. She didn't need anyone. Didn't like anyone. But he was so in love with the world, and his love was contagious. And she was so happy to be swept up in it, if only so there was someone else to blame for the work she didn't complete.

Looking back, her largest regret was having made him feel bad for the times he asked to spend time with her. When she should have been playing with the girls on the floor, watching them experience the world, she was thinking about her typewriter, about citric acid and artificial flavors and monosodium glutamate and most of all salt. At the time, her studies had seemed so important, had defined her, she thought. But when she'd given up all hope of finishing her degree after the third was born, she'd still maintained a sense of being. Because of them. They were never her kids and her husband; she was their mother and his wife. Without them – Walter and the girls – she was nothing. She'd forgotten what it was like to be on her own, forgotten the sound of an empty house, a peaceful bath, how to cook for one, forgotten what it was like to date, to smile, forgotten what it was like to be.

We are forged of sadder memories, and to move forward we must forget. She'd been introduced to the theatre through Ian and Pauline, whom she'd met at the local gym doing circuit training to get herself back in shape. Her doctor had raised concerns about her sedentary lifestyle. She was already at risk of osteoporosis without lying in bed all day long, not to mention the strain she was putting on her heart. Take it easy, he said. Don't be a hero right away. But if you don't get out more, I can't promise you how long you'll still be around. Ian and Pauline had moved to Lincoln from Haverfordwest, having just spent the last five years biking around the world, and were looking for some sort of new challenge. Before that, Ian had been a technician for the Royal Air Force while Pauline worked in the offices of the Pembrokeshire Coast National Park, programming events, workshops and nighttime entertainment. In their travels, they had managed to gather photographs with countless celebrities, typically by calling the respective agents and claiming they were cycling around the world to raise money for cancer research: actors, pop divas, politicians, multiple rugby and football players, and perhaps the most decorated Tour de France cyclist ever, who'd recently been accused of taking steroids to enhance his performance, left his wife for a pop singer, and was then murdered by his new mistress with the same gun his ex had used to kill herself. While the story was still being featured on the covers of most of the supermarket magazines, Ian and Pauline featured their photo of him on the wall immediately opposite the front door. Then, when tabloid attention shifted to another celebrity adoption of a Third World child, it was moved to the back with the stage actors, cinematographers, drummers and bass players.

As soon as they heard about the new community theatre, they immediately auditioned. Chris Eaton was not bold enough to audition for a speaking part, so she helped out where she could, fundraising, painting sets, makeup, driving children to and from rehearsals, running lines with them, stitching old rags to the beggars' costumes, blacking out teeth, fetching water, fetching take-out, cleaning up vomit, cleaning up worse, taking tickets, dressing wounds, stage managing, prompting applause, and even wrote a review for the *Echo*. But Ian and Pauline went for it, Ian landing the understudy role as Jack Foster in Giles Cooper's British re-envisioning of Edward Albee's *Everything in the Garden*, and Pauline, after realizing she wasn't included in the cast list, sitting home and fretting a hole in the floor. In the following years, though they both settled into their strengths and took a more behind-the-scenes part in things, they not-so-secretly harboured a desire to take the troupe in a "more contemporary" direction, and in Chris Eaton they saw the opportunity to bolster their ranks. Somehow, Ian and Pauline had managed to dig up the script to that movie they'd seen shooting in Panama, *Sloth vs. Manatee*, and had transformed it into a stage play about humanity's struggle to find its place, trying to decide between the warring creatures of the trees and of the sea, performed almost entirely underwater and/or with wire-work special effects, which they hoped might rival the shows in London on roller skates or horseback.

What they needed was a star for the marquee, which naturally led them to consider Jim Broadbent, the son of the theatre's founder and current president. Every time he returned to Wickenby, it was like the entire town lit up. And he always remembered to provide the theatre with passes to his big openings in London.

Jim, they felt, could play the politician.

They were hoping to get Ema Hesire back to play the nun.

Chris Eaton, they said, would be perfect to play the retired nurse.

PART 9

If she could do it all over again, would she? If there were a way to go back, and make different decisions, and set a new path for herself, would there be things she would try to avoid? Or would she seek out her old mistakes like comfort food? Or a fire behind glass? Some- how, despite doing everything to fight it, she'd ended up as a Phys. Ed. teacher back in Cartwright where, for some reason, the kids re- peatedly performed well below state and national averages. The kids were dumb as cattle, as a rule, but several of them were particularly challenged:

- The first was really just a home-schooler, over-educat- ed, over-protected and suffering from extensive malnu- trition of his social skills. His mother had returned to work after ten years as a real estate agent, which was unnecessary but made her feel useful. He wanted to be part of the group so badly, but alienated himself at ev- ery opportunity. He asked other kids why they were fat. He corrected their grammar. One year, because all of the other kids were doing it, he decided he wanted a Cowboys and Indians-themed birthday party, and the mother came in to supervise and made them all sign new treaties with one another.

- The second was like a walking germ factory, blowing snot at the other children on the playground as a means of self-defense or humour, she was never sure which.
- The last refused to associate with any of the other children directly, preferring to sit at the front with her on any class trips, and claimed to be a traveler from the future.

***

Although he was registered at the school as Henry Code, his real name, he claimed, was Henri Costa, the son of a Spanish meteorological scientist who had moved to Florida in the early-nineties to study the effects of global warming on the increased frequency of Atlantic cyclonic-scale storm systems. In only a few years at the National Hurricane Research Laboratory in St. Petersburg, Faramundo Costa was able to improve predictive systems dramatically via multiple reconnaissance missions, including research flights into some of the most notable storms of that decade, like Hurricanes Celeste and Emily (both 1992), Julie (1993), and Opal (1995). In 1996, Faramundo was selected to go to Antarctica under joint American-British funding to measure the effects of electrified particles on the atmosphere, in addition to seasonal temperatures, atmospheric pressure, wind speed, solar radiation, the usual. The job was largely comprised of rising each morning to recreate identical tests from the day before, not terribly interesting, if one had to admit it, almost like an old Greek penance meted out by the gods, and one of the other scientists – a Cajun American from Louisiana with an accent Faramundo could sometimes not follow – joked that it was almost as though they were the real experiments, like rats kept in mazes, which was not so different from real life, no? Indeed, said another, whose name was Garcia and came from California, all of life, and not just our work, is like being a rat in a maze, working hard for pellets and trying to avoid being electrocuted. Pointless. And although the solitary isolation at the South Pole was so difficult on their mental stability that their conversations were often like this, still they knew, deep down, that they were performing something worthwhile, something that might better the world for all of humanity, something that might give their lives definition and meaning. So they completed their tasks dutifully and with some joy until the day of the accidental *event*, which is the word young Henri Costa used to describe it, that lead to their deaths.

On the morning of January 27, Faramundo noticed a beautiful grey fog hanging over the South Pole. It seemed at first no more exciting than the smoke from a campfire, yet it was remarkable how something so ordinarily uninspiring could break up the monotony of so much blank space. He told the Cajun, who was supposed to be working with Faramundo on collecting core samples. And the two of them stood still for most of the day, like insects pinned to plastazote, and soaked it all in.

The next morning, it was still there. Faramundo and the Cajun pointed it out to their cynical colleague from California, who initially brushed it off. Then, on second, third and fourth glances, Garcia confirmed the obvious, that the fog wasn't moving, just hanging in the sky like a smudge on a lens, which even he could admit was curious. So the three of them suited up, grabbed some of their equipment and headed towards it. After one further cycle, the Californian returned to fetch a weather balloon, capable of registering wind speed, temperature and air moisture, seeking to prove it was some sort of optical illusion, possibly something like an astronomical mirage, light reflecting back and forth between the ice and an approaching comet, creating a vision akin to staring at two facing mirrors, a dull, southern brethren to the myriad-coloured northern lights. And on the morning of the 29th at precisely 10:13 A M (Coordinated Universal Time –4 hrs, the same as Chile), Faramundo, Garcia and the Cajun released the balloon, which soared upwards and immediately disappeared.

The men were frantic. Almost immediately, they began to argue about whose fault it had been. They began to pace. They began to argue about the best ways to hide it. They began to despair. Almost immediately, they began to argue about who would take the fall. So as not to jeopardize their funding. And this immediacy monopolized so much of their thoughts that it took some time to realize the balloon wasn't gone at all, or at least had to be up there somewhere, just out of sight, because the rope holding it was still taut in mid-air, attached to nothing, but taut, which was definitely empirical evidence of a sort. The Californian breathed a sigh of relief and turned on the mechanical winch. When the rope still didn't budge, all three of them added their body weight as leverage. And only then did the Cajun sound the alarm, rousing the entire beast of the camp to wrestle the device back to earth.

None of the data seemed particularly out of the ordinary. But whatever forces had managed to so violently resist the winch must have somehow damaged the balloon's equipment, because the chronometer still displayed the same day, but the year had been jarred forward three decades.

According to Faramundo's reports, this phenomenon was repeated several times over the next few days.

They reported their findings The White House.

And no one was allowed to visit the South Pole again.

* * *

For the scientists, it seemed impossible that the government could ever cover it up. The Cajun went public first, going about it all wrong by first approaching his local newspaper, run by failures and the embittered, who tackled the issue from the angle of a disgruntled employee, upset at being wrongfully dismissed. So Garcia sought help through a friend at a cable news show and arranged a real press conference, with representatives from all the major networks in attendance and a clear message that the government was working on a secret weapon. For nearly a week it seemed a hot topic. But The White House merely spent the next year ignoring the question, hoping it might be relegated to the portion of their daily briefs devoted to other conspiracy theories. Thankfully it was an election year and the first Republican caucuses in February took complete hold of the media's centre stage, particularly when Louisiana jumped the gun on Iowa's right to be first. To put the icing on the cake, TWA Flight 800 exploded just south of Long Island on July 17, and just over a week later, a home-made bomb went off during the Summer Games in Centennial Olympic Park in Atlanta. That's when the last remnants of public interest in the fog and time travel dissipated entirely. No one even covered the strange death of Garcia, who was allegedly mugged one night on his way home from a movie, stabbed when he put up a fight over his wallet even though his wife claimed he never carried more than twenty dollars in cash on his person at any time; or the equally fishy end of his colleague Dr. Shane Caravito, who checked into a random B&B in Cape Cod, unpacked all of his clothes, made reservations for one at the seafood restaurants he'd read about in the in-flight magazine, and then drowned himself in the ocean nearly sixty-three miles away. Within the course of five months, a total of nine scientists from the project met with curious ends. One died of poisonous mushrooms, most of which were still in his mouth, on a well-used trail in Oregon. Another in a car explosion, while parked, overlooking the Grand Canyon. Several simply vanished off the face of the planet.

***

By the time these deaths and disappearances had become news, Faramundo Costa had already made great inroads into solving the mystery of the grey fog on his own. Before boarding the plane home from Antarctica, he'd assembled all of the data he and Garcia and the Cajun had collected, as well as any relevant research on electrified particles, and copied it in code into the margins of the only book he'd brought with him for pleasure: *Notae*, a book of lists kept by famous scientists and other notables throughout the ages, from total birds killed by Audubon for his drawings to a diary of breakfasts by Darwin (mostly soft-boiled eggs, with a ranking system out of five), Daniel Rutherford's original suggestions for naming nitrogen, the bones of the Elasmosaurus, as well as a surplus of grocery lists, sometimes enlightening, more often hilarious and reaffirming, compiled by Rich Savard. The code was not complex, replacing letters with each other in a rather predictable pattern, but all the CIA men did when they searched him was hold the book by its spine and shake to see if any floppies fell out.

For years he kept up appearances, accepting his old job back at the National Research Lab, buying a home and a dog, volunteering for as many storms as possible, even getting married to a woman named Celeste from Quebec who he met at a truck stop near Flagstaff, Arizona, proposing on the spot because he considered her name – the same as his first storm – to be an important sign. Very soon she was pregnant. To everyone on the outside, they seemed the happiest couple alive. Then one night when he was supposed to be chasing a storm on the East Coast, he woke her with a hand over her mouth. Pack your things, he said. Trust me, he said. And she did. People were watching him, he said. They kept breaking into his computer at work. He'd even tried changing his password every hour, and still his coworkers made sly comments that could only be references to what he knew, what they knew he knew, and what he knew they knew he knew. He was on the verge of something so big, he told her, that men were surely coming to stop him. Three nights later, Faramundo delivered the baby himself, in the bed of a stolen pickup, with nothing to clamp the umbilical cord but a set of jumper cables. Their child asleep in his arms, he thought momentarily about smothering him, worried that the boy might hold them back, convinced in his mind that he could one day return, after he'd unlocked time's secrets, to stop himself from doing it. But the boy looked so much like him that he couldn't carry through. Plus, he didn't think Celeste would understand. So the three of them existed together on the lam for nearly nine years, until Faramundo died and little Henri was forced to take over where his father had left off.

* * *

It was all ridiculous to Chris Eaton. Henry Code was only nine, which seemed an improbable age for someone to discover the secrets of time travel or even, given the possibility that he may have come from a time where time travel was more prevalent and that every second home had their own machine, to have been trusted with the keys to one. But this was, as he explained to Chris Eaton, the curse of being his father's son, seeking to atone for acts he'd never done, looking to fix the wrongs of the past, and of his own hubris. On the run, Faramundo was able to continue his experiments unhindered, possibly accomplishing even more because he no longer had to keep up any pretext. As it turned out, time travel was remarkably simple. Predicting where the greyness would manifest itself became as simple as predicting a rainy day. They were there all around us, these fourth-dimensional holes. But they were mostly suspended in the air, having come in contact with humans only a small number of times, on the rare occasions that their presence had coincided with passing planes, sometimes damaging them to the point that they fell from the sky and other times causing them to vanish completely, which finally offered a plausible explanation for The Bermuda Triangle.

Henry was never quite sure where his father had hidden them for so many years, but from years of his own research, he knew that his needs would have been very specific: computers more powerful than what he could safely and affordably order for his home, materials which at that point only existed as rumors and hearsay, rooms large enough to house various superconductors, and a large radar dish. And this narrowed his list of possibilities down to only a few

303

locations, all of them decommissioned military stations, like the site in Montauk, NY, in the abandoned underground Air Force base under the wildlife preserve where they'd supposedly been conducting electromagnetic experiments on homeless and runaways for decades before finally giving it up. Faramundo still spent most of his time in the field hunting the manifestation down, and would leave his wife and newborn alone for weeks underground, returning with new data and freshly shoplifted sandwiches. Once, Faramundo was able to find a buyer for some abandoned military technology he had found, and this financed their travels for at least a year or two, but the guilt that followed him after that was too great to try it again. So they returned to living hand-to-mouth.

On these trips to the fog, Faramundo first experimented with sound, shouting messages into the sky that he thought might be useful if they reached him in the past: "The secret is in the Norse variant!"; "Marry Celeste!"; "Don't kill the boy!" But there was no way to measure success. Then he realized he could wrap notes around rocks, with coded dates on them and instructions for the finder to mail them to a secret post office box or, in the case that they traveled back to before he could register one in his name, to his childhood address back in Spain. In case they went back even further, he provided additional instructions for whomever received it to hide it in one of his favorite childhood spaces. It was logical to assume none of these experiments had actually reached that far, because he couldn't remember finding any notes from himself back then, but he supposed it was also just as likely that someone from the past had merely balked at such intricate directions and huffed the rock back into the woods or river where they'd found it. And eventually he gave that up as well.

The real problem was the effect the grey fog had on everything inside it, not only clocks, obviously, which only measured the time differential, but on all organic material as well, which held on to the present like a man falling off of a cliff. The key, he'd always believed, was the Norse variant, which was a theorem put forward by three

Scandinavian mathematicians in the late-nineties relating to what they called zenotic conclusion points, a reference to a combination of the Achilles and the tortoise paradox and the arrow paradox. They felt that it was possible to be completely motionless, and in fact, believed that motion and uniqueness were both illusions, that all was one and continuous and if one could break down this illusion/paradox, the whole world would be opened up through a limitless supply of undiminishing power: *zero energy*. This *zero energy*, he believed, was the main force at work in the fog. By harnessing it one could do almost anything because slowing things down to a perfect standstill opened up Einstein's theory of relativity to infinite possibilities on most other planes. By remaining perfectly still, one could be instantly transported to any place or any time.

The only issue was the matter of *zero time*. The exact moment in time at which a dimensional shift occurred would act as a reference point for the mind and body, like an elastic band, creating greater tension in psyche of the traveler the further he or she moved from the reference point of their departure. Although it was possible to shift *zero time*, especially in inanimate objects, the human mind tended to lock itself to its original timeline; the concept of moving in time is, otherwise, too much to accept. Most humans can not move with *zero time*, cannot flow in synch with the time shift without it affecting them relatively, so that, if you travel to the future, you don't emerge from the fog as the same young man who entered it, but as the older man you might become had you progressed through the same years like anyone else. Imagine tracing a line on graph paper and then suddenly lifting the pencil from the page and dropping down somewhere else. Despite not having travelled all that distance from the starting point on paper, you are still now the same distance as you would be had you actually drawn the line in the first place. The measurement would be the same, but void of memories. Faramundo's first guinea pig, the Cajun, was no spring chicken, but he died because his body could not handle the forty-year leap forward and he suffered a stroke in transit. On Faramundo's second experiment, the volunteer only traveled forward a few days; but when he reappeared, someone had parked a car in his arrival spot and the roof severed him in half. Finally Caravito, whom they thought was safe because he was young and they had discovered a fog out over the water, he just couldn't handle the concept of himself as a drastically older man, could not reconcile the idea that he was even twenty years older without any memory of how he'd gotten there. The person he saw in the mirror was not him. And because memories are our link to ourselves, our identity, our anchor, he returned a complete vegetable, unable to perform even the simplest tasks like breathing. Because of the loss of memories, he forgot who he was, what he was. He lost himself. A person is not a point on two or more axes, but the sum total of everything in between. Without any in-between, we are empty vessels, unable to survive, blowing away like formless smoke.

When Caravito's body was discovered off the coast of Massachusetts, it would have been impossible to trace DNA or fingerprints back to Faramundo. His previous record was as clean as a fresh gold sample plate. But he was also far from competent when it came to disposing of his failures, renting the boat to dispose of Caravito on a credit card, or thinking it might be enough to empty Garcia's pockets before tossing his body in an alley behind a movie theatre, and eventually this was what caught up with the Spaniard. When he was finally captured and arrested for pocketing twelve dollars worth of chocolate bars and soda, the police officer realized that the quiet man in the back of his car had been the subject of a massive manhunt for years, suspected of multiple murders and/or kidnappings.

As he was put to death for his crimes, his wife and child still underground and unaware of his situation, his main regret was that he had never achieved a full understanding of the exact trauma of time travel on the human experience.

* * *

"I never felt like a real person," Henry said. "Always hidden from other people, in my own world, outside of the real world, and I suppose, in some ways, I never really existed at all. I had no birth certificate, no passport, had never been treated in a hospital or registered in a school or daycare. My mother schooled me underground, and there was never any chance of me becoming sick or injured because I was so insulated from the rest of the world. No viruses, no stairs, no playgrounds, no early sexual experimentation. My room, in fact, was a padded cell, left from the days when so many of the base's experiments would go mad, with a door that essentially disappeared into the rest of the padding when it was closed, and even though I obviously must have slept on the floor, because I am well aware of gravity and how it works, I would often wake up and wonder if, during the night, not that I could even tell night from day in this place, I had rolled up onto the wall, or the ceiling, so identical was any one aspect of the room to any other. I was, in effect, in a world without the general rules of the first three dimensions, with nothing to tell me that I was even under New York, or Arkansas, or Colorado, or Atlantis, and lived only in the fourth.

"The only thing that I knew was the time (which was displayed in most rooms and hallways, to the second, via large, rectangular boxes with blocky, red, digital numbers) and the year (which was sometimes displayed in similar boxes but also because of a calendar my father kept in his main workshop, checking off each day to monitor how long we'd been in hiding), without contact with anyone outside, without direct sunlight. At any given moment I knew precisely *when* I was, but not *where*, which was the opposite to my later problems.

"When my father failed to return from his last trip, my mother insisted we stay put and wait, although I suspect she knew something was up, because to pass the time she told me stories, mostly about my father, but also my uncles and aunts, of which there were many, at least on her side, my grandparents, and even about people before that, as if knowing my place in history might somehow help me discover who I was. Of course, I already knew my place in time and longed mostly to get outside, but I listened to her whenever she tried to distract me because she was my mother. And I loved her. And really what else did I know? Then, once she was satisfied that I knew my personal history, she took me to my father's lab and sat me in front of his notebooks, where I learned about all of his discoveries as well as the murders. You couldn't call them by any other name.

"If I had never known any other world, then it's also safe to say the only language I knew was my father's research. I effectively took over exactly where he left off and became him.

"In my mother's suicide note, she made it clear that the future of my father's legacy was up to me.

"But I wasn't nine when I discovered the secrets of time travel. Nor was I twenty-nine, or even forty-nine, but more than seventy years old, subsisting on a nearly unlimited supply of powdered food I had discovered on a lower level, possibly left there in case of nuclear attack. Unable to find an exit, I worked on creating my own machine, using my father's collected data to approximate the effects of the fog in the lab, sending small inanimate objects forward or back by a minute, or registering a three percent slowdown in time on symmetrical crystal oscillators. Small victories, I know, but still, I was encouraged to continue. Then after nearly fifty-six years of looking at the same numbers on the same blackboard, while God knows what happened in the world above me, whether or not it even still existed, I suddenly had it, the Norse variant, staring me in the face like it was a signpost. The rats I discovered with the food survived all tests, and within another few years I felt I was ready. Unfortunately, even with the years of proof-checking, I had still miscalculated in certain key areas, still not covered every base. My father's partial successes had all been trips to the future, because that's what the grey fog seemed most often to do, but I was going back. I had a job to do. Had I simply decided to travel back in time a few years, or even a few days, perhaps looping and looping those days ad infinitum, I might have eventually discovered a way out, and then made a killing on the stock market, or betting on the Super Bowl, or even the National Spelling Bee, for that matter, it didn't matter. If personal gain had been my goal, breaking the fourth dimension could have been my equivalent of a blank cheque. To prove to anyone what I had accomplished, however, what *my father* had accomplished, I had to go back further. Predicting several years of sports winners would be tacked up to luck or coincidence, a party trick, like catching coins off your elbow, or downing someone's drink without touching the glass.

"I needed more, needed to solve the mystery of what had happened to my father, and even more so, needed to save the men who had given their lives in trust to his calculations. I had to go back further. So I set the date of my *anacronópete* to April 9, 2001, and made calculations to hopefully place me somewhere above ground, and the next thing I knew, someone was changing my diapers.

* * *

It took Henry several years to figure out what had happened – years of rehabilitation in which his body refused to function properly, unable to hold a pencil or chalk or use any other sort of computer. All calculations had to be done in his head, which took even longer, and led to more mistakes. He was discovered in a ditch. Someone he never knew brought him to the local police station, who brought him to family services, who stuck him in a home. Eventually, he was adopted by a couple who could not have children because one was barren, or the other had been previously married with children, or had had an operation, or perhaps it was some reason they wouldn't discuss with him. Eventually he realized the problem of travelling to the past, that not only had his body gone back in time but, unable to separate himself from the movement of time, it had also reversed itself in its growth. It was lucky for him, in fact, that he hadn't tried to go further, or he might have ceased to exist entirely. And so he considered himself fortunate, even if he was now trapped in this useless body without any access to his workshop or many of the materials he would require that wouldn't even be discovered for another decade or more, and no means to go searching for his father to warn him even if he did have access to research that could help him find where his father – and his mother, and yes, even himself – might be hiding.

Then he realized how much this new couple loved him, how much his involuntary smiles brought joy to their lives, and every morning when he woke he couldn't wait to see them, so he called out in his primitive cry, and when they entered his room, he kicked his legs uncontrollably and rolled partially from side-to-side, and laughed, until he was able to communicate with them in small ways, faking a cough to get their attention, or rubbing his eyes to say he was tired. And when his teeth began to force their way back through his gums, they held him. And when he spat up in the middle of the night, filling his nose so that he nearly choked on it, they were there to hold him again, and nurse him, and sing to him and swing him until he fell asleep again. And gradually, he gave up on the idea of being able to change the past and began to enjoy his new present.

It was all crazy, Chris Eaton said. It was insane. She asked him a series of questions. Who was the President in his time? Who won Super Bowl L? But he only bowed his head and apologized for not having paid more attention. Also: Why hadn't his mind also reverted? How was it that he was still the same man, with the same memories and capabilities, just in a child's body? He shrugged. A soul, perhaps? Or perhaps our consciousness exists on a plane with further dimensions still. Maybe this is who we really are, and this body is nothing different than a car or airplane, some kind of irrelevant vehicle. His was not to wonder why but to use what he had been given, and take full advantage of a life surrounded by loved ones and experiences instead of the one he had lived before, trapped alone under the ground for seventy-odd years. Besides, it was all the same life, wasn't it? Once upon a time he had been Henri Costa, but now he was Henry Code, and he supposed, since *zero energy* really removed all dimensional barriers, he could just as easily have come back as his father, or the president, or a bug, or her. Time travel is not only possible, he told her, it has already occurred. Over and over. In our past. In our future. In fact, past, future, they're both the same thing, each one ending where the other begins, and there's this monumental event, this Big Bang, which is supposed to explain how everything began, these rivers and deserts and tear drops and secret longings, except it really only creates more questions. Like what was there before that? And before that? And what about us? Our births? Does our identity come into being in those first moments of corporeal existence? Or does it exist in some prior form? Like a seed? Or a soul bank? Does it exist after us, before us, or does it even matter? Are we any different from one another?

Far in our future, as the universe completes its massive birthing contraction, progressing and compressing, growing and dying, it will contract black holes like chicken pox. The universe only needs to shrink to the smallest fraction of its normal size for the relative density to make black holes as common as humans, or flies, viruses, each one a singularity among many, and then eventually there will be an explosion, like the trapped fumes of a corroded Simca van, all you need is one tiny spark, jumpstarted by two stray molecules eventually colliding with each other, the space between them rendered infinitesimally small and unavoidable, and the spark will set off a chain reaction, in the centre of one of those singularities, at the centre of a universe so small we'd probably never notice it, and the shock waves will actually travel along the tendrils of the singular wormhole back in time to what we think of as the first three seconds and it will start all over again. The Big Bang. God.

But that, of course, is just one possibility among infinite, and these millions and billions and kajillions of singularities are all operating simultaneously, starting over and over and over, opening themselves up to countless repeated lives, always room for one more, out of sequence, taking you back three days, then three years, then thirty, then a minute, then a million, as if filling in the gaps, like defragging a computer, or the memory of a dying man, until all the pieces make a life, and even if the life you're currently living is horrible beyond belief, none of it really matters because eventually your life is gone as you know it, like the busking magician brought before Napoleon who was told that his life was over unless he could produce true magic, in one year, a wand or elixir or magic coin, that could make the emperor feel happy when he was sad, and sad when he was feeling happy, so dramatic had his mood swings become that he sought to control them just as he had seized control of all Europe, and the street huckster, who up to now had made a living off people with three cups, a ball and some clever distraction, was sent back out into the city, and naturally he thought about running, just maintaining his vector right out of Paris and France and Europe and who knows, maybe eventually reaching China or Africa or Siberia or the Atlantic, he wasn't sure which direction he was even pointed, but he knew, as all Europeans knew, that the Emperor would eventually find him, that Napoleon had achieved everything he had ever set out to do, so running was futile, and he turned his mind to the task at hand. For one year the magician travelled France and Europe and who knows, not running or hiding but searching, out in the open, seeking out the wisest men of every village he encountered and emerging with nothing but directions to a man in a neighboring village that was said to be even wiser, consulting with doctors and shamen and witches and priests, fortune-tellers and conjurers and clairvoyants and even an exorcist, all of whom had nothing for him, and when he returned to Napoleon's palace on the anniversary of his sentence, he could not even look up from the floor, and he said, Emperor, My Emperor, for the past year I have traveled all of France and Europe and who knows, and I have spoken to doctors and shamen and witches and priests, and even an exorcist, and in all of that searching, I was unable to find anything for you. Until, that is, I was on my way back to the palace, and I was stopped by a blind idiot trying to peddle his wares. He had no answer to my question, but offered me one of his rings, which were all identical, because there is always one thing that each person can do well, even a blind idiot, with the same inscription that he had pressed into it himself, and suddenly I knew the answer: We're all in the same boat.

By the time she was ready to leave the hospital, she could no longer trace the line of her life from the accident to the present moment, was no longer even sure why they'd been in the car that day of the accident, and she began thinking of her life not in the straight line of biographies, but passing in quantum leaps, so that the various stories of her existence were not linked by logic at all, but sat alone like cutlery in a drawer, ready to nourish or cut her, linked only by her own imagination. So one minute she was leaving the hospital in a wheelchair (institutional policy), and the next she was in a bar in Panama City (on her honeymoon?), watching a mediocre jazz band and waiting for her plate of carpaccio to arrive. She was eleven. She was seventy-two. Sometimes it didn't even feel like it was her. Sometimes it felt like she was underwater, perhaps drowning, and she blinked and was immediately jerked to another instant.

She theorized this aimlessness as the result of losing her family, her anchor. Without them, she was drifting through nothing. She was a child, begging her own mother to get her saxophone lessons, drum lessons, dancing lessons, dance camp. She had to go to dance camp. And as soon as she arrived she called home crying because she wanted her own bed, and something recognizable to eat, and for the instructors to stop being mean to her. For the other girls to stop being mean to her. She'd been told she had malformed feet, not a dancer's feet, and so she refused to remove her sweat socks before addressing the bar. Her mother refused to bring her home but did get another room down the hall in the same university residence for herself and Chris's sister.

Then she was up all night cramming for finals.

And buying groceries when she dropped the bottle of milk on the floor.

And being touched longingly for the first time.

A flash of being chased through the house by her mother with a wooden spoon. Laughing. A hint of the pride in her first dishwasher. In the grocery store again. And the first time she saw her future husband. After the crash, Chris Eaton spent many years without leaving her home. She paid a neighbourhood boy to mow her lawn. Her groceries were delivered. She had subscriptions to nine publications for the crossword puzzles. On several occasions, she wrote letters to them about words not appearing in her *Collins*, which seemed unfair to her. She was fairly certain, for example, that *banjax* could not be a word, and inserted *banger* instead; but that would have made the across words into *tag*, *ame* and *mir*, all of which were certainly words, and some of which might have been poetic metaphors for "a symbol, to some" and "goes to great depths," but certainly not a word that meant "crossbreed."

It was Ian who then reminded her of the international space station, with its multinational crew, and she felt much happier.

Living with Jules changed his life entirely. To the point where he was sure the Chris Eaton he had been in New York – or the Chris Eaton in London, or Barcelona, or even across the bay in St. Petersburg as a child – would not have recognized him. Through Jules, Chris Eaton became more involved with the Bay Area homosexual community, an advocate for lesbian, gay, bisexual and transgender (LGBT) culture, joined Equality Florida, was elected as secretary to the Gay and Lesbian Center of Tampa Bay, and worked for a short time for the Tampa International Gay and Lesbian Film Festival, which had grown out of the city's annual Pride events to be one of the largest in North America. He also went back to school, just barely making the cut-off point to transfer his credits from his first attempt, enrolling in a Psychology

314

BA at The University of Tampa, and under the tutelage of an amazing professor progressed directly into the Gender Studies Masters with a focus on heterosexual psychoanalysis. He graduated in a swift ten months, but just barely, and he suspected that they might have approved his thesis simply to be rid of him. He'd been quite vocal about not continuing to his doctorate, so displeased and frustrated was he with the political nature of the academic world. Instead, he withdrew from that world entirely, and he began writing a column for *The Weekly Planet* called "Each Is Torn," attempting to address the tensions and confusions between members of the LGBT and heterosexual communities, which was syndicated in several other regions of the U.S. When that other Chris Eaton ran for the Florida House of Representatives in 2002, there was naturally some confusion, and to some degree, because it allowed him to talk about gay politicians and the way many of them try to hide their sexuality, he sometimes played it up.

* * *

Then, in a letter to his column, after he'd allowed it to become more and more sensationalist over the years, a reader inquired about watching gay porn, wondering if getting turned on by it necessarily made him gay, too. The writer had been watching a lot of straight porn with the same actor in it, had gotten to really relate to that guy, to feel more like, when that guy was doing some chick, so was he. It just felt more real somehow. But then he rented a video starring the actor that must have been placed in the wrong section, because the story didn't work the way it should have, with the two construction workers talking about being tense and then maybe one of them gets called into the portable by the foreman who happens to be a chick with big boobs, and instead just stayed on the two construction workers. *Who knew*, the letter ended, *that Ian Dowd used to be queer?*

What do I do?

Chris Eaton spent the next week in a daze, unable to even mention it to Jules. Angelo was alive and had made the switch to straight porn? It made no sense. Surely the letter was a joke. But who would know him well enough to know that he knew Dowd/Angelo? And who would want to play something so cruel on him? Jules? It made no sense.

Besides: he'd heard from some common friends that Angelo had never come out of his coma.

But that had been years ago...

He went to a video store that wasn't his own, and lurked around the gay section for some time before casually slipping over to the breeder shelves, as if he'd happened on them by accident, picking up random titles without even looking at them. He found a handful of titles with Dowd in the credits, but no photo of him on the front, as is normally the case with these things. So he was forced to rent them. Only, when he brought them to the desk, the chubby Chinese girl asked him for a credit card to secure a membership and he was too afraid she might recognize his name so he left empty-handed.

He turned to the Internet. A photo search, much like looking at the video dust jackets, produced mostly just shots of splayed women, but some of the pages also provided short scenes on video, and many of those featured pairings with the aforementioned Dowd.

Definitely not the same person. But then what was the letter writer talking about? It made no sense. He told Jules. Wasn't that strange, he said. The same name, he said.

It's a play on words, Jules said. And not a particularly clever one. Why would you be so surprised?

And he wasn't sure. He replied to the letter in the next issue and tried to forget about it. From work, he decided to call Angelo's uncle Ernest, but couldn't find a listing for him, so he looked up the hospital and they told him that there was no longer anyone there by that name.

Can you look again, Chris Eaton said.

We have no one by the name of Angelo Monterossi.

And he began to show doubt. Was this not the age of plastic surgery and witness protection programs? Was it not possible to completely change one's identity, if that were the goal?

Over a five hundred dollar debt to you? Jules asked.

But the obsession was already planted. Even if this man weren't Angelo, he now had a firm place in Chris Eaton's being. There was so little he could find about Dowd's life on the Internet, however, where he had come from, or even complete lists of his work. Most entries on male porn stars were for the gay ones, with fairly useless and probably inaccurate information about penis length. What he did find was contradictory and overblown, based entirely on rumour and conjecture. Dowd had been born in Missouri, or Indiana, or Ohio, or Alberta. There were *even* stories of him being Russian, snuck across the border as a baby in the tights of one of those monstrous female Cold War weightlifters that were defecting to the US in the eighties in herds, looking like no more than a third glute, and reaching his own epic proportions by suckling straight from her steroid-shrivelled breast. *Or* he had been born to a new initiate at a nunnery in Italy, raised in the eyes of God by the Sisters themselves, until the sight of young Iago became too much of a temptation. His nickname of Woodpecker was perhaps the greatest clue that he was actually American, because it seemed to point towards him coming from Ohio, where he supposedly played high school football for the Woodville Woodpeckers. But there was also one story of him taking on the name before dropping out of college in St. Louis, because he was originally from Raicheston, Missouri, whose most famous progeny was the creator and voice of the early Woody Woodpecker cartoons, Ben Hardaway (although if that were the case, you'd imagine he might have taken on the animator's name as his porn handle, too). Then there were the rumours that he'd received the name simply because so many of his co-stars were forced to take short sabbaticals after appearing with him and said in interviews that he could drill holes in trees with that thing.

In any case, this other Dowd seemed to have lead the life that Angelo had always sought before his accident, only with different sex positions. He had somehow managed to walk off with all of Angelo's lucky breaks while Angelo had been napping, or drinking, or apologizing for not being able to get it up.

Desperate, he decided to search for Dowd in academic writing. Porn studies was such a growing field and he was already familiar with a lot of the current academic heavyweights. All he could find on Dowd through the university library, however, was a passing mention in the thesis of a colleague at the *University of California Santa Barbara*, about gay men of colour in porn and how these stereotypes have affected the romantic lives of other gay men. In addition to some very poignant and precise insights of her own, the author had interviewed dozens of actors and industry insiders, including a woman named Tina Cerosh who told how Dowd was naturally not his real name, and that he had chosen it as a post-modern homage to the gay industry, much in the same way that, as the celebrity obsession of the nineties took over, there came a trend of gay porn actors naming themselves after the real names abandoned by the tinsel town elite. Names like Thomas Mapother, Joe Levitch and Carlos Ray, but also Francis Gumm (largely in tranny flics) and Robert Zimmerman. This coincided with similar names with women in straight porn, which saw the rise of stars like Tara Patrick (the real name of actress and popular softcore model Carmen Electra), the predictable flood of actresses with the name Paris, and the exotic DP-specialist Israel Baline, star of such a broad range of pornographic genres like the rare British-style musical comedy *Oh, How I Hate to Get it Up in the Morning*, the ass-to-ass lesbian classic *Cheek to Cheek*, and *Anyone You Can Do (I Can Do Better)*, a sort of Olympic-style reality film with the aforementioned Patrick and a cast of amateurs. She wasn't entirely sure where he'd first come across the name Ian Dowd, but she believed that he'd heard it at a party in New York City where he'd seen a wall poster for a brilliant parody film with the name on it.

She also claimed to have been Dowd's lover.

But finding Tina Cerosh wasn't nearly as simple as he had imagined it would be. Mostly because, as he discovered later, despite the fact she was living in nearby St. Petersburg, Cerosh was not, as it turned out, her real last name.

* * *

Tina Cerosh, née Wax, after a horrifically fatal automobile accident in which certain vehicle parts should have been recalled but were not, was raised by her Albanian-Jewish grandfather in Celebration, Florida: Walt Disney's fantasy town on the outskirts of his fabled Disneyland. Her grandfather, James Wax, had worked for The Walt Disney Company for years – several years before its inception, in fact – as one of the artists who fashioned the wax representations of Disney's cartoon creations for use in his rides. An undeniable master, Wax was responsible for many of the original figures on rides like *Mr. Toad's Wild Ride* and *It's a Small World*, for which he was also on the crew when it was originally created by Pepsi for the 1964 New York World's Fair. As soon as Walt Disney laid eyes on it, it's said he hired the entire team on the spot, and James Wax, at the ripe old age of 54, went from fifteen years of relative obscurity in small-town museums to an extremely comfortable career in the most wonderful place on Earth. When plans for Celebration were first announced, Wax bought the first home, where he planned to enjoy his retirement. But moving day, which should have been one of the more exciting days of his life in 1996, was tragically marred by the death of his only son and daughter-in-law.

* * *

James Wax loved his granddaughter in the way that grandfathers will: to excess. Anything she needed, he got her. And when he couldn't afford it, he went to Roy Disney and asked for a favor, which he very nearly always got. He called her Cricket, presumably after Jiminy. And she called him *Zdziz*, which he told her was Albanian for Grandpa. Because he was retired, they played together most days like they were schoolmates. In fact, he took her out of class on multiple occasions to go fishing, to make art, or just to ride on the Disney attractions, to which he had lifetime free access. Sometimes he tried to scare her with stories about people being thrown from the Space Mountain roller coaster. But he'd also been on it so many times that he had the entire route memorized. And when they rode it together, they'd sit at the front and scream out the direction they were going before they hit it, ruining it for everyone.

When she became a teenager, they grew naturally distant. She rebelled and began using drugs. She wanted to be a writer and felt that, in order to be genuine about it, she had to scratch every seedy underbelly she could. She and her friends would often take trips up to New York without even telling him, and he would not sleep for days until she returned. Once she walked almost the entire length of Seventh Avenue, alone, wondering what she might do if she were suddenly rushed by young thugs from an alleyway or subway entrance. A homeless man asked her for a dollar. She said all she had was a subway token and showed it to him, and the man offered to buy her a boat later, once he got back on his feet, if only she would only give him that token. I need it to get home, she told the man. It's my last one. And he said: Girl, I will *buy* you a *house*. I will *buy* you a *mansion*. And they walked and talked some more. He followed her for the next fifteen blocks and never once asked her for money again, only licked his lips and stretched his hands and talked about the mayor, made a dated joke about an old basketball player with AIDS, and told her how he once worked in a processing plant for chickens and how you should always wash chicken when you buy it 'cos it never mattered if they dropped that shit on the floor, they just picked it up and wrapped it in plastic and hoped some rich, white fuck would eat it.

At one corner, the homeless man saw someone he knew, so he asked Tina to wait. He ran across the street and spoke quietly to the other man, occasionally glancing or pointing back across at her. She waited. Then they kept on walking, and when they reached her friend's apartment, she shook the homeless man's hand and gave him the token.

Her Zdziz, it can be presumed, would have been proud of her, had the friend not been a gay man who worked in porn. Perhaps he would have been proud of her regardless. It is difficult to say because he never knew where she went and what she got up to. Nor did he ask. And for many years she took him for granted, this rock in her life that would always be there for her, her anchor, until one day he took sick, bedridden and powerless. And when she realized she might lose him – would lose him – she spent the next three months at his bedside, feeding and cleaning him and basically keeping him company as the Parkinson's took hold. He fell into fits, began to hallucinate. Called her strange things like Danootah. Or Matoosh. Told her where she should send the clean sheets when she was finished. Spoke in a language she didn't understand. And his final words to her were proud and defiant: Our name is Cerosz. We will not back down.

**

One morning in 1939, although he had been doing nothing wrong, Zdziz Cerosz was arrested. He had been working as a chandler near Gdansk, as his father had before him, as his grandfather before his father, and so on. He had a wife, two children, and a plot of land given to his great-grandfather by the occupying nobility of the time, at the greater proliferation of the incandescent electric bulb, for his years of devoted service. Cerosz, only half-awake, sat half-upright in his bed and said: Who are you? There was laughter in a neighbouring room. And he was taken, quite roughly, by hand and then by cart, to the Long Market square for due process.

Despite his great-grandfather's servitude to the Prussian Duke, the occupying Germans classified Cerosz as third category in the *Deutsche Volksliste*, with most other Kashubians, and he was given the choice of either joining the Nazi forces or being sent to a concentration camp. After witnessing the torture of his neighbour, Cerosz chose the former to protect his family, who were permitted to stay on their land, but he was sent back to the Reich as a labourer. The army, thank God, would not take him; his right hand had been horribly burned as a child when he'd crept into his father's workshop and grasped instinctively for the brightly coloured pot of wax. And so he was stationed in a hospital in Holland where they tended specifically to the Wermacht's non-German soldiers, assigned to laundry for the first several years until the situation became more desperate and he was suited up, armed with nothing but a pistol and bayonet, both useless to him with his mangled hand, and stuffed in another train bound for the front.

Of course no one, not even his wife back home, knew that he was actually part of the Polish resistance, and that the hospital in which he laboured was a major hub in supplying intelligence to the Allies in Britain. Highly classified information, including the location, composition and movement of German forces was smuggled from the Western Front to Cerosz in the clothing of injured Poles, who were rarely coherent enough to be seen as a threat and searched. The doctors, mostly captured from Canada and France, were terribly understaffed, and so with every delivery, Cerosz was asked to help prep the men for surgery, undressing them and taking their clothing to be washed. Quickly pocketing what he found, Cerosz then spent his evenings in the linen storeroom, using his skills with wax to painstakingly retrace the information to clean articles of clothing with the ends of blunt candles. When these seemingly white articles of clothing were intercepted by other members of the Polish Underground on their way to the Eastern Front in the Ukraine, smuggled to the other side and doused with fresh pencil shavings by the Brits, the secret messages revealed themselves.

This re-con is largely considered to have been a major reason for the Allied victory. But it was so secret, for the safety of everyone involved, that as the war progressed, even Cerosz's family had grown to hate him. When he finally made it back to Gdansk following the German surrender, he discovered that his wife Danuta had remarried, to a communist who raised their children to think of Kashubia as a fairy tale, their language and culture of birth nothing more than folklore, and their father as a traitor. Before the war was even over, unbeknownst to most of the Polish resistance, the Allies had agreed to give Poland to the Soviets, as the Russians had already occupied the country and placed high-profile communists in its interim government. Many returning Kashubians like himself were arrested for treason and sent to work in the Silesian mines. And so he changed his name to James Wax and left for America.

After the death of her grandfather, Tina Wax officially changed her name back, to grant what she believed to be her grandfather's dying wish. But believing her Zdziz was Albanian and not Kashubian, she misspelled it as Cerosh.

* * *

The few Americans Chris Eaton could locate with the Cerosh surname had no relatives named Tina. All of them were also related and claimed to know anyone with the name in the U.S. So after weeks of searching in vain, Chris Eaton went back to the thesis. The Santa Barbara thesis bibliography took some time to navigate, but eventually he dug up another reference, in the memoir of Dick Ho, that detailed how hard it had been for himself and others in the porn industry to make the break to mainstream cinema. *Even (Ian) Dowd was having problems. And if that guy was stuck, what did that mean for the rest of us?* On the Internet Movie Database, Chris Eaton found an Ian Down, an Ian Dold, two by the name of Dodd and a remarkable five by Dowding. Most were non-actor listings – cinematographers, camera operators, grips, visual effects, a few in the music department and one mysterious "miscellaneous crew" – all of which he could discount almost immediately because they were too old to be Angelo (who would definitely be more likely to lie about his age in the other direction), or had worked prior to the mid-nineties, before he left New York, or even had fairly long careers in their respective fields. These were also jobs that Angelo, a purist, would never have deigned to perform. He was not above schlepping for his uncle making mannequins, but working in the movie business in any other capacity but actor or director would have been a fate worse than death.

Then he noticed one of the Dodds, despite a long career with the electrical department, had a single, fairly recent listing as an actor, in a sci-fi flick called *Earth Coins* (2004), about two stoners who can't scrape enough money together to buy pot so they cook up a scheme to become astronauts, reroute the rocket to Mars, and exchange their rare pocket change on the interstellar black market for premium grow, and Chris Eaton felt there was at least a chance that this might be a typographical and/or data entry error. The director, Chaise Torn, had been extremely successful with music videos, particularly with two genre-breakers for the punk band Heroin Cats and the experimental Christian songstress Ani Torches, and had been given the green light from 21st Century Fox for whatever feature project he had in his head. Because of his time making music videos, it was rumoured that he preferred working with non-traditional actors.

Torn was relatively easy to find. Despite a huge marketing push and some truly innovative filmmaking, *Earth Coins* was panned by most critics, and after that, he could barely find work again, not even in music. Posing as a reporter from *Entertainment Weekly*, Chris Eaton was able to reach him in a matter of three phone calls and soon they were meeting for coffee in New York. Unfortunately, Torn knew very little about where he might find Dowd. But what he did provide, however, was Ian Dowd's unfinished autobiography, provided to him

324

by Dowd on the set because he thought it would make a great biopic.

The manuscript, tentatively titled *The Bigger They Come, the More Money They Make*, was woefully lacking in many areas, unless you were particularly interested in Dowd's thoughts on wine; or his theory that it was Shakespeare who had actually written the King James translation of *The Bible* because, published on the bard's forty-sixth birthday, the forty-sixth word from the beginning of Psalm 46 is *shake*, and the forty-sixth from the end is *spear*; or that Kennedy's assassination was a cold-served revenge killing for Lincoln; or in the lists of some of the more spectacular collections he had gathered over the years, including a nearly complete set of official Superbowl Championship caps for all the losing teams since they were first introduced in 1966 (or rather, three years later, because it wasn't until then, after The New York Jets had created such an upset over the Baltimore Colts the year prior, that both teams went into the final feeling that optimistic). After the defeats, most of these hats (which were made solely for the players) were immediately destroyed, rushed as the clock officially struck 00:00 by the most trusted members of the cheerleading squad from their spot in a box behind the bench to a special incinerator installed in both dressing rooms before the game. Someone always managed to keep one for sentimental reasons, though, if not a retiring cheerleader then one of the manufacturers, which meant there was also always a price at which they could be purchased. The only exceptions appeared to be: the 1989 Broncos, because their coach was too superstitious to tempt fate in that way; the 1983 Dolphins, who took extra precautions to make the hats themselves, by hand, and then quickly devoured them on the bench as the last seconds died away; and the 1990 Broncos, who were so convinced that they had no chance of winning that it's said they didn't even bother making them.

It said nothing about his youth, or anything prior to the film that really broke him – *Hung Gary, Hung Ross* (1993), about "a team of well-endowed backdoor-to-backdoor salesmen," best known at the time for featuring the record number of unique penetration shots in any porn film, with 138 in only 100 minutes, just short of one per minute, including everything from oral to anal to pumpkins and indeed several shots of things like hands reaching into briefcases, stir-sticks in coffee and pencils in sharpeners, which has recently called the record into question, especially by the rival director who had held the record previously. It was as if he'd just materialized out of thin air.

The film's success led to an entire Hung series of films, including:

- *Hung Out to Dry* (1993);
- *Hung Jury* (1993);
- *Hung Dinger* (1994);
- the Hung detective saga that began with *Gary Hung: Private Dick* (1994), cycled through a number of parody-style offers like *The Naked Hung 9 ½"* (1996) and ended with his death at the hands, mouth and everything else of his nemesis, Anita Kvicky, in *Hung Over* (2000);
- and a vampire porn, banking on the popularity of a television drama for teens, bringing our hero Dick Hung back from the dead in *The Hunger* (2001).

The sequels and spinoffs became even more ridiculous, transforming Hung into everything from a cigar-smoking Cuban freedom fighter to a triad of martial arts films – *Hung Fu* (1994), *Hung Pao* (1995) and *Hung Kong* (1997) – which were less than sensitive on the racial front but did manage to create a strong political statement with regards to England's transfer of sovereignty of the island-state back to the Chinese government.

The book unfortunately contained no contact information, and he had to admit that the search for Dowd was likely over. At the very least, the chances of him and Angelo being the same person had grown increasingly slim.

Then he flipped over one of the pages and saw it had all been printed on letterhead from a company in California called Decter-American, purchased in 1999 by Silvestri USA.

Chris Eaton grabbed everything he could carry and caught the first bus for the opposite coast.

There were places, on his missions, that he avoided at all costs. As a child, he had heard the story of a seventeenth century Frenchman named André Pujom whose name, when anagrammed, became *pendu à Riom* (in those days, the letters *j* and *i* were often interchangeable), which translated as *hanged in Riom*, a township approximately three days from his birthplace of Saint-Rémy-de-Provence. As this was also the birthplace of Michel de Nostradame, more commonly known as Nostradamus, it was near impossible to grow up outside the influence of the burgeoning industry of the occult. And yet, the young Pujom leaned heavily on the side of contrariness, and rejected all forms of divination that were presented to him, all of which seemed to point in the same direction, including the old midwife who, on the power of a vision from his placenta, wrapped the umbilical cord around his newborn neck, and the phrenologist who jokingly remarked that the perfect roundness of his skull, without a bump on it at all, seemed ideal for the passing of a noose. He refused to believe that his life could be so predetermined, not even when the gypsy dropped all nine needles into his bowl and let out a long, low whistle. When his mother passed, they tossed her ashes into the air and they were carried by a gust of wind and hung there long after he had given up and gone home. There were astrologists, of course, and numerologists. More than he could count. And there were others who attempted to reveal his end through the tarot, his aura, the burning of figs, flocks of birds, mashing exotic fruits like kumquats, or avocados, water currents, rainwater, swirling water in a cup, passing water, falling in water, firing arrows into the sky, dogs, smoke, dogs who smoked, dripping wax, fields of light, gongs, the raving of lunatics, random shouts heard in a crowd, opening the dictionary to random words, the number of raisins in a brioche, ants in an anthill, beetle tracks, fish behaviour, dice, dominos, the I Ching, Ouija, voting, small objects, large objects, the palms of the hand, the soles of the feet, the buttocks, things found at the beach, the flipping of a supposedly magic coin. And each one he shrugged off like a shawl on a hot day and went about his daily business of orneriness. But the anagram of his name, for some reason, a combination of temurah and onomancy (as opposed to oinomancy, which was divination through wine), was one that he could not ignore, and he was more angered than opposed to the idea that something as simple as a name could decide his fate. It plagued his thoughts through day and night, night and day, causing him to live in fear for much of his life, until one day he decided to take it upon himself to set things right, packed his bags and hired a coachman to bring him directly to Riom itself.

The plan was simple. He had, in fact, done nothing wrong. So it should be simple enough to approach a judge and convince the man of his innocence. Through the entire circuitous route through Grenoble, Geneva, Lyon and Saint-Esseintes, he rehearsed his speech to the coachman, who did not hear a thing because he was partially deaf and prone to sleeping while his horses followed their familiar route. By the time they reached Riom, Pujom was sure he was free of his destiny forever. The judge, who was more than a little startled and confused by the fiercely strained young man, nevertheless agreed to grant him a special decree of innocence, something he drafted on the spot on the back of a paper napkin, more to be rid of him than anything else. Free at last from his curse, Pujom decided not to push his luck any further and set out for the Americas, searching for gold in Costa Rica. Within a year of settling in Limón, he had found no gold but had managed to accrue quite a fortune trading illegally with New Granada, until one day he went out with his mestizo wife for a picnic, became lost near the village of Moin, and eventually starved to death.

The story was equally bad for Holland's Jan du Pruom, who knew nothing of his predicted fate when he came to Riom the day after the Frenchman and was nearly run over in the market by the coach taking Pujom to the coast, which forced his horse off the road where it trampled a poor washerwoman to death. He was hanged later the next day.

* * *

Thus, Chris Eaton never traveled to Norway, for fear of contracting High Altitude Cerebral Edema (*HACE*) *in Stor*. He cut a wide path around Wales, including Chester, else risk being *shot in Caer* (the Welsh name for that British city, as well as the general word for a fortress). He even made a rule, as ridiculous as it seemed, not to travel to the islands of Micronesia, so he wouldn't be involved in a *crash in Eot*, though many of the inhabitants of the smallest island had probably never even seen a car anywhere, let alone on the island itself. This particular combination also precluded travel to Spain and Holland, specifically the villages of Teo and Oet, where crashes were much more possible.

But that was only the version of his name that he went by most commonly. So, as Christopher Eaton, he also had to be anxious about Spain around the seaside, and zoos, and any sort of unidentifiable foliage, else he be mauled by a *cheetah in Port Ros*, or if he considered Chris Avard Eaton – and this one was more uncomfortable than life-threatening – develop *a rash in Corterva*. (Rashes were also a risk in the U.S., at least in Corter, VA.) He risked equal discomfort in New Zealand, India and Finland, with the possibility of being *chased in Ratorva* (site of one of the country's famous geysers), it being *overcast in Harda*, or being *scarred in Vaahto*. More crucial, naturally, was steering clear of Germany, Hungary and Mexico, where he might become a *cadaver in Sörth*, be *charred in Sovata*, or *starved in Arocha*. And despite the logical side of his brain saying there was nothing to fear, he bypassed both the villages of Stava and Vasat in Central Serbia and Turkey, in an attempt to ward off an attack by a potential *orca herd*. If he were to ever set foot in the French village of Orvès, he would expect both *a parched throat* and *a hatched raptor*.

Of course, writing these locations off his travel itineraries did not reduce Chris Eaton's stress. Because these were only the anagrams he had figured out. He also had to worry about aches in some location using the letters *o*, *r* and *t*. There might also be *a crash in Ovedart* (or some other location using those letters that actually existed), or likewise *a crash in Ovedarttopher*. In what location, using the letters *a-r-c-o-v-a*, might he eventually be trashed? Where in *a-d-o-v-a-t* would he be ambushed by archers? *Roasted in a-c-h-a-r-v, shaved in t-r-a-r-o-c-a, tarred in c-a-s-h-o-v-a, retards in a-c-h-o-v-a*: it was nearly enough to keep him from leaving the house. And he spent hours and days, when back in St. Petersburg, poring over atlases and encyclopedias, searching for potentially lethal arrangements.

Certainly, like Pujom, he never predicted getting excessively fat in one of the indigenous territories of Central America.

***

His plane departed for Kuna Yala at six thirty in the morning, the only plane of the day, acting more like a city bus as it touched down at several of the Kuna islands on its tour. The smell of rotting mangoes that hung over the city – the trees were everywhere, and the fruit struck the ground with a rhythmic regularity – was nowhere to be found on the islands. The fruit trees found it more difficult to exist in the sand and salt water. And so the islands were nearly devoid of plant life; most agriculture was grown on the mainland and then paddled over daily, just like the fresh water. In fact, one of the more respected jobs for islanders was to fetch water, and the ones who were chosen made the trek several times a day and then came back to watch television. (During the prior rainy season, some Colombian smugglers had run their charge onto a ridge of coral and jumped ship, and since there was no way anyone could complain about it, elders had decided to outfit the entire town with the contraband sets and vcrs.) One day Chris Eaton helped some women carry the massive plastic jugs from the dock to a home at the centre of the island and in return they provided him with a stalk of sugarcane that he might have used as a real cane, and he chewed on the end for several hours, sitting on the edge of a ship and spitting the fibrous bits into the water where they floated among the rusting batteries and human waste. He learned later that the men on the boat were also Colombian smugglers and had discussed killing him, but he had misunderstood them to be talking about their mothers.

The community he had gone to explore for a potential future mission was called Hersop Trvandi, located on one of the smaller islands in the Corregimiento de Carti. His guide, who spoke fluent Spanish, Kuna and some English, was poor at holding his liquor, which he found far too often in a place where alcohol was not allowed. But he was nice enough for it, if perhaps a little too clingy and cloying when he was most under the influence. Chris Eaton stayed with his family in a home that was made almost entirely out of sticks, with cans of beer holding the thatched roofs out from the beams to prevent extra seepage. He spent much of his time there cocooned in his hammock, pretending to be asleep. In it he could see nothing, and was periodically bumped by what he imagined to be the dog he had seen earlier wearing a necklace, which just made him miss his own dog Bolivar even more. He got Bolivar in the north, on a trip to Nova Scotia with a girlfriend whose name he could no longer remember. They'd decided to canoe the province's National Park, and they'd both bought tobacco pipes at the Duty Free to complete the pastoral. She had worn her hair in a bob and had enjoyed aerobics, with a weakness for other vices, too. "So long as they aren't super-addictive, you know?" For most of the trip, around joyful coughing fits that frightened away nearly all of the wildlife, she had insisted on calling him Bumbridge, and had told him stories about her time in the Boer War, her paddle drifting unenergetically at her side as she stopped, once again, to relight. He had chosen for her the name Bigglesworth, and had spoken of converting tribal pagans. She had laughed. She enjoyed his irony, she had said. And he had no idea what she was talking about.

On the canoe back to the ranger station, they had passed another couple with a Lab perched regally in the canoe's bottom. Already bored of his date and immediately smitten with the canine's regal nonchalance, Chris Eaton had asked them where they had bought her, and they had told him of a woman just the other side of the border into New Brunswick. Despite the breeder's reluctance to sell a dog for what she deemed the wrong reasons ("Folks should never buy an animal on impulse," she warned him), she had also felt there was no harm in dealing with someone who wouldn't bother making a trip this far back just to return him.

Chris Eaton and Bolivar had been together ever since. Even on most of his missions. Particularly to South America, where the name Bolivar still really meant something. But he'd been warned that the dogs in Panamanian towns were particularly feral, with a pecking order to their street-living that Bolivar might not readily adapt to. And he'd become too old to go through the quarantine procedure on the way back. So, this time, he decided to leave him at home.

***

One morning on Trvandi, Chris Eaton woke with a pain in his back, and a slight fever, and he didn't roll out of his hammock until noon. His guide took him to a neighbouring island to snorkel, and the white sand and beautifully clear water made him feel so natural and pure that he momentarily forgot his aches. But when he climbed back into the boat, the guide made a clicking noise with his cheek and said they needed to see a woman when they returned. She looked reassuringly like a tree stump. And she moved almost as slowly, with a bark that gave off threatening cracks as she scowled around the hut. Whatever traditional clothing the Kuna had once worn had, over the years, been replaced by remaindered lots of clothing from American Kmarts and Zellers, and her t-shirt said *Blondes have more fun*. She was an expert in lancing boils, and she stuck Chris Eaton with various needles, none of which made him feel any prick, nor did they make him feel better. Nothing could make him feel better. He knew he was dying. His limbs were so swollen that they felt like flippers. He found it difficult to breathe and longed only to throw himself back in the water. Was this the end, he wondered? How would he be remembered? He began a list of regrets, at the top of which, almost trivially, was not praying more, not maintaining closer ties with his sister, not making the trip to a friend's wedding. He regretted making that joke during the debate at the Suncoast Tiger Bay Club. He regretted that he had mistakenly started as a Republican and was later seen as indecisive. He regretted having supported John Edwards in the 2004 Primary or perhaps not having supported him more.

Most recently, he regretted leaving Bolivar with a service instead of a friend, although he'd been too proud to ask for help in that way. He could imagine Bolivar whimpering in the corner of the kennel, unused to the noise of so many other animals. When he'd made the decision, he'd only been thinking of himself. He also regretted some of the relationships he'd fouled in various ways, telling Julie that he loved her, for example, or never telling Emily at all. Letting Melissa take that job. Leaving Chanté to die in that earthquake. Before leaving for Panama he had dated a woman named Tina Cerosh. She said she was a writer but he'd never had a chance to check out anything she'd produced. The date had gone well but he had been too preoccupied with his pending trip to call her before leaving. If he ever made it out of here, he vowed to himself, he would make a point of asking her out again on his return.

***

He recalled a story about two entomologists he had read about in the tourist guide, documenting the Hora insect, a tiny beetle closest in resemblance to the Malachite (which is actually quite plentiful in the mountainous areas of Panama but not in the coastal jungles

333

where they encountered the Hora) and with a similarly acidic defense mechanism to the Black Blister beetle or Meloid only much more fatal. Their names were Juan Chorea, from Portugal, whose grandfather was the first to develop a neurological disease that they later named after him, and Albert Nits, a Brit whose main claim to fame before the Hora was not that he had survived the sinking of the Titanic but that he had arrived too late to get on it, thereby narrowly avoiding what many people would call his fate. Chorea and Nits had actually been tracking a mythological species of ant called heroic ants, or *antioch ers*, after an archeological discovery in a heavily eroded Mayan pyramid north of La Libertad in Guatemala. The mound-like pyramid had actually been discovered by German officials who had gone to Mexico to convince the locals to rise up against the potential threat of the United States to enter the First World War. They thought they had stumbled upon evidence that the Central American indigenous groups were actually the Biblical thirteenth tribe. After the Germans were forced to flee, however, a team of British anthropologists was sent to excavate and study, and when the tunnels suddenly opened up beneath them, they knew they were looking at something much different, something much more confusing and spectacular, something no one had ever seen before. The structure of the underground tunnels, for one, was far more complex than anything the Mayans had ever created, with occasional, rough-hewn, circular chambers and tunnels that dropped straight down without any perceivable mechanism for raising and lowering. They found one hundred and thirty-five of these chambers before abandoning the project. The vertical spiraling shafts descended, as far as they could tell, for approximately six or seven kilometres, exceeding any mining operations before or since.

Then they found the engravings, the sight of which made their Guatemalan guides bolt off into the surrounding jungle: ants the size of men, battling what they assumed to be the Mayans on horseback, carved directly into the rock and still dripping with a mucus that shimmered in the torchlight. That was when Chorea and Nits were brought in. Chorea discovered traces of chemicals that could not conclusively be disproved as ant pheromones. Nits confirmed the markings seemed not incongruous with the mandibles of something like a bull ant, if said bull ant happened to be over a metre tall. They were convinced, and hastily sent a letter off to the Royal Entomological Society in London. But what had happened to them? These heroic ants? Most ants are known to carry their dead back to the nest for proper reverence. Without any bodies or graves, Chorea assumed they must have voluntarily packed up their wagons and moved on. Nits agreed. The question was where. So they spent several months studying the wall markings, scraping their torchlight across every rounded inch until they discovered another hidden antechamber. Images on that wall included a *cucaracha*, or cockroach, and there was a tiny roach inset that seemed to claim the heroic ants had merely sensed a change in global temperature and headed south. Nits and Chorea followed. In Honduras, an old Miskito woman told them in her Creole English of a legend where large, wasp-like aliens had visited their king and shared secrets of building temples. A Nicaraguan elder also spoke of a black, shiny people who "arrived first from the sky" and taught them how to domesticate animals. By this point, the presumed exaggeration of their numbers seemed to have been cut in half. In fact, in one local story, the aliens seemed slow and lethargic, ill. They had been struck by a sickness, it seemed, which had caused them to first lose their wings, and then, two at a time, their extra legs. By the time they appeared in the mythology of the peoples of Costa Rica, they were merely shiny black men and women with antennae, imposing and silent.

The trail finally ended in the coastal regions of Kuna Yala. There, Chorea and Nits found no heroic ants. Instead, they found the Hora. Or rather, the Hora found them. Nits woke up feeling as though he'd been shot in the backside, so great was the pain that erupted from his posterior, particularly when he attempted to sit. The British, however, are a modest troupe, and so he refrained from showing his ass to Chorea, or even discussing it. Meanwhile, Chorea could not believe the pain between his shoulder blades, on the back of his neck, and even behind his ear. He reached back and found all three areas swollen and wet. But this was not entirely surprising since they hadn't stopped sweating since they arrived. Over the next several months, they studied multiple colonies of the Hora, and realized that the bright beetles were extremely careful not to mix, not even to take members of neighbouring colonies as slaves. Another characteristic that seemed rare in the insect world was the existence of multiple queens in one hive, and that, although they did live together, the progeny of one queen was unlikely to ever interact directly with the progeny of another. They performed experiments where they extracted the queens and tried transplanting them to different hives. Was one queen the same as another? They expected the soldiers to attack the new intruder, and possibly defect to another of their hive's own royalty. But remarkably, it seemed to have no effect. Everything carried on exactly as it had before.

Then Chorea and Nits realized the affected Hora were no longer reproducing. The queen, for all of her resilience in producing eggs, was not having them fertilized by her male counterparts. And eventually they came to the realization that the queen could only mate with the males she had, herself, produced. This Hora incest was, naturally, an evolutionary problem that possibly explained why their numbers were so low and why they had never been discovered before.

Other intriguing characteristics of the Hora included their diet, which seemed to include nothing but the gigantic carcasses of beached whales. But the one thing Chorea and Nits never seemed to figure out was that the Hora excreted a pheromone when they walked, squeezing it from underneath the sclerite plates that covered their bodies, in a trail wherever they walked. The multiple sores that eventually killed Chorea and Nits were the direct result of their first encounters with the insects, and their repeated handling of the creatures without gloves. By the end, they had blisters all over their hands, and any-where they later scratched, which meant most of their arms and face. Their bodies bloated to such an extent that they looked like manatees, and thirsted for water as much as air. They were in a constant state of hallucinatory fever and one night, as we know from the discovery of his journal in the mid-eighties, Nits was sure their camp was visited by a small party of *antioch ers*, who probed him relentlessly for hon-eydew thinking he was a gigantic, pale aphid. After some Kuna chil-dren found them in their hut, some Colombian smugglers apparently agreed to take the bodies away for a fee. But it is believed that they were simply dumped in the water once the islands were out of sight.

* * *

By the next morning, Chris Eaton's fever had broken. So they ar-ranged to take him immediately back to the city, and then place him on the first plane back to America, which happened to be destined for California. When he eventually exited the hut, he surprised the dog with the necklace and another dog fucking. In their embarrass-ment they tried to extricate themselves but only succeeded in stick-ing themselves fast, their rumps practically pasted together, and he was reminded, no doubt like Pujom, or even Nits and Chorea, of the inevitability of fate.

And then it all came rushing back. According to the 1962 book by Hadice Kiebler-Krauss called *The 4 Stages of Loss*, the four stages of loss, as Chris Eaton experienced them, were:

1 regret,
2 anger,
3 sadness, and
4 acceptance.

The first was the hardest because he felt as though he had done something wrong, that he was somehow responsible, that he might have done something to save her. The second was simple, a flood of energy that he had merely to allow, focusing all of his energy, as he had in the past, on that one point of comprehension, so basic and real, which he believed to be true because it was the only fact on which he could lay total understanding. The third – a return to frustration – was marked mostly by the realization that his anger would never truly allow him, as he had first imagined, to make any sense of the world, and would most certainly never bring her back. And the fourth was by far the easiest because all he had to do was hire the hitman, which he did under the reluctant recommendation of a man named Joseph Herre, whom he had kept under retainer for the past two years.

*　*　*

Joseph Herre was part of a long line of Joseph Herres. Or rather, a long line of Josef Herres. Germans. Also, a long line of bankers, until he met Erkki Varisto in Vermont, where both Varisto and the German – second generation American, as a matter of fact – were attending college at Bennington. Varisto was on a temporary exchange from Stockholms Universitet and also the son of a son of a banker. His parents were both of Finnish descent, only in Sweden for his father's work with MeritaNordbanken after the two Nordic banking giants merged to begin their swift acquisition of other financial institutions across Scandinavia, but Varisto told everyone at school that his parents had moved to the Swedish arctic circle to more accurately track the semi-nomadic patterns of the Northern Saami. It was Varisto who planted the idea in Jospeh Herre's head that they should become private investigators, and soon after graduation the two of them set up shop in New York City as Herre Varisto. It wasn't until they were joined by the Frenchman, Pierre-Jules Chapot, that their agency really took off.

Pierre-Jules was a second cousin of the Chapot family of Olympic equestrian fame, but as a child he was thought to be afraid of horses (in reality he had a very rare condition called micro-acrophobia: a fear of small heights), and so he spent most of his time around the stables hiding in the hay. It was through this clandestine observation that he came to know many things about his family that he might not have otherwise discovered, including any and all acts of infidelity, cruelty to the animals and disgusting bodily habits, but also just the general way people behave. He came to understand the psychology of people in a way most others did not. And by the time he joined Erkki and Joseph in the U.S., Chapot had made his own name in Belgium and France as the lead investigator on several previously unsolved crimes, including: a mysterious case in a coastal town of Southern France, where the local baker had mistakenly poisoned the entire town by using bleach in his recipe to meet the demands of the French to have the whitest bread imaginable; the kidnapping of the exiled first Malagasy President, Philibert Tsiranana, in 1975 off the streets of Paris shortly after his declared intention to return to his homeland to free the people from military dictatorship, which turned out to be a plot sanctioned by both the French government and the Parisian mafia; and the capture of the glamorous Russian jewel thief, known widely as The Countess, who had escaped justice for her crimes when she had first committed them in 1927, and who was thus nearly a century old when he captured her and no longer quite as glamorous. In European detective circles, he was actually quite a celebrity, while Herre Varisto were really just spying on spouses and locating lost pets. But when they met at a conference in Brussels, Chapot was having trouble accessing the proper paperwork to shift his business to the more profitable, litigious, North American market, so they decided to sponsor him and offer a partnership.

Chris Eaton approached Varisto, Herre and Chapot with a case that never ended well. In fact, Chapot, who had built his business on a foundation of integrity, voted that they refuse it immediately.

But Varisto, who was more travelled and thus prone to waxing philosophic in such instances, preached tolerance, prudence and acceptance. Who were they to dismiss a potential client as a crackpot? Who were they to play God? Besides, as the Finn rightly pointed out, this guy was made of money, the recent recipient of a huge legal settlement from a Swiss pharmaceutical company owned mostly by the Japanese called NeoChartis. Mrs. Varisto, he added, could use a new dishwasher.

The settlement, as it turned out, was Chris Eaton's second in as many years, the result of a gross malpractice during the latest round of federally funded and recommended flu vaccinations. Their client – because Varisto had successfully convinced Herre to take it on – had lost both his wife and newborn to the illness, and the Swiss/Japanese claimed a gross miscalculation at the plant in Central America, mistakenly filling several vaccine shipments with ten times the recommended dosage, effectively infecting Chris Eaton's pregnant wife and several people in California with an advanced stage of the hybrid flu rather than protecting them against it. They took full responsibility and offered as many synonyms for condolences, sympathy, commiseration and prayer that they could fit in one masterfully executed press release. Chris Eaton had received the settlement (enough to ensure that he would never have to work another day in his life) after lengthy negotiations through his lawyer Archie Nots, who Herre quickly discovered was not exactly who he claimed to be. The man had actually never graduated from an accredited law school and had been suspended in several states. But this wasn't what Chris Eaton was after – why he had hired Joseph Herre and company – at all. Not to look into the practices of NeoChartis, and not to expose Archie Nots. Instead, he wanted them to prove one of the most outlandish conspiracy theories Joseph Herre had ever heard, involving the treason of a high-ranking government official with the goal of culling the American population and placing the country at war, first with negligible forces like Afghanistan and Iraq but eventually India, France and Canada, followed by Australia, Mexico and Chile, for which Herre had to ask for confirmation three times to make sure he'd heard him correctly. Let's forget the salt thing, Chapot suggested to Herre when he finally accepted they were going to take it all on. Let's just concentrate on linking Secretary Chi to either the Pentagon crash or the vaccination deaths. Because if this Chi treason is true, then we'll be uncovering one of the greatest American traitors since Benedict Arnold.

Unfortunately for all three partners of HVC, not to mention their client, despite using every trick in the book and a few others besides, Chi always came out clean. Even with what was going on in California, the official word from Health and Human Services was that, without the swift and concerted action on the part of the government and medical teams, things could have been much worse. With any kind of disease on such a large scale, there were bound to be a certain number of fatalities. And due to American determination and alertness, Chi was sure the economy would be back on track in no time. If anything, she was an American hero. Untouchable.

Chris Eaton, as Chapot had predicted, became even more distraught and confused than before. The thing he couldn't figure out was this: If Chi knew he had spotted her that day at the Pentagon, why was he still alive? Clearly she felt he was important for something, needed him for something in the future, and had killed Julie and Brandon as a warning. It was the only thing that made sense to him. She also felt she had that much power over him that she could just leave him alone until he served her purpose, whatever that might be. And the worst thing was she was probably right.

A week after Chris Eaton dismissed his team and explained his new plan (I give up, he said. I am a lamb voting with two wolves on what to have for lunch. What else can I do?), Chapot returned and slipped him a business card with a name written on the reverse.

You didn't hear it from me, he said.

***

The name on the card: Charriat deSavon, literally, *transporter of soap*, but from what Chapot told Chris Eaton, the name most people called him was Mr. Clean, a hitman who specialized in murders so creative no one would ever see it coming. He was, at once, the best- and worst-known man in France; every police inspector had heard of him but no one seemed to know any details about what he looked like, where he lived, where he'd come from. He was assumed to be in-volved with many of the country's unsolved murders, as well as many of the deaths by natural causes, but no one had ever pinned him on anything. It had taken some work, Chapot claimed, just to get this card. But if Chris Eaton really intended to go through with his plan, this was the man he needed to pull it off. On the card's reverse were careful instructions on how to find him, or rather, for him to find you, involving Internet searches, chat groups, aliases and an email Chris Eaton initially mistook for a Nigerian lottery scam and then realized the numbers (the strange windfall amount, the ticket num-ber, the serial number and even the date: Feb 24, '85) were actually code, to be deciphered as the flight number, time, and longitude and latitude of their destination and meeting place. Two days later, he was in Paris, drinking a *chocolat chaud* at a small café on the fair banks of the Cabanne, wondering which of the passersby looked hard enough to be a killer. He ate a third croissant, and another half-hour passed. He wondered if he was being watched. And when the killer eventu-ally did approach him, Chris Eaton said: I was beginning to think you'd never show. And deSavon replied: Well, I suppose I didn't. By which he meant that he was not, in fact, deSavon, but an assistant of sorts, named Poisson, because it would not really do for someone like deSavon, whose job required him to be invisible, to just walk up to clients in broad daylight, particularly Americans, who were anything but subtle, especially when it came to assassinations. And Chris Ea-ton said: Why do they call you Poisson? And the man named Poisson said: Why did your mother call you Asshole? But then he said with a wink: I am slippery. And then, with a look over his shoulder: I am also deadly. By which, he explained, it was a name he'd been given by deSavon because the man liked games, and *poisson* was the French word for fish, while the similar *poison* was the word for poison, and then he said: It is a funny thing, that the word for fish in so many languages is so close to another forecasting danger. Like in Spanish, where the fish is *pescado* but *pecado* is a sin. And Italian, where *pesce* can become *pece*, meaning black as night. In Japanese, *sushi* can be transformed into tooth decay, or *ushi*. And Swahili, *samaki* becomes *amaki*: an artist. He chuckled at that, like ice cubes in an empty glass, then: And what we are left with in all cases is an ess, which he drawled out in such a mockery of a Southern American accent that it sounded like ass, staring straight at Chris Eaton. And Chris Eaton laughed, like an engine full of air, failing to start. And Poisson lit another cigarette and took a sip from his Belgian beer and stretched slowly across the table to Chris Eaton's manila envelope and took a quick peek at the mark inside, looked back up at Chris Eaton, disapprovingly, back at the photo, back at Chris Eaton, tossed the envelope back down and said: *C'est rien que de la merde, connard.* And when he saw that Chris Eaton clearly did not understand, he smiled and translated: You want to kill your twin brother?

* * *

You should be a man about it, Poisson said, by which he was referring to Chris Eaton's request for a safe word. The plan was for deSavon to wait one year, and then kill Chris Eaton however and whenever he saw fit. But there were two caveats: it had to be fast and it had to be completely by surprise. He did not want to feel fear or pain or even a stunned bewilderment. He did not want to shit his pants with a knife at his throat. Thus, if he so much as heard a turning latch or snapping twig, there would be a safe word that could call the whole thing off, with a reboot period of at least one week. Poisson spat over the railing and into the river. A safe word? Did he think this was some kind of joke? Did he not comprehend the sanctity of a profession like this? Why don't you just commit suicide? Pick a fight with a wild bear. Or better yet, a train, I have a schedule.

Now, he wants a safe word, Poisson said out loud. And before? He wants a joke. You need a safe word that is a joke. Chris Eaton had not been aware of the precedent for his idea in film. Nor had he considered the problems that could arise for a man like deSavon, for whom creative murders had become a sort of calling card, if he were to, as Poisson put it, sink so low that he started stealing from Warren Beatty, or any of the other million films that had used such a boring premise, you should pick a fight with a woman on the rag. Poisson did not see many movies, he said, because he found them to be mostly a waste of time. (They did little to better his soul, he said. Often, he read *The Bible*. Or other books so long as they weren't written in the first person.) But even *he* had seen a half dozen movies with this idea. It was a joke. (*Leche moi et fait moi jouir.* Do you understand that?) They had used such a device in a recent film about Esther Chan-Poirot, the imagined daughter of the legendary Charlie Chan and Hercule Poirot. It had bombed. This could make deSavon a laughing stock. A laughing stock! They should not do it. But then there was the money. Perhaps if there were more money. Chris Eaton said: How much would he need? And Poisson said: *Va te faire enculer.* But also: Much much. And: Much much much. And after pausing for a moment longer, he wrote something down on the napkin, snatched the envelope from the table and walked away, saying: The word is the man from the movie. It will help me remember.

Chris Eaton folded it without looking and placed it in his wallet, and by the time he'd boarded his plane back to Washington he'd decided that Poisson was right, and that he should be a man about it, and so he tossed the paper from the window of his taxi and elected never to look back.

344

***

Over the course of that year, Chris Eaton did all the things you might expect: he spent a few more days in Paris, took in some Andrew Lloyd Webber in London, bought a lot of train tickets, thought about climbing some mountains, and then got bored and went back home. He had actually hoped to send all seven summits, but he blamed his eventual inaction on the debates between the Messner and Bass lists, which featured different peaks in Australia depending on whether you wanted the highest altitude or the hardest send, not to mention getting mired in the political implications around the exclusion of Mont Blanc in Western Europe. Likewise he had planned to spend three weeks hiking the poorest parts of Africa, living with the locals, just for perspective on how good he had had it in America, but they lost his luggage on the way to Cairo and he spent at least half of that waiting at the hotel near the airport for it to arrive. When he returned, he spent one last month trying to explore his own country, visiting every large amusement park he could remember before eventually deciding he rather preferred being at home.

Whereas the first six months might have been categorized as focusing almost solely on new experiences (aside from *Cats*, of course, which he had seen before on Broadway), the second half became much more introspective. He pulled out all the old documents and photo albums he'd collected over the years, including a shoebox full of ribbons from competitions he could no longer remember, a bag of stuffed animals completely faded on their backs from sitting on his windowsill, an embarrassing teenage attempt at a fantasy novel, a complete box of letters he'd received from all of his high school friends while he'd been in Scandinavia on an academic exchange, a bag of foreign currencies, a collection of joke books, action figures, old novelty '45s, and then, once he had categorized them by various time-periods, interests and endeavours, he began assigning one year of his prior life to each remaining week, lumping most of his infancy into the first seven days. He almost immediately found the exercise ridiculous, and he nearly stopped, but as he moved from his childhood to his teens and once he reached his twenties, he found reliving those years quite therapeutic. Events that had seemed catastrophic at the time now emerged as transformative, and he was grateful, some because they were actually fortuitous at the time (though he was not yet skilled enough in life to recognize it), and some because the catastrophe was, indeed, true and fierce, and he was able to navigate through it with something he recognized in retrospect as dignity, forcing him to dig deeper than he ever had before that, and to plumb the depths of his own strength, his resilience, his acceptance, and sometimes his own potential for compassion. All of the time we waste worrying about what might happen, pursuing things for the life we want to lead, without spending time to enjoy the life we have. Even an illness can remind us of who we are. Even pain can reassure and remind. He began to wonder, in fact, as he crept closer and closer to the present, if the most recent events in his life might one day, if his days weren't already numbered, lead him to some equally life-affirming lessons. Was it worth his time, he wondered, to keep hating Senator Chi the way that he did? Was it worth it to focus so much concern on things he could not control? Falsehood, delusion, illusion, fantasy, lies, deceit, and other assorted facets of bullshit and fuckery were confusing to us, in the best case, causing us to chase our tails, waste time, and become disoriented. In the worst case, they resulted in wasted, unhappy, and perhaps harmful, toxic lives that brought only pain and suffering, to the one living the life and to everyone and everything with whom they come into contact.

And it only gets worse.

The truth was that we all share the same sacred underpinnings of life, and silence, and consciousness, and it was only through compassion, tolerance and kindness that he might be able to break through it all, to access his true self beneath all of the layers of pain, hurt, sadness, and other afflictive emotions that he'd built up as a result of liv-

346

ing his inauthentic and delusive lifestyle. There was a moment, while celebrating the 30th anniversary of friends in Panama, watching them renew their vows and recalling his own wedding to Julie, when he nearly forgot the personal assassination he had arranged. His life, he realized, was now perfect, or at least nearly. He was free from worry, from greed, from hate, from aspirations. He saw now that, although their physical bodies were gone, the essences of Julie and their child would continue to be a part of him. The way he laughed at the MC's jokes, snorting so slightly at the end, was something he had picked up from Julie with great resistance. Even Brandon, whose life had been so short, was still conjured whenever he stretched out of sleep. He was not a single force in the world, but a combination of every life that had ever made an impact on his. He was happy.

Then he realized it could all end at any second.

***

The part that made it so horrible was that he didn't know when it would happen. And while he briefly considered that this was the same for everyone, for all deaths, the main difference was that he *knew* that he didn't know, and most other people just live their lives believing death is somewhere in the distance, so it either hits them before they know it or they become so sick that they can adequately prepare for it mentally. Also, with his new revelations about Julie and the baby, if he were to die now, would there be anything left of them in the world? He tried to pass those pieces of them on to others. He visited his parents much more frequently. He made special trips to visit friends in far-off places. He began to enjoy his life again. He felt much more present, more real, more himself. And wouldn't it be tragic at this point of self-realization to lose it all, to re-enter his prior stage of nothingness, where he wasn't dead but might as well have been, and by which have his life defined by loss rather than gain. His only hope, he now saw, was to catch the assassin in the act, to implement the safe word. It wouldn't guarantee that he could reach deSavon again to cancel the hit, but at least it might buy him some time.

If only he could remember it.

All he had to go on was Poisson's assertion that the word was "the guy in the movie," and the only one he could really remember was the Warren Beatty project from 1999 called *Bulworth*, because Poisson had mentioned him specifically. But a quick scan of cast and characters provided nothing that seemed like it could be a safe word, which he assumed had to be a noun or adjective, so he kept searching. In an interview with Beatty he found in an old issue of *Teknoföhn*, the actor claimed he'd been inspired by an old silent film called *Flirting with Fate* (1919), but once again the list of actors and their roles produced nothing of use, except perhaps Jewel Carmen, but Poisson had definitely said "guy." He despaired. Time was running out. There was no reason to expect that the Frenchman had been referring to something from Hollywood, so he broadened his search to specialty film stores, querying the clerks about foreign works. Was it not possible that he had seen something in French, such as *Les tribulations d'un chinois en Chine*, whose main character, Lempereur, provided the first possibility. Mickey Rooney, he discovered, had starred in a Spanish film in the seventies called *Juego sucio en Panamá*, which otherwise featured mostly Spanish names. In Canada in the early-eighties, Gabe Kaplan had made a film called *Tulips*, which produced both his character's name and also the name of a revered Canadian actor. A German film from the thirties contained the potential Kitty. He also found a recent novel from Russia, by a man named Andrei Raschatov, which had even more recently been made into a film, also Russian but translated loosely into *The Orphan Riot's Cadaver*, about a man running an orphanage who makes a deal with two of his boys to off him during a staged children's uprising. One of the boys in that was nicknamed Sloth. In John Woo's *Qian Zuo Guai*, there was a character named Fatso.

Of course, he'd never be sure if his research had been exhaustive enough, so he tried to make sure he was never alone, treating friends to dinner in popular restaurants, or sometimes, when no one was available, approaching women he saw on the public transit, or in the grocery store, where he would also frequently hang out for hours on end, because it was very crowded and well lit. He installed security cameras, eyebeams, infrared detectors, hired a company to stand guard around his new fence. And even then, he felt unsafe. Could he trust all the men in his hire? Might one of them be employed, simultaneously, by deSavon? There were times, when he was alone at night, dozing off in his armchair, pipe smoke circling his head, that he would whisper the mantra over and over until he fell asleep.

Fatso. Wax man. Emperor. Sloth. Avocado. Tulips. Kitty.

Fatso. Wax man. Emperor. Sloth. Avocado. Tulips. Kitty.

Fatso. Wax man. Emperor. Sloth. Avocado. Tulips. Kitty.

Perhaps, on one or more of these occasions, it actually worked.

The second book Julie found on his desk was Johann Scheuchzer's *Lithographia Helvetica*, originally published in 1728 but reissued towards the end of the nineteenth century as part of a larger textbook, in combination with several later works by Cuvier, Collini, Brongniart and Gessner, among others, all of which attempted to put the history of paleontology in context, compiled in 1854 by one of Cuvier's students and used in the early paleontology program at the nascent University of Montana by the Irish professor and geologist Nigel Neill. It is not Scheuchzer's most famous work – that title would belong to his *Beschreibung der Naturgeschichte des Schweitzerlandes*, an exhaustive nine-volume study of the whole of Switzerland, which begins with the original trio of texts summing up all there is, or was, to know about: (1) the Swiss mountains; (2) the Swiss rivers, lakes and mineral baths; and (3) a more general text about geology and meteorology; before moving on to (4) the Swiss flora; (5) fauna; (6) the shortest volume, about the Swiss glaciers, which should probably have been included in Volume 2 anyway; and petering out in the last three, when it seemed he had little better to write about than (7) knives; (8) chocolate; and (9) fondue – but it is perhaps his most infamous, if not certainly the most scandalous.

Chris Eaton had purchased it from a specialty shop in Amsterdam on a work trip, vertical fishing for giant zander in the Volkerak. The trip's production assistant, who was present on the trip solely to ensure they did not go over budget, was an Italian named Noah Cresti, brilliant with his flare for numbers but also a staunch vegan and thus firmly against the idea of fishing at all. This caused no problems until the shoot was complete, because he spent most of his time below deck listening to music and reading *The Collected Poems of Giacomo Leopardi (1823–1831)*. But when they capped off the trip with celebratory beer and *jenever* at a bruin in the capital, Cresti could no longer resist, particularly as the general conversation devolved, in inverse relation to the amount of alcohol he had consumed, from basic small talk to the ranking of Dutch ales against other beers of the world (particularly German and American) to women and finally to acts of bravadic angling, which set a line of opposition down the group, with nearly everyone – including the largely Dutch technical crew, the Asian Canadian director and host, the host's assistant/girlfriend, and a handful of other top fishermen/consultants from Holland, a Brit, a South African and Chris Eaton – on one side and a slurring Cresti on the other. Cresti zeroed in mostly on the professional anglers, baiting each into circular arguments about morality and evolution, and finally Johann Scheuchzer. The world is not a factory, Cresti berated them. And: Animals are not products for our use. And one of the Dutchmen said: I thought we were speaking of fish. And the rest of them laughed. And Cresti said: Intelligence is sadly only recognizable to those who have it. And the crew, who had worked with Cresti and seen him drunk before, shrugged their shoulders and toasted him, anyway.

Cresti scowled, but the Dutch were already in full disregard, so he merely readjusted his chair and continued, as if he and Chris Eaton were the only ones present. Had Chris Eaton ever heard of Scheuchzer? ("The painter?" Chris Eaton asked. And the Dutch crew laughed again.) Although a medical doctor and professor by trade, Johann Scheuchzer had been, in the late-seventeenth and early-eighteenth centuries, an avid proponent of the study of fossils, and their existence as keys to the past, an understanding of our origins and that of the Earth. But while some saw the remains of giant reptiles, or dinosaurs, Scheuchzer was a man of science, unwilling to believe in the dragons of myth, and having, in fact, spent several years in the service of the Roman Catholic Church debunking the claims of many early paleontologists across Europe, he laid forth, in various scientific papers submitted to the Royal Society, that the majority of these petrified remains were actually those of large fish. And because the typical fossil deposit was located on land and not in the oceans, he also believed that their existence was proof of the great Biblical Flood. Much of his published work from this period has this theory as its focus, including his fabulist *Piscium Querela et Vindiciae*, in which fossilized fish hold mankind on trial and berate us for not understanding their message of harmony and conservation. And Scheuchzer had many supporters, particularly in the Church. But the one piece of evidence that he and his colleagues were missing, according to those firmly in evolution's camp, was the remains of a man, *homo devilus*. If God had decided to wipe out those sinful humans and start from scratch, should they not have been, like all other fossils, deposited deep into the rock by the forceful tides of the Noachic Cataclysm? Scheuchzer's detractors claimed he would never find one because they did not exist, while even his proponents were unoptimistic, arguing that fossilized mammals were extremely rare, due to their size and fragility. Thus it was a surprise to everyone when, on Christmas day in 1725, Scheuchzer submitted to the Royal Society that he had done it, marking his discovery in a quarry near a cloister in Germany where the St. Hecarion monks, who had up to that point made a weak living off cultivating yeasts for bread and beer, had recently leapt on the bandwagon and begun creating their own *faux-sils* for profit. He'd planned the trip to put a stop to this practice, but on closer inspection of the area, he instead unearthed the holy grail of paleontology, the partial skeleton of a man, or apparent man, unlike any he'd ever studied, with a vertebral column that extended from its slightly flattened skull like a curved bell, culminating in stumpy lower limbs and "even some vestiges of a liver," which he used to calculate the approximate year of death at 2306 B.C. *It is certain that this is the half,* he wrote, *or nearly so, the proof we have been waiting for: that the substance even of the bones, and what is more, of the flesh and parts still softer than the flesh, are incorporated into the stone. We see there the remains of the brain... of the roots of the nose... In a word, it is one of the rarest relics we have of that cursed race which was buried under the waters.*

In no time at all, *Philosophical Transactions,* the *Journal des Scavans,* the *New Memoirs of Literature* and other periodicals were all proclaiming that the war against prehistory had finally been decided. Copycat findings were unearthed across Europe and Africa, but Scheuchzer debunked most of those as well, either as an attempt to augment the importance of his own specimen or to reinforce the objectivity of his critical faculties, legitimizing only the report of the Bohemian Captain Janek van Toch on a small island in Sumatra, purely on hearsay because that sample had actually been lost at sea when his ship sank in Bondy Bay. Scheuchzer died as one of the most important thinkers of his age, even though the true meaning of what he had found, according to Cresti, had escaped even him. As far as he was concerned, Scheuchzer was a prophet, ridiculed, then disputed, who would eventually be recognized as a genius. Not for toeing the Catholic line, but for discovering the real missing link, that we hadn't been created spontaneously by some benevolent God – *Creationists are lunatics and butchers,* Cresti said. *The fruits of Christianity are war and oppression and the extermination of Native Americans and the introduction of Africans to slavery!* – and not that we had descended from apes – *Why miraculously decide to walk upright if our knees were originally constructed to hinge backward like a dog? Or for the climbing of trees?* – but that we had evolved from creatures of the sea, and one day we were likely to return.

***

Then – suddenly – someone laughed. Chris Eaton thought it was the host's girlfriend, but it could have been any woman in the bar. And because it was a woman, Cresti would not fight. His fuel had been abruptly cinched off and he lost all steam. Someone brought up Gessner, who had reassessed Scheuchzer's supposed arms as flippers, and the fossil as just another large fish. Then there was Cresti's own countryman, Collini, who had declared they weren't short flippers, either, but huge wings, destroyed by the sedimentary pressure on the creature's uncommonly hollow bones, another example of the pterosaurs he had discovered several years prior. When Georges Cuvier was asked to clean the specimen in the early-1800s – someone at the table said it was on display at the nearby Teylers Museum in Haarlem, if they really wanted to see for themselves – he proclaimed it a giant salamander. Much quieter than before, Cresti murmured something about otoliths. And the vestigial gills that are apparent in human embryonic development. He held his hand above the candle and directed their attention to the shape of the bones beneath it. This was what made us different. Special. This shape. This biology. Not our hopes and dreams, which were nothing more than biological impulses, brought on by various shiny trinkets and lures. What each person was striving for made no difference. It was the striving that mattered, what made people live. Humans were nothing more than shells for aimless desire. And in every case, achieving it would ultimately lead to downfall, with no more purpose or will.

But it was obvious to Chris Eaton that his heart was no longer in it. Cresti said: If you look at the other animals of the savannah today, most of them still have fur. The other beasts who had lost all or most of their fur: whales, dolphins, walruses, manatees, hippos, pigs and tapirs. And Cresti said: They are also some of the only animals who can regulate their own breathing, like humans, which allows them to hold their breath when they need to dive under water, or even when they fall in. No one was listening any more.

Do you know why they surround animals at zoos with a moat? To scare the shit from them.

...

Once a gorilla falls in over its head, he said, it takes only a half minute to die.

* * *

Chris Eaton managed to find the book before heading to the airport, and started reading it on his way home. When he had returned, Julie could tell something was different. He was distant. Distracted. He'd put on a remarkable amount of weight. And when he spoke, his thoughts ripped out in all directions like scattering birds, or startled atoms, as if linearity no longer meant a thing to him. *Had he been meant to die as a child?* he thought. To drown in a pool, on a river, in a bathtub, in a puddle? And if so, had every moment since merely been a mistake? An infinite string of wrong possibilities?

I need a rest, he said to her one morning after all the fishermen were on the trails.

Lover.... She stopped for a moment to look at him. You totally should.

I'm going back to the East Coast to visit my parents. I need to be close to home, to get some real rest, you know? Sometimes, no matter how long I'm here, I can't seem to escape it. It's a part of me....

She was staring at him: You were born in Montana.

...

...

Yeah, maybe you're right.

And the next day, he got up from his desk and never came back.

ABOUT THE AUTHOR

Chris Eaton is originally from New Brunswick but currently lives in Toronto. He also records music under the name Rock Plaza Central. This is his fourth book.

COLOPHON

Distributed in Canada by the Literary Press Group: www.lpg.ca
Distributed in the USA by Small Press Distribution: www.spdbooks.org
Shop on-line at www.bookthug.ca

BOOK
PRODUCTION
WAR ECONOMY
STANDARD

Type+Design: www.beautifuloutlaw.com

13 14 15 16 17 · 5 4 3 2 1